THE AMERICAN SPY

Images courtesy Shutterstock.

This book is a work of fiction. Any resemblance to actual events or persons, living or dead, is entirely coincidental.

"The American Spy," by Douglas Clark. ISBN 978-1-951985-94-3 (softcover); 978-1-951985-95-0 (hardcover); 978-1-951985-96-7 (ebook).

Published 2021 by Virtualbookworm.com Publishing Inc., P.O. Box 9949, College Station, TX 77842, US.

By Douglas Clark

Belfast

Take Five

Shell Game

Evermore

Critical Mass

Fault Lines

Provoke the Devil

The Irish Spy

Endgame

Hunting Odessa

The American Spy

To Josie for her invaluable editing contributions and embracing the sharing of a writer's life.

THE AMERICAN SPY

A NOVEL

DOUGLAS CLARK

PART ONE

THE SOLDIER

American Expeditionary Forces embarking for France 1917

CHAPTER 1

Berlin, Germany | July 1934

Since arriving in Berlin, Germany a year ago, the constant social upheaval no longer shocked U.S. Army Lieutenant Colonel Spencer Fleming. The reputation of Berlin as the center of European decadence in the 1920s now transformed into a depressive environment in the last couple of years. Having weathered the food deprivations during the Great War and economic collapse following Germany's defeat, the years of recovery and hopes for a democratic government collapsed under the weight of the worldwide Great Depression. Exacerbated by political tensions, violent confrontations plagued Germany.

The principle instigators of political violence were the paramilitary ranks of the National Socialist German's Workers Party. In German, Nationalsozialistische Deutsche Arbeiterpartei, abbreviated NSDAP. The English acronym, the Nazi Party. The Sturmabteilung, the SA, literally storm detachment, represented the paramilitary wing of the party. Comprised largely of former veterans of the Great War who organized first in regional bands called Freikorps, the SA provided a political outlet for those disillusioned by the 1918 armistice of the Great War. Instead of recognizing the failure of a militaristic monarchy bent on imperialistic expansion as the fault, these former soldiers attributed blame to the political left, mainly the communists and the Jews. They argued the German army was not defeated in the field.

With access to stocks of brown WWI uniforms, the SA became known as Brownshirts. Patterned after Mussolini's Fascist Blackshirts in Italy, the SA proved an integral component of Adolf Hitler's rise to power, organizing street demonstrations and directing violence against Jews and political opponents. The only political party with an organized paramilitary wing.

For a decade, the growing ranks of the SA served Adolf Hitler's political ambitions. By 1933, their ranks swelled to over 2,000,000. This compared to the strength of the regular army, the Reichswehr, of only 100,000 as limited by the 1919 Treaty of Versailles.

With the Nazi Party achieving 44% of the votes in the March 1933 election, President Paul Hindenburg had no alternative but to make Hitler chancellor in order to establish a functioning government. The SA could now exert its influence without restraint. SA storm troopers attacked Jewish-owned retail stores. Later, to enforce a boycott of Jewish businesses, storm troopers prevented entry. A week after the boycott, the Nazi controlled government passed a law excluding Jews from civil service or teaching at public schools of universities. SA thugs randomly dragged Jews into the street humiliating and often beating them. Targeted killings of Jews became commonplace.

By 1934, formations of uniformed SA marched in all major cities. Failure for anyone not to render the outstretched arm and *sieg heil* salute risked physical assault. Adding to the militaristic environment, the black-uniformed Schutzstaffel, the SS, originally organized from within the SA as Hitler's elite personal bodyguard, became increasingly obvious.

With this climate of constant political turmoil and violence, Colonel Fleming received a telephone call at his office in the United States Embassy located at Bendlerstrasse 39, just south of the Brandenburg Gate. Although a Saturday, Fleming was catching up on paperwork from a hectic week. The date, June 30, 1934, a day he would not soon forget. Who would be calling at seven-thirty in the morning?

"Spencer, this is Konrad. I tried your apartment first. Irma called off the dinner party scheduled for tonight."

What the hell has happened? There was no dinner party scheduled for tonight. This was merely a coded reference that Richter had something of importance for Fleming. Richter was Fleming's secret intelligence source within German military intelligence, the Abwehr.

"That is unfortunate. I was so looking forward to a relaxing social evening."

"So was Irma. A matter of some delicacy. Best explained personally over coffee. Can you meet me in thirty minutes at the coffee house?"

"Certainly. Tired of dealing with paperwork on my Saturday off anyway."

Richter was not acting on his own initiative. He was the conduit to his boss, Lieutenant Colonel Hans Oster. Fleming knew this from his only personal meeting with Oster months earlier. Feeding secret information to Fleming perhaps authorized from higher within the Abwehr.

Although skillfully indirect, Oster told Fleming it was important to establish confidential conduits with foreign intelligence agencies to bypass official diplomatic channels. Since the United States had no foreign intelligence service, would Fleming act in that capacity? Oster suggested dissatisfaction within the military toward certain Nazi political objectives. A subtle implication he spoke for some wider faction with the German military. Fleming remained wary. Oster might be playing a double game.

However, since that first meeting, Fleming was often able to verify independently the sensitive information passed along by Major Richter. The information was enlightening, casting the Nazis criminal enterprise growing in scope as a threat to Germany itself. Oster was clearly not purveying Nazi disinformation.

Over their months of contact, Richter candidly admitted his personal hatred for the Nazis. He supported Colonel Oster's efforts to provide the United States with information of the looming danger of this megalomaniac Adolf Hitler. Only the United States might deter Hitler from eventually taking Germany to war again. The British-French alliance of the Great War was a paper tiger.

Fleming assumed Oster represented some faction of the German military that sought to undermine the Nazi regime. Perhaps for the purpose of engineering a coup d'état. The Abwehr as the military intelligence service essential to any such subversion. They also may have ulterior reasons for providing confidential information to the United States.

Fleming arrived at their favorite coffeehouse not far from the embassy or military high command headquarters to find Richter waiting at a table in the back. There were few other patrons.

Richter stood to shake hands. Before Fleming could sit down he said, "Hours ago Hitler moved violently against the SA. Outside Munich."

Fleming was well aware of the growing tensions between the chief of staff of the SA, Ernst Röhm and Hitler. Although a close Hitler follower from the earliest days of the Beer Hall Putsch in Munich in 1923, Röhm's views now ran counter to Hitler's ambitions. In simplest form, Röhm aspired to a Germany controlled by rightwing socialism.

Hitler's political ideology differed significantly. He was even against including the word socialist in the name of the National Socialist German Workers' Party. His vision was an autocratic Third Reich as a Germanic militaristic empire ruling Europe. Hitler was now close to achieving his goal of unchallenged rule of Germany. Only eighty-six year old President Paul von Hindenburg stood in his way. Hitler actively curried favor with the conservative regular army and German industrialists necessary to his grandiose plans. Both these factions feared Röhm and his SA pseudo army of disaffected former soldiers. Other senior Nazis like Hermann Göring, Henrich Himmler, and Joseph Goebbels despised Röhm.

"What do you mean?"

"Hitler lured all the SA leadership to a meeting at the Hanselbauer Pension in Bad Wiessee a spa town in Upper Bavaria. Ostensibly to resolve growing differences with the SA. Our sources say Hitler personally led a large detachment of SS and arrested everyone, including Röhm. Looks like a purge."

****

The meeting was to take place at 11:00am on Saturday June 30, 1934. In preparation, Minister of Defense Werner von Blomberg, supporting the plot against the SA, issued a general alert. SS Headquarters ordered all units to muster at their barracks armed. After midnight, 220 SS of the Leibstandarte, Hitler's personal SS bodyguard regiment under the command of Sepp Dietrich, boarded a train south to the small railway station in Kaufering outside Munich in Bavaria.

The plan was simple. The SS was to arrest the entire SA leadership arriving in Munich then transport them to Munich's Stadelheim Prison. The Bavarian police would operate under SS orders.

Hitler arrived at Oberwiesenfeld, Munich at 4:00am in his three-engine Junkers Ju52 aircraft. Driven to the Bavarian Ministry of the Interior, Hitler issued orders to Munich Gauleiter Wagner to dispatch SS squads and Bavarian police to arrest all SA senior officers. Arriving at 4:30 in the morning in a foul mood now convinced of Röhm's treachery, Hitler was so enraged he personally ripped the epaulets off the shirt of the chief of the Munich police for failing to keep order during an SA rampage of violence the previous night. Hitler shouted that he would have the chief shot.

With two escort cars of SS and Bavarian police commanded by SS-Obersturmbannführer Michael Lippert, Hitler departed for Bad Wiessee.

Arriving at the Hanselbauer Pension at 6:30, Hitler and his armed men pushed passed a startled elderly woman at the front door. Taking up positions outside the rooms of the senior SA, Lippert led Hitler to Röhm's room.

Lippert knocked, "Chief of Staff Röhm, I have an urgent message to deliver."

Moments later the door opened and Lippert pushed it open violently forcing Röhm back into the room. Adolf Hitler stood there holding a revolver. Bewildered, the overweight Röhm looked silly in his underwear and bare feet.

Hitler yelled, "Röhm, you are a traitor! Get dressed. You are under arrest."

With that, Hitler turned and left the hotel leaving the arrests to his henchmen. To his surprise after stepping outside, a lorry pulled up discharging a fully armed detachment of Röhm's head-quarter guard arriving from Munich.

Hitler defused the potentially tense situation by turning on the charm. They did not know their commander SA Standartenführ Uhl now sat under guard in the hotel basement awaiting arrival of additional SS forces for transport to Stadelheim Prison.

Addressing the SA men, "Chief of Staff Röhm orders you to return to barracks in Munich. As your Führer, I am here to meet with the entire leadership of the Sturmabteilung. It was I who founded the Sturmabteilung in 1920 as the backbone of the Party. That has not changed. I am here to dispel rumors instigated by our enemies suggesting discord with the Schutzstaffel. The SA remains essential for achieving the objectives of German nationalism. All is secure here. Now return to Munich."

Delivered with a broad smile, Hitler raised his arm in the Nazi salute. The SA troops snapped to attention and returned the salute with a vigorous *sieg heil*.

Hitler too was returning to Munich leaving the detained SA to the fate of the SS. As a precaution, he returned to Munich by an indirect route to avoid encountering Röhm's personal guard.

Hitler arrived at Munich Party Headquarters at 10:00am, cordoned off by prior arrangement by regular army soldiers. Defense Minister Colonel-General Werner von Blomberg and Major-General Walter von Reichenau were part of the plot. Hitler telephoned Propaganda Minister Joseph Goebbels giving him the go-ahead to issue the agreed on code word *Kolibri* to Göring and Himmler. Regional commanders of the Sicherheitsdienst des Reichsführer-SS, the SD intelligence branch of the SS, opened sealed orders. Those orders called for summary execution of the listed names. Hitler wanted no show trials or protracted discussions over the contrived reason for this coup d'état. He intended to cut the head off the snake in one blow. Himmler's chief subordinate Reinhard Heydrich let loose the SD death squads. While most of the victims were SA, it was an opportunity to rid others by simply labeling them as plotters.

The public justification cited the Führer acted as necessary to protect Germany from a plot by Ernst Röhm and General Kurt von Schleicher. Described as Röhm and Schleicher, the former defense minister, conspiring to use the vast numbers of the SA to overpower the much smaller Reichswehr regular army and seize control of the government. Heydrich authored the baseless fiction believed by no one.

As additional SS troops arrived in the early morning hours from Berlin, they arrested SA leaders arriving for the conference at Bad Wiessee at the Munich railway station then transported them to Stadelheim Prison. Those from the Hanselbauer arrived to find others already in cells.

* * * *

The purge of the SA lasted three days. Ostensibly upheld as thwarting an imminent coup, Nazi propagandist Joseph Goebbels labeled the threat as the attempted *Röhm Putsch*. Back in Munich, Hitler denounced the conspiracy to an assembled group of select Nazi Party members. Simultaneously, Goebbels telephoned Hermann Göring that same morning to release Heydrich's SS execution squads to liquidate other unsuspecting targets considered a threat to Adolf Hitler.

As for the captured SA leaders now housed in Munich's Stadelheim Prison, none would escape execution. Hitler assigned this task to a favorite officer, SS-Brigadeführer Theodor Eicke, the commandant of nearby Dachau Concentration camp. A committed fanatic, Eicke enforced rigid discipline at the camp by summary execution. As for Ernst Röhm himself, Hitler ordered his old colleague allowed the dignity of committing suicide.

Eicke stood by as Lippert walked into Röhm's cell and laid a pistol with a single bullet on the table.

Lippert said, "The Führer will allow you to die with honor. You have ten minutes."

Röhm replied, "If I am to kill myself, let Adolf do it himself."

Returning after hearing no shot fired within the allotted time, Eicke and Lippert entered the cell to find a defiant Röhm. Without further words, both shot Röhm. Lippert then crossed over to the fallen Röhm to deliver the coup-de-grace shot to the head.

Lippert immediately proceeded to the gristly task of supervising the executions of the remaining eighteen arrested SA leadership. A bullet to the back of the head dispatched thirteen in the exercise yard. However, the remaining five most senior officers suffered the more protracted horror of beheading by guillotine, the method of execution reserved for common criminals. Several of the SS officers vomited at the gruesome spectacle of the heads dropping into buckets.

With no way to keep the purge secret, on July 13, 1934, Hitler justified the action in a nationally broadcast speech to the Reichstag.

'In this hour I was responsible for the fate of the German people, and thereby I became the supreme judge of the German people. I gave the order to shoot the ringleaders in this treason, and I further gave the order to cauterize down to the raw flesh the ulcers of this poisoning of the wells in our domestic life. Let the nation know that its existence, which depends on its internal order and security, cannot be threatened with impunity by anyone! And let it be known for all time to come that if anyone raises his hand to strike the State, then certain death is his lot.'

Reportedly, at least 85 people died during the purge. Consensus placed the final death toll as several hundred. The decapitated Sturmabteilung no longer represented a threat. Hitler placated the regular military, the Reichswehr, by removing the SA as a rival military organization. This now allowed Hitler to enlist the complicit Reichswehr and conservative industrial leaders in enthusiastic participation in rearming Germany to serve his territorial ambitions.

* * * *

Before even hearing Hitler's public speech, Konrad Richter provided Lieutenant Colonel Spencer Fleming further details. The entire senior leadership of the SA executed. The violent removal of the SA as a threat to Adolf Hitler's ambitions proved a resounding success. A strengthened Hitler now exploited the German power structure as willing collaborators in his dark plans.

Covert Abwehr penetration into the heart of the SS was impressive. Fleming also knew by his own interactions with Reichswehr officers, the Abwehr was predominately anti-Nazi. The Nazi SS security section, the Sicherheitsdienst des Reichsführers-SS headed by Reinhard Heydrich, viewed as a growing rival intelligence agency. Choosing to feed information to the United States with no formal intelligence agency perhaps a safer form of subversion than trusting the duplicitous British MI6 Secret Intelligence Service or the French Deuxième Bureau.

Oster had his reason for selecting a military attaché as a conduit. Perhaps the Abwehr did not understand that peacetime military intelligence held little status in the U.S. Army. Its function primarily centered on signals intelligence and code breaking. Political intelligence held no specific interest to the War Department. The military attachés little different from U.S. Department of State consular officers with a designated area of interest.

Fleming could only guess as to their objective for leaking secret information to the Americans. Perhaps nothing more than keeping options open should an opportunity present itself to bring about the downfall of Hitler?

What they did not realize by selecting him as an anti-Nazi conspirator, they got more than just a conduit into the U.S. War Department. The information Richter provided since they met held limited interest to the War Department. As to the details, background, and power struggle behind this dramatic purge of the SA, Fleming would file nothing more to the War Department than material soon becoming public. To do otherwise might suggest the information obtained through espionage, contrary to his official portfolio as military attaché.

Engaging in espionage was exactly what he was up to off the books in parallel with his assigned military duties. An arrangement made in New York before taking up the diplomatic military post in Berlin. The recipients remained unnamed State Department officials, commercial American interests, and American

Jewish organizations. Recruited for the effort by someone he met during his consulting assignment to the U.S. delegation to the Paris peace treaty negotiations in 1919. The New York lawyer Allen Dulles now a good friend. As a lawyer, Dulles also served to conceal Fleming's spying activities that appeared far more useful to American interests than his attaché duties.

Following the second meeting with Richter, Fleming placed an overseas call from the U.S. Embassy in Berlin. He assumed the military intelligence service the Abwehr and perhaps the Nazi intelligence agency the Sicherheitsdienst des Reichsführers-SS, the SD, listened to overseas telephone calls. By prior arrangement, he placed his call to the law offices of Sullivan & Cromwell during business hours.

"Extension twenty please."

"Hello, this is Hilda. May I help you?"

"This is Mr. Jones. Are you ready to take this down?"

"Yes. Go ahead."

"546325 094257 419601 633501 170226 247110 318601 438101 359801 258701 330938 343516 338701 299701 533723 360801 265801 489901 576901 674201 227401. End of message. Everything clear?"

"Yes, Sir."

Fleming disconnected the call.

For anyone eavesdropping, Mr. Jones could be anyone at the embassy. Fleming transmitted his routine reports to the War Department telegraphically by the embassy communications staff using a designated U.S. Army cipher. Lengthy less urgent reports went into the diplomatic pouch. For Hitler's purge of the SA, he drafted his opinion of the larger implications and sent off the report by telegraph to the War Department. To his New York lawyer colleague, easier to transmit brief information by telephone to Allen Dulles' secretary.

The string of numbers represented Fleming's personally created code. This short message provided only the immediate broad details of the event. Based on chess games and a reference source and method known only to him and Dulles, it used numerical representation instead of letters. This avoided the vulnerability of letter-based representation of transposition and substitution ciphers. Every language presented a frequency of usage for each letter of the alphabet. Therefore, even complex ciphers risked the potential for advanced mathematical analytical decoding methods. His experience during the Great War as an officer in the G-2 intelligence division of the AEF provided a good grounding in ciphers. Fleming's method avoided this with no single number or even two numbers representing a letter thereby removing letter frequency analysis.

This encrypted message translated '*SA leadership purged. Rohm murdered by SS on Hitler's order.*'

CHAPTER 2

El Paso, Texas | September 1915

As a graduate of the United States Military Academy at West Point, New York in June 1915, newly minted second lieutenant Spencer Fleming learned quickly how things worked in the army. Graduating in the top academic percentage of his class with a degree in civil engineering, logic suggested a posting somewhere as an engineering officer perhaps in the Corps of Engineers. Assigned instead to the Military Intelligence Division as a G-2 officer. In two months, he was to report to 8th Cavalry Brigade headquarters at Fort Bliss in El Paso, Texas.

Requesting to see the assignments officer, the explanation was simple, "You speak Spanish fluently. A skill needed with tensions on the Mexican border."

"But the cavalry, Sir? I know nothing of horses."

"Well I suspect you will quickly learn, Lieutenant."

After enjoying leave at home to Sacramento, California, he arrived by train at Fort Bliss in September. His first time in the Southwest. The train route originated from Sacramento to San Diego then east across Arizona and New Mexico. The scenery reminded him of the old silent movie the *Great Train Robbery* he saw as a young boy and the popular more recent Hollywood western films. Stark dry dusty country with rocks and no trees. What now stood out in his mind was the prospect of riding a horse at the gallop. For a city boy, it looked like a good way to suffer grave injury.

El Paso was located at the furthest western point of Texas on the border with Mexico. It looked no different from the barren terrain over which he just traveled. Disembarking at the railroad station, he got his first opportunity to return salutes of several enlisted soldiers also awaiting transport by truck to nearby Fort Bliss.

Fort Bliss was an important military post for securing the border with Mexico. When the transport truck deposited the soldiers at the fort, Fleming saw a vast expanse of tents extending over hundreds of acres. The influx of thousands of troops radiated outward from the modest collection of permanent buildings constructed decades earlier. Troop strength began swelling since the Mexican Revolution started in 1910. In April of 1914, Brigadier General John J. Pershing took command of Fort Bliss and relocated the 8th Brigade from the Presidio in San Francisco as border tensions increased with Mexico.

Assigned to intelligence, Fleming became part of a small staff headed by Major James Ryan consisting of another lieutenant, a sergeant, and corporal. In his forties, Ryan reflected the slow promotion in the Army during peacetime. After exchanging pleasantries, he learned Ryan was a veteran cavalry officer.

"Our job is to gather information and make sense of it, Lieutenant. I served in the Philippines where we used informants extensively. Difficult here since we do not cross the border into Mexico. So we must be creative. Best we can do is use cooperative sources that cross back and forth across the border doing business. I speak Spanish as does Lieutenant Turner and Sergeant Rutherford. I imagine that is why you got this assignment."

"What exactly is the situation in Mexico that is causing concern on this side of the border, Sir?"

"Not sure of all the details but it started in 1910 after a rigged election keeping Porfirio Diaz in power after thirty years of rule. Armed revolt broke out in northern Mexico. Diaz was forced out and Francisco Madero became president. His government did not work out. Although Madero was a wealthy landowner, he had leftist leanings. This provoked the conservatives and business interests with support of the military to remove Madero. Rumor has it that our ambassador to Mexico encouraged the change of regime. Madero was ousted and then murdered in 1913. General Victoriano Huerta then became president.

"Well, Huerta didn't work out either. He increased the size of the military and dissolved the legislature. Civil war broke out. The United States did not recognize the Huerta regime. President Wilson even sent U.S. Marines to occupy Veracruz in April last year. An alliance of constitutional rebels ousted Huerta but then fell out after toppling the regime. A conservative faction under wealthy landowner Venustiano Carranza emerged victorious.

"Pancho Villa with his power base in the north and Emiliano Zapata in the south formed an alliance against Carranza. Recognizing Villa as his principal adversary, Carranza tried to split the Villa-Zapata alliance. Led by an able tactician General Obregón, Carranza's forces badly defeated Villa, killing 4,000 and capturing 6,000 in April of this year. The following month Obregón again defeated Villa in another battle.

"Sounds like Villa is badly crippled," Fleming said.

"You would think so but our intelligence from sources in Ciudad Juarez just across the Rio Grande report Villa still has enough men under arms to be a factor."

"What about the other guy Zapata?"

"Zapata backed away from Villa. Some sort of disagreement according to rumors. Probably a power struggle. Whatever the story, the U.S. troop buildup is more about what's happening in the north of Mexico between Carranza and Villa."

"So we wait and see how this plays out?"

"Not exactly. Washington has apparently taken sides favoring Carranza. Politics is not my specialty but I suspect it is because Carranza is the preferred candidate between lousy choices. Carranza is a constitutionalist but also a conservative. Running out of money to buy weapons, Villa pissed off Washington by raiding haciendas and business interests in Chihuahua. Americans owned some of those business interests. Villa started to look like a dangerous socialist populist.

"Whatever the thinking, Washington is helping Carranza. We are allowing him to transport several thousand troops by rail through the United States to reinforce his stronghold at Agua Prieta in Sonora. Then we moved five of our regiments to Douglas, Arizona directly across the border in case Obregón and Villa go at it again."

In just a few weeks, the situation seemed resolved. The aggressive Villa left his stronghold base in the State of Chihuahua moving west into Sonora to attack the main stronghold of the Carranza army at Agua Prieta on November 1. Villa's intelligence failed to discover that Carranza had reinforced Agua Prieta. Expecting a garrison of only 1,200, Villa faced 6,500 protected by new fortifications and defensive trenches. Most importantly, newly acquired machine guns decimated Villa's cavalry resulting in what seemed a final disastrous defeat.

The United States refused to allow hundreds of Villa's wounded transport by rail through the United States. With his troops ready to mutiny, Villa reorganized his remaining forces and attacked the town of Hermosillo, Sonora. Promising his forces they could do as they wished after they seized the town, the attack largely failed as his troops fell to looting and rape.

Villa's army fell apart. Wounded were abandoned, men deserted, and 1,500 surrendered by accepting an amnesty offered by Carranza. Only 200 men remained loyal and followed Villa to seek refuge in the mountains of Chihuahua.

The United States recognized the Carranza government thereby allowing the flow of weapons while refusing to sell Villa weapons. Pancho Villa was just another failed populist revolutionary turned bandit. It appeared the Villistas ceased to exist. Consensus suggested this largely settled the Mexican Revolution. This however proved premature.

Villa now regarded the United States as an enemy. As he retreated east, he attacked the border town of Nogales, Arizona engaging U.S. army forces before withdrawing.

Violence escalated in January 1916 when Villa forces removed sixteen employees of the American Smelting and Refining Company from a train near Santa Isabel, Chihuahua then murdered them.

****

Fleming spent his first few months settling into military life and the different environment of the American Southwest. Rough accommodations in a high desert climate. A large tent serving to house six junior officers tested his adaptability. Two potbellied stoves provided uneven warmth with nighttime cold winter temperatures. Everyone shaved with water heated on these stoves. Whether summer or winter, the outdoor latrines were a disgusting necessity after having always lived with indoor toilets.

Fleming liked Ryan and the small intelligence team. Other than the new corporal, the others had years of military service.

Brigadier General John J. 'Black Jack' Pershing was a commanding presence. Tall, distinguished, and handsome, with a distinguished military career. He got the sobriquet Black Jack from commanding the African-American buffalo soldiers of the 10th Cavalry, distinguishing himself with the assault on San Juan Hill in Cuba in 1898. However, the name Black Jack could equally denote his fearsome command demeanor.

However, it was Pershing's poise following a devastating personal tragedy that astounded all soldiers under his command. In August as his family prepared to join him at Fort Bliss, a fire killed his wife and three young daughters. After the funerals, he returned to duty with his only surviving young son. Fleming received his first introduction to the General a week after his return to Fort Bliss. By unsaid agreement, none of the headquarters staff made any direct reference to the tragedy by offering condolences. As for Pershing, he buried his grief completely by reestablishing his command presence following weeks of absence.

Pershing distinguished himself serving in the Philippines commanding troops in several battles in the Moro Rebellion. Because of the Army's strict seniority-based system of promotion, Pershing held only the rank of captain in the regular army in 1905.

Having ascended to the presidency in 1901 after the assassination of President McKinley, Theodore Roosevelt took the 1904 election. During his time in office, Roosevelt became frustrated with the limited advancement of proven officers during the

Spanish-American War and subsequent service in the Philippines. Roosevelt therefore exercised his prerogative as President to petition Congress to promote Pershing and several other mid-level officers to brigadier general. Pershing's promotion jumped him over 800 more senior officers.

* * * *

Lieutenant Charles Turner was a Texan from San Antonio. The son of a cattle rancher, he chose a military career following in the tradition of his grandfather and older brother by attending the Citadel Military College in Charleston, South Carolina. Eight years older than Fleming, Turner saw action in the Philippines during the Morro Rebellion. He took a liking to the young West Point graduate. Turner also taught Fleming enough horsemanship to provide essential proficiency.

Frustrated with collecting third hand intelligence from civilians doing business on both sides of the border, Turner wanted to do something proactive. At a staff meeting of the small intelligence unit, Turner offered his idea.

"If the situation turns hostile in Mexico we have lousy information, Major. The maps have no topographic details. Most date from the war sixty years ago. The information on these guys Carranza, Villa, and Zapata is little better than what we read in newspapers. We just sit on our arses and compile useless reports."

"Very well, Lieutenant. You have a suggestion?"

"Yes, Sir. We do a lot of business with Mexicans supplying beef, vegetables, and horses. I have looked at the quartermaster's procurement records. These businessmen or their agents operate out of Juarez. What if Lieutenant Fleming and I began operating undercover in Juarez?"

Fleming jerked his head to look at Turner. What the hell was he suggesting? Turner never discussed this with him.

"We are not authorized to operate in Mexico, Lieutenant. It's called spying," Major Ryan said.

"Technically. But that's the only way to get useful information, Sir. Develop sources in Mexico. We can't do that from here."

"So you go into Juarez and start asking questions? Sounds like a good way to get your throat cut. Besides, the General will not authorize it."

"We go there with a perfect cover. We are a civilian procurement contractors hired to consolidate the many individual suppliers. We actually conduct business for the quartermaster. We become these gringos conveniently in Juarez to do business without them having to go through all the bullshit of dealing with U.S. Army bureaucracy."

Major Ryan laughed. "I admit it's an interesting idea. The quartermaster will hate it. The General may throw you out of his office. What do say, Lieutenant Fleming?"

"Makes sense I guess." Silently Fleming thought it did sound like a good way to get his throat cut.

Major Ryan said, "Really? Turner here looks the part of someone likely buying beef for the Army. You Fleming look like a city-slicker fresh out of college, which you are. How did you learn to speak Spanish?"

"We had a Mexican housekeeper when I was growing up. Her son was like a brother to me."

"Jesus Christ. Are you willing to volunteer for Turner's screwball mission?"

"Yes, Sir. I can take care of myself."

Major Ryan knew Fleming's record at West Point. Academically ninth in his graduating class. Middleweight boxing champion his last two years. Fencing team. Proficient in the Japanese martial art of Jujutsu. Maybe he could take care of himself.

Silently, Fleming was furious with Turner for not discussing this first before putting him on the spot. Then again, wasn't this why he joined the army instead of pursuing a different career?

To everyone's surprise, General Pershing embraced the idea. Only his chief of staff Lt. Col. Smith harbored reservations citing orders to remain on this side of the border.

"I do not interpret our orders from restraining efforts to secure vital intelligence," Pershing said. "Lieutenants Turner and Fleming do not represent a military incursion, However, I trust both of you understand the risks? If captured you could be executed as spies. Not only by Pancho Villa but forces loyal to Carranza. "

"Yes, Sir," both replied.

Major Ryan explained the arrangement to legitimize their cover. Recognizing the importance of intelligence, Pershing ordered the post quartermaster to work with Ryan to allow for Turner and Fleming to procure required goods posing as civilian contractors. Pershing even signed a fake document naming Turner and Fleming as U.S. government procurement agents. There modest expenses of buying drinks and train tickets begrudgingly covered by the quartermaster from cash reserves used for buying incidental supplies.

Within a week, he and Turner made their first foray into Ciudad Juarez. Dressed in civilian clothing, they posed as civilian contractors charged with managing the many suppliers of meat and other food supplies as well as cavalry mounts and mules to the growing U.S. Army installations on the border from Texas, New Mexico, and Arizona. Armed with a letter of authorization from General Pershing they began contacting known Mexican suppliers. Fleming suggested they print business cards and rent an El Paso post office box as their address. Southwest Livestock Supply.

The native-born Texan Turner fit into his role as a Texan businessman. Fleming would pose as his young cousin from California to account for his different Spanish accent.

Lieutenant Turner was a Texan from San Antonio. Since his commissioning in 1910, Turner served with the 13th Cavalry Regiment patrolling the border since the outbreak of the Mexican Revolution as violence repeatedly spilled over the border. He knew the border well. When Pershing took command of expanded forces on the border, Turner transferred to his headquarters staff. Fleming respected Turner's leadership for their Mexico mission.

Fleming soon relished the excitement offered by going undercover into enemy territory. The prospect of adventure in a military career off to a good beginning.

Fleming and Turner spent a good deal of time south of the border during February. They became part of the business environment. Relationships proved productive with many of the suppliers. Wary at first to be dealing with middlemen, most quickly appreciated avoiding the need to cross the border without having to lower their prices. Generous with buying drinks, Turner and Fleming made many personal connections. During these drinking sessions, they picked up useful intelligence. As businessmen, most of their Mexican contacts viewed Pancho Villa as a bandit and threat. Villa's activities became a constant topic of discussion.

Then on March 9, Villa forces attacked the border town of Columbus, New Mexico and U.S. Army post Camp Furlong with over 200 soldiers. Ten civilians and eight U.S. soldiers of the 13th Cavalry Regiment died with eight others wounded. Stealing horses and seizing weapons, including three machine guns, the raiders burned the town before fleeing back into Mexico.

However, the raid proved another disastrous engagement for Villa by losing sixty-seven dead and dozens wounded. A machine gun unit of the 13th Cavalry inflicted most of the casualties. The machine gun again proving Villa's undoing as it was for so many other military commanders in the war raging in Europe since 1914.

The rash move now made Pancho Villa a dangerous bandit and enemy of the United States. The following day President Woodrow Wilson concurred with the commander of the U.S. Army's Southern District to order General Pershing to command a military force to pursue Villa into Mexico and eliminate these raids. Wilson released a statement to the press:

'An adequate force will be sent at once in pursuit of Villa with the single object of capturing him and putting a stop to his forays. This can and will be done in entirely friendly aid to the constituted authorities in Mexico and with scrupulous respect for the sovereignty of that Republic.'

Events took an abrupt turn after Villa's raid on Columbus. For several days, there was nonstop activity at Fort Bliss headquarters. For the G-2 staff, they assembled what maps existed of the states of Chihuahua and Sonora in preparation for the campaign into Mexico. Badly outdated with topographic features vaguely detailed and rail lines missing. Making do, they manually revised maps with information collected from local sources that knew northern Mexico.

Incensed by Villa's attack on his old regiment, Turner suggested to Major Ryan that he and Fleming return to Juarez and see if they can pick up information on the latest known concentrations of Pancho Villa's forces. After consulting with Pershing, Ryan approved their mission.

On March 15, just a week after Villa's raid on Columbus, Pershing commenced moving 6,600 U.S. troops across the border into Mexico. He would make his headquarters in Colonia Dublán, Chihuahua 125 miles south of the U.S. border.

Three days later, Turner and Fleming crossed into Juarez. A principal supplier of beef and cavalry mounts to U.S. border troops kept an office in Juarez, useful for managing his shipments of cattle and horse shipments into the United States. They would try to use him to infiltrate deeper into Villas territory deeper south in Chihuahua.

Luis Moreno owned a vast tract of land over two hundred miles south of the border near the small town of Ciudad Cuauhtemoc west of the larger city of Ciudad Chihuahua. Turner and Fleming enjoyed a friendly relationship with Moreno who typically wired them when he was to be in Juarez. Intending to send Moreno a message, they were surprised to find him at his Juarez office.

"Luis, good to see you amigo," Turner said.

Seated in the small office with his local business representative, Moreno turned as Turner and Fleming entered. The face of the usually exuberant Moreno was a picture of distress.

"What is wrong my friend?" Turner asked.

"They have killed my wife. My Natalia." His chin fell to his chest and he wept uncontrollably."

CHAPTER 3

Guerrero, Chihuahua, Mexico | March 1916

Luis Moreno said, "It happened three days ago. I came to El Paso to supervise that latest shipment of 100 horses. Villa must have just returned from the raid on Columbus. The murdering pig is nothing more than a bandit," Luis Moreno said. His tears now replaced with rage.

"The Villistas came to the hacienda looking for food, horses, and guns. Natalia and several of the ranch hands resisted. Villa personally ordered them shot, including Natalia. He spared our elderly housekeeper and her husband. Told them to spread the word this is what happens to those supporting Carranza. Then he burned the home my father built."

Moreno handed Turner the telegram received that morning. Signed by someone named Juanita, undoubtedly the elderly housekeeper.

Luis Moreno was a politically active large landowner. He allied himself with the current acting head of state Venustiano Carranza, also from an upper middle-class cattle-ranching family. Although a politician not a military man, Carranza headed the Constitutionalist Army as *Primer Jefe*, supported by capable generals. Like Carranza, Moreno supported former president Madero, and joined the Constitutionalist rebellion that overthrew the military dictatorship of Victoriano Huerta. After the falling-out between Carranza and Villa, the vocal Moreno became an enemy to Villa.

"I shall never rest until Villa is dead."

Moreno could be the perfect source for gathering information on Villa. His lands were deep in southern Chihuahua. He undoubtedly had a wide range of contacts throughout the regions of Villa's support. Motivated by the murder of his wife, Moreno also provided perfect cover. A fervent Mexican nationalist, Carranza publicly condemned President Wilson's declaration to send U.S. military into Mexico as a violation of Mexican sovereignty. For Turner and Fleming, the Carrancistas therefore represented a personal threat to their mission. Their amiable relationship with Moreno offered a measure of protection.

Turner took the opportunity to make his pitch. "You of course know General Pershing has crossed the border with 6,000 American soldiers. His orders are to hunt down Villa. Fleming and I are to secure beef to feed the army in the field and provide as many replacement cavalry mounts we can find. Will you help us, Luis?"

Moreno nodded. "Of course."

"Excellent. The United States is also offering a bounty of $10,000 for information that leads to the capture or death of Pancho Villa. Will you take us south with you?"

"Yes. I leave on the train tomorrow morning. I will add my own bounty for anyone that kills Villa," Moreno said.

"We can do business together supplying Pershing's troops and work with you to locate Villa. Perhaps it is best to introduce us as your business representatives, Luis. Señor Carranza does not welcome the gringo incursion into Mexico."

Moreno said, "That is unfortunate. Villa will likely hide in the Sierra Madre Mountains to the southwest of my lands. If Mexican forces would join with the Americans, Villa risks destruction of his reduced forces if he ventures out of hiding. If Villa remains in the mountains, he will lose his following among the peasants."

They took the train to Ciudad Chihuahua 200 miles south. Transferring to another train, they arrived in the small town of Cuauhtemoc in late afternoon. The following day they would go by horseback to Moreno's destroyed hacienda to the southwest.

Turner and Fleming looked the part of their covers. Stetsons, well-worn boots, working clothes. Each sported a Bowie knife from their belts. Expecting to be on horseback at some point, they both carried saddlebags. Inside were their Colt model M1911 .45 caliber semi-automatic army service pistols with spare magazines and field glasses. Knowing something of navigation, Turner also carried a sextant and good compass for fixing latitude and longitude by striking the location of the sun or visible celestial bodies at night.

While Turner sat next to Moreno conversing on the train ride south, Fleming reflected on their changed circumstances. Forays into Ciudad Juarez right on the border hardly felt like operating in a foreign country. Heading deep into Mexico alone into a shooting war between rival Mexican military factions made this entirely different.

He and Turner discussed how they would communicate with headquarters. Telegraph the only likely method. Public telegraph in a potentially hostile country meant that any communication needed at least basic encryption to disguise the real meaning from the telegraph operator.

Fleming offered a solution. From classes at West Point, coded communications took on new importance for the battlefield. Immediate actionable intelligence must have a means of communications to be of any use. Pershing's many regiments likely moving in different directions could not string telephone wires. Wireless communications with limited range also required bulky equipment, difficult for forces on the move. That left the network of telegraph lines connecting the desolate areas of the American southwest and Mexico.

Fleming therefore devised a simple code to transmit messages to headquarters using Moreno's business interests as cover. Villa's forces referred to as horses. Locating a prize stallion for the General referred to Villa himself. Movement stated as on the hoof or by rail. The Carrancistas referred to as the completion. Locations expressed in four-digit number groups, the first for latitude followed by longitude, with the first two numbers representing degrees and the second two representing minutes. These conformed to a grid layout Fleming prepared on a map before they entered Mexico.

The telegram addressed to Moreno's office in Juarez. The message then relayed to the Fort Bliss quartermaster for immediate forwarding to Major Ryan. Ryan could then transmit any useful intelligence to Pershing in the field. With Moreno's complicity, the communications would look like normal business to any Mexican telegrapher.

Turner appeared comfortable in these surroundings. If he was fearful, he did not show it. Fleming's anxiety increased as they journeyed further from the border. Other than his quick mind and fluency in Spanish, he possessed few skills or experience of use on this mission. He was out of his element in the barren southwest. Turner had taken their low intensity spying close to the border to a dangerous level by going deep into enemy territory. Other than Luis Moreno, any faction of Mexican military was a potential threat. Now he knew what every new soldier felt the first time going into battle.

They spent the night at the home of the mayor of Ciudad Cuauhtemoc, a friend of Luis Moreno. The body of Moreno's wife lay in a coffin at the local church. The funeral mass scheduled for the day after tomorrow. Early the next day, Turner and Fleming rode with Moreno and his ranch foreman to visit the site of the attack on his hacienda.

Moreno and his foreman toured the devastation. The foreman wept as he related the experience of returning to the hacienda with several ranch hands. "As the buildings burned, we watched as a large force of mounted riders rode away to the west. I told Juan and Carlos to follow the attackers."

Moreno said, "Miguel says Villa camped ten miles west of here. My two rancheros spent the night watching the encampment. In the morning they observed Villa and over a hundred of his men breaking camp and continuing west."

Fleming produced his map for the foreman to locate Villa's first camp location.

Returning to Cuauhtemoc late that night, they needed to wait until morning to send a telegram to Pershing. Fleming composed the message and set off early for the telegraph office at the rail station. Addressed to Moreno's Juarez office, it read '*Located a prize stallion for the General. Traveling with a herd of 100 horses west. Last location yesterday 2806 by 1073. Reliable source. Signed Fleming, SLS.*'

Turner and Fleming kept to the background during the mass and funeral arrangements. Moreno told them once he buried Natalia they would began the search for information on the whereabouts of Pancho Villa.

Cuauhtemoc was a small town. The funeral drew people from the surrounding area to pay their respects to Luis Moreno. To Fleming, the mayor said, "Señor Moreno is held in high respect. Very generous. He uses his wealth to help the community and provide well-paid work."

Following mass, the town prepared a great feast of food and drink outside in spite of the cold high desert day. After making the rounds of the crowd to thank everyone, Moreno came to Turner and Fleming. "I must make arrangements to manage my business affairs from Cuauhtemoc. That will take a couple of days. Then I will begin my search for revenge. Friday we shall go by train to Guerrero further west of my hacienda. There is a garrison of Carrancista troops there. Perhaps they can mount search patrols to find Villa. I shall telephone Carranza."

* * * *

On March 24, Turner and Fleming travel by train to Guerrero with Moreno where they hoped to pick up information on Villa's movements. On arriving, Moreno immediately sought out the local Carrancista commander. Captain Delgado knew Moreno and placed a telephone call for him directly to Carranza.

"Presidente Carranza has ordered me to send out scouts and see if we can discover Villa's main body of troops," Delgado said, "Are you staying in Guerrero?"

Delgado looked at Turner and Fleming with an expression of suspicion. "Who are these two gentlemen?"

Moreno said, "They work for me in El Paso. As you know, I sell cattle and horses to the American Army."

"You know of course that two weeks ago thousands of American troops entered Mexico. Violating Mexico sovereignty," Delgado said.

"My dealings with the Americans are a matter of business. The American army is hunting Villa because we have not been able to kill this murdering bandit. Understand this, Captain, I do not care who kills Villa as long as he dies. On this, I disagree with Presidente Carranza. Find Villa for me, Captain. The Americans are offering a bounty for his head. I too offer a bounty for the murderer of my wife."

"I understand, Don Moreno. I shall begin sending out patrols."

Moreno intended to stay in Guerrero only a few days. He hoped to elicit help from other landowners. Villa was likely here in the south of the State of Chihuahua after his foolish raid on Columbus. All of Chihuahua was Villa's power base. The poor peasants that worked the land. The landowners feared Villa's populist power that threatened their economic security. Unlike Moreno, most avoided politics fearing reprisals from the Villistas. Moreno hoped to garner at least their secret support of providing information. If Villa could be located, the resources of what now constituted the regular Mexican military combined with thousands of American forces should be able kill or capture him.

They took two rooms in a small hotel adjacent to a popular cantina. Turner and Fleming shared a room allowing one to remain awake in shifts.

While Moreno had business elsewhere, they went to the cantina. They arrived early. Turner ordered a bottle of tequila. Growing up in San Antonio, he was comfortable in these surroundings. Fleming not so much.

Turner took to engaging in conversation with a flirtatious waitress in a peasant dress revealing bare shoulders and cleavage. All the while drinking a fair amount of liquor, he made no attempt at lowering his voice.

"Charlie, keep it down. Every time that waitress comes over here we get some nasty stares," Fleming said.

"Spence, don't tell me you haven't noticed those magnificent breasts on that pretty señorita when she bends over our table?"

"Christ, Charlie, she might be one of these guys' sisters or girlfriend. We don't need the trouble."

Too late. The woman came over displaying a broad smile. "Need anything, gentlemen?"

Turner burst into a broad grin and said suggestively, "Depends what you have to offer."

A man jumped out his chair and approached aggressively pushing the waitress away. "What are you gringos doing here?"

Fleming answered, "Just waiting for our boss, Don Moreno?"

"I am talking to your loudmouth friend not you," The man said staring at Turner.

Turner and Fleming both stood up. Ignoring Fleming, the man took a swing at Turner. The table overturned as the two went at it. Exchanging blows, the man drew a knife from his boot.

Afraid Turner would draw his large Bowie knife and escalate the fight into a bloody disaster, Fleming moved toward the man but someone grabbed both his arms holding him from behind. Instinctively, Fleming shifted his feet to provide leverage to break one arm free. This followed with a turn of his body while grabbing the man's other arm. Throwing the man to the floor, Fleming followed with a blow to the neck using the edge of his hand.

Fleming stepped toward the other man holding the knife. The man turned on him thrusting the knife forward. Fleming caught the wrist twisting it causing the knife to drop. Wrenching the man's arm back forced him to the floor where Fleming delivered a powerful blow with his fist to the kidneys.

All this transpired in the span of only a few seconds. Everyone in the cantina stared but nobody made any threatening moves.

Captain Delgado entered the cantina with Luis Moreno just as the melee began. Drawing his revolver, Delgado yelled, "What is going on?"

Fleming responded, "Just a misunderstanding fueled by drink, Captain. I don't think these two are injured. I will buy them a drink to make peace." He then reached down to lift the man who pulled the knife to his feet while purposely stepping on the knife. The other man by now was up on one knee rubbing his neck.

With calm returned, Captain Delgado and Moreno joined Turner and Fleming at their table.

Delgado said, "That was impressive, Señor Fleming. Where did you learn to fight like that?"

"When I was in school in California. My best friend was Mexican. His older brother introduced us to boxing. We worked out at a local gym. The coach was a professional wrestler. Mexican *lucha libre*. The guys that wear the colorful masks. Taught my friend and me wrestling throws. Combined with boxing, it made for effective street fighting when I was a teenager. Older boys learned the hard way to leave us alone."

The story partly true. Fleming left out the judo training at West Point. His earlier training in boxing and Mexican free-style wrestling provided good foundations for advancing his skills with boxing, judo, and fencing to fulfill his athletic requirements at West Point.

"A drink, Captain?" Turner said. Shaken by the incident that could have spiraled out of control, he nodded to Fleming saying, "Thanks, Spence. Didn't know you could handle yourself like that."

* * * *

The following day was a slow day for Turner and Fleming. Moreno left them alone as he traveled out of Guerrero. Because of the disturbance yesterday, they might become victims of anti-American sentiment. Fleming did not confront Turner although disappointed with his stupidity. From now on, he would exercise his own judgment. While Turner held higher rank, he was not officially in command. Perhaps realizing his imprudent behavior, Turner did not argue against staying out of site in the hotel, sending the hotel clerk out for food.

To pass the time, Turner suggested they play cards. "You play poker, Spence?"

Fleming nodded with a slight smile. Although gambling was against regulations, poker kept him in spending money at West Point. Gifted in mathematics, he applied odds in how he played and bet. Most poker players could not avoid displaying subtle *tells* which he learned to read. Playing for pennies, Turner still lost five dollars, pronouncing Fleming unusually lucky.

Moreno returned late that night knocking on their door. "I have done all I can here. All anyone knows is that Villa is likely in southern Chihuahua. Unfortunately, not helpful. Plenty of mountains where he can hide.

"But he cannot simply hide. He is a clever sonofabitch. This is where he has a following among the peasants. To preserve his army, he must keep the support the peasants. His army needs food, horses, ammunition. Only a matter of time before he must also face the Americans.

"I return to Cuauhtemoc tomorrow. Best you two return north. Too much bad blood against gringos right now. Look what happened in the cantina."

"Will you still relay any information you receive, Luis?" Turner said.

"Of course."

The next morning, Turner and Fleming waited for Moreno to join them at the cantina next door for coffee and breakfast before catching the eastbound train. The religious Moreno chose to attend mass first.

A loud noise of many horses and shouting caused the few cantina patrons to rush outside.

"Villistas?" Fleming asked the proprietor.

"*Si.* There shall be a battle with the Carrancista garrison. Best to find a hiding place."

Fleming said Turner, "On the other side of the hotel is a livery stable. Let's try to get to the hayloft."

Both pulled their service .45s from the saddlebags sticking the pistols in the back of their waistbands and exited the cantina backdoor. Outside the commotion became more chaotic. Looking into the street from between the alleyways between the buildings, they saw hundreds of Villistas flooding into the town. Yet no shooting erupted.

Turner and Fleming entered the rear of the livery barn cautiously. The stableman stood in the open large front doors occupied by watching the turmoil outside. Quietly they climbed into the hayloft unseen.

Within the hour, Villa's superior forces overwhelmed the unprepared Carrancista garrison without a shot. Earlier in the same morning, Villa did the same to the small Carrancista detachment of the village of Miñaca ten miles south.

Watching with their field glasses, Fleming and Turner looked down the street where the Carrancista garrison of about 75 soldiers stood unarmed in two rows in front of the church. Behind them stood Villistas with their rifles leveled. Other Villistas pushed three captured officers with wrists bound to the front. One was Captain Delgado.

Turner said, "Sonofabitch! That's Pancho Villa himself."

"Looks like the Carrancista garrison surrendered without firing a shot?" Fleming said.

"Looks like."

Moments later Villa took several steps backward as three of his soldiers stepped in front of the three Carrancista officers with rifles raised to their shoulders. Through the magnification of their field glasses, they saw Delgado saying something as three shots rang out cutting him off in midsentence. Another Villa soldier put a bullet into the head of each victim with a revolver.

"Fuck. Now what?" Turner said, expecting perhaps a slaughter of the captured Carrancistas. Instead, the Villistas herded the prisoners into the church placing guards at the entrances.

"At least not a massacre. But Villa will kill Moreno if he is captured," Fleming said.

"Us too."

"Got any ideas?"

"Maybe Villa will move on. He can't stay this exposed with both the Mexican Army and American Army searching for him. We wait until darkness. Might be able to sneak out of town. Problem will be evading pickets in terrain we don't know. Villa may be a bandit, but he's also a successful military commander with skilled subordinate officers."

Turner was correct. Within an hour, Villa assembled his troops numbering in the hundreds and departed Guerrero heading north. They looted the town of food and the Carrancista garrison of ordinance. Turner observed a wagon loaded with three Hotchkiss M1914 machine guns, the U.S. Army's newest machine gun. He was familiar with the weapon used by his regiment the 13th Cavalry headquartered at Columbus, New Mexico. Probably those stolen on Villa's raid just weeks ago. The machine guns greatly multiplied Villa's force potential.

The Hotchkiss replaced the monster Maxim M1904 water cooled belt-fed machine gun weighing over 140 pounds. The French developed the lighter air-cooled Hotchkiss. Usually manned by a team of three, a single soldier could operate the gun using feeding strips of ammunition instead of a belt. A devastating weapon firing an 8mm round at a rate of 450 rounds a minute. At just over 100 pounds including the tripod, it was mobile enough for easy transport. From a defensive position, these guns could defeat a superior force of attacking infantry or cavalry. Already in use by the French on the Western Front of the European war, the U.S. purchased several thousand as the country rearmed expecting possible entry into the European war.

As Villa's forces left, Turner and Fleming scanned the town using field glasses. A couple of dozen Villistas remained to secure the town and guard the prisoners in the church.

Turner remained in hiding in the loft while Fleming set off for the rail. If left unguarded, he would send a telegram to Pershing advising of the attack and the direction of Villa's departing main force.

"Be careful, Spence."

Fleming took a circuitous route by cutting south out of town to intercept the railroad tracks. From there he walked the tracks until coming to the railway station. Checking for Villista guards from several vantage points, only a single soldier was visible walking on the platform outside the telegraph office.

Sneaking through the station from the opposite side, Fleming came up behind the guard from the back as he passed the doorway. With his heavy Bowe knife, he slammed the butt of the knife down on the base of the man's neck rendering him unconscious. He then bound the man's wrists behind his back using the man's belt. Gagging him with his bandana, Fleming dragged him inside the telegraph office. No one was there. Stepping into the rail station, he saw two men talking.

Pulling his .45, he said, "Are one of you the telegraph operator?"

"*Si, Señor,*" One man answered.

Pulling both men inside the telegraph office, he handed the frightened operator the message to send. In the clear rather than concealed by code, it described Villa's raid, size of the force, direction, and the added firepower of three machine guns. Signed Fleming, SLS.

With the guard still unconscious, Fleming had the two men drag him under a wagon at the back of the station. Leaving abruptly, Fleming jogged the same route to return to the livery barn. He did not know the sympathies of the two railroad employees, but had no choice. With limited Villistas in town, he would take his chances. Once back at the livery barn, he and Turner intended to steal horses and make a run for it.

As Fleming approached the rear of the barn, he could hear loud voices from the nearby cantina. Villa soldiers eating and drinking. Perhaps the entire contingent of troops left in the town other than the guards on the prisoners in the church. Unfortunately, far too close to the livery barn for him and Turner to make an undetected escape by stealing horses. Just as well. He was not an accomplished horseman.

All he could do was sneak into the barn and climb back into the loft.

In his absence, Turner scavenged several canteens from the barn and filled them with water from the horse trough, preparing for escape once it became dark.

The situation again changed late in the afternoon. Watching from their vantage point in the barn loft, they saw hundreds of men on horseback descending on the town from the north.

Expecting possibly American troops, Turner exclaimed, "Fuck all. Might be Carrancistas. No wait. No uniforms. Shit! Looks like Villa is returning."

It was Villa. As hundreds of riders entered the town passing in front of the livery barn, it was obvious they had been in a fight. A significant number of the riders appeared wounded. A wagon transported the more serious. Officers barked orders.

"Sonofabitch. Look at those men helping that rider off his horse. Does that look like Villa to you?" Turner said.

"Could be. It's his right leg. See the bloody bandage?"

"That's the local doctor's office. So Villa is wounded. Can't ride which puts him out of action."

As night descended, Villistas occupied the barn to shelter from the cold. Turner and Fleming passed a long night in the hayloft each taking turns awake standing guard. Staying quiet, they had water but no food. Careful not to make noise, they relieved themselves in a far corner over the horse stalls.

The following morning just after sunrise, Fleming and Turner watched a wagon draw up in front of the doctor's surgery surrounded by a group of Villistas. Four soldiers carried the wounded Pancho Villa out the door of the doctor's surgery on a bed. Then a shot rang out. One soldier carrying Villa fell causing the makeshift stretcher to tilt sideways dumping Villa to the ground.

The shot came from a room over the cantina. Villistas stormed the cantina. The sound of gunfire came from inside. Minutes later, the soldiers dragged the body of Luis Moreno into the street.

After the doctor attended to Villa, his soldiers hoisted the bed into the wagon. Pancho Villa left with a dozen of his soldiers. The larger body of his forces remained to occupy Guerrero under command of General Nicolás Fernández. One of Villa's soldiers tied a rope to the ankles of Moreno and dragged the body away.

Turner and Fleming watched while sitting well back from the hayloft door opening concealed from view below. The Villistas moved about the town erecting defensive breastworks barriers from wagons, barrels, and stacks of building lumber.

"Looks like they are expecting an attack."

Turner and Fleming had no way of knowing that Villa suffered a major setback in his third attack of the day on the Carrancista garrison in the town of San Ysidro ten miles northeast of Guerrero. After capturing the garrisons at Miñaca then Guerrero that morning without firing a shot, somehow word reached San Ysidro.

Pancho Villa was a formidable military tactician along the style of Robert E. Lee. Apart from his great populist following, his style always weighted to offensive action using mobility and surprise. However, he did not appreciate the hazards of attacking well-constructed defensive positions. That shortcoming cost him defeat in four battles the previous year against Carranza's most capable general Álvaro Obregón. Although Villa had superior numbers in his attacking force against San Ysidro, the Carrancistas prepared well after learning what happened in the other towns.

Whoever was commanding the Villistas in Villa's absence learned that lesson as they prepared to defend Guerrero.

Looking through his field glasses, Turner whispered, "Look out there a couple of hundred yards to the west of town. Those rocks low on that hillside. They've mounted one of those captured machine guns."

No way for Turner and Fleming to escape. As nighttime fell, Villistas huddled inside the barn for warmth. Another night without food with water running low while still trapped in the hayloft.

At first light, they looked in the distance to the north. As the sun rose higher, they made out a large cavalry force. Two riders displayed the American flag and the 7th Cavalry regimental colors. A bugle blaring an off-note call to arms meant the Villistas also saw the threat.

Fleming said, "We must make our move, Charlie. That machine gun emplacement will cut them to pieces. Can't see where the Vallistas deployed the other two."

"Best we can do is steal some horses from below and make a run for it. But if we have to shoot our way out, our chances are lousy."

Especially for Fleming having never ridden a horse at a gallop.

At least the barn was empty of Villistas as they took up positions on the defensive perimeter. It should provide the ability to saddle two horses. Once they rode out of the barn though, Fleming questioned their chances.

"Charlie. If we make it out, we need to attack that one machine gun position. By the time the cavalry realizes what they are up against it will be too late."

"With just our .45s and that Winchester you took off that Villista?" Turner said.

"Got to make the try, Charlie. Those machine guns will be situated to lay down enfilading fire if our cavalry attacks in a charge from where they are massed."

"Learned that at West Point I suppose? Shit. Green as grass and you want to attack a machine gun position with handguns. You got balls, but shit for brains, Spence."

"Well that's my plan, Charlie. You with me?"

"Well fuck. Let's do it."

With the barn now empty of Villistas, they climbed down from the loft. Fleming stood guard at the front of the open barn door while Turner saddled two horses.

Fleming now understood the wisdom of their shoulder holsters. Being a cavalry officer, Turner knew that carrying the sidearm under the opposite armpit made for quicker access than a holster on the hip while mounted.

With the soldier's bandolier over his shoulder and extra .45 magazines in his coat pocket, nothing else to do. More worried about staying in the saddle at a gallop. Holding the reins with one hand while holding the Winchester in the other making that more difficult.

Turner opened the rear barn door. With the Villistas setting up the defensive perimeter on the north side of the town, sneaking out from the south might give added seconds before fired on.

Fleming was the first out. As they moved away from the barn heading west, a startled Villista ran toward him. Puzzled for a moment, the man raised his rifle. No more than twenty feet away, Fleming swung the Winchester using only his right hand and shot him in the chest.

As they galloped away, several shots rang out. Fleming led the way toward the machine gun position in the rock outcropping a quarter mile away. As he drew within a hundred yards, he could see three Villistas peering over a large boulder toward the sound of gunfire. Looking back, Fleming saw Turner falling behind then slumping in the saddle bringing his horse to a stop.

Hit by a rifle round as they escaped, Turner slowly stumbled to the ground trying to dismount.

Fleming kept on guiding his horse up the slope behind the rock outcropping and dismounted. Two Villistas brandished rifles while the third wrestled to reposition the Hotchkiss machine gun.

Fleming remembered his training to take a second to find his target before firing blindly. Two hurried shots from the standing Villistas missed him.

His first shot dropped one man. Realizing he was dead if the machine gunner brought the Hotchkiss around, Fleming charged the position and the remaining rifleman.

Changing the rifle to his left hand, he drew the .45 to fire maximum rounds at this close range. Emptying the magazine killed both the rifleman and the other Villista manning the machine gun.

Looking back, he saw Turner on his feet stumbling toward the outcropping. From a distance, he could see several riders coming toward Turner at a full gallop. To secure their position, he wrestled the machine gun into place to face the attacking Villista riders.

He only saw the Hotchkiss briefly on the firing range at West Point. Never fired it, yet it was his only chance to save Turner. He quickly pulled several 24-round feeder strips from an ammunition box.

Looking toward Turner only made him more frantic. Turner was now on all fours. The Villistas closing fast. Fleming only had seconds to save Turner and probably himself. Fortunately, the Hotchkiss had a straightforward design. The entry point of the ammunition feeder strip was obvious.

Now on his knees, Turner faced the approaching Villistas firing his .45. Halting their advance, the Villistas raised their rifles from no more than twenty yards away. Before they could finish off Turner, Fleming cut down all four riders and three of the horses by expending all twenty-four 8mm rounds of the feeder strip.

Fleming rushed out to help Turner.

"Where are you hit?" Fleming said as he reached Turner.

"In the back."

Fleming could see the entry and exit wound in his upper left shoulder. Must have shattered the shoulder blade. Bleeding badly but lucky to be alive by missing the lung and heart.

From a distance, they heard the unmistakable bugle call signally the American charge of the 7th Cavalry. As Fleming helped Turner up into the outcropping, he looked back to see perhaps more than a hundred Villistas riding north out of Guerrero. Looking at the larger scene, he could see the Villistas' tactic. Position this machine gun to pour enfolding fire on the attacking American forces to break an attack. Then follow with attacking the American right flank with their cavalry now coming into position.

"Quickly, Charlie." Turner let out a gasp of pain as Fleming pulled him along roughly. "Sorry. No time to do this delicately."

Back in the rocks, Fleming took up position behind the Hotchkiss and inserted a fresh feeder strip. He had four boxes of ammunition.

The Villistas did not realize their machine gun position was now in the hands of the enemy until several riders fell from their mounts. However, to Fleming's dismay, they kept coming on at a gallop. Normally operated with a three-man gun crew, having to feed each strip of 24 rounds himself caused a pause in the rate of fire for several seconds to charge the gun with new ammunition.

Exhausting the 288 rounds of the first ammunition box, Fleming turned and retrieved a second box. Turner was now barely conscious and could not help him. The firing rate decimated the front ranks of the charging Villistas blunting their attack. To the north, a great cloud of dust rose up with a charge of the right flank of the 7th Cavalry. For the Villistas, the machine gun position became the secondary threat as they wheeled around to seek defense back within the town.

Minutes later a platoon of U.S. cavalry approached the rock outcropping cautiously. Someone was waving a red bandana wildly from the end of a rifle.

Waving the rifle, Fleming stood up and shouted to the sergeant, "I am an American Army officer. Get help. I have wounded up here."

The wary sergeant walked alone up the slope with a drawn service revolver.

Looking at the three dead Villistas, Fleming propped the Winchester against a boulder. "My name is Lieutenant Fleming and that is Lieutenant Turner. Do you have a surgeon?"

"Yes, Sir." He then yelled for one of the troopers to bring medical help and ordered the others to rejoin the developing cavalry assault.

The sergeant looked to be an old cavalry trooper with the insignia of a battalion sergeant major. He hurried down to his horse and removed his bedroll and bandages from his saddlebags.

Making Turner comfortable with a blanket, he pulled open Turner's shirt and placed a bandage to the bleeding exit wound. Looking up slightly bewildered, he said to Fleming, "How did you two wind up here?"

"Long story, Sergeant."

Looking at the three dead Villistas around the machine gun, and those mowed down by the machine good, he asked Fleming, "Who killed all these fucking bandits?"

"Lieutenant Turner and I."

"Well I'll be a sonofabitch," He said with wide grin. Standing up he came to attention and gave Fleming a salute. "You fellas saved a lot of troopers today by taking out this machine gun."

CHAPTER 4

Chaumont, France | June 1917

The press hailed the Battle of Guerrero as an opening success to expectations for a short military campaign. The Villistas suffered fifty-six dead and thirty-five wounded. The Americans incurred only five wounded in a five-hour battle. Colonel George Dodd, an old Indian fighter commanding was immediately promoted to brigadier general.

However, the 7th Cavalry had insufficient troops to finish off Villa's forces at Guerrero or prevent their escape. American forces then unsuccessfully chased Pancho Villa over the next several months. By this time, the de facto government of Carranza openly threatened American forces. President Wilson eventually abandoned the unfulfilled mission and Pershing returned his 12,000 soldiers back to the United States in January 1917.

For Spencer Fleming, his exploits in Mexico earned him promotion to first lieutenant, and a distinguished service cross for valor. With his boss Major Ryan coordinating intelligence for the Mexican field forces from El Paso, General Pershing made him his field intelligence officer for the remainder of the campaign.

The Mexican campaign served as a catalyst to mobilize National Guard units around the country with the expanding war in Europe threatening to involve the United States. The President mobilized 140,000 National Guardsmen to supplement the small U.S. Regular Army. Although the Mexico expedition failed to deliver Villa, it established General John Pershing as the preeminent field commander in the Army with his prior experience in the Philippines.

With the declaration of war against Germany in April 1917, President Wilson selected Pershing to command the American Expeditionary Forces. In September 1917, Wilson promoted Pershing, at the time a major general, to a full four-star general. It signaled his superior rank and independence from War Department interference in his prosecution of the war in Europe.

Pershing now had the unprecedented task of assembling and training an army of over a million strong to enter the conflict now three years old and stalemated in static trench warfare. To start, he must build on a regular army of only 127,000 inexperienced soldiers that would eventually grow to over two million by conscription and mobilization of National Guard units.

The equally daunting task facing Pershing was the shortage of experienced field officers to command troops at every level from battalion, to regiment, to brigade, to division, to corps. Only officers serving in the Spanish-American War or the Philippine-American War at the turn of the century had combat experience. The strict seniority promotion system also did not produce a meritocracy. The American Army officer corps therefore populated at every level with incompetence.

Fleming impressed Pershing with his ingenuity in contending with the frustrating communications problem. The new wireless technology had a limited range of thirty miles proving useless in coordinating the tentacles of the various units. The introduction of aircraft for reconnaissance proved erratic because of continual maintenance problems. Fleming also got the opportunity to develop interrogation techniques of captured Villistas and Mexican civilians. Surprising how much information people would give up given decent treatment and presented with reasonable motivations rather than fear.

For a junior officer, Fleming spent a substantial time interacting with Pershing and the senior command staff. Pershing took a liking to Fleming for producing useful results through hard work during the frustrating months in Mexico.

****

Tensions with Germany escalated with their unrestricted attacks on merchant vessels, including U.S. flagged vessels shipping supplies to Britain and France. In January 1917, the British intercepted and deciphered an encrypted message from German Foreign Minister Arthur Zimmermann to the German minister to Mexico. The message offered an alliance between Germany and Mexico if the United States entered the war. On February 3, the United States severed diplomatic ties with Germany. The country moved closer to entering the war in Europe.

Fleming received a forty-five day leave before reporting to the 1st Engineer Battalion of the newly formed 1st Infantry Division. The first opportunity to use his civilian engineering training from West Point.

It had been close to a year since seeing his parents following graduation from West Point. So much different now. He felt like he found his identity. Gone was the romanticized allure of travel and adventure. Mexico was decidedly not romantic, certainly not exotic. The entire U.S. southwest and northern Mexico was a hostile wasteland devoid of water and greenery. The adventure more than bargained for. Yet the violent experience was thrilling. Tamping down the fear, his performance nonetheless met his expectations under the circumstances. The adrenalin rush reinforced by the affirmation of accomplishing an extraordinary feat left a new sense of self. The choice of a military career validated. He was coming home profoundly matured.

Fleming was close to his parents. Each was a different personality imparting their own strengths to their only child. Spencer drew closer to his mother during his father's long periods of absence working on construction of the Panama Canal. From 1905 to 1910, he saw his father only for one month each year and twice visited the Canal Zone with his mother.

As a civil engineer, Edward Fleming made his professional reputation supervising construction for the Southern Pacific Railroad. In 1905, he took a position as a senior engineer on the Panama Canal Project. His longest leave was two months to return to their home in Sacramento following the great San Francisco earthquake on April 18, 1906.

While Spencer Fleming's father was soft-spoken with a calm demeanor, his mother was a whirl of energy. Never satisfied with the traditional role of women, she pursued an education. She received her law degree in 1893 from Stanford University, its first graduation class. Her abiding ambition was the Suffrage Movement. The denial of women to a host of rights enjoyed by men was an abomination. During her tenure at Stanford, she became not only an activist but also a talented strategist in confronting male-dominated social norms.

She met Edward Fleming at a company picnic for employees of the Southern Pacific Railroad. Fleming worked with her father also a civil engineer. Sharing her passionate expressions for the rights of women, led to a romance of intellectual equals.

That relationship sustained them through the birth of their first child. The birth of Spencer Fleming proved so difficult it threatened the life of both mother and child. Fortunately, the birth was at a hospital. On the advice of several doctors, Magda Fleming agreed to sterilization since a future pregnancy would be too dangerous.

Instead of doting on her only child, Magda Fleming set out to enrich him intellectually. From her he acquired his lifelong interest in understanding the world through critical thinking. At an early age he spoke German, French, and English. With her career and the financial means, the family hired a full-time housekeeper.

Spencer then acquired a new friend at school. Carlos was Mexican. The youngest son of a widowed mother struggling to raise her two sons on a meager wage cooking at a popular restaurant. When Edward left to work in Panama, Magda offered Lucia a job as a live-in housekeeper and cook. The arrangement allowed Lucia to bring her two sons and move from the two-room rented rooming house. With his propensity for languages, Spencer added Spanish to his repertoire.

The arrangement suited the needs of everyone. Spencer now had a brother his age and an older brother Enrique. For Lucia's older son, Magda paid Enrique to make repairs on the house. With

Lucia to supervise the boys, Magda could indulge her career ambitions each day at her law office in downtown Sacramento.

His mother's work included not only women's rights but also advocacy for minority rights. Spencer therefore grew up without the prevailing prejudices directed at the large Mexican population employed in California's agriculture. Not only did Spencer become fluent in Spanish, he also embraced Mexican culture.

Spencer's friendship with Carlos earned him the attention of school bullies. After one fistfight where he and Carlos suffered bruises and bloodied noses, older brother Enrique stepped in with some advice.

Enrique was in his last year of high school. White students did not bother him for the simple reason he was an accomplished boxer. A couple of altercations settled any further harassment. Seeing the two boys when they arrived home he said, "Looks like you two got the worse of it. You need to learn how to defend yourselves. Come with me to the gym. I will introduce you to Rafael the owner. He not only knows boxing but wrestling."

When Edward Fleming resigned from the Panama Canal Project in 1910 to spend more time with his family, Spencer was sixteen. A difficult age, but the absent father and son grew close. Time to consider his future. Although influenced greatly by his mother, he held no desire to become a lawyer. Proficient in mathematics, the engineering profession of his father held more attraction. Building projects offered tangible personal fulfilment.

Being young, he also wanted to experience adventure. Perhaps like his father's participation in the great Panama venture. Twice over those five years, Spencer and his mother visited Panama. The scope of the work defied description. It was during the last trip that Spencer met Colonel Goethals now in charge of all aspects of the project. Goethals was an engineer with the U.S. Army Corps of Engineers. A West Point graduate.

The idea formed. Become an engineer by seeking appointment to the U.S. Military Academy. A first-rate engineering degree with the prospects for travel. He harbored no interest in getting married and pursuing domestic life. Upon graduation from high school two years later, he took the first step toward his chosen career. With a nomination to the Military Academy at West Point by his father's former boss Colonel Goethals, Fleming passed the entrance examination with a high score.

* * * *

Edward and Magda Fleming relocated to San Francisco in 1911 as their son left for West Point. The elder Fleming now serving as superintendent of the city's building department. All vestiges of the earthquake and fire of 1906 were gone but major building projects continued. There was even serious talk about construction of a bridge spanning the Golden Gate entrance to San Francisco Harbor.

Coming home this time was different. The year before he was a newly minted second lieutenant. Just another college graduate about to embark on a career. The Mexican Campaign proved a shocking introduction to his chosen profession. Gone were the romanticized visions of glory from history books. Overcoming fear then performing his duty boosted his confidence. The difficult conditions and the months of chasing Villa with no success were frustrating but nonetheless an adventure testing his mettle.

With the prospect of the United States joining the war in Europe, he already experienced combat earning a coveted medal for valor. With his military education, he remained troubled by the static condition of the Western Front resulting from three years of war. This was not a war of maneuver like the American Civil War or the Indian Wars. Men fighting instead from trenches. The differences from all previous wars coming about by advances in artillery, machine guns, and poison gas. Offensives resulted in massive casualties of the attacking forces. The machine gun crippled attempts to dislodge the enemy from excavated defensive trench works. A war of attrition impossible to comprehend as evidenced by staggering casualty figures. France would be nothing like Mexico.

Fleming arrived at the main San Francisco railway station at Third and Townsend, newly constructed in 1915. Both parents greeted him as well as Lucia his surrogate aunt still looking after his parents as part of the family.

Magda was the first to rush forward as he stepped from the train carriage. Tears of joy flowed freely between mother and son.

"You look older and even more handsome, Son," She said hugging him until Lucia took over.

"My lord, a year ago a second lieutenant now a first lieutenant," His father said as he pointed to the medal on his chest. "And the medal?"

"The Distinguish Service Cross. I will explain the circumstances later, Father."

To Lucia, he said, "How are Carlos and Enrique?"

"Doing fine. Carlos works for the Southern Pacific Railroad thanks to your father. Enrique is practicing law in Los Angeles. Married. Both send their love. I have prepared all your favorite foods. Look at you. Have you lost weight?"

"The Army does not cook as well as you do, Lucia. All we had to eat were jackrabbits and rattlesnakes in Mexico."

Returning to the new house in Presidio Heights, Fleming enjoyed his homecoming. After drinks and Lucia's dinner, he shared his experiences in Mexico. Rather than recount the violent details leading to the country's second highest medal for valor, he instead showed them the award citation.

Everyone was dumbstruck listening to the official commendation. His mother and Lucia both exhibited some distress trying to assimilate how their boy had become a man and a soldier.

Tears flowed unrestrained from his proud father.

Lieutenant Turner and the 7th Cavalry sergeant provided the details defined in the citation order. General Pershing presented the medal in a ceremony just before Fleming left on leave.

The conversation took a downturn with talk of the war in Europe. Newspapers foretold the likelihood of the country's entry into the war. Reports of the hundreds of thousands of casualties of French and British sent fear through any parent. Even having been through brief combat in Mexico, he realized the reality of the Western Front was something far worse. The lives he took with a machine gun at Guerrero multiplied a thousand fold.

As a way of easing his family's apprehension, he said, "My duties will likely be building things. Roads, railroads, bridges. Finally getting to apply by engineering skills. My orders are to report to the 1st Engineer Battalion of the 1st Infantry Division. If we do go to war, the engineering battalions construct the necessary infrastructure to transport men and supplies to the front in northeast France. I will be mostly working in the rear areas."

He knew no such thing. Few soldiers or even officers had any idea what this war was like. Only that it was already the greatest war in history with no frame of reference.

Near the end of his leave, Fleming received a telegram.

```
United States War Department
United States Army Signal Corps
March 1, 1917

1LT Spencer Fleming is hereby ordered to
disregard any previous orders and report by
March 15,1917 to Colonel Dennis Nolan Army
Intelligence Section United States Signal
Corps War Department, Washington D.C.

                    Colonel Dennis Nolan
                    Deputy Chief of Staff
                    Intelligence Division
                    United States Army
```

What the hell did this mean? Still assigned to intelligence? An ill-defined function of the Signals Corps. Typical of the Army. Trained for one thing, assigned to something else. His intelligence work in Mexico meant nothing. Just a stupid idea of Charlie Turner's that nearly got them killed. Going to France to do what? He chose not to share his disappointment with the family.

* * * *

Fleming reported at the War Department offices located west of the White House after the long train journey from San

Francisco. After waiting an hour, he was ushered into the office of Colonel Dennis Nolan.

"I am sure you are wondering why the change in your orders, Lieutenant."

"Yes, Sir."

"Take a seat."

"Thank you, Sir."

Nolan opened a file on his desk. "I read your DSC citation. How did you come to be in Guerrero, Mexico ahead of General Pershing's expeditionary forces?"

"Lieutenant Turner suggested we go into Mexico undercover disguised as civilians to seek information on the location of Pancho Villa's main body of forces after the raid on Columbus, New Mexico. General Pershing agreed to the mission. Turner and I masqueraded as civilian livestock brokers for the U.S. Army. Soon after, we learned that Villa's forces raided the hacienda of one of our contacts, a rancher in southern Chihuahua. Murdered his wife and burned his property. Wanting revenge on Villa, he took us to Guerrero."

"So you two were acting as spies?" Nolan asked. "That fact purposely omitted from the citation language."

"Yes, Sir. Good intelligence was hard to come by."

Nolan shook his head and smiled. "Proceed, Lieutenant."

"We got close to Villa by accident since he captured Guerrero. Turner and I hid out. Spotting what turned out to be Colonel Dodd and the 7th Calvary preparing to attack, we spotted the Villistas setting up a machine gun position. We felt compelled to participate in the action by trying to take out the machine gun."

"Amazing. The rest as they say is history. How did you come to speak Spanish?"

"Our live-in housekeeper was Mexican and her son became like a brother to me."

"What about your fluency in German and French?"

"My mother was born in Metz in Alsace-Lorraine. Mainly French speaking from her mother but her father was German. The family immigrated to the United States in 1874. My mother insisted that I should speak other languages as part of my education. From an early age I spoke four languages almost daily. Once in school, I learned to read German and French. My mother again. She encouraged me to read classics in the original language."

"I assume you are aware that in all likelihood we will soon go to war against Germany," Nolan said. "That means assembling an army on the scale of the other combatants. Many times the size of the current U.S. regular army. It means recruiting untrained men and officers. Very few experienced officers. In your two years of service, you have more experience than most officers of your rank.

"You and Turner are the only two spies in the Army. Add to that your experience in Mexico dealing with the frustrations of communications in the field. That is already a serious problem on the Western Front. You speak French and German. Moreover, you are a West Point graduate. All reasons for assignment to intelligence. Engineers are easier to find."

"Yes, Sir," Fleming said resolved to making the best of circumstances beyond his control.

"There is another reason for this assignment," Nolan said as he handed an envelope to Fleming. "General Pershing personally requested you. He is likely to be selected to command American forces in Europe should we go to war. Both you and I will become part of his headquarters' staff, Captain."

Fleming looked puzzled.

"Yes, Captain. The position requires that rank. Those are your promotion orders signed by the General."

* * * *

Three weeks later, on April 6, 1917, the U.S. Congress approved President Wilson's declaration of war against Germany and confirmed Wilson's choice of General John J. Pershing as commander. On May 27, 1917 Pershing and his headquarters staff of the newly organized American Expeditionary Forces, the AEF, sailed unannounced from Governor's Island New York on the British liner *RMS Baltic*. 50 selected officers and 100 enlisted men all dressed in civilian clothing to preserve secrecy. Every ship making the Atlantic crossing ran the risk of attack by German U boats. Captain Spencer Fleming was the youngest officer onboard.

After landing in Liverpool, the AEF traveled to London for ceremonies before leaving on June 13 for France. Although Pershing had a basic familiarity with the French language, it was insufficient for interaction at this level with native French speakers. Fleming accompanied him as aide-interrupter on the journey to Paris and eventually to the town of Chaumont where the AEF would make their headquarters.

CHAPTER 5

WWI Chemin des Dames Ridge, France | October 1917

Located 100 miles south of Verdun, AEF headquarters in Chaumont occupied a quieter sector of the Western Front in June 1917. The entire front ran 440 miles from the English Channel along the border of France with Belgium, Luxembourg, and Germany.

The Western Front now represented a static position of the combatants since the First Battle of the Marne in September 1914. French and British forces stopped the German offensive that started the war by pushing through Belgium to within striking distance of Paris. After that, the conflict soon devolved into elaborate trench defensive positions on both sides with periodic massed offensive attacks. A static war of attrition dictated by 20th century weapons technology. Long-range artillery accounted for most casualties. Offensives consisted of tens of thousands of men advancing against fixed positions of machine guns and the use of poison gas. A war fought with 19th century military tactics causing appalling casualty rates.

British forces held the Allied lines in the north and the French in the south. With America's entry into the war in 1917, its entire standing military force consisted only of 127,000 regular army and 80,000 mobilized national guard. For the United States to tip the scales in the Allies' favor required raising an army projected to several million. American entry into the conflict required as much as a year of training before sufficient numbers of inexperienced soldiers could be ready for combat.

Soon after arriving in Chaumont Fleming learned of his initial duties. With a meeting headed by Pershing and attended by chief of staff General Harbord and Colonel Nolan, Fleming and another intelligence officer received orders explaining their mission.

"Major Clark and Captain Fleming, your duties are to act as liaison to French headquarters," General Pershing said. "You have two assignments. First, to obtain information on French tactics and provide us with your impressions of their commanders. At some point, American forces will engage in offensive operations with French forces on our flank. Notice I said offensive operations. It is essential we do not fall into the failed strategic position of relying on trench defenses.

"Which brings me to my second point. Both the French and the British are nearing exhaustion with the appalling toll of casualties. Both are struggling to replenish their ranks. Both would like nothing more than to plug the holes in their depleted divisions with fresh American soldiers. That is not to be. Let me read you something.

"Understand this is top secret from President Wilson communicated by Secretary of War Baker. *In military operations against the imperial German Government, you are directed to cooperate with the forces of the other countries employed against our enemy, but in so doing the underlying idea must be kept in view that the forces of the United States are a separate and distinct component of the combined forces, the identity of which must be preserved. This fundamental rule is subject to minor exceptions as your judgment may approve. The decision as to when your command, or any of its parts, is ready for action is confided in you, and you will exercise full discretion in determining the manner of cooperation.*

"I tell you this because considerable pressure is already brought to bear. We must first create a million-man army from scratch. That requires time. I will not send untrained men to their death simply to provide weight of numbers. Your job is to reinforce this among the French command while providing this command with useful insights. What do the French do well, where do they fall short, who are the best commanders and divisions?

"General Pétain quelled the mutinies threatening the French Army earlier this year. He is now waiting to amalgamate American forces into his formations before resuming any new offensive. That will not happen. We will fight alongside the French but as a separate army. Therefore we must understand who is on our flanks."

Everything now revolved around American readiness to throw in fresh troops and tip the balance of forces in favor of the Allies. The exhausted French and British suffered reduced formations from the casualties of three years of war. Lacking reserve divisions curtailed any offensives without the Americans. In little better shape, the Germans suffered similar casualties. Replacements meant dipping deeper into the civilian population. Unlike the Allies, severe supply problems, particularly food, compound the German situation. Even German civilians subsisted on starvation calories.

Hindenburg and Ludendorff now faced their most serious enemy, time. They understood Germany could not win the war. It was a matter of how hostilities ended. Their objective was to secure as much territory as possible and consolidate a defensive line to protect the Fatherland. Time was against the Germans. Inevitably, American manpower and unlimited resources would dictate the battlefield.

By late 1917, both the French and British were down to a million troops each. Germany was building its strength to three million by conscripting both old and young men beyond the normal age range. At the political level, Paris and London pressed President Wilson to amalgamate American troops. Their argument if American forces did not come under joint command soon, America would have limited impact on the conflict in 1918. Pressure mounted on General Pershing.

While the southern sector of the Western Front remained relatively quiet during 1917, it remained a strategic pivot point as the Germans must eventually relinquish Belgium and consolidate their lines before retreating back to Germany. Rail lines vital to German supplies and troop movement converged in the French city of Sedan. Once American forces joined the conflict as a trained army, the order of battle placed them directly opposing this German pivot point with French forces supporting the American left flank. Taking Sedan meant the end of the fighting.

This larger strategy was clear to intelligence officers Major Clark and his subordinate Captain Fleming. Setting off for French headquarters at Chantilly in July 1917, those larger strategic issues would not play out until at least the following year. Only 14,000 American soldiers were now on French soil. Although committed as voluntarily enlisted soldiers rather than conscripts, none had experience in the tactical elements of the European war on the Western Front of France. None had combat experience. As the numbers of arriving soldiers increased, new arrivals were essentially untrained after only minimal basic training in the United States. Many months of training on French soil remained before Pershing could deploy them in combat. Newly commissioned officers lacked not only basic military training but had no understanding of the demands of this new warfare.

As Pershing's liaison officers to French headquarters, Clark and Fleming faced a constant onslaught of interpreting the frustrations and threats of doom from senior French officers. Mindful of their diplomatic role, they still must uncover solid intelligence to shape Pershing's strategy. The General also expected their military opinion on every issue of discussion. Strategic analysis involving whole armies from two junior officers. Their military experience remained predominately academic with Clark graduating West Point in 1905 and Fleming in 1915. Every soldier in the AEF seemed ill prepared.

As Major Clark was the chief U.S. liaison officer to the general headquarters of the French Army, principal interaction with French senior officers fell to him. With the headquarters filled with individual French liaison officers from the corps and division levels of the French Army, Fleming sought his intelligence from these officers. Often more candid, it also provided Fleming the ability to grasp a sense of the larger picture. Officers closely connected with their respective formations in the field. No politics here. Just conscientious mid-rank officers doing their best to represent their units in the field.

The morale of the French Army badly deteriorated in the spring of 1917. The grand Franco-British operation known as the Nivelle Offensive after French Chief of Staff Robert Nivelle failed to alter the Front strategically. With a combined force of 850,000, the French suffered a disastrous 187,000 casualties, the British 160,000 in three weeks. Failure to realize a strategic victory cost Nivelle his job. The French Army fell into mutiny, rebelling against generals sending them to slaughter. Of the total of 113 French divisions, the battle readiness of 48 divisions was so badly deteriorated it prevented anything beyond static defensive deployment.

Newly appointed General Philippe Pétain quelled the mutinies by instituting reforms addressing many of the grievances of the rank and file. However, Pétain could only engage in defensive warfare until restoring stability. Any offensives required to bring about German capitulation forestalled until American forces entered the conflict with sufficient numbers of fresh troops.

While lacking in field experience except for the months in Mexico, Fleming realized the finer details of combat tactics at the company and squad levels was totally lacking in the new American forces. He attended officer-training classes for several weeks after arriving in France. French and British tactical instruction was spotty at best. The few American officers with combat experience mostly in the Philippines were unprepared for this different warfare on the Western Front.

Conscripting an American army then finding enough shipping capacity to cross the Atlantic proved the first hurdle. Setting up training camps in France strained the French with their shortage of experienced manpower. The logistics of supply overwhelmed the French infrastructure. Eventually moving several million troops with a supply line stretching thousands of miles never before attempted on this scale. Food, uniforms, equipment, weapons, ammunition, medical support, communication, transport, and every conceivable necessity for an army about to engage in a war already depleting the resources of the European combatants for three years.

Fleming could best contribute by observing firsthand from the front lines.

Major Clark agreed. "Okay. Captain. Makes sense. I'm interested how the French communicate between adjacent units. The brass also plays down the problem of French morale. Pétain is waiting for tanks and the Americans. When that happens, will the poilu fight?" *Poilu* was the informal name for the French soldier.

With the French Army reasonably stabilized since the setbacks of April and May, Pétain was ready to attempt another thrust at the Germans. This time only twenty miles east of the final engagement of Nivelle's offensive in May at the Second Battle of the Aisne. Fleming chose the location expecting to take part in the forthcoming offensive.

This would be Fleming's first visit to a forward trench position. Previous tours of the front brought him only as far as secondary support trench positions. In preparation, he assembled a field kit including helmet, gas mask, food, and basic amenities. As for weapons, the concern was defensive. His role was to gather intelligence not 'go over the top' of the trenches to engage in an attack.

Recalling his attack on the machine gunners in Guerrero, he prevailed by emptying the magazine of his M1911 .45 service issued semi-automatic. Had he required reloading a new magazine, he might be dead. Instead of a heavy rifle, preferring the maneuverability of a sidearm, he added a second .45 to his arsenal. Holstering one .45 on his hip from the standard issue Sam Browne belt with magazine pouches and extra ammunition, he added a shoulder holster rig. Acquired during the Mexico campaign, the cavalry shoulder holster provided a balanced outfit for carrying a second sidearm. To the already heavily loaded Sam Browne belt at his waist, he substituted the large Bowie knife in a leather sheath instead of a conventional bayonet. The Bowie knife provided a formidable weapon. The blade was long enough for use as a short sword. Capable of thrusting or slashing. The width and thickness of the blade gave it heft. Trained in the use of a saber at

West Point, Fleming could employ the same fighting techniques with the Bowie knife.

Perhaps overkill, but he read of incidents during this war when fighting reduced to vicious in-close combat. The fact that he excelled in this area gave him little comfort. Stylized combat of boxing, judo, and fencing was not the same as a life and death struggle with a desperate opponent.

Fleming arrived at the headquarters of the French Sixth Army. Like so many strategic locations during this war, this sector was the scene of prior battles. Again, the objective was the area around the fortified position of the 50-mile long east-west Chemin des Dames ridge. Quarried for stone for centuries, the warren of caves and tunnels provided a natural fortress from French artillery bombardment for occupying German forces.

After consulting the area maps, Fleming chose to spend the days leading up to the attack on a trench network affording a forward view of the plain rising up to the fortified ridgeline. A perfect observation position from which to observe artillery effectivity and the maneuver of tanks. Careful of the fragile morale condition of the weary poilu, General Pétain intended to conduct the offensive using massive artillery barrages. Heavy caliber shells designed to penetrate the natural fortifications of Chemin des Dames, and then use tanks to push ahead of advancing infantry.

Fleming attached himself to a relief company headed to the forward trench lines on the heights of what was once the large La Royère Farm near the western end of the Chemin des Dames Ridge. The farm and surrounding villages now a scene of destruction after months of fighting.

Walking with the French company commander Captain Jacque Leroux and his first sergeant Phillipe Rochefort, Fleming struck up a conversation and they shared backgrounds. Both Frenchmen were veterans of several major battles since 1914. Three years surviving this hell. Leroux came up through the enlisted ranks. Leroux in his early thirties, Rochefort forty. Fleming in his twenties.

After arriving at the forward trench line, they spent the remaining hours of daylight situating the company for the one-week duration before rotating back to the reserve line. After setting the watch, Fleming joined them in the command bunker for this hundred-yard sector of the left end of the trench line. A heavy machine gun emplacement with three soldiers anchored the very end of the trench.

Calling it a command center suggested more than the enlarged hole off the trench it actually was. Distinguished only by a roof of planks covered with sand bags to protect against artillery fragmentation. Along with the radio operator, close quarters with the four men. Sergeant Rochefort set about making coffee outside the entrance with a barrel serving as a makeshift stove. The warmth welcomed later with a chilly autumn night.

"How is it you speak French without an accent, Captain," Leroux said lighting up a cigarette offering one to Fleming."

"No thank you, Captain. I do not smoke. Could use a brandy or a whiskey though. As to speaking French, I owe that to my mother. Her mother was French, her father German. Born in Metz. She spoke both languages throughout her life. My father has of Scotch-English heritage. So I spoke all three languages from when I could first talk."

"You know Metz was French before the Germans invaded in 1870. French territory again when we beat them back this time."

Just outside the doorway tending to the fire, Sergeant Rochefort said, "You look like you are ready for battle, Captain. Two pistols and that big knife. Have you ever seen action?"

"Some. Not like you and Captain Leroux though."

"How long you been in the American Army?"

Fleming smiled. "Two years since graduating from the military academy. Saw action in Mexico."

"Kill any enemy?"

"That will be enough, Sergeant," Leroux said.

"I don't mind, Captain. Every soldier has a right to know if the man next to him will do his duty under fire. To your question, I killed twenty-two."

"*Mon dieu!* How?" Sergeant Rochefort said.

"Shot three Mexican bandits setting up a machine gun with my .45. Then I turned the machine gun on their cavalry charging our cavalry. So I know what the French infantry soldier has faced in this war."

Rochefort took Fleming's mess cup and poured some coffee from a coffee pot.

"What is the story on that knife? Standard American issue?"

"No. Given to me by another officer experienced in the American West. Never used it but a powerful weapon if things become ugly. Better than a trench knife or bayonet. Here, let me show you. Take out your trench knife I see sticking out of your leggings. Leave it in the scabbard though."

Fleming Taking a sip of the ersatz coffee, which tasted awful. Fleming then removed the Bowie knife sheath from his belt. "Looks like you know how to use that knife. Step outside, Sergeant. I will show you what I mean."

Everyone exited the bunker to see what the Yank had in mind. The sergeant looked like a tough bugger. Fleming simply wanted to establish his credentials to these experienced soldiers that have gone through hell.

"We leave the scabbards on so we do not kill each other." The Sergeant looked puzzled. "I want you to attack me, Sergeant."

Rochefort looked at Leroux who just shrugged.

Rochefort crouched and came at Fleming with a slashing motion. Fleming parried with the Bowie then came back with the reverse side of the knife against the Sergeant's neck.

"My knife has a sharpened double edge about two inches on the back side. I just severed your carotid artery. Now go for a thrust to my midsection."

Rochefort moved in closer to deliver a thrust. Fleming stepped back swinging the heavy Bowie knife striking Rochefort's trench knife with an upward force enough to knock it from his hand.

Rochefort stood there bewildered as Fleming handed Rochefort the Bowie knife. Removing the knife from the leather sheath, Rochefort remarked, "A heavy bitch. Like a small axe."

"More like a Roman short sword," Fleming said.

"How did you learn to fight like that?"

"Used my saber training, Sergeant."

Rochefort shook his head and smiled. "Sonofabitch."

Captain Leroux slapped Fleming on the back. "Good show, Yank."

Although Fleming had toured trenches, he never had to spend a night in one. He and Leroux slept in the command bunker on slats of wood that only elevated them from sleeping on the ground. Thankfully, he saw no rats.

The following day, Fleming chose to follow Rochefort around. Without his captain, Fleming thought he might be more candid. "How is morale, Sergeant?"

"Do you mean will we fight?"

"Let me say this, Sergeant. I have read about the battles of this war. I do not have your experience, but I tell you, I question the tactics of some of the Allied offensives. Senseless slaughter using the weight of manpower as the chief weapon. Military tactics from the last century against modern weapons technology."

Fleming was sincere. The leadership of the General Staffs of all the warring parties ranged from incompetent to unimaginative. Willing to sacrifice soldiers in appalling numbers to achieve dubious objectives. Remarkable how any soldier or officer could maintain his morale while suffering years of combat with poor chances for survival. He only hoped that Pershing did not subject American soldiers to the same grim fate. While he respected Pershing, he never achieved his objective of subduing Villa in the Mexico Campaign.

"I understand what the French Army has been through. The mutinies understandable. A soldier cannot fight indefinitely without hope. Pétain apparently recognizes the situation must change."

Rochefort nodded. "My company will fight, Captain. Not for the fucking generals, for France. I have been a soldier for over twenty years I will do my duty for France. But I tell you this, if I am ordered to send my men to a certain death, I will refuse. We will fight though. So far, General Pétain does seem different. The poilu at least is better treated."

Apart from the difficult conditions of trench life, Fleming enjoyed the opportunity to interact with the average soldier. This was the essence of being a soldier. Impossible to appreciate until experienced.

* * * *

With the massing of French troops in the sector, the Germans expected the possibility of another French offensive. The British continued pressure in the northern Flanders sector of the Western Front, therefore a French offensive in the south would prevent any transfer of German divisions north. In anticipation of such a French offensive, the Germans created specialist German counter-attack divisions known as Eingreifdivisionen along the front line.

The Eingreifdivisionen were specialized storm troops. Formations organized for blitzkrieg attacks of sustained advancement. Designed for penetration, these elite troops acted without broad objectives other than to disrupt the enemy, whether offensively or defensively. Decentralized command allowed junior officers to seek tactical opportunities rather than maneuver to an overarching strategy. These were hardened assault troops using grenades and light submachine guns. Trained in close-quarter combat, they could be a terrifying enemy.

In the opposing trenches, an enterprising German sector commander decided to exploit the elite storm troops under his command. He decided to conduct harassing trench raids against demoralized French soldiers. Blunt their enthusiasm for the expected forthcoming offensive. Chose the early hours of the morning before sunrise when half the defenders remained asleep.

Several days before the scheduled French offensive on Fleming's third night at this forward position, repeated explosions woke Fleming and Leroux at 3:00am. An artillery barrage?

"German grenades!" Leroux shouted.

Both scrambled out of the bunker ready to confront the attackers. Every soldier at a forward position slept at the full ready.

The grenade explosions came from German Stielhandgranates, the percussion stick grenade. Distinct from the cast fragmentation grenade used by the British and Americans, only thin sheet metal encased the explosive. The weapon useful for close quarter use with the explosion stunning or disorienting the victim while avoiding risk of shrapnel injury to the person deploying the weapon.

The sounds came from the left. The end of the trench. The heavy machine gun emplacement. Small arms fire followed immediately.

Fleming sensed the attack was coming down the trench rather than from no-man's land in front of the three-meter deep trench. With no cover available, the best he could do was shelter half his body in the entrance to the command bunker as a firing position.

Trenches were not constructed in straight lines. They consisted of a zigzag pattern with different levels to accommodate observation and sniping positions and try to manage the water problem from rains. This meant the attacking Germans must navigate corners manned by French soldiers standing watch.

Leroux charged down the trench toward the sound of gunfire. He did not get far. The sound of a German 9mm submachine gun sent him stumbling back mortally wounded seconds later.

Looking at Leroux just feet away, Fleming instinctively chose to counterattack as his best defense. The Germans had superior firepower. His only chance was to disrupt the assault. At any moment, they might throw more of their concussion grenades before finishing off incapacitated victims.

Without hesitation, he jumped over the prone Leroux. As a German holding a compact MP 18 submachine gun came around a corner of the trench, he fired point blank. As the man fell, Fleming discharged the remaining rounds of his .45 into a second German.

Holstering the empty .45, he extracted his second .45 from his hip while proceeding down the trench. Rounding a bend, he came on a scene of hand-to-hand combat. Four Germans and three French soldiers engaged in a vicious melee with trench knives. One is Sergeant Rochefort. As Fleming approached, a German officer came up behind the fighting men and shot one of the French soldiers with his luger pistol.

Fleming shot the officer in the face from three feet then proceeded to shoot the four German soldiers battling with the French.

He then dropped to one knee and reloaded fresh magazines in both his .45s.

Without waiting for the oncoming Germans, he stood up and proceeded quickly down the trench. Thus far, his aggressive tactic produced results. The German raiders did not expect a counterattack in the close confines of the trench. The element of surprise blunting their progress. The raiders also had only a short window of opportunity to inflict damage before the French reorganized and overwhelmed them. Fleming however did not realize these were elite storm troops, highly motivated for high-risk missions. They understood their chances to return successfully to their lines dwindled if they delayed breaking off the attack too long.

At the next 90-degree bend in the trench, Fleming peered around the corner seeing several Germans advancing in strength two-abreast. In a withering barrage of fire, he emptied both .45s. Stopping the advance, he knelt to reload fresh magazines again. Suddenly the concussion of a grenade explosion knocked him back and dislodged the .45 from his hand.

Stunned and semi-conscience he came to moments later with a searing pain in his chest. Instinctively rolling to the left, he reached behind his back. The move increased the pain causing him bellow a loud scream.

His right hand grasped the handle of the Bowie knife bringing it out of the sheath while his left hand reached up grabbing the equipment belt of the German soldier standing over him. The move caused Fleming to yell again with renewed pain. He then rammed the big knife into the German's groin.

Suddenly the scene came into focus. The soldier let loose the grip of his rifle with the bayonet now imbedded into Fleming's chest to reach the wound between his legs now emptying his blood at a steady rate.

As Fleming attempted to rise to his feet. Holding the barrel of the rifle in his left hand, he tried dislodging the bayonet entangled in the canvas gas mask pouch.

Sergeant Rochefort grabbed his arm assisting him to stand. Rochefort then pulled loose the bayonet sending another wave of pain dropping Fleming to his knees. Blood began soaking his tunic.

Fleming reached down and retrieved his .45 as Rochefort helped him up. Fleming instinctively resumed his counterattack. A few yards later both Fleming and Rochefort confronted more advancing Germans. An uneven gunfight with Fleming's pistols and Rochefort's revolver against a German submachine gun. A sustained burst by the German brought down both of them.

****

In large part, it was Fleming's and Sergeant Rochefort's actions that repulsed the German raid. Of the 20 German raiders, 17 fell as casualties either killed or wounded. The remaining three captured. The French defenders incurred 21 casualties.

Reserve troops responded by flooding into the forward trench but the fifteen-minute battle by that time ended. Medical personnel attended the wounded.

Both Fleming and Rochefort suffered serious injury. Fleming lost considerable blood from both chest and leg wounds. The chest wound the most serious. Conscious, he struggled to breathe. Later he learned the bayonet broke a rib and punctured his left lung. Pressure from air entering his chest cavity collapsed the lung. Fortunately, the gas mask prevented the full thrust of the bayonet going all the way through his chest.

Rochefort took a bullet to the lower abdomen and another shattered his wrist. Both were in a bad way. The medical field station stabilized the hemorrhaging but surgery at a fully equipped hospital was necessary for both. The two-hour ride in an ambulance carrying two other wounded over rutted roads undid the temporary medical work at the field station almost killing Fleming with renewed loss of blood.

CHAPTER 6

WWI Belleau Wood to River Marne, France | Summer 1918

On arriving at the military hospital at Reims, Fleming underwent immediate blood transfusion as he descended into shock. Needing to stabilize him before beginning surgery, the doctor also made an incision in the chest cavity, inserting a tube to relieve air accumulation exerting pressure on the collapsed left lung and heart. The condition, known as pneumothorax, occurs when air escapes the lung, in his case through the bayonet penetration, and fills the space between the lung and chest wall preventing normal expansion.

Once stabilized, the surgeon began repairs to the wound. The damage proved extensive as compounded by the fractured rib. Beyond making repairs to the delicate tissue of the lung, the most serious concern remained infection. Not only bacteria from the surface of the bayonet, but foreign material from Fleming's uniform presented a risk of sepsis. In 1917, antibiotics did not yet exist. The best the surgical team could do was irrigate and treat the wounded area with alcohol.

The bullet wound to the thigh proved less threatening. The round still imbedded struck to the outside missing the major blood vessels running down the inside of the leg. It struck the femur a glancing blow to the outside splintering a section but not breaking the bone cross-section. Fortunately, the wound was from a 9mm pistol round from the German submachine gun rather than the standard German Mauser rifle. The high-powered Mauser round at close range would pass through the leg leaving a large exit wound.

Recovering slowly from the anesthetic effects of the chloroform and ether, Fleming remained groggy with the effects of morphine hours later. His first interaction was with a nurse offering a moist towel to bite to relieve his thirst but minimizing too much water aggravating the after effects on his stomach from the anesthesia.

"*Capitaine Fleming, parlez-vous français*?"

With a struggle he responded, "*Oui. Où suis-je?*"

"You are in a French military hospital recovering from a difficult surgery. Your wounds were very serious with much loss of blood. However, we are optimistic about your recovery."

Fleming's eyes fluttered shut as he fell back asleep.

The following day, with the effects of the anesthetic dissipated, he experienced intense pain in his chest. Every breath sending a fresh spasm. The throbbing of the leg wound added another dimension of discomfort.

A woman in a white coat with a stethoscope around her neck approached his bed. "How are you feeling, Capitaine Fleming?"

"Hurts like hell."

"Do you want more morphine?"

"Maybe later. Puts me to sleep. Need to know what kind of shape I am in."

Her nametag read Dr. Dominique Dumont. She repeated what she said the day before after he regained consciousness from the surgery.

"Were you here with me yesterday?"

"Yes. I checked on you throughout the night. You are my only American patient. How is it you speak French?

"My mother is French. Did you operate on me, Doctor?"

"I assisted. Our best surgeon worked on your more serious chest wound. I repaired your leg wound."

"Have you been treating wounded soldiers since the war started?" She looked to be about his age.

"Yes. My husband taught mathematics at the university. Married only a year when war broke out, he volunteered immediately for the army. I volunteered my services following the terrible carnage after the Battle of the Marne in September 1914."

"Where is your husband now?"

She sighed, "He died at Verdun a year ago."

"I am sorry for your loss."

"Thank you. Just one of so many thousands of war widows. The pain is now receded to a dull ache. My work helps. Is there anything I can get for you, Capitaine Fleming?"

"Not right now. I think I will sleep for a while. Thank you for saving my life, Doctor."

She smiled. "Rest is the best therapy. Unfortunately, we need to irrigate your chest wound with an antiseptic solution every three or four hours to guard against infection. Painful but necessary. I shall look in on you later."

The next several days proved difficult with renewed pain from the repeated irrigating of his wound. His insistence on minimizing morphine left him alert but in constant distress. Days later, he developed a fever which fortunately subsided after several days removing concern of a more serious infection.

Everyday Dr. Dumont stopped by to examine his wounds and chat for as much time as her duties allowed. After a week, he regained some strength. The pain remained but now manageable.

One evening, Dr. Dumont came by to find another patient in a wheelchair situated next to Fleming's bed. On a tray sitting across the wheelchair arms was a chessboard.

"It is good to see you moving about, Major," Dumont said to the man in the wheelchair with a cast on one arm and bandaged up to his neck. "Ready to leave soon I understand. Congratulations."

"Three more days I am told. Perhaps I can improve my game and redeem myself against this Yank."

"Capitaine Fleming is beating you?"

"No, he is destroying me. Never played anyone as good as Monsieur Fleming. Been at this for less than two hours. This is our fifth game. Lost four times already. If you know anything about chess, you can see I am in a bad way already in this game."

Dumont smiled. "As a matter of fact I do know something of chess. I concur, Major. You are in something of a fix."

Sticking a thermometer in Fleming's mouth, she chatted with the French Major. Removing the thermometer, she said, "Normal, Capitaine. I shall look in on you later after you vanquish your opponent."

* * * *

Four weeks after the French attack on what became known as the Battle of La Malmaison, the Germans pulled back from the fortifications on the Chemin des Dames Ridge. Furthermore, the French achieved the larger objective of pinning down German reserve divisions in this southern sector that prevented their relocation to defend against British offensives in the north. More importantly, the French suffered only 14,000 casualties, only 10% of the rate suffered earlier in the year with the Nivelle Offensive. A significant success with the French inflicting 38,000 casualties on the Germans and capturing 12,000.

Buoyed with the boost to French morale, medals for valor became important propaganda for the war-weary French people.

Fleming, now sitting up in bed was eating breakfast when commotion ran through the ward of forty beds. In walked General Duchêne, commander of the French Sixth Army, flanked by three other officers. He stopped at the foot of the bed of Sergeant Phillipe Rochefort across the aisle not far from Fleming.

Rochefort survived his wounds possibly saving him from further combat. Fleming was delighted when the General began reading the award citation presenting Rochefort the Croix de Guerre.

After an aide pinned the metal to Rochefort's hospital gown, the General bent down and kissed both cheeks then saluted Rochefort. The ward cheered loudly.

An aide then called out Fleming's name. Coming to Flemings's bedside, General Duchêne read a similarly worded citation. *'A grateful French nation hereby awards the Croix de Guerre in recognition of exceptional valor exhibited on October 20, 1917 in the forward trenches near the village of La Malmaison. Faced against an early morning trench raid by an elite unit of German storm troops, Captain Spencer Fleming of the United States Army acting as an observer organized a counterattack with Sergeant Phillipe Rochefort to repel the attack. With the company commander mortally wounded, Fleming and Rochefort prevented further loss of French lives by attacking the enemy with only sidearms and knives in close-quarter brutal fighting. Captain Fleming personally killed or wounded ten of the twenty attacking force thereby blunting the German assault which allowed for neutralizing the captured machine gun position anchoring the end of the trench.'*

Another surprise followed that afternoon. Traveling to French headquarters at Compiègne required General Pershing to travel through Reims. A repeat commotion stirred the ward as the unmistakable presence of the imposing General John Pershing accompanied by a brigadier general and two junior officers walked briskly toward his bed led by a flustered nurse.

"I understand you will recover from your wounds, Captain," Pershing said.

"Yes, Sir."

"Seems you have a knack for getting into difficult situations. Also a talent for resolving those situations with great courage. Major Clark made sure I received the dispatch reported by French headquarters immediately. Without question, your actions reflect the highest standards of the United States Army. Furthermore, your conduct casts particular credit on the American Army to our Allies in these difficult circumstances. For your actions on the morning of October 20, it is therefore my honor to bestow on your country's highest award for military valor, the Congressional Medal of Honor." Turning to the brigadier general, he said, "This is General Parker the new chief of the American military mission at the French general headquarters. Your new boss when you return to duty."

Parker bent down and handed Fleming the case containing the medal. The four American officers saluted Fleming. The ward again erupted in cheers. Pershing shook his hand.

"Glad to have you on my staff, Captain. Need you back to duty as soon as you are fit enough, soldier."

That was as personable as Pershing was to staff. One tough sonofabitch. Yet Fleming witnessed his diplomatic skills when dealing with his counterparts in the French and British army commands. Pershing understood compromise to achieve objectives yet did not hesitate to push back aggressively on non-negotiable issues.

Made sense that he would bring in a senior officer to liaison with French command as circumstances turned tumultuous. The timing of introduction of the AEF into combat an increasingly contentious issue with the French and British.

General Frank Parker came with impressive diplomatic credentials and a history of interaction with the French military. A 1894 West Point graduate, he served in the Spanish-American war in 1898 followed by two years in Puerto Rico. In 1904, he graduated from the French Army Cavalry School. He then served as military attaché for a year each to Venezuela, Argentina, and Cuba. Like Fleming, Parker was fluent in both French and Spanish.

Years earlier, Parker attended the French École Supérieure de Guerre, returning there in 1914 to 1915 as the war broke out. Before the United States entered the war, Parker then served as an observer with French forces in the field during 1916 and 1917. His association with Parker, the archetype of an intellectual military officer, would significantly impact the remainder of Fleming's military career.

* * * *

Dominique Dumont took more than a doctor-patient interest in Fleming. An instant attraction felt by both. Over the next few weeks, both dropped any pretext and slipped easily into a developing romance. Since seeing Fleming playing chess, this became an excuse to spend off-duty time at his bedside. She thought herself pretty good. An avid player after her deceased husband taught her strategy and tactics. Before he went off to war, she was good enough to give him difficult competition and win the occasional game.

Her first games with Fleming deflated her confidence in chess skills. Fleming played at a level far beyond her deceased husband. She liked the fact he did not let her win, but it was nonetheless disconcerting.

After their third game where Fleming checkmated her in twelve moves, she said good naturedly, "Very well, Capitaine, you obviously are not interested in flattering a woman's ego. You not only beat me but you take so little time in considering each move. How did you learn to play like this?"

"My mother."

"Did you beat her as easily?"

He laughed. "Hardly. It took me years to even beat her at all, then never easily. Even seeing her only once a year since I went off to the military academy, she never lost her edge, beating me most of the time. Good training to concentrate the mind. I become so immersed in the board that I ignore everything else but the game."

Dumont smiled coyly, "Oh my. Then I must find other means of spending time with you. I do not want you to ignore me."

Fleming quickly laid his hand over hers. "I did not say that very well. I could never ignore you …"

"Dominique. About time you call me Dominique, Spencer," She said with a warm smile and placed her other hand on top of his.

"Of course. Thank you. You must know I am very fond of you, Dominique."

"More than that pretty nurse Eleanor that bathes you?"

"What do you mean?"

"Come now, you know who I mean. Eleanor with the ample breasts tightly stretching her uniform. Enjoys making sexually explicit banter with many of her patients. Anyway she pays you a particular compliment according to gossip among the female staff."

"Compliment?"

"She remarks on a certain part of the handsome American's anatomy. Apparently, you become aroused as she bathes your genitals. The natural reaction to an attractive female massaging such a sensitive area of course produces an involuntary natural response. Specifically she finds the size and appearance of your erection most appealing."

Fleming noticeably blushed. Delighted, Dominique bent forward and kissed him on the lips for the first time. "I will be back later at the end of my shift to tuck you in."

With all the lights darkened, Dumont returned three hours later. Fleming was asleep.

Dumont put her lips close to his ear. "Just lie there quietly and make no noise."

With that he stirred awake as she slid her hand under the sheet. With her other hand she unbuttoned her blouse then guided his hand to her breast. Touching her combined with her stroking his cock, he quickly became fully erect.

As his arousal increased, Dumont slowed her stokes to keep him at the edge of climax. It only worked for a minute before she felt his impending release then increased the pressure to bring him to an explosive orgasm. With her free hand, she covered his mouth to contain his groans of pleasure.

"That will have to do until you are fully recovered and we can enjoy a proper intimate celebration alone. Sleep well, Spencer."

* * * *

The hospital discharged Fleming after Christmas. Dressed in a newly cleaned and pressed uniform, Dominique took the day off to escort him to her small apartment in Reims. The French surgeon pronounced him fit to return to limited administrative duties in two weeks. Bundled in an overcoat, he felt the bitter cold in his depleted state but relished being away from the hospital arm in arm with Dominique.

Dominique planned a special meal with a bottle of wine. As a special holiday treat, she even found him a bottle of Scotch whisky. All for later. Once inside, having shed their coats she enveloped him in an embrace.

"I have fanaticized making love to you for some time," She said kissing him while rubbing his groin. "Are you up to it? Feels like you are."

For the next hour they explored each other's bodies prolonging the pleasure before each reached orgasm.

He was inexperienced with women. His first encounter in high school and another in his senior year at West Point. Several years older and more experienced even with her short marriage, Dominique subtly took charge. He appreciated her guidance in how best to pleasure her, reinforced by her expressions of pleasure.

The following two weeks became the happiest of his life. While she was on duty, he occupied his time reading and resting. He posted letters to his father and mother. Relating his ordeal of sustaining wounds. Minimizing the seriousness and using the restrictions of military censorship to obscure the details as an unexpected encounter. He reassured them his duties were largely administrative. Most of his words instead devoted to his developing romance with Dr. Dominique Dumont.

For exercise, he walked about Reims searching to buy food. Meat was scarce, as were vegetables out of season in the winter. They made do with baguettes, pasta, and wine. Dominique was a wonder in creating sauces to make even the simplest dish appetizing.

They spent the evenings with endless talk as they prepared dinner together. Each night they made love.

A tearful farewell as he departed by train for Chaumont.

"Promise me you will not get killed, Spencer," Dominique said. Her usual confidence and assertiveness now compromised by tears freely flowing down her cheeks. "I love you and want you back."

Fleming embraced her kissing away the tears. "I love you very much, Dominique. I intend to be back and spend my life with you. My duties do not normally place me in the front lines.

"This perhaps could be the last year of the war. At the very least, it will decide the war. In a few months, there will be one million American soldiers ready to fight against the Germans. The Allies will have superior numbers and better supplied."

Standing on the steps of the railway carriage as it pulled out of the station, he reluctantly let go her hand. She smiled and blew him a kiss. A beautiful vision bundled in a fur collared overcoat and broad-brimmed hat. Underneath, her medical uniform as she headed to the hospital.

* * * *

Little happened during the winter of 1917-18 except soldiers on both sides suffered terribly. It seemed a repeat of the record cold of the previous winter. For most troops serving in the trenches, there was no shelter. Frostbite a greater danger than the enemy. Reserve units had only tents. Soldiers could not bath or wash their clothes. For German troops, inadequate food supplies added further distress.

Impassible roads hampered transportation at every turn, disrupting movement of food and ammunition to the front from railroad centers. The wholesale churning of land by repeated artillery bombardments left a landscape of shell craters and destroyed roads now frozen. The autumn rains of 1917 quickly turned roads to mud which frozen hard into furrows like a plowed field. Engine and transmission oil froze disabling trucks.

With the prospect of approaching spring, 1918 would be decisive. The Germans benefited from the Russian Revolution with the Bolsheviks overthrowing Tsar Nicholas and removing Russia from the war. The Germans able to move many divisions to the Western Front. Time however remained short before they lost their numerical advantage in force strength.

The Americans now became the deciding factor. Significant numbers of American troops existed in France in various stages of training. General Pershing would soon command an army. While lacking combat experience, the American Doughboys were rested, well supplied, and motivated. More arrived on France's west coast daily. The projection by the end March was 300,000 American troops on French soil. By July, 1,000,000 and continuing to arrive at a rate of 10,000 per day. 2,000,000 strong anticipated by the end of 1918.

Of course, as new conscripts arrived, they faced months of training before facing the Germans on the battlefield. Training in the United States woefully lacking with some new arrivals having never fired a rifle. This forced Pershing to rely largely on French and British veterans to train the Yankees. That delay in the spring of 1918 provided the Germans their only window of opportunity to improve their position before hostilities ended.

It was not possible to train raw troops and officers in the finer tactical details learned only by the bitter experience of the other combatants after three years of war. That concern weighed on the mind of every AEF commander. Whether commanding a company, a brigade, or division, the Americans must learn by their own baptism under fire.

That would come as soon as spring arrived. While the war was no longer winnable for the Germans, they had no choice but to embark on a last ditch offensive. Bring the Allies to the negotiating table before the Americans deployed on the battlefield in strength. Their objective was retaining not only the French territory of Alsace-Lorraine annexed by Germany in 1871, but protecting the German industrialized Rhineland just east of the pre-war border. At greater stake was the survival of Germany.

For the next several months, Fleming resumed his liaison duties with the French Army. Along with improving his diplomatic skills, he benefited from absorbing tactical details to pass on in the form of operational instructions useful to AEF field commanders.

While Major Clark worked from the French general headquarters in Compiègne with General Parker, Fleming again went closer to the front observing from French divisional headquarters. This time under strict orders not to expose himself to enemy action. His assignment allowed him to study French tactical practices for coordinating rolling artillery barrages advancing ahead of their attacking infantry and the use of tanks. Most importantly, he learned how the French dealt with the difficulties of communication at every organizational level during the thick of battle.

The Germans took the initiative launching an offensive on March 21. Known as *Operation Michael*, the Germans attacked over ground previously fought over. The Battle of the Somme in 1916 was an Allied offensive intended to break the back of the German line. Over three million fought over four months inflicting one million casualties. The total devastation remained unchanged. The terrain devoid of any buildings or trees with the ground torn and cratered making military maneuver difficult.

The Germans hoped to drive a wedge splitting the British forces from the French then driving the British back to the English Channel. This would severe British supplies lines.

The thrust failed, hampered by the difficult terrain. Each side suffered 250,000 casualties. Unable to recover from these losses, this proved the beginning of the end for Germany. The Americans were close to fielding their new army backed by unlimited replacement forces.

Mistakenly believing the British Fifth Army routed by the Germans, General Pétain considered retreating to defend Paris. The mistake cost the defensively inclined Pétain his job as chief of staff, replaced by the more aggressive General Ferdinand Foch. With British commander Field Marshall Haig voicing pessimistic concerns, even suggesting BEF forces consider abandoning the fight, the British government agreed to elevate Foch to Allied Commander-in-Chief in late March 1918. The move intended to coordinate Allied strategy from a unified command, including the United States.

From the onset, things did not go well between Foch and General Pershing. Foch may be the Allied Commander however, Pershing did not intend to give up his divisions to fight under French or British command. The AEF would fight as a separate army in the field. So began a political battle between Foch and Pershing with French Prime Minister Clemenceau's continual lobbying of U.S. President Wilson.

The Germans followed with further offensives along the entire Western Front between March and June. Although these actions further drained dwindling manpower and supplies, General Erich Ludendorff planned yet another final decisive offensive.

Pressure mounted on General Foch. If the Germans successfully separated British forces from the French, it could disastrously alter the outcome of the war. Paris itself perhaps in jeopardy.

Time however ran out for the Germans. With the advances made by the Germans in the spring, Pershing felt compelled to relax his position of insisting on the AEF fighting as a separate army. He took a compromise step to Foch's argument if the Americans waited any longer it would be too late to impact the outcome. Pershing also desperately needed to test the fighting ability of his inexperienced army.

The first significant engagement for American forces was at Chateau-Thierry following Ludendorff's offensive that pushed the French off the Chemin des Dames Ridge just days earlier. The United States 2nd Division, comprised of the 3rd Infantry Brigade and the 9,500 man-strong 4th Marine Brigade, distinguished themselves at Belleau Wood in June while fighting under French command.

Although Ludendorff's offensives achieved a massive salient penetration into the Allied lines, the German advance eventually stalled. Up to 500,000 cases of the virulent strain of influenza combined with massive combat losses reduced battle-ready manpower. The civilian pool added only old and very young ill-trained and ill-equipped replacement conscripts. The westward advance of the front only worsened German inability to sustain extended supply lines. The Americans now poised to shift the numeric balance of forces in favor of the Allies spelling the end for Germany.

With evidence of AEF fighting abilities, General Pershing was now ready to commit 250,000 American forces fighting as a contiguous corps as part of a larger 50-division strong French force. Allied forces totaling 670,000 strong.

As a part of the broad-front which became known as the Second Battle of Marne, the American forces pushed back German gains at Saint Mihiel. Although the Allied success resulted from Ludendorff pulling back his best divisions for use in yet another offensive, it provided another resounding validation of the fighting capacity of the AEF. Pershing then moved his forces sixty miles north into position to face the next expected theater of battle.

Ludendoff attempted a final offensive on July 15 to cross the River Marne east of Chateaux-Thierry. After two days of bitter fighting, the Allied lines held in large part to the exceptional efforts of American Divisions. Unlike most prior engagements of this long war, the Allies poised for immediate counterattack spearheaded by the Americans.

CHAPTER 7

WWI River Meuse & Argonne Forest, France | October 1918

Since January, Fleming only saw Dominique once for two days in February as he traveled from French general headquarters at Compiègne back to AEF headquarters. With the start of the German spring offensive in March, no one at AEF headquarters received leave. A few hours off duty for sleep became even a luxury. Since then, they could only exchange letters.

My dearest Spencer,

It seems so long ago since I held you in my arms. My days at the hospital are a continuous blur. So exhausted sometimes I dose off sitting in a chair when taking a rest break. I am not alone in this. The stamina of my older colleagues pushes me not to feel sorry for myself. At night, all I think of is you. I know you assure me that you no longer serve directly in harm's way. But you are a soldier and this war rages on. What is to stay you might not be thrown into circumstances of the type that almost caused your death? It is difficult to understand how soldiers do what they do knowing they face a good chance of dying. The award citations explaining your actions for valor only cite the facts. I suspect there are other details of those violent circumstances far more revealing than you modestly described.

As a doctor, I should become use to treating all manner of patients. This war however is something quite different. Endless streams of newly wounded arrive day and night. There are piles of amputated limbs outside the surgical ward. The worse for me are those men with horrific disfigurement to their faces. They will forever suffer unimaginably difficult lives. Worse than those losing an arm or leg. As a physician, I can only repair bodies not the mind. There can be no reason that justifies sacrificing the lives of tens of thousands of an entire generation. What sets loose such a cataclysm? Is this nothing more than the arrogance of old men sending young men to their deaths to satisfy ambitions for power?

I pray you are correct that this may be the last year of war. That undoubtedly means the lives of many American soldiers sacrificed. Please do not become one of those, my love. I cannot bear losing you after just finding you. That would be a fate too cruel to imagine. I long for the time we can begin our future together. Write me as often as you can. Take care for me.

Your devoted love,
Dominique

Dominique,

Dearest,I cherish your letters. I read them again each night. Letters sustain all soldiers. You raised the question about knowing more details of my violent military encounters in Mexico and France. I promise to explain more fully when I see you in person. The censors discourage exchanging such information in letters.

Many times I have reflected on why I chose a military career. An opportunity to get a good engineering education and experience travel and adventure with the prestige of an officer. Of course, every soldier understands 'adventure' might mean combat. Some even hope for seeing action. Whether for excitement or glory. An unfortunate masculine trait. For me, the thought of glory in warfare was never an inducement. I have read military history. Seen early photographs of the American Civil War over fifty years ago. Unfortunately, this war is worse. Glory in war is a myth.

Why does any soldier force himself to act knowing the danger, the chance of death or injury? Everyone has his own reasons. For some it is country. I will tell you this, it almost always devolves to the bonding with your comrades. The commitment to protect each other is the best definition of duty. The deep-seated obligation not to let down your immediate group, even to the extent of risking your own life. That bonding forces every soldier to think beyond himself.

As for my experiences, I promise to explain every detail when I see you. However, I can tell you my actions in Mexico were a simple choice. I could stay hidden or do something knowing many of my fellow soldiers would *die from the bandit's machine gun. My personal sense of responsibility left only the option to do my best. As for what happened last year in the French trenches, let me say that I was just doing my best to survive. I saw my best chances as counterattacking. In the confines of the narrow trench, the Germans surprise raid overwhelmed the poilu. I killed so many only because the enemy bunched together in the confines of the narrow trench. I survived only because I fought shoulder to shoulder with another determined soldier. We fought to save our own lives.*

The hour is late and each day is a struggle for both of us. Having you gives me the strength to carry on. This war will soon end and we can truly be together. We shall live in France or America, whichever you choose. Perhaps I will embark on a new career as an engineer.

Love, Spencer

* * * *

The final theater of conflict of the Western Front became the sector between the River Meuse and the Argonne Forest. A vital lynchpin of German railroad supply. Although exhausted, ill supplied, and with Germany on the verge of revolting against the Prussian monarchy of Kaiser Wilhelm II, the German army remained defeated. While this sector saw lighter fighting in prior years of the war, the Germans used that time to construct elaborate defensive positions in what was the Champagne region of France before decimated by war.

Now with a recovered French Army and 1.2 million fresh American troops, the Allies poised to strike a mortal blow to the exhausted German forces. The objective was the French town of Sedan, the rail center for German supply and the principal route of retreat of their forces back into Germany.

By this time every German commander, including Hindenburg and Ludendorff understood the war was lost. A negotiated armistice remained their best outcome. Territory and survival of the German Army became the new objectives.

Although the AEF could field over a million men, fundamental problems of large-scale army-sized maneuver reduced the effectiveness in this geographically confined theater of battle. Shortcomings from lack of combat experience further contributed to considerable casualties against an entrenched and determined German resistance. The majority of American troops still received only minimal training. With the exception of only the most experienced units participating in combat during previous months, the two American armies had no combat experience.

Although German ranks now included green conscripts of the very young or old, the core of their reorganized divisions consisted of battle-hardened veterans. Led by experienced officers at all levels meant that they understand the intricate maneuver and coordination tactics essential to success developed over years of fighting.

The courage and the fighting spirit already proven at Chateau-Thierry, Belleau Wood, and St. Mihiel could not overcome inexperienced leadership as additional divisions arrived fresh from French training camps. Hastily assembled from a small professional army, the AEF had too many men led by insufficiently skilled officers and NCOs. The shortage of officers resulted in excessively large military organizational units. 27,000-man divisions, 4000-man regiments, 1000-man battalions, and 250-man companies. Almost twice the size of French and British equivalent formations with inexperienced officers at every level. The sheer size of each military unit complicated maneuver. Since the Americans divisions comprised the vanguard of the offensive, independent unit maneuver was vital in exploiting opportunity and adapting to circumstances.

AEF command structure deficiencies became evident as the AEF struggled in the Meuse-Argonne Offensive with mounting casualties.

Ushered into the office of Brigadier General Frank Parker, Fleming's boss and chief of the American Mission at French general headquarters, Parker said, "Take a seat Fleming and close the door"

"Yes, Sir."

"You have done excellent work here, Captain. General Pershing recognizes your diplomatic talents. I second that. The situation though is changing as the AEF makes what could prove the final blow to the German Army. I don't need to tell you we are short of reliable officers. At all levels."

The last month proved the ending of military careers for many senior American officers. General Pershing was relieving general officers from corps and division commands for lack of battlefield performance. In many cases perhaps unfairly for reasons beyond their control, yet Pershing had no other recourse. Needing immediate results, he battled time to deliver on AEF performance. The French commander Foch and the British commander Haig still wanted to absorb the AEF divisions into their respective commands. The aggressive French prime minister Georges Clemenceau continued to pressure U.S. President Wilson. In fear of ruining their military careers, American generals practiced the same tactic to their subordinate officers.

In addition to insufficient numbers of officers and NCOs, inexperienced senior officers sequestered themselves at headquarters too far behind the front lines. Due in part because of serious deficiencies in communications, they felt it necessary to be in telephone communications with other formations in their sectors. In so doing, timely communications with their front line units did not exist since telephone lines were spotty because of continually severed lines by artillery. The alternative fell to using runners or even homing pigeons. Information therefore arrived too late to adapt to fluid circumstances in real time.

Compounding each division's isolation, unlike the French and British, the AEF did not use liaison officers from adjacent divisions at each other's headquarters. Again the shortage of officers.

Tactically, the AEF had no experience in mastering the complicated coordination of artillery supporting an infantry offensive by advancing the bombardment continuously just ahead of their advancing troops. If well-coordinated, it never allowed the enemy a break in the shelling where they could then return artillery and machine gun fire into your attacking infantry. The Americans attacked in fits of start and stop advances. As American covering artillery bombardment stopped to advance gun batteries forward, the Germans inflicted terrible casualties. Periodically halting the advance of attacking troops as they sought cover further slowed resumption of the attack. This poorly coordinated maneuver repeated with the expected devastating results.

When an American division achieves its objective, they simply stopped to rest and lick their wounds. Tactical battlefield success meant recognizing and exploiting opportunities by pushing your resources to the maximum.

Reaching his emotional limits, General Pershing became desperate to shore up the command problem. Reduced to cannibalizing his headquarters staff for trusted officers, Pershing reassigned his chief of intelligence and Fleming's former superior, Dennis Nolan, now a brigadier general, to take command of the 28th Division's demoralized 55th Brigade.

Parker said to Fleming, "My point being, you and I are now going to get our hands dirty. Our mission as liaisons to French headquarters is no longer essential. For my part I will be glad to leave Foch's bitching behind," Parker handed Fleming a piece of paper. "You are now a major. Congratulations."

"General Summerall is taking over V Corps. I am replacing him as commander of the 1st Division. A big responsibility. The Big Red One is our best division. They have achieved every battlefield objective in this war. I intend to keep it that way. You will be my G-2 officer. We are taking over the line replacing the shattered 35th Division. I need to know the status of every element of the Division in real time. I realize communication is problem. Do your best to get me timely information, Major."

****

The sector of this great Allied offensive assigned to the AEF comprised an 18-mile wide corridor bounded on the west by the Argonne Forest and the east by the River Meuse. When Parker and Fleming joined the 1st Division, the AEF already achieved the first objective. Commencing on September 26, the AEF pushed the Germans from a front stretching between the towns of Montfaucon and Exermont. Heavy casualties exposed AEF tactical shortcomings.

The next objective was the German line ten miles further north with the town of Romagne in the center of the corridor.

Before joining General Parker the following day to assume their new roles with the 1st Division, Fleming made a visit to the 1th Aero Squadron to secure the most recent aerial photographs of the sector. He also arranged for a single aircraft equipped with radio to act as spotter for controlling artillery bombardment when the Division attacked at dawn in three days. He then spent some time at the headquarters of the 1st Field Artillery brigade to try to improve on coordination of the advancing artillery bombardment ahead of the infantry. The French already developed choreographed maneuvers of the artillery batteries. Some portion of the batteries kept firing while others advanced their position to redirect fire just beyond their advancing infantry. The process incrementally repeating. Inexperienced American artillery struggled to perfect the tactic. Not much Fleming could accomplish in just a couple of hours. At least using wireless radio, he might achieve improved results from better communication directed from a forward position.

Only three roads offered conduits to move men, artillery, and supplies into the sector. Fleming was familiar with the bottleneck. The roads were hardly roads after the rains. Lack of organization reduced this critical rear support sector to what soldiers called a giant clusterfuck.

Fleming was also mindful of what a French colonel said about Pershing's tactical use of his forces in this confined narrow front. *You use too many troops, twice as many as the French would use for such an operation. It is impossible to supply that number with food and ammunition necessary for advancing infantry and artillery*. The hasty relocation of the AEF from Saint-Mihiel to the Meuse-Argonne sector just days before made the situation worse. *Saint-Mihiel was simple. This is difficult because it requires a continuous effort to support the advance against well-entrenched German defenses not likely to give ground.* The confusion and American casualties of the first week of the battle proved the French colonel correct.

With two radio operators and four homing pigeons, Fleming suggested he could better observe from the front and report directly to division headquarters. In this way, Parker's chief of staff Lieutenant Colonel Greely would have the most current intelligence from the front lines from an independent observer assessing the entire division's situation.

October 4, 1918

Parker and Fleming reported to V Corps headquarters before arriving at 1st Division headquarters on October 1 as the Division started to relieve the shattered 35th Division. Fleming chose to imbed with the 1st Battalion of the 28th Infantry regiment.

At 0525 hours, the 1st Division attacked with two infantry brigades preceded by a rolling artillery barrage and tanks. They took the town of Montrebeau by 0700 hours then crossed the Exermont ravine. This sector initially silent except for the noise of tanks and clanking of infantry gear as the troops advanced while looking up toward the heights of the *Hindenburg Kriemhilde-Stellung* defensive line. All hell soon broke loose as German artillery and interlocking machine gun fire began butchering the 1st Division's battalions.

German artillery destroyed forty-four of the forty-seven AEF tanks. The infantry dug in as the advance slowed to a halt.

Standing close to a company commander, an artillery round exploded close enough to knock Fleming unconscious by the concussion of the blast.

Recovering minutes later and covered in blood and tissue, he carefully checked trying to determine if he was injured. The pile of unrecognizable gore just feet away likely the company commander and his first sergeant. Standing near Fleming, they apparently took the brunt of the blast shielding Fleming. Looking around, he estimated that a cluster of closely spaced artillery rounds killed or wounded perhaps half the company. The Germans had months to prepare this sector by sighting in defensive gun positions.

Fleming took charge of the company survivors as he crawled through the casualties looking for his radio operators and the pigeons to communicate with division HQ. He found both his soldiers. Killed by artillery along with the pigeons and destroying the radios. So much for communications. He was now just another field officer cut off from rear headquarters.

Eventually finding a lieutenant, he said, "Looks like you're now in command, Lieutenant. I am division G-2. Going to see if I can find your battalion HQ. Should be off to the left. Regroup what remains of your company and attach yourself to whatever unit is on either flank. Come morning, we move forward again. Staying here is certain death. Remember, this is the Big Red One Division. Good luck, Lieutenant."

October 5, 1918

Fleming crawled around dead bodies and some wounded whispering, "Where is Major Wolcott?" A sergeant responded pointing, "Shell hole twenty yards over there."

Under cover in a large shell crater, 1st battalion commander Major James Wolcott sat with a captain and his senior sergeant studying a map in the pale moonlight.

"Fleming, what's the situation with Delta Company?" Wolcott said as Fleming tumbled into the crater.

"My guess fifty percent casualties. Captain is dead. I found a lieutenant. Told him to attach his survivors to either flanking unit and renew the assault in the morning. What is the status with your other companies?"

"Almost as bad. Best I can determine is at least twenty percent casualties. Charlie Company here is in the best shape. Did you send a report back to brigade or division?"

"No. Artillery took out my radios and pigeons. Do you intend to renew the assault in the morning?"

"Yes. Unless I get new orders. Both brigades are to advance together. We're in the front of the assault."

The prior day's objective was for the entire 1st Division to take Hill 240 north of Exermont and push beyond the heights as far north as possible. The hill was one of many of the Romagne hills the Germans used to form the *Kriemhilde-Stellung* defensive line.

"Another fucking bloody day unless our artillery can get their shit together," Wolcott said.

The AEF barrage failed to suppress the German batteries from cutting down the American tanks and inflicting horrific casualties. Fleming's tactic of using aircraft for artillery coordination never got a chance. He would learn later the aircraft suffered mechanical problems and turned back after one hour. Regardless, maneuver of artillery batteries to advance in concert with advancing infantry nearly impossible with the congestion in the rear supply sector. This coming day would prove even more critical to suppress German positions firing down at short-range from the heights against the AEF infantry advancing uphill.

At 0630 hours, the 1st Division recommenced the attack. The objective remained the same. Seize Hill 240, punching a breach in the German *Kriemhilde-Stellung* defensive line and consolidating the offensive by moving as far north as possible. The situational tactical challenges remained the same as the previous day. The German Army expected to continue their stubborn defense. Unable to resupply as well as maintain an escape avenue for retreat east back into Germany, defeat here meant collapse of the entire German Army.

Fleming decided to remain with the 1st Battalion of the 28th Infantry Regiment. He offered to take command of Bravo and Delta Companies suffering reduced strength through heavier casualties the day before. Both lost their company commanders. Major Wolcott would attack with Alpha and Charlie companies abreast with Fleming following behind with Bravo and Delta in reserve with only two lieutenants. Yesterday the battalion lost 11 officers, 23 NCOs, and 291 soldiers killed or wounded. A third of the battalion's origin strength.

The second day proved as challenging. Just as bloody. Although the AEF coordinated an improved rolling barrage, it failed to silence German artillery situated on the heights and reverse slope of the hill line. Artillery rounds could also not easily destroy machine guns in hardened concrete bunkers. Placed to provide interlocking fire of the approaching Allies, the wooded ground of the Bois de Boyon slowed the infantry advance taking a terrible casualty toll.

By late morning, the battalion pushed to the base of Hill 240. Through his field glasses, he could see their progress fell behind the adjoining troops on each flank. If the entire brigade did not assault the hill with maximum coordinated forces, the attack might flounder. Another night out here to face a third day could prove disastrous.

Signaling to his two subordinate lieutenants to his right and left to keep Bravo and Delta companies in place, Fleming and a senior NCO named Nansen moved forward quickly in a crouch. Ten minutes later, they came to Alpha and Charlie companies hunkered down.

Fleming grabbed the closest soldier by the collar, "What the fuck is going on? Why aren't you moving?"

"Don't know, Sir."

"Where is Major Wolcott?"

"Dead?"

"Who is in command?"

"I think Captain Campbell?"

Fleming moved forward with a sergeant named Nansen. Asking each soldier about Captain Campbell, he found the battalion first sergeant."

"Sergeant, who is in command?"

"Not sure, Sir. Probably some lieutenant. Might even be me. Major Wolcott is dead. Captain Campbell too. Don't know about Captain Ferguson."

"What's your name, First Sergeant?

"Bertoletti, Sir."

"Well, Bertoletti, I'm now in command. We will get this battalion off their asses and move forward up the fucking hill!"

"Sergeant Nansen, get back to Bravo and Charlie Companies and bring them up at the double. Tell them they are no longer reserves. Fill in the gaps."

Fleming and Sergeant Bertoletti then moved quickly ahead weaving their way to avoid concentrations of machine gun rounds striking the ground. After a hundred yards, they reached the front of battalion. The men all hunkered down trying to find cover in shell craters and the sparse woods on the long slope of Hill 240. The AEF rolling barrage by this time advancing to the German positions at the top of the hill.

Fleming raised his field glasses. American troops on either flank were a hundred yards further along in the assault.

"Bertoletti, I want three teams of four men each to go forward as recon units. Submachine guns and plenty of grenades. They're to silence as many machine guns as possible. Your best men.

"Locate any officers. Tell them to take charge of those soldiers closest to them. Forget about companies and platoons. Make it quick, Sergeant."

While Bertoletti scurried off, Sergeant Nansen arrived directing the remnants of Bravo and Charlie companies to fill gaps in the line.

A captain then jumped into the shell crater next to Fleming. "Captain Ferguson, Sir, Alpha Company."

"I have taken command. Any other officers standing?" Fleming said.

"Two that I know of."

"Send word for them to take charge of our men on each flank. We must move forward as part of the entire brigade.

"Sergeant Bertoletti is organizing recon teams to go after machine gun emplacements. We are not waiting to see how successful they are. We resume our assault with the entire battalion as soon you organize your officers. You have ten minutes, Captain."

Ferguson said, "Sergeant Ellis is already out there going after machine guns."

"Out where?"

Ferguson pointed up the hill. "He works alone. Hell of fighter in hand-to-hand combat."

"Alone? Like some Apache warrior? Is he fucking nuts?"

"Maybe. But Ellis is hell to reckon with in a fight. The soldiers call him the *Lone Wolf*."

"Well we aren't waiting for Sergeant Ellis or the recon teams to get the job done. Get the battalion moving immediately, Captain."

As Captain Ferguson shouted orders to move out, the experienced disciplined soldiers of the 1st Division passed the word quickly and the battalion resumed the attack. Bertoletti moved his search and destroy recon teams out front at a faster pace. Their tactic to separate from the main body of troops hoping to locate then infiltrate close enough to take out German machine guns with grenades.

The universal courage of these American soldiers awed Fleming. After the disastrous previous day, the carnage was little different this day. The continuous rate of machine gun rounds sounded like swarms of angry insects. Sometimes an outcry as a round found its mark. No sound from those catching a round to the head. The washbasin metal helmets meant to deflect shrapnel, offered little protection against high velocity rounds.

Every soldier doing what he recognized as his duty. The motivation personal to every man. Fleming no different. Once in the middle of a life or death struggle, quitting or fleeing was never an option for disciplined soldiers. Most could never explain why they went into the jaws of death often on ill-conceived orders from generals in the rear maneuvering troops on maps. As for Fleming, an inexplicable existential imperative beyond rational thought.

The renewed attack on Hill 240 instigated by Fleming was as bloody as the previous thirty hours of this battle. However, as the remnants of the 1st Battalion began assaulting the sloping ground there appeared the impression of a lightening of machine gun fire. In another hour, clearly evident that something changed. Now the cracks of individual rifle rounds dominated the sound of combat. By noon, the two infantry brigades of the 1st Division took Hill 240.

The division attempted to push further north but failed. The Germans fell back in an orderly withdrawal while pounding the AEF from artillery emplacements of their secondary *Freya-Stellung* line. The entire V Corps suffered a grievous toll of casualties. Yet the effort brought sight of what might be the end. The *Freya-Stellung* was the last defensive line shielding the rail center at Sedan. A final Allied thrust could bring about defeat of the German Army.

After brigade HQ ordered a halt to the advance by the end of the day, Fleming sat down on a large rock exhausted. His feelings mixed looking about trying to calculate the losses of the battalion. He could now rightfully call it his battalion. His first command over troops in the field. Satisfied he did his best.

Captain Ferguson walked over with a sergeant in tow. "Major, this is Sergeant Ellis. Thought you might want to meet him."

Ellis saluted. He looked like he had been in a fight. Sleeve torn. A serious amount of blood splattered over his uniform.

Fleming returned the salute and said, "Are you wounded, Sergeant?"

"No, Sir. Doin' okay."

"The Captain tells me you're something of a one-man military unit. You like fighting alone. Is that right?"

"Yes, Sir. Easier for me to sneak up on the enemy."

"So how did you do today?"

"Well I got a few, Sir."

Captain Ferguson interrupted, "More than a few is what I heard, Major. Unofficially he silenced eleven machine guns."

"Eleven? Are you serious, Captain?"

"Yes, Sir. Got all sorts of reports from different soldiers."

"Remarkable. Care to share my seat and chat awhile, Sergeant Ellis?" Ellis sat down holding his rifle between his knees. "How the hell did you pull off something like that?"

"Working by myself, it was easy to get into the rear behind their machine gun bunkers. After that, I had 'em by surprise. Working alone, if I screw up I don't cost someone else's life."

"Wished most generals thought that way," Fleming said. "Tell me about yourself, Sergeant."

Sergeant Michael Ellis went on to earn the Medal of Honor with Fleming's recommendation. He and another medal of honor recipient, Sergeant Alvin York of the 82nd Division, became celebrities of the bloody Meuse-Argonne Offensive.

Fleming received the Silver Star for taking command of the shattered 1st Battalion contributing significantly in the taking of Hill 240. A good deal of the battalion's success was the extraordinary actions of Sergeant Ellis. To Fleming, a good deal more remarkable than the action that earned him the medal of honor a year earlier.

After taking Hill 240, the commander of the 28th Infantry Regiment remarked, "The enemy machine gunners held their posts until bayoneted. Remarkable how our lads prevailed."

In a week of some of the bloodiest fighting of the war, the 1st Division again achieved its objects but at a staggering cost of 9,400 killed and wounded while advancing only four miles. A thirty-five percent casualty rate. On October12, the 42nd Division relieved the 1st Division where they then passed into the First Army's reserve sector for rehabilitation and assimilation of replacements to bring it back to strength.

One month later, hostilities of the Great War halted at 1100 hours on November 11, 1918 as the effective date of the Armistice.

CHAPTER 8

Paris, France | December 1918

Following the Armistice, Fleming like every American soldier was in a high state of euphoria. While his brother officers must wait for weeks or even months before rejoining wives or lovers in the United States, Dominique was within reach by a short train ride. He expected to receive a leave before Christmas.

The AEF would remain in Europe until the details of terms of Germany's defeat became codified by treaty. The Armistice was not a cessation of hostilities among equals. Germany capitulated under terms yet to be determined by the victorious Allies. Surrender in all but name. Depending on disarmament terms imposed on Germany, the largely conscripted AEF would demobilize and downsize to fit peacetime circumstances. With Dominique now in his life, continuing a career in the military and returning to the United States was no longer certain.

Fleming spoke by telephone to Dominique at her hospital twice since the Armistice. An exchange of letters spoke of plans for the future. Family was important to Dominique. Apart from her parents, the war changed the lives of her two married sisters and an older brother. One sister with a young child also lost her husband in 1915. Dominique's older brother suffered the loss of an arm at the Battle of the Verdun where she also lost her husband. A close family, leaving France for the United States a difficult transformation for Dominique.

With only his parents as family, Fleming's circumstances suggested making his future in France. He could give up his brief military career in favor of beginning new as a civil engineer. Fluent in French, reconstruction opportunities should abound. His military experience as a decorated officer should qualify him for managerial opportunities. An entire generation of young Frenchmen killed must leave shortages everywhere.

That decision became easy after receiving devastating news. A letter from his old housekeeper Lucia.

Mijo,

I have the saddest possible news. This terrible influenza spreading everywhere has taken both your mother and father. They died only days apart. Worse yet a proper funeral service was not possible. People not permitted to be together in large groups even wearing masks. No burial service even at the gravesite. The funeral people overwhelmed with so many dead from the disease. But I am told that Magda and Edward will be buried in a nice place on a hill overlooking the ocean.

You are like one of my own sons. Your mother and father were so proud of you. So much more of life to share with you. I was not allowed to see them before they passed but I know you must have been in their last thoughts.

Forgive me for not finding better words. Please take care of yourself. Carlos and Enrique send you their love.

Love, Lucia

Sharing his grief with Dominique, Fleming felt terribly alone. Having her took on even larger meaning. He looked forward to spending time with her family over Christmas. The unexpected death of his parents made up his mind to stay in France. A Christmas present to Dominique. Troubled over not receiving a letter from her for over a week, he placed a call to the hospital since she did not have a telephone in her apartment. More troubling still after finally connecting to someone in hospital administration.

"Dr. Dumont has not reported into work for over a week."

"Why is that?"

"I do not have any further information, Monsieur. The duty roster just carries the notation not available for shift scheduling."

"How can I get more information? I am Dr. Dumont's fiancé. My name is Major Spencer Fleming. I am stuck here at American Army headquarters and cannot get to Reims. I have not heard from her on over a week."

"I understand, Monsieur. We are overwhelmed with inquiries about loved ones. I will try to obtain more information. Please give me a couple of days and call back again."

That proved unnecessary. The following day Fleming received a letter at headquarters. Thinking it from Dominique, he ripped open the envelope in anticipation.

Dear Major Fleming,

I am Dominique's sister. She shared with me her joy of falling in love with you. Not having a specific address, I addressed this to the American Army headquarters hoping it would make its way to you. Regrettably there is no easy way of telling you this. Dominique is gone. The circumstances of her death are as appalling as any Greek tragedy. You see, Spencer, Dominique's husband she thought killed at Verdun unexpectedly returned. He shot Dominique then took his own life.

The grief of our family is beyond description. I do not know what caused Marcel to do what he did. I can only imagine his emotional state took a tragic turn when Dominique explained how her life changed after hearing of his death. Having survived his ordeal the last two years, no telling his state of mind. You see he turned up first at my home before seeing Dominique since he did not know where to find her. Thinking him dead, she moved from Paris to live with me for several weeks while coming to terms with her grief. As a doctor, her sense of duty compelled her return her to work at the hospital in Reims where she met you. Marcel explained to me the events following his capture by the Germans. Perhaps this accounted for why he was not identified as a prisoner of war until much later by the International Red Cross.

With the hundreds of thousands of fallen French soldiers, easy to understand misidentifying many of the dead. Moved from the first POW camp after only a couple of weeks, he escaped during the relocation. Remaining free for weeks while trying to return to France, he was again captured. This time the Germans shipped him further east to another POW camp populated largely with Soviet prisoners. A much worse place with little food and no visits by the Red Cross. His fate unknown until repatriated soon after the Armistice.

Eventually arriving at their former apartment in Paris, he discovered she no longer lived there. Dominique left no forwarding address once she joined me in Dijon after the letter from the War Ministry arrived advising her of her husband's death. It was only *after Marcel telephoned me from Paris that I told him she was working at a military hospital in Reims.*

When I reached Dominique by telephone, she fell apart. With a bright future ahead with you, her entire world shattered. I cannot imagine the conflicted emotions she experienced. Marcel understandably felt his world also destroyed once she obviously told him of her present circumstances. That all happened over a period of a week. I never spoke again to Dominique before her death so I can only imagine the despair that drove Marcel to do this.

There are no words that can comfort any of us that loved Dominique. My sincere wish is that you fondly remember our Dominique while you move forward with your life.

Claudine Renault

Sitting in his small office with the door open, Fleming leaned forward over his desk holding the letter in both hands. The horror of the letter transfixed him in a state of shock.

A junior officer entered seeing him still staring down at the letter. "Excuse me, Major. Do you have a moment?"

Fleming raised his eyes but made no response.

The look on Fleming's face with tears running down his cheeks caused the lieutenant to stop short as he approached closer. "Is something wrong, Sir?"

With still no response, the lieutenant turned abruptly closing the door gently behind him.

Ten minutes later following a gentle knock on Fleming's closed door, Brigadier General Nolan entered and closed the door behind him. "Are you all right, Major?"

"Ah…no, Sir. Just received …more bad news."

Returned to intelligence duty at AEF headquarters, he now worked again for Nolan his first boss. Fleming always liked the soft-spoken intellectual Nolan.

Fleming covered his eyes with one hand and silently wept. Nolan knew of the loss of both Fleming's parents. Another family member perhaps?

Gaining a semblance of composure, Fleming managed, "My fiancée. She too is now dead."

Nolan sighed, "I am profoundly sorry, Spencer. So tragic following the loss of your parents. Would you like me to call the chaplain?"

"Thank you, Sir, but that won't be necessary. I would just like to retire to my quarters if I may, Sir."

****

Two days later, in the outer office area of headquarters there was a rustling of chairs and a shout of "Attention!" Fleming also stood up from behind his desk as General Pershing walked in. Fleming saluted, "Good morning, General."

Pershing closed the door. "Please sit down, Major." Pulling up a chair across from Fleming, "My condolences for your grave losses. I believe I can understand the depth of your sorrow. You know of course I lost my wife and my three little girls before the Mexican Campaign."

"Yes, Sir."

"There are no words that will provide comfort. No homilies, no religious invocations, no philosophical explanation to mitigate the unrelenting emotional anguish. Just as in war, it is up to every soldier to decide on his actions. Do my duty to myself or give up? There are only two choices in war or life. Stand and fight or surrender.

"You have proven your character, son. Not only in the heat of battle but your contributions to our enormously difficult task. We won the shooting war, however I fear that will not be the end of hostilities in Europe. The war settled nothing. It likely established new animosities.

"What do you plan on doing now that the war is over?"

The pragmatic directness typical of Pershing, Fleming looked at him with a questioning look. "Sir?"

"I refer to your military career. You have great prospects. The Army needs officers with your proven intellectual abilities. The war destroyed the archaic seniority system of the Army. Merit will hold sway just as it did here in France. Only the intelligence and skill of officers like you at every command level transformed the AEF into a first rate army. We turned untrained troops into an effective army the equal of any other on the field.

"Yet for a career soldier these next decades will prove challenging. The army must downsize from millions to some peacetime level. You certainly will have a place in the office corps. West Point, civil engineering degree, distinguished combat record, fluency in four languages. But your options may still be ill suited to your intellectual interests. You also greatly impressed your bosses, Generals Nolan and Parker. They too are thinkers with a range of skills.

"Since Mexico, I recognized your abilities. Plodding along with a glut of mediocre officers clogging the seniority system, you likely would leave the Army eventually. With the coming of the war, I took advantage of the circumstances to bring you along in rank. You may not know that following my service in the Philippines as a major of volunteers, I reverted to my permanent rank of captain in the regular army in 1901. Stuck there until President Roosevelt promoted me four ranks to brigadier general in 1906.

"I bring that up because if you return to duty in the United States, you will revert to your regular army rank of captain. I have an offer that may be more attractive. It requires remaining in Europe. My motives remain the same. The Army needs officers with your intellectual skills. The next war will undoubtedly be different. Technology will advance. Weapons and communications. Warfare becoming far more complex."

"What is the American Army's role in Europe with the war now over, General?"

"Enforce whatever will be the terms of the Armistice. Keep a close watch on the Germans. The country is economically destroyed. Millions of soldiers with poor prospects of work. Shortage of food supplies. Ripe for revolution. Communism is a threat. Perhaps keep the French from reigniting a military conflict. Clemenceau wants to exact revenge on Germany. President Wilson is even coming to Paris. He will push his own peace plan. I suspect that will include a U.S. military presence for some period.

"That of course depends on what is decided by the peace conference which will begin shortly. Let me get to what I am offering you. President Wilson is bringing an American delegation to Paris within weeks. The terms of what amounts to Germany's defeat will be decided by France, Britain, Italy, and the United States. I understand Germany will not take part in the negotiations. That alone will cause future problems.

"The American peace commission consists of politicians and academics. They need military advice. The President asked for my recommendation. I named General Summerall. He requested as his deputy, Brigadier General Parker. Parker speaks French. West Point and French War College graduate. An intellectual with a unique understanding of the French. Parker requested you as part of the military advisory staff. It's a high-profile posting, good for your career."

"I appreciate General Parker's confidence in me. May I have a day to think it over?"

"Of course. Given your recent losses, it must be difficult to focus on career objectives. If I might offer some fatherly advice, this is a good opportunity, Fleming. I looked at your fitness reports while you served as liaison to French army headquarters. French senior officers speak highly of you.

"To sweeten the offer, I told General Parker I will see you are promoted to major in the regular army. While I want to keep you in the Army, I sincerely believe you will find these duties more appealing than participating with downsizing the Army and some dreary peacetime assignment stateside."

* * * *

General Parker spoke to him as candidly as General Pershing. Where Pershing was paternal, Parker was more the experienced uncle. He and Parker had much in common. Parker also accepted the detached assignment as military adviser to the American Peace Commission as a preferred option to taking part in the unrewarding duty of downsizing the Army. Pershing even nominated Parker for promotion to major general. Congress however stopped all promotions of general officers after the Armistice.

Over cognacs in Parker's office, he said, "I can assure you, Spencer, this assignment will at least be interesting. The principal heads of state, the Big Four, all have different agendas. I suspect there will be some lively arguments. Even the American commissioners might test our diplomatic skills?"

"What do you mean, Sir?"

"President Wilson likely will push his advocacy for his League of Nations aided by his personal adviser Edward House. House is low-key backbench manipulator of the highest order. Robert Lansing U.S. Secretary of State does not share Wilson's enthusiasm for this League of Nations. Rumor has it House and Lansing despise each other. That should prove great theater.

"Besides we shall be in Paris. You shall spend several interesting months. Make powerful contacts that won't hurt your career.

"Alsace-Lorraine will undoubtedly revert back to the French. My well-placed French sources say Clemenceau wants control of the Rhineland. That would mean French occupation."

"Which therefore probably demands American participation to keep the peace between the French and Germans," Fleming added.

"Precisely. Very perceptive. That's why I need you. Such an American military presence requires difficult diplomacy. Just the sort of work suited to you. If you decide later to leave the Army, you have measurably added to your already impressive curriculum vitae."

While the initial shock of his losses subsided, Fleming could not shake the depression. Difficult to make an objective life decision, therefore following the advice of Pershing and Parker made the choice for him. He needed time to process how to move forward while his emotional wounds healed.

* * * *

Fleming served as a military adviser to the American Commission until July 1919. While interesting as Parker suggested, it was equally frustrating. The bickering, posturing, the forming of alliances within the American delegation as contentious as the higher-level negotiations going on among the principle four heads of state. Acting as an adviser, Fleming's diplomacy often amounted to avoiding unintentionally contributing to individual delegates' bias.

Above his level swirled the competing interests of France, Britain, and the United States. The Big Four also included Italy, however their influence proved marginal.

Britain was in the best place since circumstances with the defeat of Germany satisfying many of what might otherwise become negotiated demands. The German navy and merchant marine coming under restriction. Even without British pressure, Germany would undoubtedly lose all their colonies. Britain also remained physically separated from Germany by the English Channel, protected by the dominate Royal Navy.

With the war fought largely on French soil, and with a common border with Germany, the French position was more aggressive. From the onset of negotiations, they wanted punitive reparations along with security-related measures. Strategically, they pressed for a weakened Germany, whereas Britain preferred a stable Europe on the continent rather than a single dominate country. British-French relations were rarely amicable during the prior two centuries.

The United States stood as the leading financial power in the world. Little damaged financially by the war, the U.S. suffered only a fraction of the casualties suffered by Britain and France with its later entry into the war. The U.S. now possessed the best combat-ready army having fought in major engagements for only the last six months of the war. It was America that tipped the scales against Germany. President Woodrow Wilson intended to use that leverage to promote his own world-view. In an address delivered before a joint session of Congress, Wilson presented a Fourteen Point Plan for restoring Europe and maintaining future peace. Point number fourteen was Wilson's obsession. *A general association of nations must be formed under specific covenants for the purpose of affording mutual guarantees of political independence and territorial integrity to great and small states alike.* It did not necessarily embody many key demands of the other Allies, particularly those of France. Fleming thought it naïve and unworkable.

Adding to divergent objectives, the principal functionaries dictating the terms of this peace treaty dramatically differed in personality. British Prime Minister David Lloyd George was gregarious, engaging, a talented negotiator, and great orator with the ability to sound spontaneous. French Prime Minister Clemenceau was irascible, short-tempered, blunt, and aggressive. It was Clemenceau that demanded Paris be the location of the peace conference rather than a neutral country since they suffered the greatest injury from German aggression. U.S. President Woodrow Wilson was aloof, introverted, professorial, self-righteous, priggish, and arrogant. Clemenceau disliked both Lloyd George and Wilson. Their contrasting tones permeated down to all levels of the various negotiating sub-commissions.

* * * *

The best part of the assignment was living in Paris for many months. General Parker knew the city well and the two often dined together. Like Fleming, he also spoke Spanish from years of service in Puerto Rico during the Spanish-American War and successive military attaché assignments to Venezuela, Argentina, and Cuba.

One evening in early May while sitting outside a café, Parker said, "The Commission will soon advise Germany of their fate. The conditions will make clear they suffered defeat. Allied demands will infuriate them. One article will particularly inflame their sense of sovereignty. Included in the final document, the

Allies will occupy German territory west of the Rhine, including the bridgeheads, for fifteen years."

"Sounds like something Clemenceau demands. Not only a buffer between Germany and France but a way to ensure German reparation payments from their most important industrial region."

"Correct. General Summerall and I both think this an ideal assignment for you. Largely a diplomatic assignment. Might lead to later assignments as military attaché. I found my attaché assignments interesting and stimulating.

"Anyway, we submitted a letter of recommendation to General Pershing since he technically still commands the AEF Third Army currently headquartered in Koblenz on the Rhine. Dramatically reduced in troop strength, it still has sufficient presence to demonstrate American resolve to enforce the peace."

The months spent in Paris with the intellectually challenging work for the peace commission served to dispel Fleming's overwhelming depression. The deep scar to his soul would always remain, but the pain eased enough for him to compartmentalize his grief.

He loved Paris. Felt at home here. Although vast areas of villages and farmland little more than 100 miles from Paris suffered complete destruction, Paris was physically unscathed by the war. The frequent sight of men with missing limbs served as a constant reminder.

Returning to the United States and remaining in the Army held no attraction. Postponing any decision to leave the Army while staying in Europe appeared a good interim alternative.

On June 28, 1919, all parties signed the Treaty of Versailles. Specifics defined in 435 articles running 240 pages. With no choice, Germany signed under duress.

Within days, Fleming received orders to report to the newly formed American Forces in Germany replacing the former AEF Third Army. On German soil, the AFG headquartered in the 19th century Prussian Ehrenbreitstein Fortress on the east bank of the Rhine where it joins the River Moselle, overlooking the town of Koblenz. Fleming's orders read: *You are to assume the position of intelligence officer to American Forces Germany as part of the commanding officer's personal staff. As the AFG commander also serves as the United States Commissioner of the Inter-Allied Rhineland High Commission, you shall also perform additional duties related to the maintenance of working relations with other Allied occupation commands and German civil and military administrations as directed by the AFG commanding officer.*

The American Army in France was rapidly drawing down as soldiers began shipping back to the United States at a rate of 300,000 a month. The American Forces in Germany command occupying the American sector in the central area of the Rhineland expected to number only 20,000 by the following summer. France controlled the largest sector of the Rhineland occupation with much larger numbers of troops, including 25,000-40,000 colonial French troops from Africa. Britain and Belgium occupied the northernmost sector of the Rhine industrial basin.

* * * *

While in the process of vacating his office at the Ministère de l'Europe et des Affaires Étrangères on the Quai d'Orsay, a well-dressed man stood in the open doorway. "Might you have a few minutes, Major Fleming?"

Fleming turned from filling his briefcase on his desk, "Yes, I… I recognize you. You're with the American delegation. Sorry I don't recall your name."

"Allen Dulles, State Department."

Dulles extended his hand.

"What can I do for you, Mr. Dulles?"

"Secretary of State Lansing asked if I might have a word with you. Nothing official, just an informal chat since we have shared objectives in our duties representing the United States. Am I correct you are being posted to Koblenz to AFG headquarters?"

"How is it you know that, Mr. Dulles?"

"We have broad sources of information. I also know you will be the G-2 officer on the staff of the new commander of the AFG, Major General Henry Allen. No relation. However, Secretary

Lansing is my uncle by marriage. Therefore, he asked me to speak with you. Now that the war is officially over, the State Department must assume a new role in a cooperative effort with the War Department."

"Very well, Mr. Dulles, what's on your mind?"

"How about we discuss this over drinks. My favorite bar is located just across the river on the other side of the Louvre in the Hôtel Regina. Quieter than the more popular Hôtel de Crillon congested with too many dignitaries attending the peace conference."

CHAPTER 9

Koblenz, Rhineland Region, Germany | April 1920

Seated at a small table in the small wood-paneled bar at the Hôtel Regina, Allen Dulles asked, "What is your take on the Treaty, Major?"

Sipping a good single malt Scotch, Fleming replied, "Short sighted. The terms ensure Germany will someday again become a problem. Lloyd George and Wilson caved into Clemenceau's demands for retribution. The French position understandable but a weakened Germany ignores the threat of Russia on all of Europe. Germany is the essential buffer."

"I agree. I believe a good many of the American commissioners also agree. What about all the other articles? Wilson got his League of Nations. What's your opinion on that?"

"Utopian. Idealistic, Impractical?"

"Why's that?

"No major power will relinquish their interests to collective arbitration. Goes to the heart of sovereign prerogatives." Fleming set down his glass. "Why did the Secretary of State send you, Mr. Dulles?"

"Sorry, I must sound like my brother the lawyer. He also works for Mr. Lansing as part of the delegation. Before I get to why we are seeking your help, indulge me a moment to set the background."

"Who exactly do you represent, Mr. Dulles?"

"Secretary Lansing and certain other senior American foreign service professionals."

"Okay. Go ahead."

"The United States is the only major country without a foreign intelligence service. There is no indication that will change. The entrenched isolationism of the United States breeds a sense of ignoring the constant changing political dynamics throughout the world. Knowledge is power. Secret knowledge is supremely powerful. As the most powerful country now in the world, the United States needs a continuous flow of intelligence to understand what is happening in the rest of the world.

"At present, the only intelligence organizations we have are the Military Intelligence Division of the Army and the Office of Naval Intelligence. Perhaps to a lesser extent, the Treasury's Secret Service. The only foreign sources of intelligence are military attachés and diplomatic staff.

"The information gathered is largely by observation and publicly available. Channeled back to Washington according to its category or relevance. Military, trade, economic, etc. No formal analytical process on the receiving end. Intelligence of vital national interest is a combination of all types of information necessary to create a coherent picture."

"So this background you are explaining serves to make the argument for the State Department as the center for U.S. intelligence." Fleming said,

Dulles smiled. "Very perceptive, but not quite what we are after. You see, State already receives intelligence from the MID, ONI, and the Secret Service. Second hand without the ability to vet the integrity by understanding the source. These agencies are also concerned with narrow avenues of information. Political intelligence largely absent. The world however revolves around politics."

"I appreciate the civics lesson and this fine Scotch. Now tell me what you want from me."

"Of course. Thanks for indulging me. What we are asking is your assistance in providing the State Department whatever political intelligence you come across in your duties with the occupation forces in the Rhineland."

"Without telling my military superiors I assume?"

"Obviously. That might be awkward."

"Why me?"

"Because of your experience. Going all the way back to your undercover venture in Mexico, to your diplomatic work as liaison to French headquarters during the war, and your work with the American peace delegation. Your reputation as an original thinker. A decorated soldier that does not shy from challenge.

"You are strategic. Likely to see beyond provincial bureaucratic constraints. That is my assessment after researching you. Secretary Lansing gave me the assignment to recruit you."

Fleming interrupted to signal a waiter for another round of drinks.

With fresh drinks, Dulles resumed his selling. "You are correct that Germany will be problematic. The Treaty will eventually become an excuse for future German militarism. It is in their cultural makeup. No telling what may evolve from their present political and economic chaos. You speak fluent German. Your official duties will place you in immediate proximity to interact with all levels of German society."

"It would be my career should the Army discover me going outside of channels. If I agree to spy for the State Department, do I communicate only with you? No one else would know me as the source?"

"Spying is too harsh a word. All we are asking is your personal observations on political and social circumstances in Germany. Nothing violating your military duties."

"Really? Communicating official information to a foreign service officer at the State department?"

"I'm suggesting something more indirect?"

"I should hope so. Not only indirect but it must stand up to scrutiny as seemingly personal correspondence. The content kept entirely separate from my official military duties. I will not share anything I feel as classified. Any information I provide will be restricted to political observations. If ever discovered, nothing that cannot be explained as personal observations to a friend."

"Are you agreeing to help us, Major Fleming?"

"Conditionally. The State Department is a bureaucracy. The top guys are political appointees. Not comfortable with that. If I agree, you must assure me that only you know me as the source of the information I provide."

Dulles thought for a moment before responding. "Right now the only ones that know about this other than Secretary Lansing, my uncle, is my older brother John. In fact, it was John's idea to approach you. What about I restrict knowledge of your helping us to just my family?"

"That makes me more comfortable. How then can I disguise my correspondence?"

"What I meant was using someone outside the State Department as intermediary. I have a younger sister, Eleanor. Intelligent, adventurous. BA from Bryn Mawr. Spent two years working for relief organizations in France during the war. Back in college now at Radcliffe working on her masters in economics. A serious woman. What about a romance by correspondence? She would relish the intrigue."

Fleming considered everything. The concept made sense. Still serving the interests of the United States. Not like spying for a foreign government. The MID focused largely on signals intelligence, encrypted transmissions, and battlefield intelligence. They possessed no capacity or interest for analyzing political intelligence. In peacetime, a military backwater. Regardless how General Parker hyped the Rhineland assignment, it sounded boring. Moonlighting for the State Department might add an interesting sideline while doing something meaningful.

Collaborating with Dulles did not conflict with his military duties. He exaggerated the concerns over confidentiality simply to avoid controversy. Voicing his opinions was his business. Not even sure he intended to continue a military career.

"Very well. I will give it shot."

* * * *

After enduring almost one year stationed at Koblenz, nothing of interest ever happened. His duties indistinct. A military intelligence officer with nothing militarily going on. The occupation sector assigned to the Americans consisted of the central portion of the Rhine. To the north, the Belgians occupied German territory to the west bank of the Rhine. The British a smaller area situated on both sides of the Rhine. The French occupied the largest geographic area to the south containing the major cities of Frankfurt, Wiesbaden, Mainz, Mannheim, and Karlsruhe. Civilians only. The German Army prohibited from the occupied Rhineland.

The Treaty of Versailles also restored Alsace-Lorraine to France after Germany seized the area following the Franco-Prussian War in 1871. Fleming's mother's mixed French and German background coming from Metz that now reverted back to France.

The American sector was comparatively quiet. While the Allied occupation forces were there to ensure no German military adventurism, Germany still controlled all civil governmental functions. The French sector suffered periodic incidents of clashes with the German population, largely from the significant use of African colonial troops. People anywhere resent a foreign military occupying force yet relations in the American sector remained peaceful.

Information of intelligence value proved scarce both to the U.S. Army as well as for Allen Dulles at the State Department. Most of Fleming's reports came from his official duties interacting with his counterparts of other occupying countries, and accompanying the American commanding general to meetings with German civilian government groups. Fleming took the opportunity to engage the Germans unofficially, promoting social relationships. Although acquiring a broad cross section of German opinions, he could find very little of intelligence value to provide to Dulles.

During that first year, his most useful information came from the German Reichswehr liaison officer to the Inter-Allied Rhineland High Commission, Oberstleutnant Ritter von Strobel.

A Prussian from an aristocratic military family, Strobel commanded an artillery regiment during the Great War. His war record and high regard of fellow officers allowed him to remain in the German army restricted to only 100,000 by the terms of the peace treaty. A career officer, Lieutenant Colonel Strobel came from a heritage of army officers stretching back generations. Two years before the start of the Great War, Strobel graduated from the prestigious Prussian Staff College in Berlin.

Fleming and Strobel struck up a friendship. Both shared common intellectual interests, While they held differing opinions concerning the war, their views aligned far more than their differences. Both gathered insights from their respective countries. It was from Strobel that Fleming gathered useful information for reporting. Not military secrets, but a sense of the political and social issues of Germany from Strobel's unusually objective viewpoint. Like Fleming, Strobel was an independent thinker arriving at his own conclusions.

With Koblenz located centrally, General Allen offered to provide offices for the representatives of the German Weimar civilian government and the Reichswehr, the German Army, within the massive Ehrenbreitstein Fortress serving as American headquarters. The arrangement proved helpful to Fleming to cultivate relationships with German officials.

Soon after arriving in Koblenz, Fleming's aide escorted Colonel Strobel into Fleming's office. The office being large, Fleming had a small round table with two comfortable chairs better suited to conversations than from behind his desk. On the table sat an ivory chess set.

Fleming's fluency in German surprised Strobel. After exchanging pleasantries, Strobel said, "That is an interesting painting hanging behind your desk. Rather unusual. Impressionist?"

Fleming turned to look at the painting, "Yes, I see what you mean, Colonel. However, the artist is not someone of note. It depicts the great San Francisco earthquake and fire of 1906. My father purchased it since he took part in rebuilding the city. My mother and I lived through those terrible several days. They are both deceased so it is a valued possession."

Strobel nodded. "And the fine chess set? Do you play?"

It too was a prized possession. A gift from Dominique after his release from the hospital. "Yes. Every opportunity I can. Has the effect of completely consuming my concentration. The perfect diversion when wrestling with a difficult problem."

Strobel smiled. "Well put, Major. Since General Allen was kind enough to provide me office space in this vast building, perhaps we might play occasionally."

"Excellent idea, Colonel. I am at your service."

After losing the first three games to Fleming in their first match, Strobel remarked, "My compliments, Major. I consider myself a player of some skill. At least I thought so. You however are in a different class. I do not believe I made any disastrously bad moves yet you repeatedly outmaneuvered me. Remarkable."

It was not long before their chess matches became a frequent event over lunch when both were in the headquarters building. Strobel commented jokingly, "Of course I prefer to win, but losing to someone as good as you at least does not deflate my ego."

With a wife and daughter in Berlin, Strobel was also a stranger to Koblenz. He and Fleming fell into an easy social routine over drinks and dinner when possible. Although unspoken, both understood their friendship had a professional component by providing useful information for their respective governments. They did not exchange secrets but found no reason not to be candid in their opinions, even when critical of their own country's position.

Fleming introduced Strobel to his favorite watering hole, Gruenewald Taverne, a small tavern not frequented by American Army personnel. Although regulations stated U.S. soldiers must always be in uniform and armed, as intelligence officer, the commanding general exempted him. Fleming's argument that his duties included interacting with Germans where dressed in civilian attire set a more amicable environment.

Gruenewald Taverne also provided another diversion. The proprietress was a thirty-year-old beauty named Eva Gruenewald with a curvaceous figure.

****

After staying close to American headquarters or traveling to the other Allied occupation headquarters for the first few months in Koblenz, Fleming felt confined. The work was boring. The same faces of his fellow officers, generally grumbling over what amounted to garrison duty after being away from the United States over a year, did little to improve his mood. The emotional distress following the loss of his parents and Dominique subsided into a general malaise.

The antidote was getting outside the headquarters complex and mingling with the local population. To assess German compliance with the terms of the treaty, Fleming began driving about the American sector enjoying the mild spring weather.

Mindful of orders to venture about always armed, he sought out a local shoe repair shop to fashion a belt arrangement for his shoulder holster. The cavalry arrangement secured the holster under his left arm by a belt around his chest. For concealment under a civilian suit, he needed an arrangement that looped under each armpit to hide the harness. Once equipped, he began exploring Koblenz in civilian attire. The purpose was not to avoid his identity as an American Army officer, just not to advertise it. Blending in with the civilian German population set a more congenial tone augmented by his fluency in German.

Avoiding the haunts of fellow American soldiers, he ventured south of American headquarters to where the right-bank tributary River Lahn emptied into the Rhine. Here he found a perfectly located bar with a large outside seating area. The view was spectacular. Across the Lahn situated on the left bank of the Rhine on a hill was the Stolzenfels Castle. A gleaming white Gothic Revival palace constructed in the 19th century over the ruins of a 13th century castle. Not far on the right bank of the Rhine sat Lahneck Castle, an intact 13th fortress situated on a steep rock outcropping.

He discovered Gruenewald Taverne on a sunny late September Sunday afternoon. A bustling place with people returning to a semblance of normality after of four years of war. Beer and wine in good supply but meat remained a scarce commodity. The Gruenewald however compensated with a hearty vegetable stew and fresh bread. Sunday was a special day to take the family for a modest outing.

After enjoying a late lunch with several steins of beer, an attractive woman came up to his outside table.

"Welcome to my tavern. I do not believe I have seen you before. I am Eva Gruenewald," She said extending her hand.

Fleming stood and took her hand, "Spencer Fleming. Your food is excellent. The view spectacular."

Gruenewald pulled up a chair and sat down opposite Fleming. "Where are you from Herr Fleming? I cannot place your accent."

Fleming smiled, "American. I work for the American Army in Koblenz."

Gruenewald's expression went through several changes from surprise to distaste to curiosity.

"How is it you speak German so well?"

"My mother. German and French heritage from Metz. I therefore spoke English, German, and French interchangeably growing up."

"Interesting. What is it you do for the American Army?"

"I am an officer on the commanding general's staff."

"So you are here as part of the occupation forces?"

"Yes. Not sure I agree with the occupation but a soldier obeys orders."

"You fought in the war?"

"Yes."

"I lost my husband early in the war. My father was too old but they conscripted him anyway when the need for replacements became urgent. He died six months before the fighting ended. So I run the family business."

Nothing Fleming could say. Her story like so many others with the millions of dead suffered by all the warring powers.

"Thank you for coming, Herr Fleming. Perhaps I will see you again."

With that, Gruenewald stood up abruptly and returned inside the tavern. Their brief exchange disappointed Fleming. It appeared the woman resented him as a reminder of the enemy that took her husband and father. She was the first woman to stir his attention since the death of Dominique a year ago. Undoubtedly just lust, but nonetheless it made him feel alive after a year of depression. Large expressive dark eyes and curly dark hair made her look more Italian than Teutonic. Overtly sexy with large breasts and long legs, she understood the effect she had on men by dressing to accentuating her assets.

With access to a staff car, he made the five-mile drive often. The view of the castles and Eva Gruenewald a pleasant diversion. Subsequent visits seemed to temper her earlier resentment. Perhaps mistaken that first visit as she eventually turned to flirting. Both felt a sexual attraction.

It was not long before they became intimate. Arriving late one evening, she greeted him with a warm smile.

"I missed you, Spencer. Been almost a week."

"I missed you as well, Eva. Finally escaped a boring dinner with the General."

"Must you get back tonight?"

She touched his cheek with the back of her hand.

"No. In fact I am off duty tomorrow."

Bending down to whisper in his ear, "Then we shall not only enjoy the rest of the night but spend the whole next day together. Give me just a few minutes. Otto can close the tavern tonight."

Eva reappeared with a wrap to cover her shoulders from the chill of the autumn night and took him by the arm.

"Where are we going? You will be cold without a coat."

She stopped to embrace and kiss him passionately. "We are just going around to the staircase in the back. I live above the tavern."

Feeling the butt end of his .45 service pistol under his jacket, she looked into his eyes with a look of surprise. "Is it so dangerous to be among us Germans that you must go armed?"

"Just following orders. The only danger is the effect you have on me."

He touched her face and kissed her again, running his hands along her hips.

Once inside her apartment, she grabbed his head in both hands, "I have not been with a man since my husband died. Why you?"

Fleming held much the same question. What he felt was not the same as the emotional connection with Dominique. With Eva, it was about sex. An antidote for his indefinable emptiness. Perhaps for her as well.

Eva Gruenewald provided a perfect escape into sexual pleasure. Too many conflicting circumstances existed to likely develop into something more serious. Yet the carnal pleasure made for good therapy.

Both quickly learned to avoid politics or discussing the war. Like so many Germans, she voiced the commonly held view of German victimization. While accusing the new government, the generals, and the communist-Jews betraying the German soldiers, she never cast blame on Kaiser Wilhelm's ill-conceived military adventurism.

Fleming saw a more complex set of circumstances. To a great extent, civilians and soldiers of a warring country suffered because of the actions of those controlling their country's government. Patriotism if you agreed with the sacrifice, but if you did not, you suffered regardless. Most gave their lives simply because they had no choice. Older men sending younger men to their deaths for power, glory, or hubris. The United States was no different. President Wilson authorized various laws denying constitutionally guaranteed rights to American citizens cloaked in terms of national emergency. Censorship. Dissent criminally charged as sedition. For Germans, *stabbed in the back* was a simplistic excuse for a complex set of circumstances leading to self-inflicted ruin.

Fleming chose to talk about less contentious subjects. What America was like. His exploits in Mexico. They spoke like strangers avoiding obvious controversial issues. Their time together revolved around sexual intimacy as a means to celebrate the end of their respective despair.

An occurrence one evening illustrated the divide between Fleming and Gruenewald.

Colonel Strobel arrived midday at the Gruenewald tavern with Fleming. Both dressed in civilian suits. They took a table outside. A sunny day.

"An extraordinary view, Major," Strobel said. "How did you find this place?"

"A local in Koblenz told me of these two castles close by. This is actually the city of Lahnstein. That is the River Lahn in front of us as it joins the Rhine. The magnificent white castle is the Stolzenfels on the west bank of the Rhine. The other is Lahneck Castle. So I stopped to take in the view over lunch."

A waitress came over. "*Guten tag,* Major Fleming."

"Two beers, please, Johanna."

"*Sehr gut.* And I will let Eva know you are here."

Strobel raised an eyebrow. "A regular?"

"Fairly often. What better place to take a drink and good meal?"

Strobel noticed Eva Gruenewald walking briskly toward their table. "Is she perhaps the other reason?"

Fleming just smiled as Gruenewald touched Fleming's shoulder possessively.

"Eva, let me introduce Oberstleutnant Strobel of the German Reichswehr. We work together." Turning to Strobel, "This is Frau Gruenewald, proprietress of this fine establishment."

"Welcome, Oberst Strobel. Will you gentlemen be taking lunch?"

"Of course, Eva. We already ordered beers from Johanna."

"Wonderful. Please enjoy," She said touching the back of her hand against Fleming's cheek.

As Eva walked away, Strobel laughed, "Frau Gruenewald adds to the view. You appear a very favored patron."

From across the outside seating area, A man signaled to Gruenewald. Her expression turned stern as she approached the man's table. "Fritz, what brings you here?"

"Been awhile. Klaus sent me. Of course, you were my first stop. How are you, Eva?"

Fritz Reiner was a close friend of Eva's brother Klaus. Both veterans of the Great War. Both served in elite Sturmtruppen battalions. Bitter over the terms of the armistice, both became deeply involved with the right wing Freikorps. Comprised of disgruntled soldiers, the Freikorps stood in violent opposition to socialists and communists.

Following the end of hostilities in November 1918, revolution broke out. The political left gained considerable traction with the population for the sufferings endured during the four years of war. Against this popular uprising stood the remnants of the defeated German army and the conservative aristocracy still holding power. Along with remaining Reichswehr troops, the paramilitary Freikorps proved critical to stabilizing shattered German institutions. It took until August 1919 for the new republic to suppress the leftist revolution. Yet political tensions remained heightened amid worsening economic and social dislocations.

In addition to their active affiliation with a Freikorps unit in Munich, Fritz Reiner and Klaus Gruenewald also became politically active. Klaus wrote to his sister about a mesmerizing speaker named Adolf Hitler. The leader of a right wing political party known as the Nationalsozialistische Deutsche Arbeiter-partei, the National Socialist German Workers' Party. The NSDAP. Both enthusiastically joined the Nazi Party.

"I am getting by, Fritz. What brings you here?" Eva Gruenewald did not disguise her displeasure. She only tolerated Reiner because of his friendship with her brother. More assertive than her brother, Reiner relished the violence of the Freikorps as an excuse to attack leftists and Jews under the color of authority.

"Political affairs. I noticed your attentions to the man over there. A boyfriend perhaps?"

"None of your business, Fritz."

"Does Klaus approve?"

"Approve?" Gruenewald slammed both hands flat on the table in front of Reiner. "It is none of my brother's fucking business either. I could use his help running this place. I support our mother who needs constant medical care. Money is tight so business is a struggle. You and Klaus want to play soldier rather than work. Both of you are useless shits. You lost the goddamn war! Get over it!"

Gruenewald made no attempt to lower her voice. Fleming saw her walk away briskly. The man she yelled at stood and starred at Fleming for several moments.

Minutes later the waitress Johanna brought their steins of beer.

"Fleming said, "Is everything alright, Johanna? Who was Eva yelling at?"

"His name is Fritz Reiner. Friend of her brother. Both live in Munich. Involved with some political group. Still involved with those ex-soldiers in the Freikorps. After the war ended, they stayed in Munich. Reiner was always interested in Eva but she did not like him. He must have said something to upset her. You know, Eva."

Strobel said, "Looks like you have competition for the affections of your lady friend, Major. To be expected with a woman who looks like that."

Fleming changed the subject. "With the revolution put down, are the Freikorps still active?"

"Not officially. They did not go away of course."

"What about this political party in Munich, this National Socialist German Workers' Party?"

"Just another extremist right-wing party, not yet large enough. However, a group to keep our eye on. Very militaristic. Dress up in old khaki uniforms so the newspapers call them Brownshirts. They call themselves Sturmabteilung, literally the storm detachment. A bunch of thugs. Comprised mostly of former Freikorps. Contrary to the name, nothing socialistic in their agenda. These are right wing Fascists. Known for their virulent anti-Semitic ideology claiming the Jews are the source of all Germany's problems.

"I assume you don't agree with their political views?"

"Of course not. Germany lost the war for clearly practical reasons. Underestimated the enemy repeatedly. Overestimated the pathetic Austrian Army. Tried to prosecute a war on two fronts. Insufficient resources to maintain supply. Underestimated the

British naval blockade. Stupid decisions brought the United States into the war. The resources of manpower and goods of the United States ultimately proved overwhelming. A failure of leadership. Nothing to do with socialists, communists, or Jews."

CHAPTER 10

Koblenz, Rhineland Region, Germany | July 1920

"The political situation appears to continually disintegrate in Germany. As a military officer, where do you stand, Colonel?" Fleming asked his friend Lieutenant Colonel Ritter von Strobel of the Reichswehr. They sat outside on a pleasant summer evening enjoying beers at their favorite venue the Gruenewald Taverne.

"The situation to be expected. Germany lost the war. The victors took their revenge. As a military officer, I continue to do my duty. The Army is the only institution holding Germany together."

By early 1919, the strength of the German Army, the Reichswehr was only 350,000, reduced through demobilization from several million. More than 250,000 of those demobilized enlisted in the volunteer Freikorps paramilitary units. The German government supplied and repeatedly used Freikorps formations to put down communist uprisings after the war. The terms of the Treaty of Versailles required Germany to reduce its armed forces strength further to 100,000 by March 1920. Demobilized former soldiers of the Freikorps forced to disband. Yet as militant former soldiers, now mostly unemployed, many joined right wing political organizations.

The Social Democratic Party of Germany, the German Democratic Party, and the Christian democratic Centre Party, dominated the new Weimar Republic coalition government.

In March, the beleaguered centrist government faced an attempted coup by rightwing nationalists, monarchists, and many within the military. What became known as the Kapp-Lüttwitz Putsch was an attempt to take over the government by Freikorps troops and units of the Reichswehr. Spectacularly, the coup failed with the population going on a general strike, including most government bureaucrats. With every facet of German society paralyzed, the coup collapsed. Still plagued by communist popular uprising, a left wing revolt following the general strike broke out in the Ruhr Valley.

Fear of a populist takeover of Germany remained the greatest fear of the both the centrist government and ring wing factions. The government reshuffled some ministerial positions, removed the putsch leaders Kapp and Lüttwitz from their official positions, and amnestied the other participants. Having made peace with the right, the government now unleashed the Reichswehr and Freikorps coup perpetrators on leftist strikers in the Ruhr Valley.

Fleming's question therefore held significant weight for his friend holding high military rank.

Strobel continued, "I did not support the Kapp-Lüttwitz Putsch. A return to an autocratic militaristic government will doom Germany eventually to another war. We must break that cycle and find the means to coexist with other European countries."

"What about the Ruhr uprising?"

"Necessary to put it down. Communism threatens not only Germany but hope for a peaceful Europe."

"Do you then favor a democratic republic?"

"Is this the sort of intelligence you report to Washington?"

Fleming smiled, "Of course. Not actually intelligence though. Just my gathering of the opinions of others. The kind of intelligence usually ignored unless it fits preconceived bias."

Strobel smiled and nodded his agreement. "To your question, I favor a democratic republic. The problem however, this current government has little chance of success. Those that understand economics point to the debt caused by the war and the impossible reparation demands. Inflation already on the rise. Soon this will limit the ability for people to buy food. Unemployment remains the most pressing problem. The same circumstances that brought about the fall of the Russian Tsar. Germany could suffer such a popular revolution. Starving people are apolitical."

"I agree. The problem remains the French and Belgians. They understandably demand compensation for invading their countries. They also fear a remilitarized Germany."

"Therein lays the problem. Equilibrium on the international scale is a chimera. Tell me, Major, what is the American mission in this occupation of the Rhineland?"

"Just policing a demilitarized zone to protect France and Belgium from German remilitarization. Garrison duty. The worse kind of duty for a soldier. As head of intelligence for the AFG, I do nothing of real meaning. Best I can do is to communicate my observations. Probably nothing more than what Americans read in newspapers."

"Dealing with you Americans and the British is much different from the French and Belgians. I too am a soldier. Doing what I feel is honorable duty. Yet like you, gathering soft intelligence of questionable value."

"Good evening, Colonel. So nice to see you again," Eva Gruenewald said coming up to the table standing next to Fleming.

Strobel smiled broadly. "Major Fleming has excellent tastes. Everything about your establishment is delightful, Frau Gruenewald."

"Thank you, Colonel. Please enjoy your evening, gentlemen." To convey her possessiveness she touched Fleming's cheek with the back of her hand as her usual gesture of affection or possessiveness.

As Gruenewald walked away, Strobel turned to watch her behind. "I would come here just to watch her walk away. Makes garrison duty more bearable I should imagine."

Fleming laughed. "Eva is a real beauty. Intelligent but the war has left emotional scars. With you, I can delve into sensitive German political and social subjects. Not with Eva. She wants to argue anything conflicting with her views. Accuses me of not understanding Germany. She subscribes to the stab-in-the-back view. Hates the French. Makes an exception for me as an American.

"Speaking of provocative subjects, her brother is a member of the paramilitary Sturmabteilung branch of a right wing political party in Munich, the NSDAP. Their leader gets lots of play in the newspapers. What can you tell me about them?"

"Thugs. Uneducated working class. These SA storm troopers are mostly refuges from the disbanded Freikorps. Their leader, Adolf Hitler was a corporal in the Great War. A demented little *arschloch*. Energizes his membership by fiery oratory generating a mob response. Violently anti-communist and anti-Jewish. Herr Hitler preaches the German Army was never defeated. The fighting stopped by treacherous defeatists from the left and of course the Jews. He is an ultranationalist."

"Do they represent an important movement?"

"Not at this time. These Sturmabteilung however make them unique. Recruitment is easy with so many unemployed veterans without prospects. A chance to put on a uniform and feel important again. A chance to take out frustrations violently against perceived enemies. Who is to say what a political party with a private army might achieve?"

"I ask because, Eva's brother is a member of this group."

"Well, if she sides with her brother, I suggest you avoid disusing their political ideology. It will not be conducive to your romantic relationship, my friend."

* * * *

A month later, Fritz Reiner returned to Koblenz to visit his parents. Like so many others, their circumstances difficult. His father unemployed following injury at his railroad job. His mother semi-bedridden with kidney disease. Reiner contributed what he could from his meager salary working for the NSDAP. His family circumstances further fueling his hate.

Obsessed for years with Eva Gruenewald, Reiner spent each evening at the tavern since returning because of his mother's declining health. He was doing more than stalking Gruenewald.

Having learned from a waitress that she had taken up with an American Army officer, his obsession turned darker. Every night he came to drink beer while waiting for the American.

Twice he observed the American sneaking off with Eva Gruenewald up the outside stairs to her apartment. Camped outside he seethed with rage as the lights went out. Both times the American remained for several hours before leaving in an American Army sedan.

After a week, Reiner could not constrain himself. After several hours of drinking, he drifted off toward the rear of the building as Gruenewald closed the tavern. Waiting for Gruenewald to ascend the stairs, he waited twenty minutes. Slightly drunk he hoped that Gruenewald might have by now undressed getting ready for bed.

Reiner knocked on her apartment door.

"Spencer, is that you?" She said through the door.

Reiner said nothing.

Moments later, Gruenewald opened the door. "What the hell do you want, Fritz?"

Reiner stepped forward forcing his way inside the apartment.

Gruenewald retreated. "Get the hell out of here!"

Reiner guessed correctly. Gruenewald stood there in her bare feet wrapped in a robe. His stare gravitated to her exposed cleavage. The effects of alcohol and being this close to Eva Gruenewald likely naked under her robe proved too much. His swift movement caught Gruenewald by surprise as his hand grasped the belt to her robe pulling it open as she stepped back. His eyes widened as she stood there with breasts and pubic area exposed.

Instead of worrying about covering herself as Reiner moved closer, she raked his cheek viciously with her fingernails.

"Ah!"

Her attack enough to draw blood and stem his advance allowing her to quickly retreat to the kitchen. Finding a butcher knife, she turned on him while pulling the robe around her with her left hand.

"You fucking pig! You think I would ever screw you?"

Clutching a handkerchief to his cheek, Reiner said, "But you are screwing this American. Does he pay you for sex?"

"Not necessary. I fuck him for free. I even suck his cock to get him very hard. He has a beautiful cock. Circumcised, not the disgusting foreskin covering the head of the penis like you Aryan assholes. Perhaps he is Jewish. That would be something. Tell Klaus I am fucking a Jew. Imagine him having to explain his sister sleeping with a Jew. Piss on both of you and that Jew-hating piece of shit Adolf Hitler he talks about in his letters.

Reiner took a step toward her.

Holding the large knife, she did not retreat. "Come any closer and I will stick this between your legs, Fritz"

"I will tell Klaus his sister is a whore to a filthy Jew."

Still enraged, Gruenewald lunged forward sticking the tip of the butcher knife into Reiner's forearm.

Reiner stumbled backwards quickly opening the door. "It does not end here, Eva. Scum like you must be eradicated."

* * * *

Reiner immediately returned to Munich. Eva no longer a sexual obsession instead became an object of personal revenge. He adopted as reality Eva's sarcastic reference to Fleming possibly being Jewish. His rage over rejection further distorted by the conviction that her American lover was Jewish. In his anti-Semitic fog, no greater sin.

Fritz Reiner and Klaus Gruenewald shared a small apartment in working class Munich, not far from NSDAP headquarters at Schellingstrasse 50. Walking straight from the train station, he was waiting when Gruenewald arrived.

"Ah, you are back, Fritz. How was the trip? Did you look in on Eva?"

Reiner shook his head and sighed. "Yes. However, I have distressing news, Klaus."

"What? Is she all right?"

"Nothing like that. Unfortunately she has taken a lover."

"A lover? How do you know this?"

"From the tavern staff. Then I watched her. Eva makes no attempt to conceal the affair. Rather scandalous. Consorting with our enemy, Klaus. Her lover is an American Army officer. A major."

"Shit. And you saw him with Eva?"

"Yes. Twice I observed him spending hours late at night in her apartment with the lights out. I confronted her knowing I must provide you some explanation.

"It went badly. Eva has never liked me. She turned angry. Said what she did was none of her brother's business. Then she said something truly shocking. Obviously intended to hurt you knowing your feelings about Jews. Her lover is Jewish, Klaus. She delighted in describing how they have sex. Described how she liked a man that was circumcised. Scratched my face when I called her a whore."

Klaus Gruenewald stood there dumbfounded. Reiner poured him a glass of schnapps.

Gruenewald drank the liquor down in one gulp. Shaking his head in denial, "This cannot be true, Fritz. Eva is strong minded but I cannot believe she took up with Jew."

"I am afraid it is true, Klaus. She made a point of wanting you to know. Enjoyed telling me intimate details."

Gruenewald replied, "The stupid arrogant bitch. Always flashing her tits and ass, thinking she can control everything. Resents working so hard and taking care of mother. Thinks I should be doing more to help out. Sounds like something she might do to spite me."

Reiner said, "You cannot leave it at that, Klaus. As a member of the Sturmabteilung, you must take action. Should this become known, it will ruin your career."

"So how do I fix this?"

"We kill the Jew of course. After that, you must teach Eva a lesson. I will help you, Klaus. Go to Hauptsturmführer Schreck. Tell him you have an urgent family problem. Your sick mother. We board a train in the morning. I am still on leave therefore I will go with you."

"What do we do when we get to Koblenz?"

"We have comrades from our old Freikorps unit. I have an idea of who might help. Then we find this Jew that is defiling Eva. Together we help you redeem your honor by killing him."

* * * *

Less than a week after the incident between Reiner and Eva Gruenewald, Fleming left her apartment late at night following their usual intimate liaison. As he walked the short distance to his car, two men in working clothes confronted him. In the light of a full moon, both held short lengths of metal pipe. One man repeatedly slapped the pipe into the palm of a gloved hand.

"What do you want?" Fleming said.

Immediately, one of the men moved cautiously toward him. Fleming closed the distance in three steps instead of retreating, surprising the assailants. The man closest attempted to bring the pipe down on Fleming's head. However, Fleming's move allowed him to catch the man's upper arm preventing the blow. With a rapid shifting of his weight, Fleming dropped the man to the ground with a classic judo throw. He followed with a powerful straight on blow breaking the man's jaw.

Rising to confront the second assailant, Fleming met with a nasty blow of a pipe slamming into his lower abdomen as he half turned. Using the same aggressive counterattacking tactic, he captured the assailant's arm welding the pipe in a hold. This time Fleming opted to deliver a blow to the man's nose with the heel of his right hand. Delivered with enough force, the blow crushed the man's nose removing any further resistance as the man fell to his knees clutching his face streaming blood.

Two other men then appeared brandished what looked like trench knives.

Fleming picked up one of the pipes ready to confront them, confident he could contain the situation before matters turned more violent.

However, from off to the side, two additional men appeared both holding pistols. In the bright moonlight, Fleming recognized one as the man Eva shouted at months earlier. The friend of her brother.

Fritz Reiner said, "Very impressive, but it will not save you. We cannot tolerate a Jew defiling Aryan women. Klaus, you may have the honor of killing this American Jew for defiling your sister."

No escape now without escalating this to deadly force. He was not about to be cut up by these goons.

"Wait a minute. Let me explain," Fleming said as he dropped the pipe. Rubbing his right side with his left hand, he groaned and dropped to his left knee. "I think my ribs are broken." The move intended to conceal drawing his sidearm quickly before being shot.

"Klaus, get on with it," Reiner said.

Fleming looked up as Klaus Gruenewald took several steps toward him pointed a Lugar at his head. With no choice, Fleming reached inside his suit coat and in a fluid motion extracted his .45 Browning firing two rounds into Klaus Gruenewald's abdomen from close range.

Reiner fired one hurried shot, missing Fleming. Fleming replied with a well-placed single round into Reiner's sternum.

The other two assailants took flight. Fleming hesitated from shooting. Unlikely to be successful at the distance. Best not to expand the incident further. The dead and injured assailants easily argued as self-defense.

It was just before the midnight closing of the tavern. A couple of late drinkers and the staff rushed out to investigate. Fleming yelled to the first person to arrive at the scene to call the police. Minutes later, Eva Gruenewald appeared.

Seeing Fleming, she started toward him before looking down at Fritz Reiner with his shirt soaking in blood. Then she saw her brother also a bloody mess and gasped. Holding her hand to her mouth, she kneeled down beside him to touch his face.

* * * *

When the German police arrived, Fleming showed his military identification. Refusing to answer any questions, he ordered them to bring the American military police to the scene. All this time, his .45 remained concealed in the shoulder holster under his suit coat.

When an American sergeant and another MP arrived, Fleming explained the essential circumstances of the situation. *He was leaving the tavern when accosted by six men. The injured attempted to assault him with steel pipes. Having failed, the two dead displayed firearms. Armed, he defended himself when one assailant ordered the other to kill me before realizing I was also armed. For some reason they called me a Jew. I believe that might be the cause of this attack.*

Fleming then explained to the German police that ultimately this was an American matter. They could advise their superiors that a full report would be forthcoming. With that, he ordered the sergeant to follow him back to American headquarters at Koblenz. They could join him as he reported the incident to the American military police commander.

* * * *

To his superiors, Fleming spun a distorted version of the circumstances. He admitted to a sexual relationship with this woman who became a source while pursuing his intelligence duties. Citing associations within the local German government and the industrial community, Eva Gruenewald's tavern provided a perfect social location for developing sources of information.

In so doing, Gruenewald revealed her brother's affiliation with a violent right wing political party based in Munich. He suspected the Nazi Party possibly had members of their paramilitary wing the SA based in the American occupation zone. He knew remnants of the disbanded Freikorps populated the American occupation zone. Learning the Nazi SA recruited largely from former Freikorps veterans, he wanted to investigate political right wing activity here in the Rhineland. Eva Gruenewald proved an unwitting source into this clandestine world.

To General Allen, Fleming said, "I appreciate the delicacy of our mission, General. Unfortunately, engaging in intelligence collection sometimes gets messy. Although succumbing to human weakness, my venture ultimately proved successful. It exposes the threat of right wing political activity in this important industrial sector of Germany. We have not seen the last of German aggression, General."

For Fleming, if this did not blow over it might make his decision to leave the Army. Therefore, he forcefully asserted his position rather than pleading a defensive case.

General Allen was a tough old bird. While serving in the Philippines, he organized and commanded the Philippine Constabulary. Known as the Iron Comandante, he had a police mentality. Regardless of extenuating details of the incident, a gang of thugs attacked one of his officers with deadly force. The German authorities registered no official complaint. Both the military police commander and General Allen signed off on Fleming's report.

Fleming likewise passed along a similar sanitized report to Dulles. Since this was in the form of a contrived letter to his girlfriend. Eleanor Lansing Dulles in New York, he omitted Eva entirely from the narrative of the violent confrontation.

Since that night, Fleming never again saw Eva Gruenewald. Although experiencing some guilt for whatever emotional involvement she may have felt for him, they were not in love. They had only sex in common. The affair to eventually end anyway. Having killed her brother clearly made any attempt at reconciliation impossible.

As much as these fanatically racist Nazis obsessed about Jews, there seemed no reason to think he was Jewish. Perhaps the incident nothing more than Fritz Reiner planting disinformation to get rid of a rival for Eva Gruenewald's affections disguised as anti-Semitic violence. A mystery he would leave buried.

CHAPTER 11

Warsaw, Republic of Poland | August 1931

Taking office in January 1921, the new administration of United States President Warren Harding began steadily drawing down the American Third Army occupying the Rhineland. The American withdrawal into isolation again taking shape with the country focused on its immerging prosperity. Fleming received orders to take on a new assignment as observer with Spanish forces engaged in a colonial war with Berber tribesmen in Morocco. He was only too glad to leave Germany. With the tragic events surrounding Eva Gruenewald two years earlier, his duties turned increasing boring.

The War Department's interest lay more with intelligence he could glean from the French and British military positions. Intelligence on their allies. Therefore, he spent most of his time socializing in their respective occupation sectors. All very gentlemanly since there were few secrets to unearth. Germany represented European concerns. Meaningful intelligence could only come from within Germany. Without an established agency to gather political intelligence, the U.S. had no capacity to recruit German sources for confidential information.

The Rhineland occupation largely centered on economic interests of France and Belgium enforcing the punitive terms of the Treaty of Versailles. The United States had little interest in the Rhineland reflected by its relatively small military commitment. U.S. isolationism began taking hold.

Granted an extended sixty-day leave because of his extended service in Europe, he chose to spend his time in France before reporting to the U.S. military attaché at the U.S. Embassy in Madrid. Unlike Germany, France largely recovered from the visible effects of the Great War in the last four years. An extended trip using the French railway system allowed a leisurely way to see the beauty of France. In Provence, he leased a car to explore the many hilltop villages.

From Marseille, he began the long train journey to Madrid in October of 1922. One week later, he took a train to Malaga on the Spanish southern coast. From there he boarded a Spanish naval vessel for Ceuta, Morocco on the northern coast of Africa across the Strait of Gibraltar.

Morocco held no attraction other the adventure of the unknown. Better than returning to the United States and a boring military posting.

The sweeping reorganization of former countries defined in the Treaty of Versailles ignored centuries of cultural identities to create artificial countries to satisfy the interests of the victors of the Great War. Europe and the Middle East forever changed. Anyone knowledgeable in history could foretell instability. Staying close to Europe held his interest. Morocco at least a new experience.

Arriving in Ceuta, on a Spanish troopship he reassessed his decision to remain in the Army. Even by contrast, with poorer Spain compared to the rest of Europe, Morocco proved a shock. The disembarkation port on the Mediterranean coast was exotic but dirty. Yet he was about to venture into the mountainous interior where circumstances were much more primitive. This colonial war a throwback to some earlier era of warfare in its barbarity on both sides. Compared with the European Great War it transformed those horrors into something evocative of Dante's *Inferno* by one journalist's account.

Fleming imbedded with the 1st Legion Bandera commanded by Lieutenant Colonel Francisco Franco. The Spanish Legion represented the shock troops fighting alongside the larger numbers of the Spanish Regulares consisting largely of conscripts.

Fleming arrived in 1922 one year after Spanish forces suffered a staggering defeat losing over 8,000 casualties at the hands of a united Berber guerrilla army only a fraction of their strength. The defeat punctuated the pathetic fighting abilities of the Spanish Army. Half the conscripts were illiterate. Officers of all ranks corrupt to the point of selling arms and supplies to line their own pockets.

Strategically, the Spanish Army of Africa chose to occupy the remote lands of the Berber tribes by erecting hundreds of remote outposts each occupied only by a squad of soldiers. These squalid outposts led to the further undoing of the Spanish. The Rif Valley insurgents easily picked off these isolated positions, impossible for the Spanish to supply and reinforce.

Fleming could barely keep up with his observational critiques in his reports. The filth and deplorable conditions far worse than his rough experience in Mexico. Yet it was the war itself that captured his abject disgust. Both sides took few prisoners resorting to torture, summary execution, and mutilation. Neither side recognized the value of obtaining actionable intelligence from interrogating captured enemy combatants.

After ten months in this shithole, Fleming speculated this unattractive assignment was possibly a reflection of his unremarkable record with the American Forces in Germany. As intelligence officer, he had little means of providing the War Department with anything of real value within the narrow confines of that corner of Germany. The violent confrontation the only entry of note into his service record for the period.

Stuck in the Moroccan backcountry with no meaningful role, resigning his commission a daily thought. The Great War over and neither his duties in Koblenz nor certainly this disgusting colonial war in Moroccan made further military service attractive. New orders then arrived making it easier to postpone leaving the Army. Instead of a boring assignment, an invitation to attend the United States Army Command and General Staff College. Surprisingly, the telegram was signed General John Pershing, U.S. Army Chief of Staff.

Perhaps about time he returned to the United States after five years abroad. An interesting academic opportunity. Likely to improve chances for promotion. Even the posting to remote Fort Leavenworth in Kansas welcomed after his conflicted experiences in Germany and the purgatory of Morocco.

New York City 1929

Sitting in the study of Allen Dulles' eastside apartment, Fleming enjoyed his coffee and brandy.

"Clover's wonderful cooking and your first-rate liquor always a special treat, Allen. How do you manage that given Prohibition?"

"A minor client who is a major liquor smuggler from Canada."

"Well, seeing you and Clover is a welcome experience."

"Both of us enjoy your company, Spencer. Given any further thought to leaving the Army?"

No longer with the State Department, Allen Dulles earned a law degree George Washington University Law. His extensive foreign service background made him ideal for the unique services of New York Law firm of Sullivan & Cromwell, where his brother, John Foster Dulles, was a senior partner.

The venerable law firm specialized in creative business services. The firm provided legal guidance for the creation of General Electric and U.S. Steel. They invented the concept of a holding company as a mechanism to circumvent anti-trust laws. In an era predating bankruptcy laws, William Nelson Cromwell rescued many insolvent companies through innovative restructuring.

Internationally, the firm represented European banking financing of U.S. railroads and other infrastructure projects. At the turn of the 20th century, Cromwell personally represented French interests in financing their early efforts to construct a canal across Panama to connect a shipping channel between the Caribbean with the Pacific. He later represented America in the creation of the Panama Canal Authority following completion of construction in 1914.

Following the Great War, John Dulles was instrumental in devising an international financing plan to reduce German reparations by American financial institutions lending money for German investment. The profits earned from the investments then served to make reparations payments to Britain and France that in turn served to service the debt on their American war loans.

With offices throughout the world, the skills of internationalists like Allen Dulles provided a unique depth to their services. Dulles recognized Fleming's talents during their brief association during negotiations of the peace treaty following the Great War. Subsequently, Fleming's willingness to provide political intelligence to the State Department displayed his range of knowledge beyond narrow military interests. That the intelligence proved nothing more than confirming much of what appeared in the news media and from U.S. foreign-based diplomats, was not the fault of Fleming. Restricted to the American occupation zone limited Fleming's scope of information on German political turmoil.

Since that time, Fleming enhanced his academic credentials. Attending the U.S. Army Command General Staff College earned him a Masters of Military Arts and Science degree. That led to an appointment as a lecturer at the Military Academy at West Point, New York. Fleming explained to Dulles the rather boring assignment came with an attractive side benefit.

Someone senior in the American Army obviously pulled strings to pay his tuition and twice-weekly 120-mile commute by train to Columbia University in Manhattan. For the last two years, Spencer Fleming was a doctoral candidate pursuing a PhD in history. The working title of his dissertation *Maneuver Warfare in the 20th Century*.

Dulles read drafts of Fleming's progress. Well researched and scholarly. Fleming used not only U.S. military sources but also those of France and Britain through his connections from the Great War. The war appeared to change the strict seniority-based conservativeness of the American Army giving officers like Fleming merit-based advancement. Future large-scale conflicts involving advances in technology dictated wholly new strategic objectives and tactical methods. According to Fleming, General

Pershing was his benefactor. With the command difficulties Pershing encountered during the Great War, not surprising that he viewed the need for intellectual officers like Fleming.

Of course, Dulles would like to see Fleming join Sullivan & Cromwell. Probably a hard sell for someone without a law degree. Although his older brother was a senior partner, Allen Dulles did not carry that kind of clout within the firm. However, Dulles' value came from his extensive network of contacts throughout the world and the American foreign service. As a rising star in the U.S. Army with international and linguistic expertise, Spencer Fleming might eventually prove a valuable asset with his upward trajectory in the Army.

* * * *

The following year of 1930 proved a watershed for Spencer Fleming. The crash of the stock market in September and October of 1929 began the distressing economic decline into the Great Depression that would dominate the decade. Production and employment already in decline from the late 1920s combined with stock speculation, an inflated bubble in utility stocks, and leveraged margin buying. A perfect storm of disastrous circumstances.

Any thoughts of leaving the Army now held increased uncertainty. Attractive positions in the civilian environment now scarce. He did not want to teach which ruled out academia. He intended his educational credentials for direct application in some interesting endeavor. With the State Department, he would join at the bottom of the civil service ladder. Allen Dulles hinted at the possibility of some position with Sullivan & Cromwell, but was never specific. This was not the economic climate to pursue a new civilian career.

All of these alternative career moves became moot with a convergence of countervailing events in 1930. Columbia conferred his PhD degree. With that came promotion to lieutenant colonel followed by acceptance to attend the U.S. Army War College. Again the result of a high-ranking benefactor. This time, General Summerall serving his last year as Army Chief of Staff.

Summerall sent a personal letter stating similar sentiments to that of General Pershing. Both men remained close and held the conviction the Army needed officers with intellectual skills as well as experience. The Great War was a bridge between 19th century tactics and immerging 20th century technology. The next war would place currently unrecognizable demands on military leadership.

Graduation from the War College with a Master's Degree in Strategic Studies added to his impressive academic credentials. Orders again sent him abroad. This time as military attaché to Poland.

* * * *

Poland did not exist as a sovereign nation from 1772 to 1918. In a final partitioning in 1795, the former lands of the Polish-Lithuanian Commonwealth were divided among Prussia, the Habsburg Monarchy of Austria-Hungary, and the Russian Empire. Stitched back together as one of many new nations by the Treaty of Versailles following the Great War, Poland remerged as a country rather than simply an ethnic culture.

Although restored, Poland remained in a precarious situation 1931. While recovering defeat in the Great War and the economic deprivations of the 1920s, Germany remained an unstable neighbor on their western border. In the 1930 election, the ultra-right NSDAP went from 12 seats to 95 seats in the Reichstag, second only to the centrist Social Democratic Party. The immediate future clearly held political instability.

Although Poland became a sovereign country only in 1918, the Poles did not secure their eastern borders until 1920 after defeating the Red Army of the new Soviet Union. An expanded Russia with the inclusion of former east European countries became the Soviet Union. The feudal rule of the last Russian Tsar now replaced by an equally brutal autocratic regime. Soviet dictator Joseph Stalin clearly had aspirations to expand his regime westward.

It was not likely the 1919 Treaty of Versailles would offer lasting protection to these two historic enemies bordering Poland on the east and west. However, in 1931, the Soviet Union having grown in military strength under Joseph Stalin appeared to pose the more serious threat to Poland.

Welcomed by the Poles, French and British intelligence maintained a strong presence in Warsaw. To this mix, Lieutenant Colonel Spencer Fleming represented the lone intelligence equivalency for the United States.

All manner of intelligence interested the French and British whereas the United States Army was concerned with only military-value intelligence. The posting to Poland however allowed Fleming to learn firsthand the methods of human intelligence gathering, often behind enemy lines. Modern day Poland began developing its intelligence capabilities in 1914 with the secretive Polish Military Organization. Founded by the patriot and father of the Second Polish Republic, Józef Piłsudski, intelligence took on high importance by 1931. Biuro Wywiadowcze, the Intelligence Bureau of the Polish General Staff, deployed extensive networks of domestic and foreign informants. Intelligence proved vital to Polish success in the Polish-Soviet War of 1919-1920. In 1931, Polish intelligence operated networks from their consulates in Moscow, Kiev, Leningrad, and Minsk.

After Fleming's frustrating intelligence gathering experience in Koblenz, Warsaw promised to provide an educational experience in intelligence gathering methods.

Within a week, he made his introductions to Polish Military headquarters. Ushered into the office of a tall distinguished-looking officer in his late forties, he greeted Fleming warmly in English. "Colonel Fleming, welcome to Warsaw. I am Colonel Ludwik Czajkowski, Polish Intelligence," Obviously a chain-smoker by the stale air and overflowing ashtray.

"Glad to have an intelligence officer representing America. Your predecessor was an agreeable officer but lacked your background. I must say your background is unusually impressive. For a staff officer, you distinguished yourself on the battlefield. How does an intelligence officer receive multiple citations for valor?"

"In each case, I wanted to see the situation from close up. Got too close but also got lucky."

Czajkowski smiled. "I doubt that luck was the only factor. Not three times. A remarkable record."

An aide arrived with a tray and two cups of coffee. Czajkowski lit another cigarette offering the cigarette box to Fleming.

"No thank you, Colonel, but please feel free to smoke."

"Good for you. Unfortunately a habit I am unwilling to abandon."

After adding a heaping spoonful of sugar to his coffee, Czajkowski said, "By your academic background, I hardly need to tell you that Polish sovereignty remains precarious. America is the most powerful nation in the world. While Germany struggles with its own internal problems, the Soviet Union is an ever-present threat. The Red Army is now vastly stronger from when we defeated them a decade ago. We look to not only France and Britain, but especially the United States for support. I understand there are a million Polish-speaking citizens in America. We are culturally very much joined with America."

"During the last part of the prior century, great numbers of Poles emigrated to America," Fleming said, wondering where Czajkowski was leading.

"Joseph Stalin represents the greatest threat to Europe. Russia already stretches to the Pacific. His communist ambitions lie to the west. Soviet industrialization will eventually provide him the military means to confront western Europe. Poland will become his first target.

"Intelligence on the enemy is at the heart of Polish defense. I joined with Piłsudski when he formed the Polish Military Organization in 1914. We were a secret intelligence unit. It was important fighting the Russians when we were part of Austria-Hungary during the Great War then again in 1919 fighting the Bolsheviks."

"Or the Germans," Fleming added.

Czajkowski made a dismissive wave of his hand. "Perhaps. Germany appears less an immediate threat given their political turmoil and the restrictions imposed by the Treaty of Versailles."

"What about this Adolf Hitler and his National Socialist Party? They did well in the last election."

"So did the German Communist Party. International communism controlled from Moscow by that megalomaniac Stalin threatens not only Poland but the entire world."

"I will defer to your judgment, Colonel. Stalin is obviously a concern. However, the United States feels Germany once rearmed remains of equal concern. My time while serving in intelligence in the occupation of the Rhineland was enlightening. The victorious allies wanted to punish Germany for the Great War. Understandable, but shortsighted. The longer view suggests future problems.

"At the end of the Great War, you Poles even had to fight a defeated German army to seize control of ethnically Polish Poznań and Silesia as part of the new Polish Republic."

"I can see why they posted you to Warsaw, Colonel. Let me introduce you to Major Kaczmarek. He runs the German desk. A native of Poznań. He shares your concerns about Germany. He fought in the Greater Polish Uprising."

* * * *

Major Feliks Kaczmarek looked the part of a rough character. Unusually dark eyes, black hair, mustache, with a nasty scare running from his forehead down his left cheek, interrupted by an eyepatch. According to Czajkowski, Kaczmarek earned the wound at the Battle of Kostiuchnówka in the Ukraine in 1916 facing a Russian offensive of twice their number. Following the war, Kaczmarek then saw combat fighting the Germans immediately following the Armistice. A military insurrection proved necessary to restore the former Prussian Grand Duchy of Posen to the new Polish Republic.

Kaczmarek grew up under Prussian rule in the city of Poznań. Fluent in German from childhood, his family had a long history of hatred of all things German. With the outbreak of the Great War, the young twenty-year old law student escaped conscription into the German Army. Fleeing south to Galicia and the Carpathian Mountains, he joined the semi-independent Polish Legions.

Comprised of ethnic Poles, they fought alongside Austrian-Hungarian forces. Although allied with Germany, the ethnic Polish Legions fought solely to defeat Russia and restore a Polish state from historically Polish territory. They had no investment in the war against France and Britain on the Western Front.

The Great War altered both the geographic and political landscape of Europe. The victorious allies reorganized the territory of the Central Powers of Germany and Austria-Hungary in an attempt to satisfy ethnic ambitions of previously subjugated peoples. Polish insurrectionists led by the Polish Military Organization further expanded Poland's western borders through two years of bitter military confrontations with remnants the German Army.

Russia fell into revolution before the ending of war. Reconstituted under communist rule, civil war preoccupied the years following the war. Russia had no say in the Treaty of Versailles, therefore relinquishing their long occupation of historically Polish lands.

Kaczmarek was an intense character. A fierce Polish nationalist, he hated the Russians and Germans equally. Told of Fleming's combat exploits, he embraced Fleming as a fellow soldier rather than the desk-bound diplomatic military attaché types of the British and French.

"Why do you Americans not have a foreign intelligence service?"

"You mean separate from the Army? I am in the Army's intelligence division."

"Yes, of course. Every army has intelligence departments. Directed to battlefield information. By the time armies take the field, you are at war. Early warning comes from clandestine foreign political intelligence on your enemy."

"Not sure why America does not have a foreign intelligence organization. Perhaps complacency because of our isolation by two oceans. Canada and Mexico also present no threat."

Fleming felt the real reason was American hubris. Dangerous in today's interconnected world. Allen Dulles' law firm made a business out of offering international business services based on economic and political intelligence. The government of the United States could benefit from a secret intelligence organization rather than relying on a few foreign service officers scattered about embassies. The collection process of information just random with no analytical process. As the most powerful nation in the world, that made no sense.

Changing the subject, Fleming said, "Colonel Czajkowski says you run the German desk? What exactly do you do, Major?"

"Espionage. I spy on the fucking Germans. Do you have any experience with spying, Colonel?"

Thinking about his military experiences, the answer was no. The brief episode in Mexico `behind enemy lines hardly qualified as spying. Everything else was essentially observational intelligence. Even Koblenz. "Very little. Just one time in Mexico when I went undercover."

"Then you at least know something of what clandestine operations involve."

"I did my research before coming to Warsaw. Both the British Secret Intelligence Service and the French Deuxième Bureau hold your Polish intelligence service in high regard. Without a corresponding intelligence service, I must represent the United States. Without compromising your confidential procedures, I hope to understand something of your methods."

* * * *

"Most Poles believe Russia to be our principle security threat," Kaczmarek said to Fleming. "Whether true or not, it ignores that Germany also remains a threat."

Fleming was sitting in Kaczmarek's office two months after his arrival in Warsaw. Not only did he and Kaczmarek hit it off, Germany was Fleming's professional interest. He also felt it was Germany that immediately compromised Western European stability more than Soviet Russia but wanted to hear Kaczmarek's views.

"Stalin is a brutal pig and certainly a future danger to Poland, but he has his hands full at the moment. He wants to industrialize

Russia at any cost. To get rid of any opposition, he is in the process of creating forced labor camps in Siberia. Tens of thousands already deported.

"He is raping the great bread basket of the Ukraine as part of his Five-Year Plan. At the center is collectivization of privately held farmland. Serves multiple purposes. First, he sends anyone owning land to Siberia. Gets rid of political opponents. Forces the peasants into these state-owned collectives governed by political overseers. Steals the grain for the growing urban population needed for industrialization. People can barely survive in these agricultural collectives. Thousands then migrate to the industrial centers seeking work. People in Ukraine are starving in vast numbers. Serves to get rid of a troublesome peasant class."

"You summarize what is appearing in the Western press very well, Major. Yet you think Germany is more a threat than Russia?"

"Not necessarily. More immediate I believe. You see Stalin has a long way to go to first stabilize his rule. People are starving not only in Ukraine but also in the agricultural areas of the Northern Caucasus, the Volga Region, and Kazakhstan. Russian industrialization, while trying to achieve economic stability, will occupy Stalin's attention for a long time."

"You could say the same for Germany. The Weimar Republic is in constant political unrest. The military drastically reduced. Economically in terrible shape."

Immediately following the end of the Great War, Germany suffered terribly. The British blockade of all goods going into Germany continued until signing of the Treaty of Versailles in 1919. German civilians continued to die of starvation by the thousands. War debt, unemployment, and a whole generation of skilled workers decimated on the battlefronts, stifled gross national product output recovery. Hyperinflation set in. By the mid-1920s, Germany recovered a measure of stability. Berlin thrived, even becoming the capital of decadence in Europe. However, the stock market crash of 1929 triggered the worldwide Great Depression. As everywhere, Germany descended into another period of economic distress.

"What makes you think Germany represents an immediate threat to Poland?"

Kaczmarek's single right eye flashed with passion. "Not necessarily immediate, a good intelligence officer takes the longer view. This National Socialist German Workers' Party raises concern. Led by a fucking madman, Adolf Hitler. Dangerous as Stalin. The bastard even has his own private army. A quarter of a million and growing. Twice as large as the regular army."

Fleming commented, "The Nazi Party is now the second largest party in the Reichstag. It seems this Hitler fellow has come a long way in the last ten years."

Fleming went on to relate his experience in Koblenz in 1921, leaving out Eva Gruenewald's involvement.

After listening, Kaczmarek nodded and smiled before saying. "Remarkable. Your dossier, Colonel, makes no mention of this incident. Now I see the pattern that led to medals in combat."

Fleming said, "These Nazis are a nasty bunch of thugs. The Sturmabteilung Brownshirts are responsible for the organized violence inflicted on German Jews. How is it they represent your concerns for Polish security?"

"Since your encounter with the Nazi Sturmabteilung, this paramilitary group has spawned something more sinister. Few people know of the Schutzstaffel, the SS. Adolf Hitler's personal guard. You see the Sturmabteilung predates the rise of the NSDAP. Its leader, Ernst Röhm, a former infantry captain, found Hitler. Röhm recognized Hitler's oratory skills to move a receptive group. The Sturmabteilung needed a political platform. Hitler turned the tables on Röhm and took control, making the SA his personal military force.

"Tension has existed for some time between the Nazi leadership and the Sturmabteilung leadership. Early on, Hitler moved to consolidate his personal power. The SS formed as a personal bodyguard unit to protect Hitler as far back as 1923. Following the failed Munich Putsch and Hitler's early release from Landsberg Prison, Hitler elevated the SS to an elite unit of the SA. Selective entry requirements. Oath of alliance personally to Hitler. Last year, the SS essentially became independent of the SA. The new chief of the SS, Heinrich Himmler reports direct to Hitler."

Fleming said, "Are you saying the German threat is not the Nazi Party, but specifically Adolf Hitler?"

"Exactly. Hitler is the Nazi Party. A dangerous demagogue. My sources report continuous expansion of the SS, both in manpower as well as responsibilities. At some future time, Hitler will use the SS to take control of the SA. Remember, the Nazis are the only political party in Germany with a private army.

"I read Hitler's book, *Mein Kampf*. He wrote it while in prison after his failed coup in Munich in 1923. That should have finished him off politically but he resurrected like some mythical monster. The book is a blueprint of his plans should he come to power. Destruction of the Jews. Blames them as behind the stab-in-the-back of the German Army and the principal cause for defeat in the Great War. His platform preaches ignoring the punitive restrictions of the Treaty of Versailles that panders to most German sentiment. Rearm and return Germany to greatness.

"Yet there is another theme that bears directly on Poland. Hitler strongly embraces *Lebensraum*. Increasing living space and natural resources for Germans. The same policy Germany pursued in the Great War. Annex Belgium, parts of France, and Russian Eastern Europe. That means Poland. A remilitarized Germany is not likely to repeat invasion in the West. Invading eastward into Poland and other Eastern European territory is the logical conclusion. Agricultural land, mineral resources, and most importantly oil in the Caucasus region."

Fleming was familiar with *Mein Kampf* published in 1925 as part of his research for his PhD thesis. A badly written tract that read like a stream of consciousness. At the time, he dismissed it as political fringe nonsense. However, with Hitler's political party holding close to twenty percent of the seats in the Reichstag, he could understand Kaczmarek's concern for Polish sovereignty.

"I see your point. What are the chances that Hitler might come to power?" Fleming asked.

"Difficult to predict. The Social Democrats and the Catholic Centre Party combined have about forty percent of the Reichstag seats. Unless the Nazis can gain a majority in the next election, not likely they can form a coalition government. The other conservative parties shun the Nazis. The government only remains functional because of President Hindenburg. At age eighty- five he has few years left."

"Without revealing any specifics, do you have well-placed intelligence sources in Germany, Major?"

Kaczmarek considered the question. The United States could be a useful ally to Poland. Colonel Czajkowski complained about failed attempts of the Foreign Ministry to find a sympathetic ear among U.S. diplomats. Political appointees with no grasp of larger political and cultural issues in Eastern Europe. Fleming's predecessor as military attaché no better. Educated in international affairs, Fleming appeared different. Fluency in German perhaps made him more interested in the threat Germany might represent.

"When we first met, I told you my job was spying on Germany. Let me say that I have productive sources. Penetration of an enemy is of course a work in process. Whatever we learn is never enough. Unlike the British and French, your interest appears more directed toward Germany than Russia."

Fleming responded, "Let me answer your question this way, Major. I am new to this role as military attaché. As I see it, it is a diplomatic role where you pick up information through interaction with the military of the host nation. In the United States Army, there is no formal training for military attachés. I am an intelligence officer. Trained to analyze disparate information to form a larger picture. My bland reports to Washington consist largely of just disconnected observations. As to Germany, it appears of more immediate interest to the United States."

"I assume you would like something more substantive than easily obtained information on Germany?"

"Yes. I share many of your concerns. I can offer to transmit the information you provide to the U.S. War Department. There are senior officers in the General Staff interested in information on clandestine German rearmament activity."

Kaczmarek said, "If I agree, I must not be identified as your source. How can you explain secret information only obtainable through an espionage network operating within Germany?"

After a few moments considering the problem, Fleming said, "Do you exchange information with British Secret Service and French Deuxième Bureau agents?"

Kaczmarek grinned. "Occasionally." Kaczmarek could have added, when it suited Polish interests. "Colonel Czajkowski does not totally trust the British or French. You might have met their agents in inter-embassy diplomatic functions. The Brit is the passport officer. For the French, the trade attaché."

Kaczmarek seemed to be offering the product of active espionage against Germany with selective exclusivity to the United States. If Kaczmarek could be trusted. As a spymaster, he traded in subterfuge. Not likely to reveal sources or methods which seemed essential for authenticating the information. Fleming would deal with that later.

"There is the solution then. I socially befriend these fellows. Find some common bond. I also speak French. They just think I am the harmless U.S. military attaché since I never acknowledge knowing their real jobs. What is happening in Russia becomes the dominate subject of political conversation. They undoubtedly see their military attachés as diplomats. When necessary, my reports imply the information attributed to intelligence agents of our former allies operating from Warsaw using me as a backdoor conduit. After all, it is information they might otherwise share if the United States had a foreign intelligence service."

"Sonofabitch! An absolutely convincing cover. You are made for this game, Colonel."

PART TWO

THE SPY

Nazi SS marching at Nuremberg Party Rally 1933

CHAPTER 12

Warsaw, Republic of Poland | August 1932

It was a year since Spencer Fleming arrived in Warsaw. The duties of military attaché were ill defined. Largely diplomatic, Fleming's early efforts of cultivating contacts within the Polish military paid dividends. His intuitive ability to engage people set him apart as more than simply a diplomatic functionary of the United States mission. The association with Major Kaczmarek developed into a personal relationship. With their common interest in Germany, Kaczmarek convinced his superiors to use Fleming as a backdoor channel to Washington. Even realizing his reports to the War Department had little impact on U.S. policy, access to espionage product of Kaczmarek's German network engaged Fleming's interest. A mystery why the United States did not engage in foreign espionage.

In July, the political situation in Germany took a dramatic turn.

In the spring, there was growing concern about the SA Brownshirts. This private political army now numbered 400,000. Four times the strength of the regular army the Reichswehr. Led by the bombastic Ernst Röhm, even Adolf Hitler had trouble controlling the SA.

Röhm harbored ambitions to have the SA become the German army. His revolutionary pronouncements frightened German conservative elements, including industrialists and the

Reichswehr. Elements of the German power structure Hitler was trying to cultivate. In April, Chancellor Heinrich Bruening invoked Article 48 of the constitution and issued a decree banning the SA and the SS.

Playing his own double game, Hitler did not protest.

In May, General Kurt von Schleicher, an ambitious army officer met with Hitler. Wanting to ensure political supremacy of the military, Schleicher planned to use the Nazi Party in a scheme to topple Bruening. Schleicher offered to remove the ban on the SA and SS, dissolve the Reichstag, and call new elections in return for Hitler's support of a conservative national coalition government. Hitler agreed.

Schleicher's treachery undermined an already beleaguered Bruening. His economic policies failed to improve the overwhelming effects of the worldwide Great Depression. Repeatedly invoking Article 48 of the constitution allowing him to ignore the legislature failed to break the political stalemate.

Bruening's ineffective leadership also forced aging President Paul von Hindenburg to run for reelection at age 85 against Adolf Hitler. The former Field Marshal could not allow the presidency and therefore the fate of Germany to fall into the hands the despised Bohemian Corporal.

As a check on the power of the legislature, the Reichstag, the Weimar Constitution provided for a president elected independently from the Reichstag. As the chief executive, the president held broad powers. He could dissolve the Reichstag or suspend civil liberties in case of national emergency. Political responsibility rested with the chancellor who served at the pleasure of the president.

Nudged by Schleicher's scheming, Bruening proved too much of a problem for Hindenburg. Calling for his resignation, Hindenburg appointed little-known Prussian aristocrat Franz von Papen as chancellor. Schleicher proposed Papen with Hitler agreeing to support a Papen coalition government. All parties viewed Papen as a weak figurehead without a political base.

Hindenburg dissolved the Reichstag, called new elections, and lifted the ban on the SA and SS.

With elections only weeks away, roving groups of SA Brownshirts let loose an unprecedented wave of murder and violence across Germany. Communist and socialists the targets. Papen as chancellor then invoked Article 48 to stem the chaos.

In open defiance, Hitler said to Papen, "I regard your cabinet only a temporary solution and will continue my efforts to make my party the strongest in the country. The chancellorship will then transfer to me."

Sitting at Kaczmarek's favorite restaurant, Fleming listened to his friend's diatribe while both consumed too much vodka.

"There it is. The final putsch. Adolf Hitler and his Fascist Nazi Party are now close to controlling all power in Germany. The political center has collapsed. Only Hindenburg stands in Hitler's way. At age eighty-five, possibly suffering senility, Hitler does not have long to wait."

* * * *

With the flow of confidential information flowing from Major Kaczmarek on German political turmoil, Fleming's more substantive reports tended to be those concerning Germany rather than the Soviet Union. With few questions for follow up clarification from Washington, he determined his reports to the War Department did not reach the right audience. Secret information on the workings of the German government held little immediate value for the U.S. Army.

Fleming regularly corresponded with Allen Dulles since leaving York. In a recent letter, Dulles stated he would be in London and Paris in the autumn. Perhaps Fleming could join him? With his continued involvement in foreign affairs since leaving the State Department, Dulles undoubtedly knew people interested in the kind of intelligence product produced by Kaczmarek's German network.

Allen,

My year in Warsaw has proven a useful experience. Thinking this diplomatic posting likely to prove boring, it turned out to be most enlightening. My academic work in history given practical application.

Military affairs in Poland hold little strategic interest. However, this new republic created from historically ethnic Polish lands sandwiched between its previous occupiers has adapted its defenses. Suffering as other nations under this terrible economic downturn, the Poles do not have the means to create a modern army from scratch. Aircraft, artillery, and mechanized armor too costly. They have instead turned to intelligence to provide an edge should either Russia or Germany become a military threat in the future.

The depth of their intelligence penetrations into the Soviet Union and Germany are impressive. I have little in the way of comparison. However, my British and French attaché counterparts speak highly of Polish intelligence operations. This largely comes from penetrations into the restrictive sphere of territories under Soviet domination where Western intelligence agencies are at a disadvantage. As military attaché, difficult to understand American reluctance to engage in foreign political intelligence. Such covert knowledge *obviously necessary for strategic decision-making. I sense my dispatches to the War Department have little effect.*

I am more interested in Germany as I think you are. My meager intelligence while in the Rhineland was only a precursor to where Germany is today. Newspaper reports suggest Germany is poised to revert to a totalitarian regime. Adolf Hitler and his Nazi Party may very well prove a future threat to European security. Their violent exercise of anti-Semitism is only one expression of this extreme political movement. Now with the greatest number of seats in the Reichstag, their private army of stormtroopers provides the manpower to intimidate any opposition to ensure absolute parliamentary control of Germany.

None of this is undoubtedly news to you. I have the fear there will soon be a totalitarian regime in Germany to rival that of Stalin's in Moscow. I have tapped into a source of secret information within the power structure of the Nazi Party. I need to find a means of sharing this information with those in America that see our country's interests in an international context.

From your prior correspondence, I can meet you in Paris the first week of September. If that is agreeable, wire particulars.

Spencer

* * * *

Apart from the principal reason for the trip, Fleming looked forward to the week in Paris. His time spent in Paris during the treaty negotiations remained forever memorable. Reuniting with his old friend Allen Dulles added to the feeling of being on holiday.

As planned, he was to meet Dulles at the Hotel Ritz bar in the afternoon. From the young foreign service officer Fleming met during the treaty negotiations in 1919, Dulles advanced professionally over the last few years since the time they spent together in New York,

Dulles did not boast of his professional success, but cited details of his work in his correspondence. Fleming knew his friend and understood the reason for his influential rise. Simply put, Allen Dulles was eminently likable. Approachable, people became drawn to his intellect and the breadth of his knowledge. No longer the junior attorney, his abilities quickly found him a niche role in the unique services offered by Sullivan & Cromwell. While he may have joined the firm due to his older brother John the managing partner, he forged his own place.

Whereas his brother John was stiff and blunt, often compared to a stern preacher with his conservative dark suits, Allen was always at ease looking relaxed. He favored tweeds and smoked a pipe. Success stemmed from his demeanor that put people at ease. Allen Dulles excelled in continually expanding his wide network of associations of influential people in the United States and Europe.

Unfortunately, these same traits also extended to women. Fleming winced as Dulles referenced openly some of these personal relationships in his letters. Fleming liked Clover Dulles and wondered if she knew of her husband's affairs. A blind spot in Allen's moral fabric, but he treated it as nothing more than a part of his life.

Fleming smiled as he walked from his modest hotel on Saint Germain on the left bank of the Seine. A beautiful sunny day in

Paris. The five-star Hotel Ritz was on the right bank. Dulles obviously enjoyed the perks of a generous expense account.

Arriving early, Fleming ordered a Scotch while watching the rich and beautiful entering the bar at cocktail hour.

A short time later, Allen Dulles arrived and warmly embraced Fleming.

"So good to be with you here in Paris, Spencer. How is Warsaw?"

"Different. A disadvantage not speaking Polish. Cuisine a little on the heavy side. Probably accounts for the penchant of washing it down with copious amounts of vodka. The Poles are warm people though. Consumed with their ethnic identity. That extends to their military. Which leads to the reason why I am here."

Interrupted by a waiter, Dulles ordered a Scotch and another for Fleming.

"I developed a relationship with the Polish intelligence officer in charge of the German desk. Major Feliks Kaczmarek. He is sharing with me intelligence gathered by Polish covert sources in Germany."

"Good lord. Why?"

"Kaczmarek says they do not trust the British and French to support Polish interests."

"By *they*, who does he mean?" Dulles asked.

"At least the head of intelligence, Colonel Czajkowski, who I have met many times. Most friendly to me and has made comments supporting Kaczmarek's claims."

"Why you rather than the diplomatic staff at the embassy?"

"The ambassador is a political appointee of dubious stature. Kaczmarek does not trust foreign service officers. Cannot determine how his material acquired by espionage sources will make its way unfiltered to American decision makers."

"Then why you, Spencer? As military attaché, you are essentially a diplomat."

"According to Kaczmarek, I was chosen somewhat by default. First of all, because the United States has no intelligence agency. As he explained, intelligence agencies are structured to analyze information to synthesize into summaries directed to policy makers in their respective governments.

"Second, he liked my background. The fact that I possessed academic credentials reflecting an appreciation of European history, and fluency in German and French suggested I might be a substitute conduit.

"Polish intelligence wants to establish a backdoor to share intelligence with the United States. I would guess their foreign ministry is simultaneously pursuing the same objective through normal diplomatic channels. Poland sits in a precarious situation between the Soviet Union and Germany."

"That they do. Historically lots of bad blood between their neighbors. I am sure Stalin would like to return Polish territory to Russian control."

"My friend Major Kaczmarek believes Germany presents an equal threat."

"How's that?"

"Adolf Hitler. Germany becoming Fascist. Undoubtedly remilitarized. Another Italy. Of course, Kaczmarek runs the espionage network in Germany so that's where he perhaps sees the greater danger."

"Interesting. You trust your Polish spies?"

"Generally, yes. The intelligence they provided so far seems borne out by newspaper reports. It largely centers on Nazi government officials, the Schutzstaffel, Hitler's personal paramilitary elite guards, and the Reichswehr. The level of detail, the Poles have well-placed sources."

"What are you suggesting, Spencer?"

"You told me back in New York that Sullivan & Cromwell had clients with business interests in Germany. You are a former foreign service officer. You are also the Director of the Council on Foreign Affairs. Therefore, you know those in Washington interested in what is happening in Germany. My reports to the War Department have little chance of informing U.S. foreign policy decision making."

"Goddamn! You want me to pass along the product of Polish espionage on Germany?"

"Exactly, Allen."

A long evening of enthusiastic discussion commenced. A lot of Scotch before breaking for dinner. An excited Allen Dulles only picked at his expensive French dinner.

"As part of your official duties, I assume you have been passing this intelligence along to the War Department. From the sounds of it, hardly material you would pick up within diplomatic circles."

"Thought the same thing, Allen. Therefore, I released the German material interspersed with Russian stuff and the usual reporting on the stature of the Polish military.

"In case anybody in Washington thought this a still a bit much for military attaché reporting, I had a fallback plan if questioned. You see I know the diplomatic cover identities of the British MI6 and French Deuxieme Bureau station officers in Warsaw. Minor consular staff. Made a point of meeting them and pursued casual social contact. Never revealed I knew their real functions. Therefore, I can always say they passed along the information they received from Polish intelligence."

Dulles remarked, "Very good. Impossible to challenge."

"Of course, nobody ever raises the question. In fact, I receive almost no inquiries from Washington. That's why I'm talking to you, Allen. This is political intelligence. The Army has no capacity for evaluating or influencing U.S. decision making in peacetime."

"Well, I have people very interested in political information. They will have endless inquiries. Will your fabricated association with these British and French intelligence agents hold up?"

"For a time. However, my name is never to come up to anyone, Allen. I rely on you as the conduit because I know you. You have the perfect excuse for secrecy for shielding your source."

"Which is?"

"You are a lawyer, Allen. Attorney-client privilege. Besides, it's the kind of stuff Sullivan & Cromwell deals with all the time for your clients."

"You have thought this through. So let me ask a practical question. How can you secretly transmit the material to me?"

"Tell you what. Before getting into those specific details, I think you should see for yourself if the information has value." Fleming reached over retrieving a wrapped parcel from an adjoining chair and handed it to Dulles. "Take a look at this. The product I received over the last six months. Reports from Kaczmarek's team. Names of sources referred to only by a number."

"And you passed this on to the War Department?" Dulles asked.

"No, Allen. That would raise questions that I was indirectly mucking around in espionage. Which of course I am. My reports are sanitized summaries of this material.

"It's getting late and you need to evaluate this material. Determine if it is worth the trouble. How about I meet you back here for lunch tomorrow?"

* * * *

The following day, Dulles was waiting in the Ritz dining room. As Fleming shook hands and sat down, Dulles reached over placing his hand on Fleming's forearm.

"This is extraordinary material, Spencer. Your Polish friends have accomplished a remarkable feat of penetration into the workings of the Nazis. Herr Hitler has moved beyond the fanatical rabble-rouser. Reading this material, it is clear he is playing a more nuanced game beyond that of a populist outlier.

"These references to military and conservative business interests suggest he is pursuing a coalition essential to consolidating power."

Fleming added, "Backed of course by the threat of this SA private army. Perhaps even more interesting is this personal Praetorian Guard unit called the Schutzstaffel. Their loyalty personally to Adolf Hitler. According to Kaczmarek, the SS has grown from nothing to the power behind Hitler. For all the wild rhetoric of Hitler's rants, the SS is the force to translate the ideology into practice. Kaczmarek says if you want to know Hitler's thinking, look to what Heinrich Himmler is doing."

Dulles said, "I see what you mean. A good deal of these reports deal with the SS. Should Hitler make the next leap to chancellor, the SS might become the dominate administrative force."

"Are you interested in getting involved, Allen?"

"Absolutely. There are career foreign service professionals in the State Department who will understand the importance of this intelligence. We most likely will have a new president and administration in the fall. Regardless the election outcome, the potential for a Fascist German state like Italy should provoke concern."

"Very good. Makes me feel I am doing something useful. Now to the matter of how to transmit material secretly to you. Know anything about ciphers, Allen?"

Dulles shook his head, "Hardly."

"Since I want to stay anonymous, I've given the problem considerable thought. Remember, I started my military career in intelligence. When I came to France, I reported to the head of intelligence. The majority of the intelligence work related to communications. Keeping our communications secret while listening to enemy telegraphic and wireless transmissions. Among Pershing's G-2 staff was another captain. Brilliant fellow named Parker Hitt.

"Hitt took over signals intelligence. The guy even wrote a manual on military ciphers. How to encrypt communications as well as methods for decoding enemy ciphers. Hitt enjoyed problem solving. Taught me a lot about ciphers. I can explain the differences between transposition and substitution ciphers. No expert but I know enough to understand the pitfalls. The problem becomes a tradeoff for ease of use balanced against the level of security. According to Hitt, every cipher is vulnerable to decoding.

"The vulnerability of most ciphers is the letter frequency used for a given language. Decoding therefore becomes a mathematical process in statistics. It can be highly complex, but somebody practiced like Hitt could unravel ciphers I thought unbreakable."

"So what's the solution?"

"The solution is to remove the statistical association with language letter frequency. To do that you need to establish a common reference key for both sender and receiver. Difficult to accomplish on the battlefield where time for encryption and decoding is vital. We do not have that constraint."

"Okay. How will you transmit the information, Spencer?"

"By telegraph. A string of groups of numbers. That is how most ciphers appear. The difference is the basis for establishing the conversion from numbers to letters then words."

"Won't that be a little obvious if you do that from the embassy?"

"Not necessarily. I already encrypt the material into an army cipher. The cipher I developed looks very similar therefore will not appear out of the ordinary."

"Where do you send it to reach me?"

"To your office at Sullivan & Cromwell. The cover is my old friend and family attorney. Why in code? I'm just a secretive guy being in army intelligence my entire career."

Dulles smiled broadly. "You appear to like this intrigue."

"Let me roughly explain the concept. It is a chess-based encryption method based on each party using a common reference. I based the encryption key on documented chess games as cataloged in *Charousek's Games of Chess with Annotations* by Phillip Sergeant. Published in London by G. Bell & sons in 1919. I will give a copy with a detailed set of instructions including examples. It sounds more complicated than it is. Once you get into the rhythm, the decoding moves along quickly. I will also keep the messages concise without unnecessary words."

Fleming took out a notepad from his suit coat pocket and sketched a chessboard. Each square is identified by a letter a-h from left to right as viewed from White's side, then each row number from 1-8.

"This is the modern depiction of algebraically identifying all the squares of a chess board. Moves identify the chess piece moved to the designated square. For example, Be5 indicates bishop moved to square e5.

"The specific chess game becomes the key to decrypting the message. Therefore, also encoding the specific chess game for a given message adds another layer of encryption. Impossible to decode without knowing the key."

"Good grief, Spencer. You expect me to grapple with this. You are the chess expert."

"This has nothing to do with understanding chess. Let me finish then I will show an example of decoding.

"So to select the game from this book," Fleming said handing Dulles the chess game anthology, "the chess opening is first defined by describing the first three moves of White. This is converted to a six-digit number using a grid where the chessboard squares are numbered 11-81 as in this diagram. Each move represented by a two-digit number. For example, the White opening three moves of the Ruy Lopez opening becomes 546325.

"From there you need to do a little more work to identify the game. The 6-digit code consists of identifying the move expressed as the first 2 digits and the positions of the two moved pieces after that move. By example, the 1910 game between Alexander Alekhine and Akiba Rubinstein becomes identified by the Ruy Lopez opening and move number 9 followed by the two pieces moved to d2 and e7. The six-digit code therefore becomes 094257. This identifies the game that becomes the key for decrypting the message.

"The message itself consists of six-digit number-groups, each representing a word or individual letter from *Webster's Revised Unabridged Dictionary,* 1913 edition. Best if you read the instructions rather than me explaining it verbally."

"Is this really necessary, Spencer?"

"Hard to say. Better to error on the side of caution. I am in a precarious position as a diplomatic officer for a country that has no foreign intelligence service. The material impossible to transmit in the clear. Simpler codes are insecure. Besides, all codes require a degree of work to decrypt. You deal in confidential information all the time as a law firm. Delegate deciphering to a smart secretary you trust."

"Very well. I will give it a go. You struck a rich vein of information with your Polish spymaster friend. This is important intelligence on the state of affairs in Germany. The United States damn well needs to take notice. Communism is not the only threat."

"Thanks, Allen. When I return to Warsaw, I will send you a test message by wire. Call me by international telephone after you decode it. If the method appears workable, simply say *you enjoyed our visit in Paris* and *your financial affairs remain in good shape.*"

****

A most productive trip for Allen Dulles. The Polish espionage material painted a distressing picture of Germany's future. Not only the likelihood of a right wing government backed by the Army and the industrial sector, but administered through the truly sinister Nazi Party. That was the real substance of Fleming's intelligence.

The sinister element of the Nazi Party was the immerging power of the Schutzstaffel. These black-uniformed paramilitaries already began taking on the shape of a secret police. Dulles knew the name of Heinrich Himmler heading the SS. Assuming the Polish network material Dulles read was valid, it suggested the Poles had well-placed sources inside the SS.

To corroborate the Polish intelligence, Dulles had his own network of international journalists and foreign service staff of several countries. At the least, he could confirm the general context of the Polish material with other publicly known facts. However, what he read already fit into a broader profile of the changing landscape of German politics.

Within the last two years, those interested in events on Germany expanded. Other than senior career foreign service officers in the State Department, a number of American corporations and financial institutions had business interests in Germany. Several were clients of Cromwell & Sullivan. American banks held significant outstanding German public debt. A Fascist takeover might involve nationalization of essential industries, particularly in pursuit of rearmament, and possible debt payment default.

Among Sullivan & Cromwell clients, Dulles recently took on a new client. The American Jewish Committee, dominated by the wealthy and conservative American German-Jewish establishment, sought information and strategic advice on how to assist

German Jews undergoing increased persecution. Adolf Hitler as chancellor meant the end of German Jewry. Dulles also read *Mein Kampf,* dominated by Hitler's obsessive views towards Jews.

* * * *

Dulles realized Fleming occupied a unique position. He was the only U.S. government employee with access inside the political underbelly of this emerging German Fascist state. In contrast, the U.S. foreign service produced little more than information reported by newspaper correspondents.

If Fleming could be reassigned as military attaché to Berlin, he could be close to the Nazi beast threatening to consume Germany. No reason he could still not continue to receive the product of Polish intelligence. The Poles could secretly communicate using Fleming's chess game-based secure encryption code.

How to orchestrate Fleming's reassignment without revealing the reason would test Dulles's skills at manipulation and subterfuge. The key might be with the change of administrations. Polls strongly indicated the Democratic candidate Franklin Roosevelt defeating the incumbent Republican President Herbert Hoover in November.

A new administration meant a new ambassador to Germany. A sensitive appointment. The situation in Germany demanded an individual with specific skills rather than just selecting someone as a political favor. Dulles hit upon the tactic of inserting the idea in the right places of the Berlin diplomatic mission benefiting from the services of military attaché expert in German affairs. How to pursue a campaign to influence an army appointment remained unclear.

Roosevelt won a landslide election in November against the unpopular Hoover. Dulles calculated the only way of getting Fleming assigned to Berlin was pressure from the new White House. Although the developing economic downturn seemed to overshadow everything, foreign affairs increasingly made news. A major trading partner, the aggressive Japanese military regime threatened the entire Far East. Leading Fascist Italy, Benito

Mussolini massively rearmed the country since the Great War. A totalitarian Soviet Union lead by strongman Joseph Stalin threatened expansion of Communist ideology. Artificially created states from previous territory of the defeated Central Powers all suffered political and social unrest. With the expected consolidation of power, Hitler would soon create a Fascist Germany.

Only fifteen years since the end of the Great War, the world was again precariously unbalanced. Roosevelt had a taste of foreign affairs after serving as Assistant secretary of the Navy during the Great War. Dulles correctly figured that staffing the post of secretary of state and diplomatic postings of ambassadors to trouble spots would receive high priority on Congressional nominations. Roosevelt would rely on his transitional team to suggest qualified candidates. As a foreign policy wonk, Allen Dulles knew those closest to the new president advising him on foreign policy.

Through his extensive network of contacts, Dulles developed a strategy. His targets were two known trusted advisers to President Roosevelt, both instrumental in his election success.

Born in New York City, Sumner Welles was from a wealthy politically connected family. A family friend of Franklin Roosevelt advised him to enter the foreign service following graduation from Harvard. Welles was connected to Dulles' close friend Hamilton Armstrong, the managing editor of *Foreign Affairs* for the last ten years.

Dulles confided in his close friend Armstrong to assist in his lobbying efforts to get Fleming appointed to military attaché to Berlin. Perhaps divulging more than Fleming wished, Dulles however did not reveal that Fleming now actively participating in espionage against the Nazis.

The other person of influence was Louis Howe, Roosevelt's longtime adviser. A former New York journalist from a prominent family, he attached himself to Roosevelt's early political career in 1909. Howe became far more than a political adviser after helping Roosevelt through the difficult years after Roosevelt contracted polio in 1921. Howe even advised Eleanor Roosevelt on political matters.

Although Dulles was not a Democrat, he knew Howe from Howe's fund-raising for Roosevelt's presidential bid, having met several times at social functions involving clients of Sullivan & Cromwell. In Dulles' position as Director of the Council on Foreign Affairs, Howe engaged with him often on issues of foreign affairs.

As for Fleming, the violent attack by Nazi SA thugs ten years earlier might add a personal motivation to actively work against the Nazis from Berlin. So began a process to persuade the White House to request Fleming's appointment as military attaché to Germany. Dulles knew these gentlemen and President Roosevelt shared a profound concern over another totalitarian state threatening European stability. United States interests indirectly at stake.

Even with allies of Armstrong, Welles, and Howe, Dulles remained concerned that suggesting Fleming's appointment might likely become lost among the filling of hundreds of personnel appointments by the new administration.

Filling the ambassadorship to Germany however proved a problem and unexpectedly an opportunity. From Welles and Howe, Dulles learned that Roosevelt's first choices for the typical patronage posting turned down the offer. Both political heavy weights, they saw Berlin as a hornets' nest. Hardly a sought after ambassadorship posting.

Armstrong telephoned Dulles in early February. "Just received a call from Sumner Welles. The appointment of Adolf Hitler as chancellor of Germany last week dismayed Roosevelt. That and the difficulty of finding someone with suitable credentials willing to serve as ambassador. Welles also believes the current foreign service staff in Berlin lacks the ability to deal effectively with the regime. Therefore, the White House is moving forward with the reassignment of Colonel Fleming to Berlin as military attaché to bolster the consular staff."

Howe independently telephoned Dulles. "Colonel Fleming already has proven his diplomatic skills. Extraordinary war record. Medal of Honor recipient. Intelligence expert. Speaks fluent German. Educated. Holds a PhD. A perfect asset to whoever becomes the new ambassador. The President even remarked sarcastically, *maybe this fellow should be the ambassador.*"

Unknown to Dulles, Fleming's official reassignment happened quickly by a call from Welles to Army Chief of Staff General Douglas MacArthur's senior military aide, Major Dwight Eisenhower. After Eisenhower looked up Fleming's service record, he recalled his fellow classmate of the West Point Class of 1915. Although not close friends, he remembered Fleming as academically gifted.

Fleming's record spoke for itself. A somewhat unusual request, but a reasonable request from the White House to place a competent well-qualified military attaché in Berlin. General MacArthur signed the order prepared by Eisenhower.

CHAPTER 13

Berlin, German Reich | Spring 1933

In mid-March, Fleming received orders reassigning him to Berlin as U.S. military attaché. Typical of the Army, there was no accompanying explanation. He immediately placed a call to Allen Dulles.

"Not surprising, Spencer. Things are heating up in Germany. Hitler is getting close to fulfilling his ambition to control Germany. A totalitarian regime more dangerous than in 1914. Many in the U.S. government believe Hitler and the Nazis are a populist anomaly lacking sufficient support among the military and industrialists to achieve success. Others like me and certain advisers to the President feel otherwise. Hitler is a clear and present danger to European stability."

Fleming interrupted, "Therefore, a danger to the United States. Hitler is already chancellor. Hindenburg has no direct political party affiliation other than being a conservative. His power comes only from his personal stature. He reluctantly made Hitler chancellor. At his age, not likely he will be able to hold Hitler in check."

"My point exactly. The Roosevelt administration is also having difficulty finding an ambassador willing to wade into the German environment. Our consul general in Berlin since 1930 is trying to hold the fort. He agrees with our dire assessment regarding Hitler. The Roosevelt administration needs help in Berlin. Certain people close to the President believe you can bolster our diplomatic mission in Berlin, Spencer."

Fleming reflected for a moment. "Did you have something to do with this, Allen?"

"Yes, but only indirectly. Your background makes you ideal for the assignment. If you are looking for something more interesting, what better place than Berlin?"

"Really? Someone once suggested a tour as observer in Morocco during the Riff War was also interesting. Turned out to be a disgusting experience. Could say the same about Berlin right now." The sarcasm intended.

"On a separate note, will you be able to continue sending the other material of interest?" Dulles said referring to Fleming passing along the product of Polish espionage in Germany.

"I expect to. Will let you know, Allen"

* * * *

"The move makes sense, my friend. You can now witness firsthand Germany distorted by this Nazi malignancy," Major Kaczmarek said. "I hope the information on political events in Germany is proving enlightening to the American government."

"More than enlightening. It paints the Nazis as a criminal enterprise."

"Something far worse I believe. What feedback do you get from Washington?"

"Very little. The United States government does not know what to make of Adolf Hitler. Isolationist mentality combined with complacency I suspect."

Other than the information on armaments figures and directly related military information, the War Department made few requests. The flow of information for Allen Dulles' *clients* was also largely one-way other than the occasional follow up inquiry.

"I shall miss you, my friend," Kaczmarek said. Their professional association by now a personal friendship. Fleming felt a special bond reflected in Kaczmarek's trust to share the product of Polish espionage into the Nazi Third Reich.

"As will I, Feliks. I will of course continue to relay your intelligence on Germany to the American government. However, that becomes more difficult for us once I leave Warsaw."

"Yes. Obviously, we must use a cipher. Considering what we are both doing, best not to use either known U.S. or Polish codes."

Fleming smiled. "Way ahead of you. I of course transmit some of your intelligence to the War Department. Material of military interest. Easily disguised as just the work of a good military attaché. I transmit to Washington using the standard U.S. Army code.

"However, the real value of your espionage is political intelligence on Germany. That requires a different audience. For that, I use a trusted source, an old friend. Someone with a wide range of contacts within the American government. Decision makers. Your intelligence at least reaches the right ears, Feliks.

"I already use my own proprietary cipher to send your intelligence product to my trusted friend. I have a familiarity with ciphers. Enough to understand most methods of encryption are susceptible to cracking given the right expertise. The only truly secure method is to remove the frequency relationship of letters for a given language. This eliminates the principle basis for mathematical deciphering.

"Being an avid chess player, I created my own cipher. Based on chess games with encryption and decryption using an obscure key. I believe the algorithm is sufficiently complex to offer exceptional security when used selectively."

Fleming spent the next hour explaining his cipher. Kaczmarek also knew something of ciphers. A quick learner, Kaczmarek instantly grasped the inherent security of the cipher.

* * * *

The German political environment transformed over the previous twelve months. Adolf Hitler's rise to power however suffered a setback when Hindenburg defeated him in his bid for the German presidency in the March 1932 elections. The following month, this emboldened incumbent chancellor Heinrich Bruening to invoke the power of Article 48 of the constitution by issuing a decree banning the SA and the SS.

Chancellor since 1930, the Centre Party Bruening sought to take advantage of the growing concern about the Nazis paramilitary forces. Numbering four times the strength of the regular army, the increasing violent SA led by the outspoken Ernst Röhm represented a direct military threat to democratic government.

Ever the astute and scheming politician, Hitler ignored his party's outrage and did not publicly denounce the degree. Hitler knew the current government was teetering on the edge of collapse because of the worsening economic situation of the Great Depression. Hitler also had no wish to use the SA to seize power. He realized that within the SA and even the Nazi Party, there was little consensus on political strategy. A pack of individually ambitious dogs fighting for prominence. He alone held the political movement together.

Hitler intended to acquire power through constitutional means. Convince the conservative elements of business, banking, and the military that he was the only viable solution for leading Germany out of this economic morass. The growing unchecked membership growth of the SA ran counter to that strategy, therefore a threat to Hitler's ambitions.

An ambitious army general, Kurt von Schleicher, recognized an opportunity in the Nazi Party to orchestrate a political coup to install a conservative nationalistic government to replace the centrist Bruening government. The first step in dismantling the democratic republic forced on Germany following the Great War.

Schleicher secretly met with Hitler. He could ensure the lifting of the ban on the SA and SS, dissolving the Reichstag therefore triggering new elections, and removing Bruening as chancellor. This in exchange for Hitler and his Nazi Party joining a conservative nationalist coalition following new elections.

With Schleicher's considerable influence with the eighty-five year old President Hindenburg, he easily exploited Chancellor Bruening's vulnerability. Hindenburg blamed Bruening for his lack of economic progress and the political turmoil that forced him to run against Hitler who he despised simply for the good of

Germany. Schleicher offered Hindenburg a solution he could not ignore.

Playing on Hindenburg's conservatism and military background, Schleicher suggested a path to not only dump the politically centrist Bruening but to move the government to the right while bringing Hitler and the Nazis under control.

Schleicher proposed a little-known conservative politician, diplomat, Prussian aristocrat, and former army officer as chancellor. After Hitler agreed to support Franz von Papen as the new chancellor and join a collation government, Hindenburg agreed to Schleicher's scheme. He sacked Bruening, dissolved the Reichstag, lifted the ban on the SA and SS, and scheduled new elections for July 1932. Schleicher grossly underestimated Adolf Hitler.

What followed was a scale of violence hardly seen before in Germany. Let loose, SA Brownshirts went on a rampage. With their sizable numbers, they roamed the streets unchecked by the police. They beat Jews, murdering many. Rival political party offices attacked. The worse violence reserved for the communists. Hundreds of gun battles took place throughout Germany.

The new chancellor Papen reverted to Article 48 proclaiming martial law in Berlin. A largely hollow threat since Papen lacked sufficient police resources to quell the SA.

Although losing his bid for the presidency, Adolf Hitler increased his hold on the government in the July 1932 election. Campaigning with fanatical energy across Germany, Hitler promised stability built on German nationalism. The Nazi Party increased their seats in the Reichstag to 37% making them the largest and most powerful political party in Germany.

With this new political capital, Hitler immediately made his demands known to Schleicher who was now defense minister in the Papen cabinet. Hitler understood that Schleicher engineered the entire scheme to remove Bruening and install the puppet Papen as chancellor. Hitler now demanded Papen's removal and he be installed as chancellor.

The decision rested with President Hindenburg. Distrusting Hitler, Hindenburg refused.

In a rage, Hitler chose a parliamentary tactic. With Hermann Göring the new president of the Reichstag, he maneuvered a vote of no confidence of the Papen government. The result triggered another election called for November.

The country tired of the constant cycle of elections. Factional differences within the Nazi Party diminished the energy of a renewed campaign. The result still returned the Nazis as the leading party in the Reichstag, but with a loss of 34 seats. However, the Nazi Party was still large enough to block the formation of any coalition.

With no workable coalition possible to form a government, Papen resigned. Hitler approached Hindenburg renewing his request to become chancellor. Hindenburg tried to convince Hitler to work instead with the other parties for the good of Germany, but from a lesser role than chancellor. Hitler refused.

Days later Hitler again approached Hindenburg. In a prepared statement, he claimed the failure of parliamentary government with only the Nazi Party capable of standing against the communist threat. Hindenburg again refused Hitler the chancellorship.

German government ceased to function. Adding to the pressure on Hindenburg to resolve the crisis, a group of influential business leaders and bankers pressured him to install Hitler as chancellor as necessary for restoring economic stability.

Hindenburg succumbed instead to Schleicher's continued scheming to make good on his promise to split the fractious Nazi Party. If successful, Schleicher could muster enough votes from a fragmented portion of the Nazi Party to form a conservative national coalition, excluding Hitler.

Hindenburg made Schleicher chancellor. Schleicher immediately met secretly with Gregor Strasser, an original founding member of the Nazi Party. Strasser had been at odds with Hitler for some time. Now with the Nazi Party in disarray after losing millions of votes and in severe financial straits, Strasser felt the Nazis should compromise and share power in a Schleicher coalition government. Göring and Goebbels preferred a hardline. Hitler accused Strasser of stabbing him in the back.

Strasser then resigned all his party duties sending another blow to the already unraveling Nazi Party. To those around him, Strasser remarked, "Whatever happens, mark what I say. From now on Germany is in the hands of an Austrian, who is a congenital liar, a former army officer who is a pervert, and a clubfoot. Göring is a brutal egotist who cares nothing for Germany as long as he becomes something."

With the political landscape appearing to end Hitler's aspirations, came another surprise. The seemingly ineffectual Papen refused to shrink into the background.

The major industrialists and bankers still favored bringing Hitler to power as a strongman. Papen now mustered their support and jointly approached Hitler with an offer. Universally mistrusted and unable to form a coalition government, Schleicher was now isolated and vulnerable. Papen and influential business leaders joined to convince Hindenburg to oust Schleicher in favor of a Papen-Hitler jointly led government. Hitler agreed but insisted on being chancellor while vowing to work with ministers from the Papen constituency. Papen naively agreed thinking his broader coalition could control Hitler.

Unable to overcome the tide pressing against him, the conniving Schleicher tried to convince Hindenburg to declare a state of emergency to crush the Nazis, then dissolve the Reichstag and suspend elections. Hindenburg refused. Outmaneuvered, Schleicher resigned.

With no alternative for establishing a functioning government, President Hindenburg reluctantly named Adolf Hitler chancellor of Germany on January 31, 1933.

* * * *

What followed reflected the failure of every political faction with a stake in Germany to forestall the catastrophe by allowing Adolf Hitler to come to power. While fractured with internal power struggles, Hitler *was* the Nazi Party. His oratory, his indefinable magnetism, his innate ability to manipulate competing ambitions of his chief lieutenants, made the fragmented movement appear cohesive. The power of everyone in the Party accrued directly from Hitler. He wasted no time in consolidating that power.

On February 1, as requested by Hitler, Hindenburg dissolved the Reichstag and called for new elections on March 5. Learning from the shortcomings of the last election, Hitler set out to insure a different result this time.

On February 2, to strengthen his base, Hitler secretly met with senior military commanders to lay out his plans for German rearmament in defiance to the hated terms of the Treaty of Versailles.

On February 20, Hitler secretly met with two dozen leading industrialists to raise campaign funds for the Nazi Party in the upcoming election. The solicitation little more than extortion.

On February 27, fire totally destroyed the Reichstag building. A single Dutch communist the only person convicted in the arson. Few people believed this to be a communist plot. As Interior Minister of Prussia, Hermann Göring commanded the investigating police, adding suspicion that the perpetrators likely were Nazis. The chief of the Berlin fire service later gave testimony implicating Nazi involvement in setting the fire and inhibiting resources to fight the fire.

On February 28, President Hindenburg used Article 48 to sign the Reichstag Fire Decree into law. This suspended most civil liberties in Germany including habeas corpus and freedom of expression in any form. It further invested the government with policing power to imprison anyone considered in opposition to the government. A virtual police state emerged.

The election of March 5 returned a small majority of deputies to the Reichstag for Hitler's coalition government though not a majority for the Nazi Party. All of which was academic. The Reichstag would soon cease functioning as a legislative body.

On March 24, the Reichstag passed the Enabling Act. Meeting in the opera house, the Nazis overtly intimidated deputies of the other parties to pass the legislation. The law gave the chancellor and his cabinet the power to enact new laws and overturn existing laws for a period of four years unless renewed. Hindenburg signed the law the same day.

Over the next several months, all opposition parties to the Nazis disbanded or went underground. Adolf Hitler now held unchecked power.

* * * *

Into this political swamp, Spencer Fleming arrived by train at Berlin's Hauptbahnhof station at the end of March 1933. The last hour of the trip spent reflecting on the German border guards' overtly unfriendly attitude when the train stopped at the border for passport control check.

After handing over his passport, the guard asked aggressively, "American? What is that uniform?"

Tired after hours on the train, the guard's arrogance irritated Fleming. After standing up abruptly, the guard stepped back placing his hand on his holstered sidearm in alarm sensing aggression from this foreigner.

In flawless German, Fleming said, "I recognize your rank as a corporal. How is it you do not recognize an American Army officer? Lieutenant colonel in *Englisch,* Corporal. If you do not read English, *Oberstleutnant* in German."

After returning Fleming's passport, the soldier said nothing as he made a note on his clipboard.

"Are you not forgetting something, Corporal?"

The soldier looked up, taken back as he saw Fleming's eyes flash.

"Protocol in any army is to salute a superior officer, regardless of nationality." To punctuate his point, Fleming said sharply, "*Achtung*!"

Subdued by Fleming's confrontation, the soldier instinctively clicked his heels coming to attention and rendered a salute. After collecting his luggage, Fleming took a taxi to the Hotel Adlon on the Unter den Linden near the Brandenburg Gate. A bit pricey, but it would give him a good introduction to Berlin.

On the short drive to the hotel, he noticed patrolling police accompanied by SA Brownshirts. Welcome to the new Germany.

The following morning, Fleming reported in at the United States Embassy in the Tiergarten area on Bendlerstrasse 39. The Marine guard on duty at the fenced entrance came to attention and saluted smartly. As he examined Fleming's credentials, a sergeant approached and also saluted.

"Been expecting you, Sir. I will escort you to Consul General Messersmith. Until the appointment of a new ambassador, Mr. Messersmith is the chargé d'affaires."

"Welcome Colonel Fleming. I am delighted to have someone of your experience and academic credentials as part of the Berlin mission," George Messersmith said.

"Thank you, Sir."

After an exchange of pleasantries, Messersmith briefed him on maintenance details. Arranging to present Fleming's credentials to the new German Foreign Minister, embassy protocols, and advice regarding locating a personal residence. Fleming found the soft-spoken Messersmith warm and considerate.

As their conversation moved to German politics, Messersmith appeared well informed about the Nazi Party and Adolf Hitler. In view of the difficulty in finding a high profile candidate willing to serve as ambassador, Fleming wondered why not simply elevate Messersmith with his diplomatic experience?

"I do not wish to poison you against this new German regime. However, I must also be candid. Adolf Hitler and this Nazi Party are something I have never experienced. It has all the manifestations of an organized criminal enterprise similar to what we are experiencing in America."

"You are referring to his private army the SA and his bodyguard the SS?"

"Yes, But far more. This is my third year serving in Germany. What has transpired in the last few months is frightening. A dystopian nightmare. Please forgive my hyperbole, Colonel."

"No need, Sir. My awareness of the Nazis goes back to my time when I served as intelligence officer of American occupation forces the Rhineland. The violence of the SA touched close to me.

"My posting in Warsaw for eighteen months furthered my education of the Nazi darker side. I speak of course of these black-uniformed SS. Hitler's personal Praetorian guard. I share your view."

"Interesting. Are the Poles worried?"

"Of course. Equally worried about the Soviet Union. As they should be. Reading Hitler's disgusting tract *Mein Kampf* leaves little doubt about his ambitions to the east."

"I can see why they posted you to Berlin. We can use another experienced diplomat to contend with these buggers."

"As to the Schutzstaffel, I was fortunate to have access to secret information acquired by our ally Britain. I became socially acquainted with a British consular officer. I knew him to be the station head of the British Secret service, MI6, although I never acknowledged that.

"He must have been aware I knew his real position though. He revealed a surprising depth of knowledge about the Schutzstaffel that could only have come from covert sources in Germany. My guess he was using me as an unofficial backdoor to America since we have no foreign intelligence service."

Fleming was laying groundwork should his intelligence communications about the Nazis raise any suspicion.

"What is your take on the Schutzstaffel, Sir?"

"They are of great concern. Independent now of the SA. Numbering 52,000, I understand. Heinrich Himmler is the most trusted Hitler lieutenant. Commands the police in Munich."

"What about Göring and Goebbels?"

"Göring is an ambitious buffoon. As unscrupulous as any. Theoretically the number-two ranking Nazi. Goebbels is skilled in using the media to communicate cliché-dogma to the citizenry. He lacks an organizational platform. It is Himmler that should be feared."

"Why is that?"

"Because Himmler has the means. Unlike the SA populated largely from working class disgruntled Freikorps veterans, Himmler's SS form an elite organization. A rigorous selection criteria. Many are well-educated. All with sworn allegiance to Adolf Hitler personally.

"Whereas Göring thinks like a street-smart thug, Himmler thinks strategically. Within the SS, he created the Sicherheitsdienst des Reichsführers-SS, the SD. Ostensibly to police the Nazi Party, which obviously takes on new meaning now that Hitler is in complete power. Heinrich Himmler is Hitler's enforcer."

Through Kaczmarek's espionage network, Fleming already possessed considerable detailed information on the chief of the SD, Reinhard Heydrich. Close to Himmler and respected by Hitler, the organizationally talented Heydrich translated Himmler's vague instructions into results.

"With Göring controlling policing functions in Prussia and Himmler in Bavaria, the Enabling Act transforms Germany into a police state. Himmler has already created what they call Konzentrationslager, or KZ. A concentration camp near Dachau. A tangible reality of the suspension of due process allowing the Nazi regime to imprison people without trial. I suspect more such installations will follow."

"How does this intensifying persecution against German Jews fit into Nazi objectives?" Fleming asked.

Of all the Polish intelligence passed on to Allen Dulles, this subject provoked the most inquiries for further information. The anti-Semitic crisis in Germany began to look like the worst of the Jewish pogroms in the late 19th century in the Russian Empire. Jewish organization clients of Sullivan & Cromwell seemed the only Americans interested in what was going on in Germany. The apathy of distance and isolationism.

"Hard to say. In Hitler's political beginnings, he blamed the Jews as largely responsible for German defeat in the Great War. The stabbed in the back excuse letting the military off the hook. Then Hitler coupled the Jews with the communist threat melding them together in a racial conspiracy pitting Slavs against mythical Germanic Aryans."

"Yet politically, the Jews are not important," Fleming said. "Estimates suggest there are only 500,000 German Jews out of a population of 67 million. Having achieved power, there seems little political reason to devote effort to their continued persecution."

"There doesn't have to be logical reason. Hitler is a rabid anti-Semite. Perhaps nothing more than the twisted whim of a demagogue. Anti-Semitism exists everywhere, including the United States. So Hitler proceeds with only token international condemnation."

* * * *

Once settled in at the embassy, Fleming presented his credentials to the office of the Foreign Minster as his first official act. The first secretary to the minister received him with little ceremony.

That afternoon, he presented himself by appointment at the Reichswehr Ministry only a short walk from the U.S. embassy. A bit more cordiality afforded, probably out of deference to another military officer. A colonel greeted him warmly then ushered him to the office of Defense Minister General Werner von Blomberg.

From Polish intelligence, Fleming knew Blomberg to be a fervent Nazi. He became defense minister in the new government formed by Adolf Hitler in January 1933. Kaczmarek's network reported Blomberg's appointment foiled a possible military coup by the scheming current Chancellor and former Defense Minister General Kurt von Schleicher. Blomberg and Schleicher personally loathed each other.

Kaczmarek's network reported fragmented rumors of a plan calling for kidnapping President Hindenburg and launching a military coup. If successful, preventing Hitler from becoming chancellor as announced by Hindenburg with Schleicher assuming supreme power as head of a military government.

An archenemy of Schleicher, Blomberg got wind of Schleicher's maneuvering and when recalled from his post in East Prussia, he immediately met with Hindenburg's son Oskar instead of reporting to Schleicher. Accepting the position of defense minister in the Hitler cabinet, Blomberg ensured the Hitler chancellorship and foiled the scheming Schleicher.

Blomberg immediately set out to purge the Reichswehr of senior officers allied with Schleicher.

Expressing regard for America, the brief visit with the cordial Blomberg belied his conspiratorial background known to Fleming.

Before departing, Fleming said, "I am well acquainted with one of your senior officers, Sir. His name is Oberst Ritter von Strobel. We worked together following the Great War during the Allied occupation of the Rhineland. A diplomatic challenge for both of us. Might his office be here in this building?"

"Why, yes. Oberst Strobel is the executive officer of the Operations Sector on General Beck's staff. I will have my adjutant escort you to his office. Welcome to Berlin, Oberstleutnant Fleming."

Interesting to learn how Strobel fit into this new regime. When he represented the young German republican government to the Inter-Allied Rhineland High Commission, he appeared a political centrist. Certainly not the typically conservative stance of a Prussian aristocrat. He supported putting down the right wing Kapp-Lüttwitz Putsch in 1920. Conversely, he remained virulently anti-communist and anti-socialist. Back then, Fleming had the impression Strobel even grudgingly favored a republic despite the struggling Weimar government faced with insurmountable obstacles.

The republic was now gone. Hitler and the Nazis represented something far more to the political right than merely a conservative government. The German military was critical to Adolf Hitler moving his power closer to a dictatorship.

General Ludwig Beck was Chief of the Truppenamt. Translated as 'troop office', it was the cover organization for the German General Staff. Prohibited under article 160 of the Treaty of Versailles, Fleming knew this from Kaczmarek's intelligence. If the Poles knew this, then so did the British and French. An open secret, yet impossible for the former Allies to challenge.

Ritter von Strobel was now at the center of the German Army high command.

* * * *

Strobel knew his former associate from the Rhineland thirteen years ago was the new United States military attaché. He looked forward to renewing their friendship. Someone outside the paranoid chaos of the Reichswehr caused by the Nazi government. Every senior officer finding it necessary to take a political position. Career limiting if careless enough to share candid views to the wrong person. Strobel disliked Adolf Hitler when he first came to national attention over a decade earlier. Now his worse fears realized with Hitler's swift consolidation of power.

As an aide ushered Fleming into Strobel's office, Fleming came to attention and saluted.

Strobel returned the salute and came around from behind his desk to shake Fleming's hand while embracing his forearm with his left hand. "So good to see you after all these years. Now a lieutenant colonel. Very good."

"The Army has also been good to you. Not only surviving the demobilization and downsizing, but promoted to full colonel," Fleming said. "A difficult time for Germany this last decade."

Strobel's expression turned sour. "Far more than difficult. Yet Germany survives. Largely because of the Army."

However, not an army with a unified political perspective. Choosing to avoid putting his friend on the spot with any direct questions related to Strobel's views about the Nazis, Fleming said, "Germany has made great strides economically,"

"In spite of the Treaty of Versailles."

Fleming replied, "I know what you mean. As you know, I served as a military consultant to the American delegation. Clemenceau of France was the principal driver for the economic penalties. Along with Britain, they wanted to hobble German power in Europe."

Strobel shook his head, "Not only power, but eliminate economic competition. Inhibit German export capabilities. Relegate Germany forever to inferior status."

"Perhaps. Certainly, the French wanted to cripple Germany. Because of my background during the war, I spent a lot of time interacting with the French."

"What about the Americans?"

Fleming now shook his head. "Wilson was a misguided self-righteous meddler. Deluded into thinking he could reshape national borders throughout the world. Had no appreciation for underlying historical and ethnic antagonisms. Wilson's interest lay with creating the League of Nations. So he instead laid the foundations for future problems around the world while letting the French and British have their way in punishing Germany."

Strobel sighed then smiled as a way to change the subject. "So much to talk about. I enjoyed our times in Koblenz. How about we catch up over drinks and dinner this evening?"

CHAPTER 14

Berlin, German Reich | October 1933

The flow of intelligence from Major Kaczmarek increased. The material principally centered on the rise of the Schutzstaffel. The SS began in 1925 as a small formation within the SA. Originally formed to provide security at Nazi Party meetings, it grew from several hundred to over 50,000 by late 1933. More importantly, it provided the backbone from which Adolf Hitler exercised power over the quarrelsome factions within the Nazi Party and the threat of the bloated ranks of the SA.

Fleming understood the workings of the SS better than others of the Berlin Embassy diplomatic staff. Kaczmarek's Polish network produced a surprising level of secret detail from within the SS. Not only personal details of the leadership, but their influence over other political sectors of Germany.

Conservative factions and the Reichswehr believed they could control Adolf Hitler. From the beginning, they badly miscalculated. The Reichstag fire in February became the first indication. Kaczmarek's network never discovered direct evidence incriminating the Nazis, yet no one believed it the work of communists. The greatest suspicion fell on the President of the Reichstag, Hermann Göring, one of the first to arrive on the scene.

A month later, with Communist Party delegates already suppressed, Göring and the Nazi delegates intimidated enough other Reichstag delegates meeting at the Kroll Opera House with violence to pass the Enabling Act. The legislation provided the chancellor and the cabinet plenary powers to rule without legislative involvement of the Reichstag. The declining President Hindenburg signed the act into law, moving Germany closer to complete Nazification.

With the Reichstag Fire Decree abolishing most civil liberties now combined with the Enabling Act, Germany ceased to be a republic. In effect. Hitler became dictator. So began the Nazification of every aspect of the government. Where convenient, Nazi Party organizations such as the SS took over what should be governmental responsibilities. Hitler's last obstacle was the aging and ill President Hindenburg.

* * * *

William Dodd was an unusual choice for ambassador. He was not wealthy or politically influential. A professor of history at the University of Chicago. His only distinction for the posting was fluency in German acquired when he pursued a doctorate at the University of Leipzig. Hardly even a compromise candidate after several prominent political figures turned down the ambassadorship. No one wanted the job.

The sixty-four year old Dodd arrived in Berlin with his wife and two adult children. From the onset, Dodd appeared out of place. Notoriously underfunded, U.S. foreign missions typically required independent financial means of the ambassador to uphold the prestige of a major nation. The ambassadorial salary usually inadequate. Dodd's frugality quickly became obvious. He even shipped his Chevrolet from the United States instead of acquiring a Mercedes favored by most other ambassadors.

A strange family entourage. A matronly wife, unaccustomed to continual rounds of diplomatic entertaining, a twenty-eight year old son using the opportunity to pursue a PhD at the University of Berlin, and twenty-four year old recently divorced Martha. Martha soon proved a challenge for the new ambassador. His attractive and vivacious daughter immediately plunged in the Berlin party circuit. Within her sphere of those involved with government, the flirtatious Martha found many attractive men to satisfy her intellectual and sexual proclivities.

Most of the foreign service officers found Dodd awkward in his job. Professorial with little talent for diplomacy. Fleming shared the general view but personally got on well with Dodd from the beginning. In contrast, Fleming possessed diplomatic skills developed over his military career. He believed Dodd regarded him as a fellow academic with both holding PhDs in history.

Dodd's primary objective was to pressure the German government against the likelihood of defaulting on loans from U.S. banks in exchange for lowering interest rates from 7% to 4%. A tall order pitted against the new dictatorship of Adolf Hitler. The same financial institutions were also clients of Allen Dulles' law firm Sullivan & Cromwell.

Having been in Berlin for several months, Fleming saw the threat of Nazi Germany as something far greater than debt default. In return for high interest rates, the American lenders understood the elevated risk. The intelligence coming from Kaczmarek's network pointed to increased spending on secret German rearmament. Hitler's best play seemed to be debt default. The United States held little leverage.

With all the intelligence Fleming passed along, not to mention the daily outpouring of news media reporting, everything pointed to the heighten threat of a rearmed Germany. Adolf Hitler now held the power to pursue his militaristic ambitions.

Toward the end of October, Ambassador Dodd hosted his first reception at the embassy. German dignitaries included, Vice Chancellor Franz von Papen, Foreign Minister Konstantin Neurath, Minister of Finance Schwerin von Krosigk, and Minister of Propaganda Joseph Goebbels. All second tier officials, perhaps signaling how the Nazis viewed the United States.

To a lesser degree, the reception was to introduce the new American military attaché Lieutenant Colonel Spencer Fleming into the social fabric of the diplomatic environment. Fleming was delighted to see not only Colonel Strobel but his boss, General Ludwig Beck, chief of the Truppenamt, the camouflaged General

Staff of the Reichswehr. Military attachés of other countries attended as did a collection of mid-level German officers representing different branches of the Reichswehr.

Strobel introduced General Beck, "Colonel, this is Generalleutnant Ludwig Beck, Chief of the Truppenamt. May I present Lieutenant Colonel Spencer Fleming, Sir."

Beck said, "Oberst Strobel speaks highly of you. Told me something of your background. Tells me you hold certain views sympathetic to Germany."

Fleming's expression suggested he did not understand Beck's comment.

Strobel interjected, "Your views regarding the terms of the Treaty of Versailles we discussed years ago during our association in the Rhineland."

"Ah, yes. I am a historian, General. I would frame my views as critical of the Treaty for being shortsighted. Caving into French sentiments for imposing punitive measures and imposing harsh limits on German remilitarization. Unrealistic. Not conducive to a rehabilitated Germany resuming a place in a new European order. I believe we are seeing the failure of many of the Treaty articles contributing to current international difficulties."

The blunt spoken Beck smiled. "Spoken like a true diplomat. I can see why they chose you for this assignment. You also speak excellent German." Before Fleming could comment, Beck changed the subject. "As military attaché, What do you hope to learn about Germany's military stature?"

The truthful answer for any military attaché is to learn what the host country prefers to hide. Fleming instead said, "Let me answer by first expressing my personal views. Certain Treaty articles are emotionally based rather than pragmatic. Restricting Germany to a 100,000-man army, with no general staff, and no capital ships indefinitely without modification by the League of Nations is not realistic. It does not recognize German sovereignty essential for future parity with its European neighbors.

"As for reparations and loss of territory, I have mixed views on those issues. Suffice it to say, I believe the Treaty of Versailles highly flawed. Shortsighted. A recipe for future international discord."

Fleming was thinking of the naïve creation of new sovereign states and colonial mandates for the British and French. He chose to let Beck think he meant future discord with Germany.

"As to your question, General, I hope to learn of German military stature after all these years since demobilization following the war. If I were in a position of command in the German military, I would test the boundaries."

Beck offered a slight grin, "Thank you, Colonel. I appreciate your candor rather than diplomatic evasion. Yet Strobel says you were involved with the American treaty delegation in 1919."

"One of several military consultants. I doubt our input carried much influence. President Wilson was overwhelming focused on his League of Nations."

"Do you then agree with Germany withdrawing from the World Disarmament Conference and the League of Nations?"

This happened just a week earlier. Fleming understood the underlying issues. Another extension of the animus between France and Germany. France wanted Germany military inferiority to ensure French security. The United States and Britain declined to offer commitments to France to ensure their security if France reduced their offensive military capabilities. Yet the United States, Britain, and Italy agreed Germany should be allowed equality of arms. Disarmament negotiations broke down.

"I understand Germany's argument for parity. However, leaving the League of Nations sets Germany at odds with the rest of the world. Equivalent to abandoning diplomatic relations."

Beck raised his eyebrows. "We must talk further sometime, Colonel."

"I am at your service any time, General. A pleasure meeting you."

Strobel gave a slight affirmative nod as he shook Fleming's hand, and then moved with Beck to mingle with the other reception attendees.

"Colonel Fleming," Martha Dodd said to get his attention while approaching. With her arm intertwined with a German army officer, she held a flute of champagne in her other hand.

The officer, a handsome young major appeared uncomfortable with the flirtatious physical attentions of this pretty young woman. Dressed in a blue dress flattering to her figure with stylish hair and perfect makeup, Martha Dodd relished the male attention as one of only two women at the reception.

"Colonel Fleming, this is Major Konrad Richter," Dodd said.

Richter clicked his heels and extended his hand. "Colonel. A pleasure to meet you."

Dodd interjected, "Major Richter is with the Abwehr. German military intelligence, the same as you, Colonel Fleming. You should have much in common."

Martha Dodd continued standing close to Richter as she made small talk. "Berlin is wonderfully electric. Everything in a bit of a swirl. Unlike Chicago where everything is so dismal. The best to hope for there is the end to Prohibition coming soon."

Richter obviously uncomfortable with Dodd's continued touching of his arm, replied, "Glad you find Berlin to your liking, Fräulein Dodd. Unfortunately, what you find exciting is largely unsettled political turmoil."

"Unsettled? It seems Herr Hitler and the National Socialists are firmly in control. No more of this continual succession of new elections," Dodd said.

A dark expression came over Richter's face. "Germany continues to face great uncertainty. Events this year point to deep divisions. Rather than resolving these problems, emergency measures by decree only heighten the problem."

Fleming could not agree more, however surprised by Richter's candor expressed to a foreigner and social gadfly like Martha Dodd. Perhaps becoming paranoid by reading the intelligence reports of Nazi criminal behavior from Kaczmarek's network and observing the trappings of the Nazification of Germany. Hermann Göring's merging of various Prussian police organizations into a secret police, the Gestapo. The continued growth of Heinrich

Himmler's SS. With Hitler holding all but absolute power, dissent in any form could be dangerous.

Fortunately, for Richter, Martha Dodd diverted her attentions with the arrival of Joseph Goebbels. Making her apologies, she left Richter with Fleming.

In German, Fleming smiled knowingly at Richter. "Fräulein Dodd can be a little overpowering. Beautiful women can be that way."

Richter was still a little off balance. Perhaps just awkward around forward women.

"I hope you develop an appreciation of the complex circumstances facing Germany, Colonel. Colonel Strobel speaks highly of you. Says you are sympathetic to Germany."

"Perhaps empathetic is more accurate, Major. You now have a totalitarian nationalistic government. To the rest of the world, that can mean a threat to peaceful coexistence. For Germany, that may hinder economic progress."

Richter nodded as if in agreement. "My boss Oberstleutnant Oster asked me to attend this reception in his absence. He sends his compliments. At your convenience, he would like to meet you. Our offices are close by. Adjacent to OKW headquarters at 78 Tirpitzufer.

"Meaning no disrespect, your predecessor seemed somewhat aloof. Hardly spoke German. You on the other hand have an understanding of Germany. Educated in history. Extensive European experience. A soldier and diplomat. Colonel Oster believes we may share common concerns."

"Convey my regards to Colonel Oster, Major. I look forward to meeting him at the soonest.

Once Richter departed, Fleming resumed his mingling. The other woman at the reception soon approached him. Watching her from afar, Fleming observed that she knew everyone in the reception room, and they appeared to know her. A confident woman, fully comfortable in the environment of influential men.

"Colonel Fleming. Welcome to Berlin. I am Bella Fromm. Columnist for *Vossische Zeitung*," Fromm said in German.

Fromm was an attractive woman about Fleming's age. Not the vivacious beauty like the younger Martha Dodd, but nonetheless attractive.

Fleming reciprocated in German,"A pleasure to meet you, Frau Fromm. I know your name from our embassy staff. They speak highly of your reporting."

"Oh my. As an intelligence officer, you should know better than to believe in gossip."

"Hardly gossip. Genuine respect for your journalistic work. George Messersmith is amazed at the breadth of your contacts. Says you get interviews denied to many of your male counterparts. Foreign diplomats of all nations, heads of state, and of course the new leadership of Germany. George called you the best-connected and most respected German political journalist in Berlin. "

Fromm smiled, "Thank you, Colonel. George is a dear."

"Is it true you are Jewish?"

"Oh yes. And *Vossische Zeitung* is part of the Jewish-owned publisher *Ullstein Press*."

"Extraordinary. Given the rabid anti-Semitic stance of the Nazis, how is it possible they grant a German Jewish woman interviews?"

"Good question. Male hubris undoubtedly plays a part. Perhaps uncertainty about my standing in the diplomatic community therefore unwilling to create unnecessary controversy. A German Jew rather than of Slavic ancestry probably helps. The Nazis hate Eastern Europeans. Possibly just some perverse desire to get close to a vile Jew. Who is to say?

"I can trace my Jewish genealogy back at least 500 years when some distant ancestor emigrated from Spain. For most of that time, Jews lived in relative peace among the larger Christian population in Bavaria where I am from. That changed after the Great War."

Fleming said, "Hitler looking for a scapegoat. Manufacturing a conspiracy with the despised communists in league with Jews. A revolution in search of an enemy. Are you safe with all this violence perpetrated against Jews?"

Fromm remained silent for a moment. "Relatively speaking. At least for now. May not be able to work as a journalist all much longer though. By the first of the year, Jews become banned from working at newspapers other than Jewish publications. That too will only prove temporary. I expect to be silenced soon. I also have a grown daughter whom I must consider. Then the question of where to go. Jews seem not welcome anywhere. Did you know American conservative factions viciously attacked George in your press for issuing a visa to the Nobel Laureate physicist Albert Einstein?" With a sarcastic chuckle, "What chance for a troublesome Jewish woman journalist?"

"What about your husband?"

"Divorced."

"We are both in similar professions, Frau Fromm. We both seek to uncover confidential information either hiding in plain sight, or extracting it from those willing to talk. Not by definition spying but discovering consequential information lies at the heart of our work. Might I contact you from time to time? Get your read on those in the government involved with military matters?"

"Of course. Since we are both in the information gathering business, I will be glad to share anything helpful. George briefed me on your background. He was right. You are someone I should get to know."

"My portfolio is obviously military related information. Besides interacting directly with the Reichswehr, that means an interest in German industrial capabilities geared to rearmament. Among your extensive network of sources, are you acquainted with any important German industrialists?"

"Of course. Many are among my best sources. Most possess the arrogance of the privileged, and therefore often the most candid. Fritz Thyssen, Gustav Krupp, Hermann Schmitz of IG Farben, Ernst Brandi chairman of the Ruhr Mining Association, Hjalmar Schacht President of the Reichbank to name a few of those I know personally."

"Impressive. May I use your name as an acquaintance to get interviews with some of these industrialists?"

"Better yet, say I am a good friend. We also must talk further, Colonel."

"I look forward to that. At your service anytime, Frau Fromm."

"Some of my foreign correspondent colleagues are throwing an early birthday party for me. Frankly, they worry about me. The Nazis dislike any reporting casting them in a bad light. The intimidation is often overt. Some journalists fear possible physical violence. Several foreign reporters unsympathetic to Nazi Party propaganda have received threats. With Göring's Prussian Gestapo and Himmler's SS with their stupid death's head emblem on their caps above the law, that makes those concerns real.

"Knowing our political bent, would you like to join me and chat with a bunch of anti-Nazi reporters?"

"Delighted. Are you sure I will not be intruding on your celebration?"

"Nonsense. You can be my escort. A boost to my ego showing off a handsome American officer on my arm."

"Sounds like a stimulating evening."

"Wonderful. This Saturday at seven o'clock." She extracted a business card then wrote the address to her apartment on the back with a gold fountain pen.

"You will enjoy the venue. A place called the *Geisterstunde* on Leipziger Strasse. The witching hour in English. One of the last surviving pleasure palaces of the decadent twenties. Economic problems followed by the narrow-minded Nazis closed down the wild clubs catering to jazz, sex, and opium.

"The *Geisterstunde* only survived because the new owner turned the nightclub into an upper class night spot a couple of years ago. The owner is a magnificent singer backed by a talented orchestra. The food and liquor are exceptional. The prices ridiculous. Beautiful waitresses dressed in evening gowns. A refined atmosphere that attracts the wealthy and influential. I trust my journalism colleagues are funding the evening with generous expense accounts."

* * * *

Fleming's first visit to the *Geisterstunde* proved a most interesting evening. His first surprise was Bella Fromm. She looked elegant in a cream-colored fitted dress with plunging neckline and pearl necklace. A matching wide-brimmed hat and jacket offset the ensemble. He sensed her attention to fashion served her well by declaring her equal status when interviewing the aristocratic and influential.

"My compliments. You look stunning, Frau Fromm."

He presented her with a dozen red roses.

"Oh my. These are beautiful. Please call me Bella. Frau Fromm sounds like my mother."

"Then I am Spencer,"

By agreement, Fleming wore his dark blue dress uniform with matching overcoat and leaf embellishments on the visor of his peaked cap signifying his elevated rank.

Out of habit, he always went armed. The random acts of violence on the street against people not rendering the outstretched arm Nazi salute for passing SA or SS formations disgusted him. He did not recognize them as soldiers, therefore he would never render that stupid Caesar-like gesture. Nor would he back away from physical attack. Since his M1911 Browning .45 service pistol was too bulky to conceal under his uniform jacket, he opted for a smaller German 9mm Walther PPK, easily concealed in his overcoat pocket.

The exterior of the *Geisterstunde* was understated simplicity. Sculpted bushes accented with offset lighting adorned the light colored masonry exterior. Inside a tuxedo attired maître d' confirmed reservations. A beautiful hostess in an evening gown then escorted Fleming and Fromm to a large round table already occupied by four men. As they approached, the men stood.

Fromm greeted each with a kiss to the cheek then said, "Let me introduce Lieutenant Colonel Spencer Fleming, the American military attaché. Fear not, he shares our critical views on the current government."

The interior of the *Geisterstunde* reflected understated elegance. Fine linen and tableware. Crystal chandeliers. The walls festooned with heavy curtains with strategically located large-format oil paintings. All in good taste, but with a subtle undertone of sexual decadence.

"Once seated after shaking hands and making introductions, the correspondent for the New York Times said, "I noticed your campaign ribbons, Colonel. Am I correct that you are a recipient of the Medal of Honor, the Distinguished Service Cross, and the Silver Star?"

"Yes. I saw some action in the Great War."

"Bella, in case you are not aware, Colonel Fleming holds the highest awards for battlefield valor. Those other ribbons suggest a distinguished career."

Fleming remarked, "Been in the Army since 1915. Those medals come from being in the wrong place at the wrong time."

"You are too modest, Colonel," the correspondent from the *Chicago Tribune* said. "I covered the war in 1918. Where did you receive these citations?"

"Different places. One in Mexico in 1916 before coming over with the AEF. I am an intelligence office. So the wrong places I referred to came from sticking my nose into dangerous places just like all of you."

Everyone laughed then nodded with serious expressions.

"That is the ugly truth," The correspondent from the *Manchester Guardian* said. "I replaced my predecessor a few months ago. He returned to London following rumors that the Gestapo was plotting to kill him."

"Not that farfetched. Colonel," The older correspondent from the *Daily Mail* said. "Recently the Gestapo arrested two of our colleagues. Each spent a horrific week in prison before being expelled from Germany."

They were interrupted by their waitress, another attractive young woman provocatively attired. "May I take your drink orders? Frau Kaplinsky is about to start her first show. She disapproves of distractions when she is singing."

With a new bottle of champagne replacing the empty in the tableside ice bucket, the dining room lights dimmed and theatrical lighting illuminated the stage.

Valeska Kaplinsky made her entrance in a sequined black tight-fitting gown with a long slit up one side revealing a shapely leg as she walked onto the slightly elevated stage. The room burst into applause. Fleming's first impression was Kaplinsky's face. An angular face framed by a stylish short hairdo. A real beauty even viewed from the distance of their table.

Fleming was surprised to hear Kaplinsky begin with a series of excerpts from several soprano arias sung in Italian. Although not particularly knowledgeable in music, he nonetheless could appreciate the beauty of her voice. Her small orchestra consisted of a string quartet and piano. Perfect accompaniment to her voice and musical repertoire. Thirty minutes later, she launched into a medley of popular music.

Her first selection was *Wenn Ich Mir Was Wünschen Dürfte* in German, a sultry song made famous by Marlene Dietrich. Usually sung in the contralto lower voice register, Kaplinsky's rendering as a soprano lost nothing in its sexual overtones. She followed with *Stormy Weather* and *Night & Day* in English. Intermingled with personalized banter with the patrons, she concluded her first one-hour performance with *April in Paris* sung in French.

Most of the male patrons stood to give her a resounding round of applause.

Fromm remarked, "Valeska Kaplinsky is a remarkable singer as well as businesswoman. Note the minimal songs sung in German. My guess, it is her attempt to internationalize the experience, catering to the sensibilities of her influential clientele. Look around. Everyone here has money or power. Perhaps with the exception of our table. More importantly, she is carefully avoiding running afoul of Nazi cultural restrictions."

"What do you mean?"

"Hitler's cultural tastes run to the banal or ugly. Notice Kaplinsky chose no arias from Wagner. The one German song she sang flirted with defying the boundaries. No Negro jazz or energetic dance tunes popular during the last decade. No artistic expression that offends Hitler's prudish sensibilities allowed."

The nightclub's patrons, mostly men, consisted of every age but few under the age of thirty. A scattering of women. Everyone well dressed. Several senior army officers. Three SS officers in their distinctive black uniforms sat together at a table.

Fleming asked Fromm, "How do then reconcile these attractive waitresses in revealing gowns."

Fromm looked at Fleming with a knowing expression. "Look around you. Mostly male patrons. Sex sells. Kaplinsky can push the boundaries as long as this remains the haunt of the very powerful while avoiding anything overtly offensive. Joseph Goebbels, the Minister of Propaganda comes here occasionally. He has a more eclectic appreciation of art than Hitler but he still represents the cultural police."

Kaplinsky was making the rounds greeting patrons. Fleming observed with some amusement the awestruck expressions on these men of power making an elaborate show of kissing Kaplinsky's hand.

As Kaplinsky approached close to their table, he understood the effect she exuded. Up close, left no question that this was a woman of confidence. Her dark eyes spellbinding as she looked directly into your eyes.

Kaplinsky recognized Bella Fromm. "Bella, so good to see you."

Fromm introduced her fellow journalists and as she came to Fleming, Kaplinsky interrupted and said, "And this handsome officer? What army do you serve?"

"*Oberstleutnant Spencer Fleming, United States Armee. Meine Komplimente. Du hast eine wundervolle stimme,*" Fleming said in German to Kaplinsky's surprise as she extended her hand.

"Delighted to have you at the *Geisterstunde,* Colonel. Please be careful of Bella. Her sometimes imprudent comments can be dangerous."

Kaplinsky smiled at Fromm and moved on to another table. Fleming sat back down. He wondered if he now looked slightly awestruck after being close to Valeska Kaplinsky.

CHAPTER 15

Berlin, German Reich | January 1934

Valeska Kaplinsky sat in her office in the late afternoon. A cozy environment furnished with style. A fire burned in the fireplace. After finishing a light meal, she sipped coffee as her way of relaxing before each night's performance. Dressed in a silk robe she began fixing her makeup. Across her desk sat a short man in his forties dressed in an inexpensive suit also drinking coffee.

Thumbing through a sheaf of typewritten papers, he looked up at Kaplinsky. "Remarkable how these men talk. Gossip like a bunch of old women."

Kaplinsky said, "Men try to impress pretty women. Make themselves appear important. Especially where sex is involved."

"Good material, Valeska. Any problems?"

"Not really. The clientele has changed. Many of the old regulars no longer come. The old moneyed aristocrats. The clientele now more aligned with the new regime. More government officials. More SS. Which for you I guess is good."

With a sigh, he said, "Yes, of course. Which reminds me." Reaching inside his jacket, he extracted an envelope. Major Kaczmarek is increasing your retainer."

"Thank you. That helps. The Nazis are lousy tippers."

Bruno Goettner was a Polish espionage agent working for Major Feliks Kaczmarek. His cover was a sales agent for a wine and spirits distributor. Goettner was Kaplinsky's control. The source of her intelligence was her escort service. Expensive prostitutes arranged by appointment only.

The attractive women working as hostesses and waitresses at the *Geisterstunde* were available to hire for sexual services. Their looks and demeanor suggested some came from privilege. Dreadful circumstances now brought them to prostitution as a means of survival. Several of the women were Jewish as defined by Nazi racial laws.

The escort service was common knowledge but never openly discussed. The clientele of the *Geisterstunde* were the wealthy or powerful, many socially prominent. The breadth of influence of those that also indulged as sexual clients ensured a collective confidentiality from embarrassing disclosure. Many were senior Nazis adding to that security. Hitler and Himmler possessed prudish and mystical attitudes of Aryan racial superiority.

Other influential Nazis, including high-ranking SS officers, observed no such restrictions. They frequented the exclusive *Geisterstunde* with many hiring the services of the waitresses for sex. Among those aficionados, dining at the *Geisterstunde* provided the ability to shop for the desired girl and boost of the extravagance of both experiences. Kaplinsky went to great lengths to keep the *Geisterstunde* nightclub separated from the escort service. Although rumored, it only added to the allure of the *Geisterstunde*.

Ambition and the ability to exercise unchecked power for personal gratification provided a rich opportunity to harvest intelligence from men. No ordinary exchange of money for brief sex at a bordello, these liaisons were expensive engagements spanning an entire evening with the most attractive young women in a place of the client's choosing. Polish Major Kaczmarek's Kaplinsky Network was among his most productive penetrations into the upper echelons of the Nazi Third Reich.

"Being close to Heydrich, this Sturmbannführer Pfeiffer is turning out to be a productive source on the SS. Genevieve Meier is proving talented in drawing out information from Pfeiffer," Goettner said.

"Her body and sexual talents likely have much to do with that," Kaplinsky said sarcastically. "That and being Jewish. Her hatred for the Nazis great enough to overcome the disgust of engaging in sexual relations with someone like Pfeiffer. She sends money to support her family."

"Good thing Pfeiffer comes from an affluent family. Spending what you charge for a night with Meier with his regular frequency is well beyond his officer's pay."

* * * *

Valeska Kaplinsky was born in 1896 in the city of Wroclaw in Silesia. Although ethnically Polish, Silesia was part of the German Empire at the time. As a sovereign country, Poland ceased to exist from 1795 until the end of the Great War when reestablished by the Treaty of Versailles in 1919.

Her father was descendant from an obscure branch of Polish aristocracy. It provided nothing more than a modest career as a Prussian army officer. When war broke out in 1914, Major Tomasz Kaplinsky commanded a battalion in a Prussian regiment. At the time, Valeska was studying music at the Universität der Künste in Berlin.

The Great War destroyed the Kaplinsky family. Her father fell in 1914 leading an infantry charge in the First Battle of the Marne. An older brother enlisted in the German Army in 1916 which by then turned into a stagnate war of attrition fought from static trenches on the Western Front. Alternating offensives from opposing trench positions soon claimed her brother.

As the war went badly, her remaining sibling, a younger brother, reached conscription age. Soon after he left for the front, their mother fell seriously ill. Suffering respiratory ailments all her life, food and heating fuel shortages contributed to pneumonia. Valeska returned home from Berlin after receiving the news. Unfortunately, with the trains dedicated to troop transport, obtaining a ticket delayed her journey for several days. She arrived too late. Her mother died the previous night.

Valeska took stock of her desperate circumstances. Selling the meager household belongings did little more than cover payment of the family's debts and funeral. What little funds remained would sustain her living expenses only to the end of the current academic year.

There was no available work in either Wroclaw or Berlin. Germany was losing the war. Food became increasingly scarce. She had no skills other than her music. Yet there was no demand for a concert violinist or a developing operatic soprano. Her best hope rested with returning to the university. Well regarded by the college of music faculty, it was her only alternative. Perhaps she might find some means of supporting herself in the only environment she knew.

An emotionally devastated Kaplinsky returned to her small rented apartment close to the campus. Her dismal prospects made worse by a miserable gray, cold winter's day in December 1917.

By carefully watching her dwindling funds, she managed to complete her studies and receive her undergraduate degree in May of 1918.

Circumstances by now became desperate for German civilians in the final year of the war. Throughout the years of war, the civilian population suffered severe food shortages. Meat became an impossible luxury. A significant percentage of the cattle and hogs slaughtered because too costly to feed. By 1918, average daily food consumption dropped to 1,400 calories a day. Fully one-third of foodstuffs diverted to the black market. Urban areas suffered even greater shortages. People began starving in alarming numbers.

Lack of nutrition contributed to disease. The Influenza Pandemic reached Germany as elsewhere in the world. Tuberculosis in the cities rose 90%. Cases of typhoid doubled in the last two years. Everyone suffered from various degrees of malnutrition. Throughout the war, the British naval blockade exacerbated the German food crisis. Although defeated, German only signed an armistice, not surrender. The British blockade therefore remained through 1919 until signing the Treaty of Versailles codifying terms for what amounted to a German defeat. Three-quarters of a million German civilians died of malnutrition and its effects during the war years.

Armed with only an undergraduate degree in music, Kaplinsky faced the real dilemma of survival. Although distasteful, her only solution became obvious.

In addition to her exceptional voice and musical talents, Valeska Kaplinsky was a beautiful woman. More than that, she possessed the indefinable quality of sex appeal. Her musical talents alone did not account solely for her favored status among many of the faculty. That included, the director of the College of Music.

A noted performing violinist before the war, Ludwig von Albrecht came from wealthy Prussian aristocracy. Family connections, including marriage into another wealthy family propelled him to the directorship. The same connections and the excuse of poor eyesight allowed him to avoid conscription.

Albrecht was a handsome man of good stature in his early forties. His fine features only slightly diminished by rimless eyeglasses with thick lenses. The effect made him appear professorial.

Attracted to Kaplinsky because of both her physical charms and musical talents, he undertook to find reasons to interact with her as much as possible. He offered to tutor her personally each week. To further her voice development, he assigned two faculty members to work with her regularly in voice training and Italian language opera.

Regardless of Kaplinsky's musical talents, Albrecht's intentions soon turned romantic. Considering the professional risk of scandal, likely an obsessive attraction. He also knew of Kaplinsky's limited financial means.

"Fräulein Kaplinsky. You are a talented student. Perhaps good enough to eventually advance into the professional ranks. Those possibilities might come about now that the war is over. However, you still need to advance your studies. Develop your considerable skills further. My sincere recommendation is to continue your studies by pursuing an advanced degree."

Kaplinsky lowered her head and sighed, "I understand Doctor Albrecht. Unfortunately, I do not have the money to continue my musical education. I have no family. My father and two brothers died at the Western Front. My mother of illness. I must look to some means of supporting myself."

"I am aware of your unfortunate family circumstances. A talent like yours however must not go to waste. I asked you here today to offer a solution. I have at my disposal, a scholarship grant. Sufficient funds for you to complete your education."

Kaplinsky looked at Albrecht with surprise. "Is it possible for me to qualify?"

Her riveting dark eyes put him slightly off balance, "Ah ...of course. I mean you already qualify. You see, this scholarship fund is from an anonymous benefactor to the School of Music. It am entrusted to distribute the grant at my discretion."

Kaplinsky broke down at the welcoming news. "Thank you, Doctor Albrecht. I do not have the words to ..."

"No need to thank me Fräulein. It is your talent and efforts that qualify you. The scholarship will provide a stipend for room and board and cover tuition. To provide you with additional living expenses, I am also offering you a teaching assistant position throughout your term of study. The entire faculty looks forward to the day when you appear on a major European stage."

There was no scholarship. The funds came from an inheritance from Albrecht's great-uncle. He periodically funded a cover account from which the bank automatically mailed a check to Kaplinsky each month.

The naïve young Kaplinsky only learned the truth behind her financial windfall one evening in Albrecht's office after coaching her on a difficult violin piece.

In a sudden outburst, he confided his undying love for her. He would bring her out into the performing world once she was ready. He had the contacts and the money to promote her career. Meanwhile, he would see to her financial welfare. A better apartment. Fine food. Clothes. They would become lovers.

The revelation shattered the complacency of her newfound life over last several months. Admittedly, she was fond of Albrecht. Even the occasional romantic fantasy intruded into her thoughts. His highborn wife dying suddenly. Taking her place after a suitable time. Living a life of affluence and culture. Pursuing a career in the arts with a gifted, supportive husband. A fantasy grounded in financial security not sexual intimacy. That fantasy now turned to the unfortunate reality of becoming a kept woman. A mistress. Trading sex for survival in devastated Germany.

Her feeling of betrayal eventually subsided. Better off than most young women. She was a survivor. The arrangement proved agreeable once she reconciled to the practicality. Albrecht was a handsome man and proved a considerate lover.

Over the next two years, while her violin technique improved, it was her voice that developed into real performance quality. All this while moving closer to completing a master's degree.

Another setback then again changed the arch of her career. Somehow, Albrecht's wife discovered the affair. Likely through some carelessness, or perhaps a jealous faculty member. Keenly aware of the attractive Kaplinsky, several young professors may have guessed the affair with the music school director.

Regardless, a much-deflated Albrecht confronted Kaplinsky with the prospect of scandal. His wife was willing to ignore his indiscretion if he ended the affair.

Kaplinsky asked, "What is to become of me?"

"You must leave the university. Leave this apartment. I shall give you enough money to relocate and live for a year."

"How am I to survive given the hyperinflation of the Reichsmarks?"

Realizing he must ensure her silence and not expose the scandal, he said, "Very well, Valeska. Find new lodgings. I will fund an account in your name at a Swiss bank in Zurich. You can draw funds as required by wire transfer in stable Swiss francs. All I ask is for you to keep silent about our past relationship."

Kaplinsky pushed back. "What about finishing my degree studies?"

"I shall see you are awarded your degree. But you must leave the university."

That was that. Hoping to launch a professional career with the help of Albrecht no longer possible. Yet philosophically she did manage to survive these last two years while improving her professional prospects.

* * * *

Circumstances in Germany remained chaotic. Hyperinflation created violent political upheaval. Goods remained in short supply. Food availability improved but specific shortages continued. Unemployment remained high as the country struggled to assimilate the six million demobilized military. Other countries continued to boycott German goods further impairing economic recovery. War reparation payments added further strain.

Yet the war was over. Prospects no longer clouded by the inevitable certain defeat. Although suffering continued to foment social and political strife, the great catastrophe of the war was now behind Germany. As difficult as recovery remained, expectations existed for resumption of normal existence. Venues for entertainment soon flourished as the need for emotional outlet became of part of German life once again.

* * * *

The stipend from Ludwig Albrecht to keep her silence kept Kaplinsky afloat until the period of hyperinflation eased. In January of 1925, a new currency issue replaced the worthless former German mark. This returned the value of the mark to its pre-war conversion rate with the British pound and U.S. dollar. Her insistence on Albrecht paying her in Swiss francs allowed her to survive during this period where German currency had no value and people starved.

There was still no work. Her attempts to pursue her career in opera met with failure. Regardless of her talent, there simply were no opportunities. She considered leaving Germany but was unsure what she could do to earn a living. Risking her meager resources in Swiss francs that Albrecht might discontinue at any time, staying in Germany seemed a safer choice. Although repelled by the idea, perhaps she might turn to teaching music or tutoring.

By 1925, the German economy began to stabilize. Entertainment returned to Berlin. Gone was the pre-war conservative social environment. As if in rebellion, Berlin quickly turned toward every expression of decadence.

As everywhere in the world, women experienced freedom from the fin de siècle oppressive confines of buttoned to the neck, angle-length dresses worn over absurd layers of non-functional undergarments. Woman now showed their legs to above the knee in lively colored dresses, or tight-fitting gowns showing as much bare skin as possible for eveningwear. Use of makeup became more pronounced. Women smoked and drank cocktails. American jazz became popular. African-American jazz and energetic dancing became the international rage among younger Germans.

The cabaret was born. A place to party, be entertained, and indulge in a range of vices including liquor, opium, and sex. Hedonistic escapism in every extreme imaginable. Kaplinsky's voice and looks made her stand out. However, Berlin was a city full of attractive young women making competition fierce. The cabaret was as much stage performance as vocal abilities. The crowd often noisy and more interested in the booze and their friends. While you could be popular, competition depressed the fees entertainers could demand. The German cabaret was a combination of American vaudeville and Prohibition speakeasy spiced with overt sexual performance.

Kaplinsky eventually landed at the *Geisterstunde*. Billed as a venue for sophisticated entertainment and dining, it was less raucous and decadent in its style of entertainment. The quality of Kaplinsky's voice with her classical training made her a perfect fit for the more refined ambience attracting a different clientele. Within weeks, she became the featured performer.

Jakob Asner, the owner of the *Geisterstunde,* was a young entrepreneur. From an upper middleclass Jewish family, he purchased the *Geisterstunde* a year earlier. Converting the club's image remained a work in process. The décor not yet commensurate with the food and drink prices. The entertainment uninspiring until Kaplinsky arrived. The best thing going was the pretty waitresses dressed in the latest "flapper style" offering eye candy.

Kaplinsky, coming from the cultured world of serious music, immediately concluded that Asner failed to achieve the necessary atmosphere for the *Geisterstunde.* Stuck instead somewhere between a palace of implied vice and an aspiring five-star restaurant.

Asner unfortunately possessed a large cocaine habit. As a result, the *Geisterstunde* failed to prosper through lack of his attention. It was insufficiently upscale to command its premium prices. Carrying the business largely through her singing, within a year Kaplinsky threatened to move on unless paid much more. With profits tight, Asner instead offered her a piece of the business.

Unfortunately, Asner's addiction worsened. Following hospitalization after an overdose, Kaplinsky took charge of the club's business affairs.

Once Asner recovered, Kaplinsky told him she was leaving. Realizing the *Geisterstunde* would fail without Kaplinsky as the draw, Asner made her an equal partner. Months later Asner died of another overdose induced by excessive alcohol. Having insisted on surviving partner rights in the partnership agreement, Kaplinsky inherited the *Geisterstunde.*

She set about to correct the faults of the *Geisterstunde.* Reinvesting the modest profits, she began transforming the place. The makeover included new lighting, crystal chandeliers, and new tableware. She upgraded the quality of musicians and installed a piano. The musical repertoire reset to vary from contemporary to classical. The repertoire geared to sophistication. Her two nightly performances alternating between operatic arias and selected international songs. She hired a maître d' and new head bartender. Every detail directed at differentiating the *Geisterstunde* from the cabaret popular entertainment venue to one of refinement catering to the wealthy and influential.

The final change came to reinventing the waitresses. First came getting rid of the drug users. She replaced the flat-chested unsexy flapper attire with revealing low-neckline gowns with appropriate hair and makeup. Since sex sells, it was a question of stylish display complimenting the overall environment.

Well aware that many of the waitresses already engaged in sex for money as a sideline, she introduced strict rules. No soliciting at the club. Scandal will be cause for termination. Yet she understood the availability of the young waitresses for sex was part of the draw for certain of the club's clientele. Kaplinsky needed their business.

Recruiting became easier as the *Geisterstunde* reputation for better wages and tips attracted young women casting about to escape the crude debauched excesses of the typical cabaret. Yet times were still difficult. Unemployment remained a problem. Many attractive young women willing to sell sex for extra money. Restricting her waitresses from directly soliciting Geisterstunde male patrons might be counterproductive. Making a formal adjunct to the business to satisfy everyone became the obvious solution.

Creating a separate unaffiliated business advertised as a temporary employment service complete with business cards, Kaplinsky could plausibly deny involvement while adding another profit source. Not all the waitresses wished to engage in prostitution. That was up to the individual. For those that did, it became a lucrative sideline.

All arrangements made by advance appointment only and prepayment. Credit advanced to select clients. Venues for engaging in sex the responsibility of the client. Unlike typical prostitution rates charging for performing a sex act, liaisons were for a night with correspondingly steep fees. The women split the earnings from the lucrative trade with Kaplinsky. For the male client, the experience made to feel like a night spent with a mistress rather than a brief interlude with a prostitute in a shabby hotel.

Kaplinsky separated the two businesses by subcontracting the running of the escort service from the office of her lawyer who set up the business under a shell company and managed false financial records. For this he received 25%. With 50% going to the call girl, that left a 25% clear profit for Kaplinsky. It served to retain attractive young women while adding intrinsic value to the

Geisterstunde. Business increased as word secretly spread among certain of the club's wealthy clientele of a safe alternative for gratifying their sexual desires. An important supplemental profit stream without debasing the refined reputation of the *Geisterstunde.*

After finding solid financial ground, events outside Kaplinsky's control again threaten her prosperity. A worldwide economic downturn quickly followed the Wall Street stock market crash in late 1929. Just as the *Geisterstunde* began hitting its stride, business began falling off.

* * * *

In 1931, Major Feliks Kaczmarek of Polish intelligence served undercover as the second secretary working trade related matters at the Polish embassy in Berlin. Recognizing the likely rise of Hitler and the Nazi Party coming to power, his mission was to establish a network of intelligence sources.

Research produced the name of Valeska Kaplinsky. Owner of a fashionable Berlin nightclub where she appeared as a celebrated singer. Classically trained in opera and violin. Rumors circulated about her involvement with an exclusive prostitution service. Expensive call girls for hirer. A perfect means for intelligence gathering if Kaczmarek could recruit Kaplinsky.

Kaczmarek's local espionage agent in Berlin, Bruno Goettner, found Kaplinsky. He knows her from his cover as a salesman for a wine and spirits distributor. She is ethnically Polish. Father and two brothers killed in the war on the Western Front fighting in the German army. Mother died before the end of the war.

Not what Kaczmarek would call a Polish nationalist, however from her comments according to Goettner, she dislikes Adolf Hitler and his private army of thugs, the SA and SS. She also appears to hide the fact she is a Jew as defined by Nazi racial law. Church records in Wroclaw, Poland documented her Jewish mother's conversion to Catholicism to marry her father. Unknown if this might be a factor for gaining her cooperation.

"Other than her Jewish background, why should Kaplinsky be willing to provide us intelligence?" Kaczmarek asked Goettner.

"The nightclub is struggling financially. I believe the prostitution service is keeping things together with the business downturn of the nightclub. Her affluent clientele apparently affected by this economic downturn. If we could provide a financial incentive, she might be persuaded to use her call girls to pass information gleaned from indiscretions of their clients during sexual relations. Unlike most prostitutes, the client pays for the woman by the night. Many hours to engage in more than sex. The time likely filled with conversation with much alcohol."

Kaczmarek personally approached Valeska Kaplinsky to spy for Poland. Surprised when confronted with his knowledge of the prostitution service, she calmly asked what type of information he was looking for and what was he willing to pay.

"Any confidential information related to political maneuvering, German rearmament, or foreign affairs. The political situation changes every day. Who acquires more authority? Which government or military leaders are allies or enemies? Sentiments regarding officials within the NSDAP are of particular interest. Boasting and indiscrete revelations trying to impress a beautiful woman fueled by sex and drinking."

As a pragmatic businesswoman, Kaplinsky said, "Beyond a monthly retainer, I will want a bounty for any particularly important information."

Kaczmarek replied, "Very well. May I ask what cover story you will give to these women for relaying information to you?"

Kaplinsky thought for a moment. "I shall remain somewhat vague. They know the clients are influential. I shall tell them that knowledge is power. Every secret has a market. Tell them it affords protection from the police. They will assume I pass the information to the Gestapo."

Although not totally certain of Kaplinsky's motives, successfully recruiting Kaplinsky's prostitution service was an intelligence coup considering the stature of her clientele.

Intelligence was a matter of not only gathering secret information, but also finding means of independent collaboration to elevate the quality of that intelligence. A network of exclusive prostitutes could compliment information gathered by Kaczmarek's other sources within the Third Reich.

"This is the last you will see of me Frau Kaplinsky. From now on, you will communicate solely through Bruno Goettner and he will deliver your money each month, in Swiss francs as agreed. Poland thanks you for your service, Frau Kaplinsky."

CHAPTER 16

Berlin, German Reich | April 1934

Since first arriving in Berlin, Spencer Fleming advanced his range of informative contacts. The renewed friendship with Colonel Ritter von Strobel opened up many contacts within the Truppenamt, the thinly veiled cover for what served as the General Staff of the German Army. Interestingly Strobel steered him to several general officers that shared similar critical views of the Nazis as those of his boss General Ludwig Beck. Among those were Generals Franz Halder, Walter von Brauchitsch, Wilhelm Adam, and Erwin von Witzleben. Names Fleming would come to know later as more than mere critics of the Nazi regime.

Fleming and Strobel met frequently. Dinner, drinks, and sometimes with friends, mostly fellow army officers. Ostensibly, these were social circumstances, however, the talk invariably turned serious. The subject always the disastrous political situation of Germany coming under the absolute control of Adolf Hitler. While Germany was not yet a police state, the candor of the criticism toward Hitler by army officers to a foreigner was nonetheless remarkable.

Fleming and Strobel sat in the backyard of Strobel's large stately house overlooking Lake Wannsee in the southwestern sector of Berlin. The home of three generations of the aristocratic Prussian Strobel family. Old wealth. While conservative, even perhaps inclined toward monarchy, the crude populist demagogue Adolf Hitler now in power was an affront to everything Strobel held dear.

A bright sunny spring afternoon, Strobel uncorked a bottle of Bordeaux. His wife Adele inside preparing dinner. They were expecting another couple for a small dinner party.

"Before Alfred and Gretchen arrive, I want to share the latest disturbing news," Strobel said. "Hitler made his case to the Reichswehr for support in his bid to succeed Hindenburg as president. In exchange, he vows to reduce the three million-strong SA. At the same time, he pledges to increase the size of the regular military. The General Staff has signed on to the bargain.

"A deal with the devil. Many senior officers not present believe the demented corporal stifled any organized dissent. Why should they believe Hitler? It is not certain he even holds enough control over the SA. Not likely that disgusting thug Ernst Röhm would willingly reduce his power base. Röhm feels secure enough to declare his ambition for control of Germany's military. Yet if Hitler achieves absolute power, he will do as he pleases."

"Hitler seems to hold that power already. Hindenburg is too old to hold him in check," Fleming said.

"I agree. In fact, Hindenburg might die any day. The point however becomes a matter of honor for the military. No matter how ill conceived. Once pledging alliance by oath, a German officer becomes duty bound to fulfill that commitment."

Strobel paused taking a sip of wine before adding, "There is something else. By support, Hitler means something more. You see the SA is also a problem for him. Too large and unruly to control. He expects the Reichswehr to participate in whatever plan he has to bring the SA under his control."

"Therefore you are saying the Reichswehr now supports the Nazi regime?"

"Yes. Perhaps even actively. The industrialists already have pledged support. With the military behind him, there is nothing to temper Hitler's ambitions. The megalomaniac seems to have no fear of risking Germany in another future European war. Does the new American president understand that?"

"Truth is I don't know. I do know there is a sizable amount of support for Hitler among German-Americans. As for the American government, not sure there exists concern for Hitler's territorial ambitions. Isn't that more a concern for the French and British?"

"You would think so. They may talk tough but I question their resolve to go to war again over territory of other countries. If it ever comes to that, it will likely involve Eastern Europe territory."

"You clearly know by now I share your disgust with Hitler and his Nazis. As a friend, I will tell you this in confidence, Ritter. I have a well-placed close friend in America with whom I communicate regularly. As a military attaché, my official reports go to the War Department. For now, Hitler is a political problem. The War Department is concerned only with military related information.

"Introducing me to many of your likeminded senior officers has provided valuable political intelligence. That is the providence of the United States State Department. Equivalent to your foreign ministry, and of course, the President. I keep my friend informed. He is a former foreign service officer with direct connections to those close to the President.

"I pass information to my friend. Without divulging me as the source, he shares that information with those that matter. I have no way of knowing the impact. I can assure you though, people in high places see the information I provide."

Strobel nodded. "I appreciate your efforts, Spencer. May I convey what you just shared with me with General Beck? America has a vested interest in European stability. As an army officer, he prefers not to trust political appointed diplomatic staff. Better officer to officer."

"Go ahead. I trust your judgment, Ritter"

"As a knowledgeable outsider, where do you see this heading?"

Fleming sighed. "Difficult to see any good coming to Germany with Hitler in power. If circumstances get out of hand, it appears obvious only the Army can save Germany from another disastrous European war."

****

Fleming's close personal association with Ritter von Strobel largely accounted for his successful flow of information back to the War Department. Largely centered on rearmament progress. However, the political intelligence provided to Allen Dulles seemed of greater importance. Much of that came from Kaczmarek in Warsaw and from Fleming's unexpected connection to the Abwehr.

Following their introduction at the embassy reception in October, Major Konrad Richter passed along an invitation to meet with his boss Lieutenant Colonel Hans Oster. An unusual gesture for a ranking officer of the German military intelligence service to meet with a foreign military attaché.

Oster was a tall lean distinguished looking officer with captivating light blue eyes. The meeting was privately with Oster in his office at Abwehr headquarters.

"A remarkable career in the American Army, Colonel Fleming. For an intelligence officer serving on the AEF General Staff in France, your combat decorations under fire suggest unusual initiative."

Before this meeting, Strobel briefed Fleming on Oster's background. Six years older than Fleming, he entered the military as an artillery officer in 1907. After seeing action on the Western Front in the first two years of the Great War, came promotion to captain assigned to the German General Staff. Oster's talents allowed him to remain in the downsized Reichswehr limited by the Treaty of Versailles to only 4,000 officers. Oster now was chief of the Abwehr Central Division that served as the administrative center for personnel and finances for the foreign intelligence and the counterintelligence branches.

Fleming smiled, "Finding myself in the wrong place at the wrong time, I simply took necessary measures to survive."

Oster returned the smile. "I suspect there was much more involved, but appreciate your modesty. As the military attaché for the most powerful nation in the world, I have of course researched your background thoroughly.

"I therefore wish to be candid, Colonel Fleming. I have a sense of your views regarding the current political situation of Germany. For a former enemy, you have surprising empathy for Germany."

"That is true, Colonel Oster. Might I ask how you determined that?"

"Certainly. I know Oberst Strobel very well. Let me say we share many views. He sees you as not only a personal friend but someone of outstanding character."

"I consider Oberst Strobel and his wife as my closest friends here in Berlin. Without beating around the bush, we do share views on the current Nazi government and Adolf Hitler."

"Thank you, Colonel. I hope you do not resent our interest in you, but we are also aware of your friendship with the outspoken political and social columnist, Bella Fromm. Since she associates with reporters with anti-Nazi sympathies, that only confirms what Strobel says. You do realize that Frau Fromm is Jewish?"

"Yes, of course. Frau Fromm does not hide her ethnicity. She comes from an old distinguished German family."

Oster's father was a pastor of an Alsatian French Protestant Church. The same general area where Fleming's mother was born. Fleming recalled Strobel's additional adjectives describing Oster. Intelligent, charming, yet brash, cynical, and volatile. A risk taker. Known as a notorious womanizer.

"How do you view the Nazi persecution of German Jews, Colonel?" Fleming asked.

"An obscenity. We did not lose the war because of the Jews. I served with many Jewish fellow officers in the war. Anti-Semitism exists throughout the world. However, state-sponsored pogroms makes Germany look the Russian barbarians."

Hard to tell Oster's personal feelings regarding Jews but another factor placing him against the Nazis.

Oster leaned forward over his desk, "There is no secret that Oberst Strobel is no fan of the Nazis. I share many his concerns. We particularly share the fear of Hitler's territorial ambitions. The precursor to such a disaster will of course be German rearmament and increasing the size of the armed forces. Sufficient to challenge Britain and France. How will the United States react to Germany breaking the terms of the Treaty of Versailles?"

"I can only give you my opinion, Colonel Oster. My sphere of intelligence is military not foreign policy."

"I ask this because you are far more than just a military attaché. You served in the war. Spent time consulting to the U.S. delegation on the peace treaty. Then you served in the occupation of the Rhineland. All diplomatic functions.

"You are as qualified to comment on American foreign policy just as much as your new ambassador. You both possess PhD degrees in history. The difference being Ambassador Dodd is out of his element. Mired down in negotiating repayment of American loans. He does not engage the German government with the kind of strength expected from someone representing the United States. Gives the impression your government is more concerned with financial issues than the larger implications stemming from the Nazi rise to power. Dodd carries little influence with the current government.

"You however, Colonel Fleming, demonstrate a wider interest in German affairs."

"Yes I do, Colonel Oster. To your question regarding the U.S. position on the Treaty of Versailles, I do not believe there would be substantive repercussions if Germany reneges on the terms. That is more an issue for Britain and France. Isolationism from European events is manifestly present in America.

"There is also a high degree of pro-German sentiment among the American population. A large German-American population. The Great War remembered as a tragedy. America dragged into what they saw as a European affair. Not likely any interest exists for participating in another European conflict."

Oster nodded in agreement. "Your newspapers suggest those same sentiments. Do you communicate with those in your government other than the Army?"

Wary of the question coming from German military intelligence, "I have a close personal friend that was formerly in the foreign service. We share letters discussing international affairs, but nothing not already reported by foreign newspaper correspondents."

Oster reflected for several moments before getting to the reason for the meeting. "Unfortunately, the exchange of information between respective foreign services does not always resolve a crisis. The German military wants a voice in any decision that might result in armed conflict. We simply want to ensure that vital information reaches the policy decision makers of other countries. Being in the intelligence business, we feel it best to convey sensitive information through each country's intelligence apparatus to avoid political filtering by diplomats."

Fleming took the statement to mean it allowed for the military to participate directly in German foreign policy. "Since the United States has no foreign intelligence service, I therefore become the next best alternative. A backdoor circumventing normal diplomatic channels whereby you can transmit information of a certain nature."

Oster smiled. "Precisely. Of course, that must be done discretely. Perhaps Major Richter might also become your personal friend. That would make for a convenient means of providing you information."

"Very good. Let me clarify one critical aspect of our relationship, Colonel Oster. Those in Washington will surely want to understand the source of this information. What do I say?"

"Obviously I wish to conceal the involvement of the Abwehr, at least as acting officially. Deniability always paramount. However, I will leave that to your discretion should the information prove sufficiently critical that establishing its authenticity becomes necessary."

Oster's proposal stunned Fleming. He was actually proposing to pass information to a foreign power. Knowing his anti-Nazi views by his references to outspoken Ritter von Strobel, Oster was flirting with treason. No mere modest risk considering the growing power of the SS and its SD branch becoming a rival to the Abwehr.

"Thank you, Colonel, for your confidence. I shall do everything possible to guard the source of any information you provide. For that matter, I also disguise my own involvement when conveying information beyond my official portfolio."

"Perhaps an indelicate question if I may ask, Colonel Fleming. All embassies use diplomatic codes for communication."

Monitored of course by the Abwehr. Is Oster implying U.S. diplomatic communications are insecure? What about the military cipher used for the War Department?

"Do you possess a secure channel of communication to which only you have access to the encryption?"

"Yes. Having some training in encryption, I am somewhat paranoid. There are certain pieces of information I prefer to transmit by means other than the assigned cipher for sending official communications. I dislike embassy cipher clerks becoming privy to confidential material. I also understand that any code can be susceptible to unwanted deciphering."

The last comment meant for Oster in case the Abwehr could read U.S. diplomatic signals traffic.

Oster nodded. "That is good. I thank you for meeting with me and sharing your frank comments. Unfortunately, for reasons of security, it is best if we do not meet again. Let us hope that another European war is not in our future. Goodbye, Colonel Fleming."

Fleming met Oster only that one time in October. After that, Major Richter became Lieutenant Colonel Oster's intermediary and eventually a friend. While Fleming and Richter got along well, both understood their relationship was a dangerous cooperation in the uncertain business of espionage.

Now fully immersed in covert activities, Fleming understood Richter's role. He was the cutout between Oster. Should something go crosswise, Oster could claim plausible deniability. There would be no record of meetings between him and Fleming except that initial introduction with the new American military attaché should anyone in German counterintelligence ever investigate. This meant the newly formed Nazi intelligence service within the SS, the Gestapo, or even Abwehr counterintelligence. Fleming did not know if Abwehr higher command authorized Oster's overture, or if Oster was acting independently.

A year earlier, Hermann Göring founded the Gestapo as a Prussian state police force. From its origin, intended as an instrument of ruthless intimidation and violence. When Göring transferred authority over the Gestapo to Himmler, it fell under Himmler's overall authority of the SS. Himmler saw the opportunity to combine the newly created Nazi intelligence service, the Sicherheitsdienst, with the Gestapo to create a powerful secret police. Himmler's second in command of the SS was Reinhard Heydrich. As current intelligence chief of the SD, Heydrich inherited additional command of the Gestapo.

Already establishing itself as an instrument of secret police terror, the Gestapo's reach now expanded across all of Germany backed by SD counterintelligence. A seamless union expanding repression exponentially. As the military intelligence service formerly responsible for all intelligence including espionage and counterintelligence, the Abwehr would now compete for power with the SS over control of foreign intelligence and domestic counterintelligence. As chief of the Gestapo, Heydrich had the added advantage of vast police manpower with unchecked power at his disposal.

In that first meeting with Fleming, Oster shared the struggle the Abwehr faced with the rival SS intelligence service, the Sicherheitsdienst. Oster had good reason for excess caution.

* * * *

While Spencer Fleming was captivated by Valeska Kaplinsky that first evening at the *Geisterstunde,* he had the same effect on Bella Fromm. They left the nightclub at one o'clock in the morning. In the taxi, Fromm reached over and placed her hand on his thigh. "This has been a wonderful evening. I am not ready for it to end. Perhaps we could go to your apartment?"

Fleming looked at her. He had not been with a woman for some time. Not since returning to Europe. Fromm possessed all the attributes he found attractive. Good looking, intelligent, self-assured.

He laid his hand over hers and gave the taxi driver his address. Since he knew her adult daughter lived with her, he said, "Won't your daughter be concerned when you do not return at a reasonable time?"

She smiled conspiratorially, "She knows I am celebrating my birthday. I also told her I had a handsome date for the night. Perhaps not to expect me home until tomorrow. Do you find me shamelessly bold, Spencer?"

"I would rather say you are a woman that knows what she wants."

Bella Fromm definitely knew what she wanted from lovemaking. Both in the giving and receiving. A very good night. Fleming felt some return to normalcy in the depressing atmosphere of Berlin. Yet as a Jew, he knew that Fromm's situation would likely change for the worse.

Thereafter, they periodically engaged in sexual relations as the mood and opportunity suited. More a physical expression of two people that cared for each other but chose to live separate lives.

Although somewhat protected by important conservative figures in Hitler's government, Fromm understood the growing danger for Jews. After persuading her daughter to immigrate to the United States, her periodic liaisons with Fleming become a refuge.

By the end of 1934, Fromm lost her job as the Nazis shutdown Jewish publications. Writing under a pseudonym, she continued publishing articles on politics with the few remaining anti-Nazi publications. Her principle outlet began feeding information to foreign correspondents. However, the loss of sufficient income from writing forced her to rejoin the family wine trading business.

With Fromm's vast network of connections, Fleming tapped into information on the plight of German Jews. With Nazi censorship, she provided material unlikely to become public in the United States or Europe. Allen Dulles promised to distribute the disturbing material to international news services, disguising attribution as unnamed sources within Nazi Germany.

By the end of 1934, Fleming considered the extent of his immersion into espionage. His sources now reached deeply into the Nazi regime. Major Kaczmarek continued to provide material from his Polish espionage network. Fleming's friendship with Ritter von Strobel provided a window into the alignment of the senior generals of the Reichswehr. The Army representing the only possible check to Hitler's territorial ambitions that might bring about war.

With the latest overture from some anti-Nazi faction within German military intelligence, Fleming realized how far his actions went beyond the official duties of military attaché. Hans Oster was offering secret information from within German intelligence. Either committing treason or running a disinformation operation. Fleming's position in Nazi Germany now became as dangerous as any battlefield.

CHAPTER 17

Berlin, German Reich | July 1934

The purge of the SA lasted three days. Not only did it decapitate the SA, but it also provided an opportunity to settle old scores. Far more than the officially reported eighty-five summary executions, the actual number ran into the hundreds. Each of Hitler's senior henchmen, Göring, Goebbels, and Himmler had their own lists. Reinhard Heydrich organized the death squads comprised of the SD security service and the Gestapo state political police. The Army high command colluded by providing logistical support while not interfering.

The coup posed a high risk for Heydrich had the plan failed. It was largely his plan including the totally fabricated basis that Röhm was planning an imminent coup against Hitler. An audacious deceit perpetrated even on Hitler followed by a multipronged surprise attack mounted against a well-organized paramilitary adversary numbering in the millions.

Everyone on the various lists died by summary execution. With systematic efficiency, the death squads reported in by ticking off the status using the assigned number for each victim. No attempt made for any semblance of judicial process. Murder on a vast scale. Justified for the security of the state. Even though Hitler later ordered all official records of the purge destroyed, the tally of victims painted a picture of the true nature of the violent purge. By any account, the death toll ran into the several hundreds, perhaps approaching 1000. Of this, only about 200 were SA. The lists prepared by Göring, Goebbels, and Himmler eliminated selected individuals of organizations opposing the National Socialist regime. Other victims targeted to settle personal scores.

The fate of former general, minister of defense, short-termed chancellor, and scheming rival to Hitler, Kurt von Schleicher, being a typical example.

On the morning of June 30 outside Schleicher's villa in Potsdam, armed men in trench coats and fedoras knocked on the front door. They shot him twice as he answered the door. Coming into the foyer at the sound of the shots, the gunmen then shot and killed Schleicher's wife.

Because of his association with Schleicher, General Ferdinand von Bredow, deputy defense minister in Schleicher's short-lived cabinet, suffered the same fate at his home in Berlin. The Army not even immune from the great blood purge.

Fleming knew this and other specifics of the murders from Major Richter, obtained from Abwehr sources within the SS.

"Here is a bit of interesting news. Two of the victims of the purge were Kurt Ernst and Edmund Heines, both senior SA officers." Richter said to Fleming. "However, eight other lower ranking SA also fell victim. A good example of the scope of the purge not only to remove the SA leadership, but also to get rid of those that knew too much.

"You see, it was Ernst that led a squad of ten SA to ignite the Reichstag last year. Everyone knew it was a Nazi plot not the communists, but until now, the specifics remained unknown. The single former communist convicted and executed was nothing more than a pathetic dupe. Mentally disturbed, but we now know also drugged when placed within the Reichstag.

"The otherwise highly secured Reichstag building had a secret entrance. A tunnel underneath Freidrich Ebertstrasse connected the building to the residence of the President of the Reichstag, Hermann Göring. This point of entry allowed the arsonists to place incendiary devices undisturbed then make their escape leaving behind the single scapegoat, the Dutch communist Van der Lubbe.

"A fellow named Heini Gewert escorted the SA arson team through the tunnel from the President's residence then throughout the darkened Reichstag. Gewert was a Nazi delegate to the Reichstag. He knew the building well."

Fleming asked, "How did you come by this information?"

Richter grunted disdainfully. "Gewert bragged about his involvement and his survival of the Night of the Long Knives purge due to Heydrich's personal protection."

The scope and audacity of the mass killings dressed up as essential to thwarting an imminent coup to topple the government stunned everyone in Germany. There remained no question about the ruthless nature of the Nazi regime. Previous concerns over the millions of SA marauding thugs targeting Jews and opposition political parties now overshadowed by something more sinister. Every German had reason to fear the Nazi secret police.

Bedridden and dying of lung cancer, President Hindenburg remained silent. Hitler now ruled Germany with unchecked power backed by the SS. Not only the Gestapo, but also a growing private army in the SS firmly under his control backed with an intelligence service. Unlike the vast numbers of the SA membership, acceptance into the SS was a rigorous process of selection. Intelligence, racial background, physical condition, and dedication to the Führer created an elite paramilitary force.

The SS was the instrument by which Hitler began pursuing his ambitions in earnest. The SS took over or closed the early concentration camps of the SA. Himmler's plans went far beyond mere internment of political enemies. He even created a special formation within the SS to administer and guard the camps. The SS-Totenkopfverbände would elevate brutality and eventually mass murder to an industrial level. The Gestapo arrested enemies of the state and feed them into a constantly growing network of concentration camps now organized as places of hard labor. The SD became an intelligence service to monitor every sector of Germany military and political life seeking out dissidents for arrest by the Gestapo.

Unlike others close to Hitler, Heinrich Himmler was the consummate subordinate. The functionary that always delivered.

Arguably the second most powerful figure in Germany. It fell to Himmler's organizational skills and dedication to hard work to translate Hitler's grandiose pronouncements into reality. Himmler's SS was the operational backbone of the Nazi Third Reich. Good reason the intelligence passed to Fleming by Kaczmarek's Polish network and Oster's Abwehr counterintelligence network focused largely on the SS.

* * * *

The purge of the entire SA leadership not only removed a possible threat to Hitler, it allowed him to assert complete control of the ranks of the SA, now exceeding 4,000,000 members. Still useful as auxiliary police, the additional manpower expanded the reach of the Gestapo. It also represented fertile recruiting ground for Hitler's intended expansion of the army in defiance of the limits imposed by the Treaty of Versailles.

Combined with backing from the conservative German institutions of the Reichswehr and the industrialist sector, it proved a masterstroke. Interestingly, the dramatic event did not result from Hitler's megalomaniacal delusions. Through devious manipulations, Hitler's most senior deputies progressively convinced him to move against his old ally and friend Ernst Röhm. Göring, Goebbels, and Himmler all had their reasons for destroying Röhm and suppressing the power of the SA. In Reinhardt Heydrich, the conspirators had a master of organization and intrigue. Combined with orchestrating the entirely fictional basis used to convince Adolf Hitler of the treachery of his oldest ally, Heydrich developed the ruthless execution plan that proved a resounding success.

To the outside world, it was an appalling display of totalitarian violence. None of that mattered to the Nazis now drunk with power. No foreign country recalled its ambassador. Richter even passed along the content of a confidential memo from Heydrich to Himmler saying *we hear only the powerless rhetoric of weak foreign enemies against our bold action. It shall be no different as we pursue resolution of the Jewish problem.*

Of equal importance, Hitler removed serious threat to his power from the military. Complicit in the purge to rid themselves of the rivalry from the vast numbers of the paramilitary SA, sufficiently tainted them, yet not enough to make Hitler beholding to them. Every officer knew the murder of two senior generals on the pretext of involvement with the SA in a coup conspiracy was a ridiculous fabrication. The opportunity for the military to rein in Adolf Hitler came and went.

* * * *

On August 2, President Paul von Hindenburg died. On August 19, in a plebiscite, the German people approved the merger of the presidency and chancellorship into a common office. Adolf Hitler became *Führer und Reichskanzler.* The last obstacle to absolute dictatorship overcome. With the backing of the Army and the industrial sector, the purge of the SA leadership, and the total suppression of any other political parties, Hitler could pursue his ambitious agenda without domestic opposition.

* * * *

The flow of information from Major Richter and Major Kaczmarek increased following Adolf Hitler's ascendancy to Führer. The perquisite for pursuit of Hitler's nationalistic ambitions rested on rearmament. To accomplish this, he must obscure rearmament efforts until sufficiently strengthened when Germany can then ignore threats to enforce the terms of the Treaty of Versailles.

While the Nazi regime went to great lengths to disguise German rearmament, it nonetheless was an open secret internationally. Difficult however for any one foreign nation to pressure Germany effectively. The only real recourse was trade sanctions. Unrealistic as every country struggled with the Great Depression. No appetite existed among the former allies of Britain, France, and the United States to act in concert against Germany.

German rearmament lay at the center of concern for Abwehr Lieutenant Colonel Hans Oster and Polish Intelligence Service Major Feliks Kaczmarek.

For Kaczmarek, former German occupied Polish territory would become a likely target for Hitler's territorial expansion, *Lebensraum,* as openly proposed in *Mein Kampf.*

For Oster and many in the German military, military adventurism would involve Germany in another war. Given Hitler's impatience and ignorance of military matters, this would likely be premature. Placed at a potential military disadvantage, another defeat could destroy Germany. The victors would never allow Germany to rise again to a level of threat after initiating two great wars. Stalin's aggressive industrialization of the Soviet Union already made them a potent threat to Germany if they again stood with Britain and France. Although damaged by the Great Depression, the United States remained the most powerful nation in the world.

Hitler also held a warped under appreciation of a strong navy. The British naval blockade during the Great War helped bring Germany economically to its knees, contributing to defeat. However, building a German fleet of capital ships from scratch sufficient to challenge British supremacy was not possible while simultaneously rebuilding the Army. Hitler compensated by pursuing the less costly strategy of submarines. Perhaps because of Göring's influence as chief of the Luftwaffe, Hitler placed much greater reliance on airpower rather than sea power.

Oster also understood the severe shortage of vital natural resources. The economic drain of rapid rearmament would eventually converge with the realities of limited access to militarily essential natural resources. This alone would propel Hitler to take Germany to war to secure those resources in captured territory.

The flow of information to Fleming became increasing dominated by rearmament. The level of German sophistication in international finance proved astonishing. Clearly not the product of the thuggish minds of the more prominent Nazis. While fed secret information from the Abwehr and the Poles, Fleming began his own investigations. As the American military attaché, his duties gave him a certain level of access to German industry. While those executives divulged no secrets, nationalistic instincts and sheer hubris often led to candid revelations. Combined with the flow of covert intelligence, Fleming's reports to the War Department and Allen Dulles provided valuable insights.

* * * *

Having coffee at their favorite cafe, Richter said, "Here is some information those in the American financial community might find interesting. A brilliant scheme to conceal government funding of rearmament. Conceived by one of Hitler's most creative enablers, Hjalmar Schacht, President of the Reichsbank. Ever heard of Metallurgische Forschungsgesellschaft m.b.H.? In English, the Society for Metallurgical Research."

"No."

"Schacht initially intended the scheme to rejuvenate Germany's dire economic problems. With little state funds available, his idea was to issue public debt in exchange for newly produced goods. In this way, the circulation of new money balanced with the increase in gross national product. I do not pretend to understand economics but others say this unconventional idea was brilliant because it avoided inflation. By all accounts, it is working well.

"However, that same process also provides a mechanism for concealment of massive government funding for rearmament. Schacht convinced several of the largest armaments manufacturers to capitalize a shell corporation. Krupp, Vereinigte Stahlwerke, Siemens, Gutehoffnungshütte, and Rheinmetall. On paper, a private company with no direct involvement with the government. However, MEFO has only two directors. One appointed by the Reich Ministry of Defense, the other by the Reichsbank.

"Works like this. The National Socialist government issues five-year promissory debt instruments. MEFO then contracts with manufacturers, paying invoices with what are called Mefo bills. The manufacturer redeems them at any bank at a discounted value. Essentially these debt instruments become cash equivalent since they are backed by the German central bank, the Reichsbank."

Fleming said, "So this scheme hides government rearmament financing by interposing this shell company. Keeps all the transactions within the private sector and off the public books. Creative accounting. Does production activity for rearmament account for a significant portion of Germany's economic recovery?"

"I am told a large percentage," Richter said. "There is more to this. Are you aware of reconstruction loans made to Germany by the United States?"

"Only what I read in the newspapers," Fleming said. He of course knew more than that. Three Wall Street syndicates put up most of these loans. All clients of Allen Dulles' law firm Sullivan & Cromwell. All concerned about the prospects of repayment. The principal subject of Ambassador Dodd's negotiations.

With a wry smile, Richter said, "a good deal of that money is funding German rearmament. Much of it flows to armaments manufacturers obscured through these debt instruments. The private transactions hide the nature of the economic activity created by these corporations.

* * * *

Major Kaczmarek's Polish network also contributed sensitive details on German rearmament. Illustrative of circumventions of restrictions imposed by the terms of the Treaty of Versailles, one encrypted message read:

'Of interest is Deutsche Verkehrsfliegerschule. Funded by the Reichswehr. Established in 1925 as an air transport school for training commercial pilots and aircraft maintenance personnel. The number of students is inconsistent with the limited German commercial aviation industry. Instructors are al former military pilots suggesting this is training for military personnel. Headquarters and principal operational location is Broitzem Flugplatz near Braunschweig. If this is a clandestine military operation, proceed carefully with any follow up. Reports about the excesses of the secret police are appalling. Your diplomatic status might prove inadequate protection. FK'

Another coded communication addressed naval rearmament, even more restricted by the Treaty of Versailles. *'Several German shipyards set up a Dutch company over ten years ago. Ingenieurskantoor voor Scheepsbouw. IvS is a joint venture marine engineering design firm of AG Vulcan in Stettin and Hamburg, and Krupp-owned Germaniawerft in Kiel and AG Weser in Bremen. The Reichsmarine funds IvS. Sources report completed design of the next generation of the German attack submarine type VIIA. Unconfirmed intelligence indicates sea trials possibly underway in the Baltic of a prototype constructed in Helsinki. FK'*

* * * *

Fleming invited Ritter von Strobel and his wife Adele to the *Geisterstunde.* Not only a particularly valuable source of candid information on the political views of senior army officers, but his closest friend in Berlin.

In the upside down world of Berlin since Adolf Hitler's ascendency, there remained few venues for cultured entertainment. The pervasive fear engendered by the sudden decent into a police state dampened much of the enthusiasm for public entertainment. The *Geisterstunde* was an exception. Perhaps since its clientele included a cross section of the powerful and wealthy and occasionally foreign diplomats like Fleming. Perhaps for the refined entertainment.

It was several weeks since Fleming spent an evening at the *Geisterstunde.* Listening to Valeska Kaplinsky his special indulgence. Kaplinsky was the one bright exception in otherwise depressing Berlin. Dulles' generous retainer allowed him the indulgence. He assured Strobel the evening was his treat. Falsely assuring him his government position provided an expense account.

It was the first time here for the Strobels. The dinner was excellent as was the French wine. The elegant dining room appointments and orchestral accompaniment set a complimentary environment. Kaplinsky's performance this evening was totally devoted to Italian opera arias. Like Fleming, she captivated the Strobels.

With a generous tip, Fleming ensured a front row table. Finishing her first performance of the evening, Kaplinsky, dressed in one of her signature form-fitting dresses with a long slit revealing a gorgeous right leg, made her way to their table.

Fleming and Strobel immediately stood.

"Colonel Fleming so good to see again. And your guests?"

"Let me introduce my friends Oberst Ritter von Strobel and his beautiful wife Adele."

"Welcome to the *Geisterstunde,*" Kaplinsky said as Strobel kissed her offered hand.

Adele Strobel said, "A thoroughly magnificent performance, Frau Kaplinsky. I particularly enjoyed your choice of arias. Your remarkable voice can bring tears."

"You are very kind, Frau Strobel."

Turning to Fleming who then kissed her hand, Kaplinsky said, "How is Bella? I have not seen her for many weeks."

Fleming said, "Unfortunately, being Jewish, she can no longer work in journalism. A tragedy for someone as talented as Bella. She now works at her family's wine distribution business in Potsdam. Mostly avoids central Berlin. Sadly, her daughter has already emigrated to America. Bella should leave as well, but she is stubborn. Germany is her home."

Kaplinsky's expression saddened. "If you see her, please tell her to write me."

"I will," Fleming said.

"So good to meet you Oberst Strobel and Frau Strobel. Please come again."

Kaplinsky unexpectedly touched Fleming's arm. "And please do not remain a stranger, Colonel Fleming. Next time I would love to share some time with you to hear about America."

After Kaplinsky walked away to make her rounds greeting the other patrons, Adele Strobel said, "Breaks my heart that someone like Bella can be persecuted simply because she is Jewish. Will this ever end?"

"Not likely," Strobel said under his breath followed by a sigh.

The Strobel's met Bella Fromm when Fleming brought her once to a small social gathering at the Strobel residence. Her lively and often disparaging comments about many of the leading Nazis elicited much laughter among Strobel's uninhibited anti-Nazi friends.

The news about Bella Fromm distressed Adele. "Please excuse me for a few minutes," She said and then left the table for the restroom.

Strobel shook his head. "Adele will be fine. Unfortunately, her doctor for many years is Jewish. No longer able to practice on non-Jewish patients. She does not understand this persecution of German Jews.

"Let us however enjoy the rest of the evening. I promised Adele not to discuss politics. She tells me I cannot discuss Hitler without flying into a rage. Therefore, I shall change to a more pleasant subject. It appears you have made another conquest, Spencer. I believe the remarkably beautiful Frau Kaplinsky was flirting with you."

****

In September 1934, the NSDAP held its sixth Party Congress. A gigantic stage-managed rally culminated at the Zeppelin Meadows outside Nuremberg. Attended by 700,000 Nazi supporters. The purpose of the event was propaganda. A melding of spectacle, quasi-religiosity, and nationalism. The night was marked with torch-lit parades of thousands. Albert Speer devised a spectacular effect he called a Cathedral of Light by arraying 152 searchlights to cast vertical beams surrounding the grounds.

Using Hollywood-like filming techniques with many camera crews, filmmaker Leni Riefenstahl created the technically acclaimed documentary film *Triumph des Willens*.

CHAPTER 18

Berlin, German Reich | Spring 1935

Otto Decker was born to a middleclass German Bavarian family. At age seventeen, like others his age, he enlisted in the German Army in 1916. The Great War now in its third year turned into a struggle for German survival. Assigned to the 86th Reserve Regiment of the 18th Reserve Infantry Division, he saw his first action at the Battle of the Somme. The joint offensive of French and British forces intended to hasten defeat by crushing the opposing German forces. Over three million soldiers fought for almost four months resulting in over a million casualties. The conflict accomplished nothing other than an unparalleled bloodletting of attrition warfare.

Decker survived unwounded. Six months later, he was not so lucky. Now as a senior sergeant, he sustained a serious wound at the Battle of Arras putting him out of the war. As with many soldiers, he joined the Freikorps after the Armistice. Possessing an iron cross, he rose in stature to command a company of SA paramilitaries supporting Adolf Hitler's abortive Beer Hall Putsch in 1923.

Decker rose within the SA and eventually accepted into the elite SS in March 1933 with the rank of Untersturmführer, a second lieutenant. Assigned to the Bavarian Political Police, his first boss became Heinrich Müller. Later he would connect with Reinhard Heydrich who he knew from service in the Freikorps.

That year, Decker received the Blood Order Medal of the Nazi Party. Limited to participants of the Munich Putsch of 1923, the prestigious metal only added to his recognition as an able SS officer. The perfect combination of intelligence, ruthlessness, and dedication to Adolf Hitler.

In the SS, he found a new home after wandering in the wilderness of the difficult years since the Great War. Here was a new order he could follow. An officer in an elite paramilitary formation. The Gestapo political police provided opportunity for exercising initiative. Not only able to apply his intelligence, but also exercise power over those he saw as enemies. The weak functionaries that sold out Germany in 1919. The communists and socialists wishing to discard everything sacred to German identity. The perfidious Jews the worst. Already imbued with anti-Semitic feelings, the Gestapo provided the capacity to participate in organized persecution of these enemies of Germany.

When Göring handed over control of the Gestapo in April 1934 to SS chief Heinrich Himmler, it expanded from a Prussian police organization to encompass Germany nationwide. Hitler appointed Himmler chief of all political and criminal police throughout Germany. By decree, Hitler also exempted the Gestapo from any judicial oversight. Himmler named Reinhard Heinrich as chief of this consolidated state police. Heydrich now presided over the means of unrestrained Nazi repression.

Himmler and Heydrich immediately began installing their own personnel in key positions of the Gestapo. Several came from the Bavarian Police. Heydrich moved to Berlin, taking with him Heinrich Müller as his operations chief. Impressed by Decker's work, Müller selected Decker for his personal staff in Berlin.

Now promoted to Hauptsturmführer, equivalent to captain, Decker had arrived. The years of toiling through the difficult decade of the twenties now behind him. The years of breaking heads and even killing enemies of Germany brought him within the circle of the new elite. The distinctive black uniform with white embellishments emblematic of his status.

Although lacking the educational background of many within the SS, his intelligence combined with instincts elevated him close to the real power within the new Reich. As a personal aide to Heinrich Müller, Decker's power exceeded his rank. Employing hard work, he consistently impressed Müller as well as Heydrich. Not an insignificant accomplishment.

* * * *

Heinrich Müller was a singular anomaly in the SS hierarchy. As former head of the Munich Political Police, Müller became a decided enemy to the Nazis during the attempted Beer Hall Putsch of 1923. His talents were such that none of this derailed his rise to power once the Nazis seized power in early 1933. Himmler's pragmatism for acquiring professional expertise soon elevated Müller to criminal inspector in November 1933.

The reasons for this twofold. Müller was the consummate bureaucrat. A workaholic at home with reports, notes, statistics, and regulations. No mere record keeper, Müller possessed a dark Machiavellian character. His advancement stemmed from efficient use of denouncements, conspiracies, torture, and secret executions. Everything geared to his self-interests. In terms of ruthlessness, only Heydrich rivaled him. Müller's success derived from his ability to implement Heydrich's orders into successful action.

* * * *

In terms of ruthlessness, deviousness, confidence, and self-promotion, there was no equal to Reinhard Heydrich. Not part of the Nazi old guard, Heydrich only joined the Nazi Party in 1931 and the SS the same year. Quickly becoming a favorite of Adolf Hitler and indispensable to Heinrich Himmler's ambitions, he rose rapidly to the top of the growing SS. Heydrich's devotion to secrecy and intrigue even made Heinrich Himmler uneasy at times.

By 1935, Heydrich was third in the chain of command directing change within every fabric of German life. Hitler rarely gave orders, relying instead on swiping pronouncements. While

Himmler anticipated the Führer's intentions, he too was vague as to the means for translating these into tangible plans of action. Not so with Heydrich. A risk-taking man of action possessed of exceptional organizational skills, Heydrich consistently delivered. Hitler reportedly called Heydrich the man with the iron heart. Enemies and subordinates alike respected Heydrich's pragmatic ruthlessness to achieve results.

Reinhard Heydrich came from an East Prussian family of some social standing. His father founded the Halle Conservatory of Music providing the family with comfortable wealth. With his mother teaching piano, Heydrich developed a passion for music and became an accomplished violinist.

Too young to participate in the Great War, the economic distress in Germany with hyperinflation during the early 1920s hit the family hard. With the inability for families to afford the luxury of a musical education, the conservatory collapsed. The young Heydrich now needed to pursue a stable career. Joining the Reichsmarine in 1922 at the age of eighteen offered both stability and a measure of prestige in militaristic Prussia.

Heydrich served in the Reichsmarine until 1931, rising to the rank of lieutenant. The military regime suited him well. Tall at six feet three inches, he was also an accomplished athlete. Stationed at Kiel on the Baltic, he won the Baltic Sea sailing championship in a twenty-foot sailboat. Attracted to fencing at an early, Heydrich continued throughout his life to remain in world-class form.

Heydrich cut an elegant figure. Always impeccably dressed, tall, handsome, blond, blue-eyed, he cut a dashing figure. Women thought so. His appearance therefore enabled him to indulge his singular vice. Not only attracted to women, his inclinations ran to sexual obsession.

His womanizing cost him his career in the navy in 1931.

Exceptionally able, he served as an intelligence officer under Wilhelm Canaris. However, because of his arrogance, his fellow officers generally disliked him. Notorious for his countless affairs, a former lover filed a formal complaint over breach of promise after learning of Heydrich's intention to marry another woman. The allegation reached Kreigsmarine commander Admiral Erich

Raeder who dismissed the unpopular Heydrich from the service for conduct unbecoming an officer.

A devoted Nazi because of her brother, Heydrich's new wife, the former Lina von Osten, encouraged him to apply for membership in the SS. The timing fortuitous. Heinrich Himmler was looking to create an internal counterintelligence service within the SS. Although only a junior naval intelligence officer, Heydrich impressed Himmler. Overselling his intelligence credentials and aided by his outsized confidence, Himmler hired him on the spot.

Regardless how Heydrich came to his position, his many skills immediately made him indispensable to Himmler. Heydrich was perfect for translating the darkest of tasks conceived by Hitler and Himmler into action. Brilliant, clever, bold, and ruthless, Heydrich took over operational command of the Schutzstaffel within a few years.

Yet fundamental inclinations did not change. Under the guise of his prominent position as head of the Nazi Party's intelligence service and German secret police, he was free to indulge his sexual appetites. The marriage bed proved an inadequate outlet. He took every opportunity to avail himself of Berlin brothels. Who would possible dare to denounce him?

Reinhard Heydrich frequently used Kaplinsky' exclusive call girl service, often staging orgies with selected SS subordinates. He was aware that most of the prostitutes were also employees of the *Geisterstunde.* Since the Gestapo knew everything, Heydrich also knew that Valeska Kaplinsky must also be involved with her lawyer in the high-class prostitution service.

Heydrich further appreciated the *Geisterstunde* with its cultured clientele and entertainment. Kaplinsky's singing of opera arias and the occasional solo violin performance made the musically inclined Heydrich a devoted patron. For someone with Heydrich's sexual appetite, Kaplinsky's physical beauty must have also been an attraction.

* * * *

A week following their evening at the *Geisterstunde,* Fleming was enjoying wine on the patio of Strobel's villa. A perfect late spring afternoon on Saturday. Fleming was there early for dinner. Becoming a frequent guest, Adele Strobel loved his company. Out of earshot, she told Fleming that her husband considers him a close friend. Delighted to be able to discuss politics with a fellow army officer without fear of reprisal in this awful atmosphere of the Nazi secret police. As for Adele, she loved to hear about America.

Strobel said, "You recall me mentioning at the nightclub that I had some information to share. Did you ever meet Ernst Brandi during your tenure in Koblenz?"

"No. I remember the name though. Something to do with mining?"

"Brandi is the chairman of Bergbauverein, the big mining consortium in the Rhineland. We spent considerable time together back then. Brandi is your typical industrialist. A conservative of course. A monarchist back then. Today, I am not so sure, other than Adolf Hitler scares the hell out him. Anyway, while on business in Berlin, he paid me a visit to discuss his concerns."

"What specifically troubles him enough to pay you a visit?"

"Rearmament for one thing. This Gestapo secret police for another."

Fleming said, "Doesn't rearmament represent a great economic opportunity for German mining?"

"Certainly. Yet Brandi realizes that economic activity from military goods production is a dead end. It must eventually lead to another war given Hitler's ambitions. Brandi welcomes Hitler's moves to get out from under reparations and the continued boycotting of Germany exports by the French and British Commonwealth. He disagrees with most everything else about the Nazi regime. Rather see the German economy restored by conventional means."

Fleming added with a note of skepticism, "I assume he welcomed the return of the Saar Region to Germany last month."

Strobel said, "Conceptually he agrees with its return to Germany through the plebiscite. However, the 90% vote in favor of returning to Germany came as a result of violent Nazi agitation. Opposition groups harassed by provocateurs. Undercover agents of the Gestapo and the Sicherheitsdienst des Reichsführers-SS ensured the voting result.

"Hitler dispelled any question about where rearmament is heading with his announcement to reorganize the Reichswehr into the Wehrmacht representing the unified elements of the German military. Reconstitute the General Staff and introduce conscription to raise the manpower of the army to 550,000."

"That must please the Army," Fleming said.

"To the extent it removes foreign imposed restrictions. To those like me, that manpower target is just an initial number. Hitler plans to create an army capable of challenging France or the Soviet Union. Then he will use it to expand German territory by military means."

Fleming sat silently waiting for Strobel to get to the point of telling him this.

"Brandi confessed to me the substance of a secret meeting two years ago. It took place in the residence of the President of the Reichstag, Hermann Göring. Hitler, Göring, and Hjalmar Schacht, President of the Reichsbank, strong-armed two dozen industrialists to fund the election campaign of the NSDAP for the March 1933 election."

"Did they?"

"Yes. To the tune of two million Reichsmarks. Bergbauverein alone contributed 600 thousand. The others included executives or board members from Krupp, I.G Farben, Opel, Winsterstall, Siemens, and Demag. Here is a full list of all the attendees and their pledged amounts to the NSDAP provided by Brandi."

While Fleming looked at the list, Strobel continued.

"Of course these leaders of German industry saw the NSDAP as the only viable conservative alternative for a stable government. They also saw it as an investment to share in the benefits of backing a likely NSDAP electoral success."

"Why did Brandi feel compelled to tell you this, Ritter?"

"I believe to signal to me there are some in private industry that now regret enabling Adolf Hitler."

"Really? Why is that? Seems their investment is already paying off. German rearmament will be profitable business."

"I asked Brandi that same question. He only stated his personal discomfort with Hitler. Like many of us in the Army, he understands the threat of taking Germany into another war. Left to Hitler, that likely might happen before Germany possessed sufficient military strength. The man is a megalomaniac, obsessed with *Lebensraum*.

"And like many of us, Brandi is appalled by the excesses of the police state. This unreasoned persecution of the Jews invoking East European pogroms of the last century paints Germany as a country of barbarians. Like me, Brandi is a Christian. Hitler offends his morality as it does me. Brandi sees the Army as the only German institution not completely corrupted by the Nazis."

"Ritter. You must be careful. If Brandi recognizes your anti-Nazi sympathies, you are being dangerously indiscreet. Your rank in the Army might not be enough protection."

"I appreciate your concern. Hitler needs the Army. Any attempt to purge senior officers would likely provoke a coup d'état. His SS is not enough to protect him."

Possibly, yet Fleming considered the success of the Night of the Long Knives. A pervasive secret police backed by growing numbers of armed SS could embolden someone of Adolf Hitler's unstable temperament. Identify and purge a dissident cabal of anti-Nazi generals not that farfetched.

"Enough of politics. Let's play another game of chess and enjoy our wine before dinner."

Strobel reset the chessboard. "Although humbling to play against you, Spencer, concentrating on the game allows me to divert my thoughts for a time from more troubling matters."

After losing the game, Strobel said, "From here on out, I shall swallow my pride and endeavor to improve my chess skills. Yet would you be so kind to enlighten me where I went wrong allowing you take that last game? I thought I had a particularly strong position."

"You did. You played a strong game up to when your queen took the pawn."

"Had I taken the seemingly obvious move to castle, I believe I would have been in more serious difficulty," Strobel said.

"Correct. However, you had other better options. Let me show you." Fleming reconstructed the position of the critical pieces from several prior moves. "With your king and queen so far apart, easy to miss my looming threat. The flaw was the capture of my pawn by your queen. A subtle trap. It led to the unexpected discovered check in the next move, subsequently leading to the forced loss of your queen. From there you were down not only a major piece but it also destroyed the collective positional strength of your remaining pieces. Those couple of moves meant the end."

CHAPTER 19

Berlin, German Reich | Summer 1935

Those like Strobel, Oster, Richter, Kaczmarek, and apparently even certain industrialists harbored concerns of Hitler leading Germany into another war through his territorial ambitions. Those concerns not hypothetical as reflected by events in Austria the prior year.

In 1934, Hitler called on Heydrich's SD to devise a takeover of the Austrian government. Created from the remains of the former Habsburg Austrian-Hungarian Empire following the Great War, the hated Treaty of Versailles created the First Austrian Republic. Hitler coveted his German-speaking homeland. As in Germany, the years since 1919 saw violent clashes between factions of the political right and left. In 1933, the right achieved power with Engelbert Dollfuss of the Fatherland Front becoming chancellor. Unlike German Nazism, the Austrian Fatherland Front was organized along the lines of Italian Fascism and remained fully aligned with the Catholic Church.

The Dollfuss regime advocated Austrian nationalism and independence from Germany. Totally at odds with the banned Austrian German Worker's Party supporting union with Germany. As an Austrian, Hitler's first territorial ambition was inclusion of Austria within the German Reich. Direct military annexation was not yet an alternative. German rearmament was just beginning. Toppling the Dollfuss government might however bring the Austrian Nazis to power.

Following within weeks of the successful purge of the SA, an emboldened Adolf Hitler turned his sights on Austria. The plan called for supporting shock troops of the Austrian Nazi SS to storm the Vienna chancellery while other units seized radio and telephone communications centers.

The attempted coup d'état occurred on July 25 with 145 Austrian Nazis wearing uniforms of the Austrian civil guard storming the chancellery. The armed assault seriously wounded Chancellor Dollfuss. Refusing to sign his resignation, Dollfuss eventually died, but hours later. During the delay, Austrian troops and police loyal to the government retook control of the government. With the Dollfuss government closely aligned with Fascist Italy, Mussolini reacted strongly by mobilizing five divisions poised on the Brenner frontier to dissuade Germany from taking military action.

Without immediate success and consolidation, the coup failed. However, Hitler did not intend to give up his plan for annexing Austria. Reverting to the methods that brought him to power, Hitler turned to Himmler and the SS.

That meant Austria became another project for Reinhard Heydrich. He was to engineer a campaign of destroying opposition from within. The weapons included intimidation, terrorism, and selective murder of opposition leaders. With an active base of Austrian Nazis backed by a sizeable paramilitary, Heydrich's SD had resources in place to destabilize the Austrian government limited in the size of their standing army by the Treaty of Versailles.

Heydrich delegated one of his ablest senior officers to the Austrian campaign, SD Sturmbannführer Johann Pfeiffer.

Like Heydrich, Pfeiffer came from a conservative middle class educated family. After earning a law degree then experiencing difficulty finding a position during the Great Depression, he joined the Bavarian political police. Soon after, he joined the Nazi Party. In 1932, a high ranking SS officer named Werner Best recruited him to the SS. Best knew Pfeiffer from studying law together at the University of Heidelberg. Heydrich recognized talents in Pfeiffer similar to his own. A sharp mind with a decided inclination toward intrigue.

Pfeiffer's role in the failed Austrian coup was that of liaison with the Austrian SS. It was Pfeiffer that rigorously pressed the Austrians not to delay while waiting for Dollfuss to sign a resignation. Ignored by the Austrian Nazis, the hesitation failed to consolidate the coup by neutralizing army command centers that retook control with units loyal to the government. With his understanding of the dynamics in Austrian, Pfeiffer remained integral to SD covert efforts to destabilize Austria.

Heydrich also tapped him to begin a much more delicate project. Pfeiffer was to head a small select taskforce of SD and Gestapo to expand the dossiers of all senior military officers. Identify their political views and those of their families. Assess their military records to understand their behavioral traits. In particular, identify their weaknesses. That included the military intelligence branch, the Abwehr.

****

In January, the Abwehr acquired a new chief, Navy Captain Wilhelm Canaris. The outgoing chief warned Canaris about the increasing competitive pressure from Reinhard Heydrich head the of Nazi Sicherheitsdienst des Reichsführers-SS, the SD. Heydrich's ambition was to replace the Abwehr by taking over German foreign intelligence and counterintelligence functions.

By 1935, the Abwehr was an accomplished foreign intelligence service. Canaris had a long career in naval intelligence before his posting to a field command where Heydrich served as a junior officer. Canaris was every bit the cunning and conspiratorial manipulator as Heydrich. He felt confident in managing a coexistence with his former subordinate.

Irrespective of the prior association between Canaris and Heydrich, the antagonism between the Abwehr and the SD increased. At this time, Canaris appeared fully in support of the Nazi regime. Nonetheless, as a military professional, he disliked everything about the pseudo-military SS and its chief Heinrich Himmler in particular. As for Reinhard Heydrich his former naval subordinate, he recognized a talented adversary.

Cautious and aware of his new boss's political inclinations, Hans Oster excluded Canaris from his select group of anti-Nazi conspirators.

* * * *

"Gentlemen. We have a new task to take on. A far-reaching mission whereby the future of the Third Reich might rest. I am speaking about the Wehrmacht," Reinhard Heydrich said to Heinrich Müller and Otto Decker of the Gestapo, and Johann Pfeiffer of the SD assembled in his office.

"The task is to expand existing dossiers and develop new ones for every army officer of the rank of major or higher, or korvetten-kapitän of the navy. What I require is a full assessment of their political leanings, skills, and most of all weaknesses. Their habits and social environment. Sexual proclivities. Not hearsay rumors but substantive information, ideally with corroboration. More detailed the higher in rank. Look at their wives and deeply into their family history.

"The code name for the mission is *Operation Versteckter Schatz*. Sturmbannführer Pfeiffer will be in charge. The difficult part will be to conceal this from appearing a direct attack on the military establishment. *Versteckter Schatz* shall be a work in process. It will go on indefinitely. Now, I would like to hear your thoughts about how best to begin."

Müller spoke up, "Since this is a labor-intensive task, we must use all our available resources masqueraded as broad policy. That means much of the effort must fall to the Gestapo. I suggest we roll this out in the form of a new security directive applicable to background investigation of anyone in government position.

"Very good. Thank you, Standartenführer Müller," Heydrich said.

Decker added, "We define a set of criteria to filter material of particular interest to investigate that officer further. We largely ignore civilian officials unless uncovering something significant. We therefore disguise our targeted interest of the military from our own people. Eventually it becomes standard operating procedure for everyone in government service."

"While that broad effort is put into effect, I will assemble a list of those officers already with questionable loyalties for special attention," Pfeiffer said.

"Not only those with questionable loyalties, Sturmbannführer, everyone. To achieve the Führer's objectives we must ruthless deploy all devices to ensure the military follows any order without hesitation. That includes those seemingly loyal, but possibly disinclined to act contrary to other respected general officers." Heydrich said.

"Of course, Sir."

"Now that we have a new chief of the Abwehr, start *Versteckter Schatz* there," Heydrich said. "Controlling the Abwehr is essential to insuring loyalty of the Wehrmacht.

* * * *

Weeks later, Pfeiffer made his first report to Heydrich.

"You of course are familiar with the new Abwehr chief Wilhelm Canaris so I will add more recent intelligence," Pfeiffer said, avoiding any awkward resurrection of details of Heydrich's shortened naval career.

"The High Command approved Canaris as a compromise candidate with the departure of Kapitän Patzig. Reliable sources suggest Patzig manipulated the selection of Canaris as his successor. With the majority of Abwehr officers from the army, Patzig convinced Admiral Raeder that an army officer would be selected unless he backed Canaris who Raeder dislikes.

"Canaris has extensive ties to Spain. Speaks six languages. Shrewd and experienced in plots and intrigues. While aware of the background details of the Lohmann Affair, the financial scandal of misappropriations of naval funds, he avoided direct implication. Before coming to the Abwehr, Canaris was deeply involved with the Spanish involving secret German naval rearmament projects including training of German U-boat commanders.

"The elusive Canaris seems to have extricated himself from scandal. Canaris has also been a supporter of national socialism since the war. Nothing found recently changes that assessment. However, he clearly remains a military man. He shall likely remain a formable competitor to the Sicherheitsdienst. Unlike his predecessor, Canaris will not get into direct confrontations with Reichsführer Himmler, but likely will work against the Sicherheitsdienst using more subtle methods when differences arise."

Unlike Canaris whose entire naval career involved him in continual secret affairs, Patzig was more a naval commander used to direct action. Abwehr sponsored reconnaissance flights over Poland endangering Hitler's secret plans for eventual invasion of Poland by contravening indirect orders from the Führer resulting in pressure for a change in Abwehr leadership.

"Yes. I would agree with that assessment of Canaris. He is a clever old fox," Heydrich said. "The question remains, where does the threat lie within the Abwehr, Pfeiffer?"

"We have not uncovered concrete evidence, but we must keep a close watch on Oberstleutnant Hans Oster. Oster heads the Central Division which broadly controls personnel and financing of foreign intelligence and counterintelligence operations."

Heydrich interrupted, "Other than his position, what raises concern over Oster's loyalty to the Führer?"

"His associations. Oster is charming and gregarious. He maintains a wide circle of relationships within the Wehrmacht and other governmental institutions, especially the foreign ministry."

"Hardly unusual for an intelligence officer engaged in foreign activities," Heydrich said.

"No, Sir. It is more about his routine interactions with certain individuals. Several have dossier entries raising serious questions about their political views. Mostly army and foreign ministry individuals. I have added them to the list for advanced scrutiny."

"How deeply have we infiltrated the Abwehr?"

"Insufficient for our needs. Obvious by the lack of internal intelligence. I have raised it to the highest priority. Unfortunately, at the Abwehr Berlin headquarters, we have only two low-level sources currently."

"Do they understand the recipient of their information?"

"Yes, Sir. The Gestapo. Led to believe they are part of a wider group within the Abwehr tasked to maintaining vigilance for any reactionary behavior detrimental to the Reich. These two have personal reasons for betraying their military oath to secrecy. Further penetration of the Abwehr has proved difficult. I have assigned someone dedicated solely to look for existing Abwehr personnel that might be converted to our purpose."

"Very well. Anything further that raises suspicions about Oster?"

"Yes, Sir. A combination of circumstances that might suggest he harbors anti-National Socialist views. Oster is the son of a Protestant pastor. Served on the Western Front until 1916 then promoted to captain and assigned to the General Staff. Regarded as sufficiently talented to remain in the reduced Reichswehr limited to only 4,000 officers by the Treaty of Versailles. He served under Franz Halder who currently commands the 7th Infantry Division in Munich. According to sources, they remain close personal friends.

"Oster's service record labels him as brash, cynical, opinionated, and sometimes reckless. An adulterous affair led to scandal. Compelled to resign the Reichswehr, General Ferdinand von Bredow, chief of the Abwehr at the time hired him. Bredow reinstated his commission in the army with the rank of oberstleutnant."

Heydrich said, "And of course Bredow was eliminated as a co-conspirator of Schleicher in the purge last year. You feel Oster may harbor resentment?"

"Undoubtedly he will feel some sense of resentment. To the extent he might act on it is uncertain. However, considering his behavioral traits, that may be possible."

"Anything else?"

"There is another Abwehr officer, Major Konrad Richter. Works directly for Oster. He is of interest because of his close friendship with the American military attaché Lieutenant Colonel Spencer Fleming."

Heydrich interjected, "Why is that of interest?"

"Fleming's name crops up as a close personal friend of Oberst Ritter von Strobel. Fleming is a frequent visitor to Strobel's residence. Strobel is a senior officer on the personal staff of Generaloberst Ludwig Beck."

Heydrich said, "Ah, the difficult General Beck."

Beck was defacto Chief of Staff under the disguise of the Truppenamt since 1933, now officially Chief of Staff of the Army High Command, the OKH, under the reorganized Wehrmacht. It was commonly known that Beck disagreed with Hitler's plans for annexing Austria and Czechoslovakia. Beck also disliked the increasingly totalitarian aspects of Hitler's police state.

Pfeiffer continued, "Strobel is known to share Beck's views. Outspoken about his contempt for the SS. From an old Prussian military family with modest wealth. With Strobel's anti-National Socialism views, he certainly conveys his opinions to his American friend. He is at the top of our list for intense scrutiny. These mutual close associations with the American military attaché raise questions."

"Does Oster frequently meet with Fleming?"

"No, Sir. Our sources report no record of them ever meeting. Unlike Beck, Oster is an experienced intelligence officer that obviously knows how to cloak himself in secrecy. We have little information on his views or habits for the last several years other than his known wide circle of acquaintances. Even his personal habits such as his womanizing are thin on details. However, Richter may be a cutout to allow Oster to communicate with the American."

Heydrich raised his eyebrows. "Seems a stretch. You raise the question of Oster without any firm grounding and suggest the possibility of him providing confidential information to the American military attaché?"

"Only as a possibility, Sir."

"The Americans have no foreign intelligence service. Unlikely a single army officer could be conducting an intelligence operation against Germany. Regardless, continue to pursue the thread and see where it leads. What do we know of this American?"

Pfeiffer retrieved another folder. "I have opened an investigation to expand on knowing more about Colonel Fleming. At this time, we only have his submitted background from his diplomatic accreditation.

"I will just state the highlights. Born 1894 in San Francisco. Mother from Metz therefore he is fluent in both German and French. Father, a civil engineer, constructed railroads in the American west and later worked on the Panama Canal. Mother a lawyer. Both parents deceased. Fleming attended the U.S. military academy. Saw action in the border war with Mexico in 1916 winning the highest American medal for valor. Came to France with the AEF as an intelligence officer because of his language skills. Principally worked as liaison with French headquarters as part of General Pershing's staff. Details are not expansive, but he saw action in the field where he earned two additional combat citations. Served in the American sector of the occupation of the Rhineland. Well educated. Holds a doctorate in history. Known as an outstanding chess player. Never married. Parents deceased."

"What about women?" Heydrich asked.

"Information we have suggests a possible romantic relationship with the Jewish journalist, Bella Fromm. Other than that, we have no further information on his sex life until more intense investigation provides a better picture of his habits.

Knowing Heydrich occasionally frequented the *Geisterstunde.* Pfeiffer added, "He often visits the *Geisterstunde."*

"For the music or the beautiful hostesses?"

"That is yet to be determined, Sir."

"A good start, Pfeiffer. Keep me informed if something of interest is discovered."

* * * *

As Heydrich begin consolidating the German police state by identifying dissent senior officers in the military, Himmler positioned the Schutzstaffel to implement Hitler's next phase of ridding Germany of all Jews.

Since coming to power two years earlier, the Nazi regime systematically persecuted German Jews. First by physical harassment and enforced boycott of Jewish goods and services using the

SA. Legal prohibitions followed. Jews prohibited from civil service. From practicing law. From practicing medicine on non-Jews. From university faculty. From the military. Naturalized German Jews stripped of citizenship therefore subject to deportation.

On September 15, the Reichstag convened during the annual rally of the Nazi Party to pass anti-Semitic and racial laws appalling to the rest of the world. The sham single-party parliament voting unanimously in favor. The Nuremberg Laws completed the total disenfranchisement of German Jews. Marriage and even extramarital sexual intercourse between Jews and non-Jews prohibited under penalty of imprisonment at hard labor. The following month the law expanded to include Romani and broadly, people of dark skin. Only those of German or related blood qualified as citizens of the German Reich. In a supplement decree, the complex classification of Jewishness from a law promulgated in 1933 was simplified. Anyone with one or more Jewish grandparents now became a Jew.

Cynically, the Reich delayed prosecution of the laws until conclusion of the 1936 Berlin Olympic Games to avoid foreign boycotting of the Games.

CHAPTER 20

Berlin, German Reich | Autumn 1935

Fleming sat in his apartment trying to read. The late October day was sunny. The leaves turning Berlin into an impressionist canvas. The normal exuberance of the Munich Oktoberfest that normally extended all over Germany earlier in the month visibly muted this year. While the economy continued to improve, the oppressive environment created by the German police state dampened enthusiasm.

After two and a half years in Berlin, Fleming was dispirited. Witnessing the increasingly repressive Nazi regime made performing his official duties seemingly pointless. Observing diplomatic protocols with those he regarded as criminals filled him with disgust. His thoughts increasingly looked to leaving Germany.

The continuing flow of secret information from Kaczmarek, Oster, and Strobel reflected the desperation of these opposing Adolf Hitler. Their concern went beyond political disagreement. Independently, they all concluded that unchecked, Adolf Hitler would lead Germany into another war.

Listening to public pronouncements by Hitler and Goebbels made clear German territorial ambitions. Annexation of Austria. Annexation of the ethnic German Sudetenland territory of Czechoslovakia. The concept of *Lebensraum* could only mean annexation of historic Poland to the east of Germany. Once German rearmament reached a sufficient level, the threat of war by a collation of

Britain and France appeared the only check to Hitler's imperialistic ambitions. The crux of the problem lay with the lack of will of Britain and France to threaten war to ensure the sovereignty of these countries. The carnage of the Great War remained fresh. Economic recovery across Europe arrested by the Great Depression. There was no appetite for war among Hitler's adversaries.

The United States shared these same views. The American population did not universally approve of participation in the Great War. Retreating again into isolationism, weighing in on the side of Britain and France to back military action against Germany aggression seemed unlikely.

Fleming's malaise grew out of the feeling that his dangerous espionage efforts meant little toward influencing U.S. foreign policy. The fact that those like Kaczmarek, Oster, and Strobel sought passing information to a lone U.S. military attaché might influence Washington was unrealistic. Continuing his military career back in the United States however did not offer an attractive alternative. The intrigue of Berlin at least fed his intellectual curiosity but at a cost.

These thoughts weighed on his mind since receiving a telegram yesterday from Allen Dulles. *Arriving Berlin by train from Paris Friday 25 Oct 1430hrs. Please confirm available for weekend. Regards, Allen.* The perfect opportunity to discuss if his efforts served any purpose. What exactly was the attitude of the administration toward Germany? Did a rearmed Germany illicit concern? How did Americans react to the violent persecution of German Jews? Did they ignore the demented ravings of Adolf Hitler as a matter beyond American interests? Who receives his coded intelligence reports?

Adding to Fleming's pervasive angst was a body of intelligence just received from Richter. While Richter normally transferred his information to Fleming verbally for reasons of security, a week earlier he gave Fleming a thick package of documentation. Far too much to exchange verbally.

Richter went to significant efforts to devise a secure means of transfer. Perhaps unnecessary but in the current charged environment, a prudent precaution. Either of them could be under surveillance by the SD or Gestapo. As a foreign diplomatic officer, Fleming assumed the police at least nominally monitored his activities. He was always careful to engage in contacts explainable by his role as military attaché.

Over their usual coffee, Richter said, "I have something of particular interest for you. A great amount of highly confidential detail bearing on German rearmament. Too much information to encrypt. Each document must be studied in the original to understand the larger picture. Assuming you might want to review before transmitting, Colonel Oster suggested providing full size photographic prints. Do you have a secure means for getting this material to Washington?"

Fleming nodded affirmatively.

"Here is my plan for transferring the material to you. It involves Bella Fromm."

Fleming's expression turned to concern. "Is she involved with the Abwehr?"

"Not officially. She is personally acquainted with Oberstleutnant Oster. In her former capacity as a journalist, an intermediary for us to contact certain individuals clandestinely. Now of course relegated to mercantile work at her family's wine distributorship. Useful still because of her influential circle of contacts. Are you still on good terms with her?"

Fleming smiled. "Knowing my relationship with Frau Fromm, do I assume there is a dossier on me at the Abwehr?"

Richter returned the smile. "Of course. As it must also exist within the SD and therefore the Gestapo."

"To your question, I see her only occasionally since she moved closer to the family business after sending her daughter to America."

"Very well then. Call her to arrange a visit as soon as possible. Give me twenty-four hours' notice and I will arrange to deliver the package to Frau Fromm in Potsdam. You will purchase a case of wine. Under the straw in the bottom of the wooden box, you will find the package.

"The transaction must only take place with Frau Fromm. I suggest you disguise the visit as a social call. Take her to lunch.

When you return from lunch, she will give you the case of wine. Return to the security of the American Embassy. If they are watching you, this should appear nothing more than a continuation of your romantic involvement."

"Now tell me about these documents, Konrad."

"They reveal major American corporations involved with German rearmament."

"What corporations?"

"Ford, General Electric, Standard Oil, ITT, among others. Corporate documents from their German affiliates."

"Does the material directly identify production of military goods or technology?"

"In many cases, yes. Sometimes indirectly. That is why it is necessary to examine so many documents."

"What does Oster want me to do with these documents? These are publicly traded corporations. U.S. law requires disclosure of such business affiliations. Some branch of the U.S. government already knows about these business dealings. Seems like you can do more damage by publishing the details in American newspapers."

"If the American public pays little attention to the persecution of German Jews, why would cooperation between American and German business provoke any response? German rearmament is not obvious. As you know, the government conceals contracts by using the intermediary shell company MEFO masquerading as private industry. To the average person this is just normal international business."

Fleming also knew that Hitler's march toward confrontation possibly resulting in another European war was also beyond the concern for the average American.

Richter continued. "Colonel Oster hopes it might be of concern to President Roosevelt and those in his administration taking a longer view of European stability. He said, *this is not material intended to cause scandal but perhaps cause the American government to exert executive pressure on these companies to cease enabling German rearmament.*"

Fleming considered that a remote possibility unless Hitler did something unusually aggressive. Yet for Fleming, American business participating in enabling this psychopathic monster disgusted him. Of course, corporations were inherently amoral. As long as they stayed within the law, the sole objective of executives and directors was to increase shareholder value.

Nonetheless, it pissed him off. He intended to communicate his feelings strongly to Dulles. While he engaged in espionage against the Nazis, American business enabling them for profit infuriated him. At least direct Dulles to release damaging material to the American press should the administration ignore the issue.

The reunion with Bella was emotional after not seeing her for several weeks.

They lingered over a long lunch at a beautiful restaurant overlooking the River Havel, not far from the wine warehouse in Potsdam, sixteen miles from central Berlin.

Fromm became teary-eyed discussing her daughter now in the United States.

"Bad enough missing Grete-Ellen, but losing my job at the newspaper is taking a toll. I keep my hand in the game, publishing an article here and there under assumed names. Just bland crap. Who is going to publish anything critical about the Nazis? However, I am not cutout for working in business, Spencer. Nothing intellectually stimulating."

"Why not join your daughter in America? I can get you a visa."

"That's kind of you. My American journalist colleagues have also offered to help me find work should I emigrate. If I leave Germany, I will never be able to return. Sounds a silly concern considering the plight of being Jewish under these new Nazi laws. I suspect it will eventually come to that though."

"How long have you been working with Major Richter, Bella?"

"A while. You know of course it is not Richter's doing but his boss Hans Oster. Have you met Hans?"

"Once."

"Handsome devil, just like you, Spencer."

"This is way too dangerous, Bella. Oster has his own reasons for feeding me information. Though not always clear what those reasons are. However, as the American military attaché, it is my job to gather information related to German military capabilities. I also have diplomatic immunity. The Gestapo however could send you to one of these detention camps on mere suspicion. Just for being Jewish. Indefinite internment with no judicial recourse. Much worse if they believe you are working against them."

"I know. Been swimming against the Nazi tide before they came to power. Have navigated successfully so far."

"I am telling you, get out, Bella. Tell Richter you are done."

She smiled. "You are a sweetheart, Spencer." Laying her hand over his, "I want to see you again soon."

"So do I, Bella. Been too long. How about I drive down next weekend. This is a perfect setting with the view of the river and the spectacular coloring of the leaves."

"Wonderful. Come in the afternoon. Maybe the weather will still be mild. They serve an excellent dinner here. I will bring a special bottle of wine. Can you spend the night?"

Fleming placed his other hand over hers. "Of course. I would love that, Bella."

* * * *

Allen Dulles arrived at the U.S. Embassy in Berlin as scheduled.

"Good to see you, Spencer," Dulles said greeting Fleming warmly. My god how the world has changed these last few years. How are you bearing up? You've not been back to the U.S. for five years."

"A difficult environment to say the least. No matter what appears in the newspapers and even my reports, you cannot image life in a police state without living here. For those anti-Nazi Germans I interact with, every facet of life has changed. As bad as it is, they fear another war. A frightening prospect after living through the last twenty years. The deep scares of the Great War and its aftermath are still fresh."

"How do you think the majority of Germans feel about Hitler?"

"Impossible to generalize. Since Hitler came to power two years ago, things change almost daily. The average German is just trying to get by finding some comfort in finally fixing on a stable government. The circumstances of the Weimar Republic were so chaotic, democratic institutions never had an opportunity to take hold. Then the flawed constitution giving vast power to the presidency forced the aging Hindenburg to rule by decree.

"Culturally, the Germans gravitate to order. Strongly conservative with a militaristic history. Hitler brought political stability, albeit by killing or imprisoning all opposition. Noticeable improvement in economic conditions. Yet the average person does not realize a good deal of the increased economic activity comes from rearmament. The vast investments necessary for expanding the army fivefold instead of directed toward infrastructure devoted to improving the standard of living.

"Germans overwhelmingly resent the punitive measures of the 1919 treaty even if they do not buy into Hitler's propaganda about Jews and leftists stabbing the Army in the back. Yet collectively, the typical German avoids recognizing that an ambitious German militaristic monarchy instigated the Great War."

Dulles said. "So they are more than just complacent. Accepting of the Nazis by embracing Germanic nationalistic feelings and improving economic conditions while ignoring they live in a repressive police state?"

"Something like that. As long as you are not Jewish, socialist, or in any way critical of the regime. The Nazis do a good job of covering up their violent crimes. With the Nazis controlling the press, people only hear of the repression indirectly. Human nature being what it is they turn a blind eye. Keep their heads down. Obey the new laws no matter how odious as long as it does not affect them personally. An intimidated population now incapable of organized resistance."

"Looking to get out of Berlin?" Dulles said.

Fleming shrugged. "Certainly looking for a change. This unofficial diversion into espionage is stimulating but everything else stinks. The attaché work is boring. A stylized mating dance. Predominately irrelevant bullshit. As a former foreign service office, you know the drill, Allen. Making relationships with disagreeable people. Lots of liquor. Reading between the lines looking for obscure bits of information. Berlin is an unpleasant place. When I leave, it will be a relief. "

"Well, given the flow of your information, it seems you have a skill for espionage, Spencer. Is all your material coming from Polish Intelligence?"

"Not entirely, but they remain a consistent source. Are you familiar with the Abwehr, Allen?"

"Yes. German military intelligence."

"Well for the same reason the Poles approached me, someone from the Abwehr approached me. Whereas the Brits and French have intelligence services, the United States in its inexplicable xenophobic arrogance chooses to ignore foreign political intelligence. I am the next best thing to American intelligence."

"They approached you? How do you know it is not just a disinformation ploy?"

"My first thoughts. However, I became quickly convinced there is a dissident faction within the military. The level of secrecy of the information seems too sensitive to be disinformation. There is no benefit to reveal this to the U.S. other than for its expressed purpose. I also have another source in the Wehrmacht. Knew him from my tenure in the Rhineland. Hates Hitler. A significant number of senior officers also share my friend's strident views about Hitler. I am a regular among his social group of likeminded officers. None as candid as my friend but all are clearly anti-Nazi. There is definitely a strong thread of anti-Hitler sentiment within the Wehrmacht.

"Through these contacts and some of the Polish material, I independently corroborated enough of the Abwehr material to convince me their anti-Hitler subversion is genuine. The extent I do not know. These fellows are experienced intelligence officers. I only communicate through a single designated officer. Most often verbally."

Dulles expression reflected skepticism, "Even if these army officers are what they say, you are playing a dangerous game, Spencer. What is the motivation of these dissidents in the Abwehr? Engineer a coup d'état? Then what? Replace Hitler and the Nazis with a military dictatorship? Bring back the monarchy?"

"Perhaps. Their stated immediate concern is the same as the Poles and my Wehrmacht officer friend. They all fear Hitler's territorial ambitions involving Germany in another war. My Polish colleague Major Kaczmarek confided candidly that they interact regularly with British and French intelligence. If Hitler acts on *Lebensraum,* that certainly means Poland. The restoration of historically Polish lands to a sovereign Polish republic by the 1919 treaty remains an affront to the Germans.

"As for these conspirators in the military, including my friend, it is about another war. Perhaps more the prospect of Hitler acting prematurely before Germany rearms sufficiently thereby leading Germany to another defeat. The Army High Command fears Hitler's impulsiveness. Hitler possesses no military knowledge yet portrays himself as a strategic visionary. It could be many years before German military capabilities reach a level capable of threatening the former Entente of twenty years ago. They fear Hitler might act sooner."

"Why choose you as the conduit rather than the regular diplomatic channels?"

"Ambassadors are political appointees. Consular foreign service officers report through a chain of command of political appointees. These are intelligence professionals and soldiers. They want their work product seen directly by top decision makers without political filtering."

"Very well. How do these German military dissidents see the United States playing any part in derailing German rearmament?"

"They don't. That is unlikely and the German military supports rearmament. Rearmament will continue until economically unsustainable. Their issue is premature war. They want to see external forces threaten Hitler with war if he acts on his public stated objectives. He repeatedly makes clear his desire to unite Germanic

Austrian and ethnic Germans of the Czechoslovakian Sudetenland into a Greater Germany. Britain and France seem the only counterweight by threatening war should Hitler take military action. Those in opposition question the resolve of the British and French. A decisive stance by the new American president could bolster a coalition to face down Hitler."

"Interesting. I doubt there is any American will to engage in European political turmoil again. The weight of the Great Depression increases American isolationism. The Great War still fresh in the American psyche."

"I told them the same thing, Allen. However, I see Hitler and the Nazi regime from a perspective few others in American government can appreciate. This crazy bastard will take Germany into another war. Just a question of when. The United States will likely face the same dilemma as in 1917. If these anti-Nazis in the military can derail Hitler, the world is better off. For the United States to act in strength by backing the British and French seems an acceptable risk.

"Tell me this, Allen. Who exactly sees the intelligence product I send to you? You realize of course that you receive certain information I do not report to the War Department in my official capacity as attaché?"

"Why is that?"

"The political stuff would fall on deaf ears. Military intelligence is largely about signals traffic. Encryption and code breaking. Most U.S. military attachés have an intelligence background but receive no special training. Just observers gathering what they can. There is no central clearinghouse for our attaché reports at the War Department. No analysis. Does any of it ever go higher up in the chain of command? I doubt it. Most importantly, it would be clear by the substance of the material you receive that I am engaged in espionage. My orders do not extend to actively spying. That's why I agreed to your proposal, Allen. "

Dulles nodded. "To your question, I have a network of contacts in the State Department and former foreign service professionals now in the private sector. At the senior level, I regularly pass your material to an influential undersecretary of state named

Sumner Welles. Welles is close to the President. Much to the ire of Secretary Hull, Roosevelt clearly sees Welles as the central figure in the State Department. Roosevelt and Hull for unknown reasons do not enjoy a close relationship. Hull can do nothing about the awkward arrangement because of Welles' powerful political base.

"I also regularly talk to Louis Howe. I am sure you recognize the name. Probably President Roosevelt's closest advisor. Instrumental in originally getting you assigned to Berlin. Unfortunately, his health is seriously failing but he still has the President's ear.

"Another is William 'Wild Bill' Donovan. Commanded the 165th Regiment in the war. Like you, a decorated officer. Served in the Justice Department then started a law firm in '29."

"I know of Colonel Donovan. An unusually effective officer in the war," Fleming said.

"Although from opposing political parties, Roosevelt and Donovan are similar personalities. Anyway, as Roosevelt likes to operate through a few close confidential advisers, Donovan is increasingly among the President's foreign affairs inner circle.

"Donovan and Roosevelt both share an interest in Great Britain. Roosevelt developed a relationship with Winston Churchill during the war when he was assistant secretary of the navy when German U-boats threatened American aid during the war in the Atlantic. Donovan maintains a close interest in European affairs. Like you, he sees Hitler inevitably leading Germany toward another war. I know both Welles and Donovan very well.

"Then there is my close friend Hamilton Armstrong. We went to school together at Princeton. Ham has been the editor of *Foreign Affairs,* the journal of the private think tank Council on Foreign Relations of which I am a director. His publication is widely read in government circles and academia. With no American historical precedent for engaging in foreign espionage, he finds your secret material enlightening."

"What about Sullivan & Cromwell clients. What do they make of the material?"

"We have two Jewish organizations as clients. Of course, they realize the depth of the persecution of German Jews from media accounts. I offer my opinion to them that this supplemental material suggests there will never be a stabilization of Jewish circumstances. The Nazis mean to drive them entirely from Germany."

"Allen, it is much more serious. You read the reports about these concentration camps. That will be the plight of Germany's Jews. Slave labor. Under these new Nuremberg racial laws, Hitler's police state needs no further pretext. If arrested, that means a forced labor camp. Indefinitely. Brutality, starvation, disease. Not meant for survival."

Since receiving the documents Bella passed from Richter, Fleming was anxious to confront Dulles about what he knew of American corporate involvement with German rearmament.

"How about your corporate clients? What do they make of the material?"

"Discouraged I'd say. Financial institutions. Their German loans likely to default. Ambassador Dodd has been unable to negotiate an agreement at reduced interest."

"Of course Hitler will default, Allen. What leverage do American banks hold? Serves them right. Greed and hubris. Thought Germany would forever be a vassal state to the victorious allies. Everything codified in the Armistice Treaty. Wilson's utopian League of Nations has no teeth."

"Not sure I agree with that assessment, Spencer. Germany could not be left to descend into anarchy and likely communism."

"Well, besides loaning money at lucrative interest rates, the allied governments did little else to foster German recovery. German civilians starving by the continued British blockade of food imports. German export goods boycotted. Did anyone think Germany would forever remain with an inferior military to their hostile neighbors?"

"We both acted as consultants to the American delegates to the treaty conference. Wilson held all the cards yet he let the French and British dictate the punitive measures," Dulles said.

"Let me get to what has me so steamed. I have a large document dump from my Abwehr sources. It reveals active participation of major American corporations in German rearmament. It goes beyond the mere pursuit of profits. All these corporations know what business activities relate to German rearmament. You recall my earlier material regarding this shell company MEFO that disguises military related government contracts as private enterprise transactions. Not only suits German manufacturing of profitable military contracts but also certain American corporations. Those with holdings in German subsidiaries understand how this deception works."

"Which American corporations?"

"Standard Oil, General Electric, General Motors, Ford, IBM, ITT to name a few. Are any of these clients of Sullivan & Cromwell?"

"No. Our clients involved with Germany are financial institutions. How are these companies involved with the Nazis?"

"I'll give you some general highlights. The most egregious collaboration is that of Standard Oil of New Jersey and General Motors with the German chemical cartel I.G. Farben. They formed a German subsidiary, Ethyl GmbH just this year as a subsidiary of their joint venture Ethyl Gasoline Corporation. What is at stake is the transfer of technology for industrial scale production of synthetic gasoline and related products. Germany has no petroleum reserves. It relies on foreign imports for 85% of its current needs for petroleum based fuels and lubricants. A problem for a modern mechanized army and air force. With process technology and abundant coal reserves, this becomes essential for Hitler's military ambitions.

"As to Ford, not surprising that the anti-Semitic asshole Henry Ford would embrace Nazism. Fords' German subsidiary Ford-Werke A.G. imports rubber and other critical military materials. In exchange, the German subsidiary exports Ford automotive parts at reduced costs to the U.S. Since Ford Motor Company holds a majority stake in the subsidiary, it circumvents 1919 Treaty restrictions. Documents show that Ford-Werke also produces critical parts for aircraft manufacturing. Not likely commercial applications as documented by intentionally falsified records.

"Here is another example that your Jewish clients might appreciate. Not related to rearmament, it stems from corporate pursuit of profits irrespective of consequences. IBM has a German subsidiary, Deutsche Hollerith-Maschinen GmbH. In the 1933 German election IBM provided the Nazis the ability to use D11 tabulating machines to analyze census data to define campaign strategy. Most successfully by the way things turned out. Documents show IBM equipment and technology are also integral tools for searching databases for identifying Jews."

Dulles said, "Frankly, what you uncovered is not surprising. Undoubtedly, various departments of the U.S. government know of these American foreign investments in Germany. Why should it raise any questions? Any trade sanctions are fifteen-year old fine print in Commerce Department regulations. Regardless the danger Hitler might present, he appears little different then his Italian Fascist counterpart Mussolini."

"Are you saying this material will not influence U.S. policy toward Nazi Germany?"

"That pretty much summarizes it. European political turmoil is beyond the U.S. taking any direct foreign policy action. The more worrisome international problem immediately effecting American interests is Japanese imperialism in the Far East.

"By the way, if it makes you feel any better, I am here to close Sullivan & Cromwell's Berlin office."

"Really?" Why?"

"Largely my doing. My brother does not fully agree but Germany has become my particular responsibility. I agree with your dire outlook for the peaceful prospects of Germany. The firm is not interested in fostering new business relationships here. In addition to your secret intelligence reports, the media accounts of Nazi oppression are appalling. Inconceivable that Adolf Hitler will pursue conventional means of economic recovery. Everything confirms your view of rebuilding the German military to embark on his territorial objectives."

Fleming nodded. "Perhaps I am just too close to the beast. Corporate veniality should come as no surprise. Tell you what. I will get these documents to you by diplomatic pouch. How about you distribute copies to the major newspapers. At the least, it will prove embarrassing for many corporate executives and board members."

"Sure, why not. Anonymously of course."

Fleming said, "In hindsight, the Treaty of Versailles was fundamentally shortsighted. Designed to punish Germany at the expense of ignoring practical long-range interests of the victorious Allies."

"What do you mean?" Dulles asked.

"They imposed an unworkable parliamentary democracy on a defeated people while ignoring economic supports necessary for recovery. That self-righteous idiot Wilson let Clémenceau and Lloyd George inflict crippling terms with little ability for Germany to recover economically. Wilson held all the cards yet directed his intentions toward creating his vision of a new world order. Not only were the treaty terms unsustainable, but they laid the foundation for failure of the Weimar Republic."

"Isn't that Hitler's repeated claim?"

"Yes. Nonetheless, it ensured the German republic would not survive. Hated by all political factions, none of which lamented its demise. There never was any viable opposition to the rise of Hitler's national socialism. Every organized sector of German life capable of stopping this madman withdrew from active opposition. The military, business, the Catholic Church, the Protestant Church, the dominant centrist Social Democratic Party. All concerned with their individual provincial interests, never organizing in an opposition coalition. Why should we be surprised? Now it is too late. They allowed Frankenstein to set loose his monster."

Dulles smiled. "You've turned into quite the philosopher-soldier, Spencer. Your PhD is showing."

Fleming replied, "Ugh. That and getting older. Tell you what. Are you available for dinner tonight?"

"Absolutely. Any place other than the Hotel Adlon where I'm staying with all the other foreigners. Is there some place more interesting you can recommend?"

"Certainly. My favorite venue. Good food and drink. Extraordinary entertainment. Beautiful waitresses. Place called the *Geisterstunde*. The Witching Hour."

* * * *

Settled at a good table close to the slightly raised stage, Fleming and Dulles enjoyed a good Scotch as they listened to the small orchestra play jazz.

Even in New York, Fleming knew Allen Dulles enjoyed women. Made little attempt to conceal his many affairs. It always troubled Fleming since he was close to Dulles' wife Clover.

"I see what you mean about the attractive waitresses."

"Believe it or not, it is the music that brings me here. Wait until you hear the singer. A magnificent operatic voice. Italian arias."

Dulles looked up with a surprised expression then stood. At the same time, Valeska Kaplinsky came up behind Fleming and put her hand on his shoulder. "So good to see you, Colonel Fleming."

Slightly embarrassed, Fleming stood. "Frau Kaplinsky, let me introduce my good friend from New York, Allen Dulles."

Dulles responded in his terrible German. After some small talk, Kaplinsky made her usual tour to greet all the patrons. Before leaving their table, Kaplinsky said, "After my first performance, I shall join you gentlemen for a drink."

"Now I see why you like this place, Spencer. Perhaps more than Valeska Kaplinsky's voice?"

Fleming smiled then changed the subject. "Likely I will be applying for a transfer this coming year. Allen. Have my efforts meant anything?"

"Hard to say. As to the raison d'être of these anti-Nazi conspirators, doubtful that it will impact U.S. policy in any tangible way. Hitler has not yet directly threatened other nations with military force. A madman yes. Yet not an immediate threat. Little the U.S. or even the British or the French can do unless he goes off the reservation."

"What about the incestuous international financial dealings funding German rearmament? If the administration felt strongly about slowing Hitler's efforts, they could exert enough political pressure on U.S. corporations and investment banks."

Dulles shook his head. "There is no political will for anything so aggressive."

"Then why should I bother to continue gathering intelligence that disappears into a dark hole?"

"The short answer is it does not go unheeded. Your insights into the structure of the Nazi regime are eye opening. Particularly the structure of the Schutzstaffel in all its ugly manifestations. Scary material to see the actual details of the evolution of a police state."

"What's the point if it has no impact?"

"I did not say it had no impact. Quite the contrary. Your material influences those people I named as the recipients, including President Roosevelt. All of them digest your secret information with great interest. The most significant impact of your efforts is exposing the disadvantage the United States suffers by not having a foreign intelligence agency. Bill Donovan said the President even remarked about that failure.

"Look what you have accomplished as a single operative. You set in place a secret backdoor intelligence channel to the U.S. foreign policy making apparatus. That may become vital as the situation in Nazi Germany develops."

CHAPTER 21

Berlin, German Reich | Winter 1935

Like many Berliners, Genevieve Meier's life was difficult. Being Jewish more so since Adolf Hitler came to power. For twenty years, her parents struggled to provide food for the family. The deprivations of the war years followed by the dark days of the collapse of what remained of the German economy, followed later by the effects of the worldwide depression.

Genevieve was the youngest of three daughters. Both parents worked long hours in their tailor shop. When war came in 1914, her father's age and poor eyesight excused him from military service. Genevieve's sisters married when they reached age, relieving the financial burden on the parents. When Genevieve reached nineteen in 1923, hyperinflation reached its peak. With Reichsmarks holding no value, German economic life reduced to barter. With little call for new clothing, father and mother scraped by exchanging services in clothing repair and alterations for food.

Genevieve worked in the tailor shop alongside her parents. With insufficient work, she realized she was an added burden. Much to her parents' dismay, she abhorred the idea of marriage and children. The Meiers were casually observant Jews but firmly part of the larger Berlin Jewish community. Although determined to make her way, there were few options. Therefore, she must find a way to use her only marketable assets, her beauty and shapely body.

The mind-numbing toil as a seamstress in the shop and the subtle pressure to get married eventually brought her to a decision point. Anything was better than staying in this dreary existence locked into a detestable future. The glittering lights of the decadent Berlin cabarets offered the only possibility of escape.

Her looks and body easily got her auditions, yet she needed to land a job. In her room, she listened to jazz while practicing singing and dancing. He only tutor became watching Marlene Dietrich in Saturday matinee movies each week. Performance success required more than just beauty. She worked to develop a style geared to accentuating her inherent sex appeal.

Eventually landing a job as a dancer, reality replaced the glamour of entertainment. The pay as a cabaret dancer was not enough to consider leaving her humble circumstances living with her parents. Barely enough to contribute her share of living expenses. That included tips by hustling drinks and dancing with patrons between performances.

Dancing was more an excuse for men to press against her breasts and fondle her butt. She quickly learned to discern those men that were both good looking and spent freely. Like many of her fellow dancers, exchanging sex for money soon defined Genevieve Meier's professional life.

Unlike Dietrich, Meier found no opportunities in film. Appearances as an extra in two films was the closest she got. Decline of the cabarets as severe economic downturn set in deepened her discouragement.

By the time Hitler came to power, the Berlin cabaret scene declined further. The overt public expressions of the youthful sex and drug culture ran its course. Struggling for survival again like the previous generation left little time for frivolous entertainment. Meier's employment became erratic. Tips became meager. The going rate for selling her body to the few men she found attractive fell off proportionately.

At about the same time, the Meier tailor shop came under violent attack by the SA in a rampage on their street populated by mostly Jewish merchants. The SA destroyed the inventory and beat Genevieve's father. In a particular act of cruelty, a storm trooper smashed the old man's fingers with his boots.

Fortunately, Genevieve's looks and shapely figure landed her a waitress job at the upscale nightclub the *Geisterstunde*. Knowing little about the club except that it catered to the wealthy and influential, she hoped to get a job dancing or singing.

The interview with the woman owner immediately turned disappointing.

"Kaplinsky said, "I am sorry, I have no position for dancers. Do you sing?"

"Yes," Meier replied.

"What sort of music?"

"Popular music."

"Very well. Sing me something."

Terrified to fail the opportunity, and singing acapella, Meier began singing a current jazz favorite.

Kaplinsky raised her hand. "That will do. I am afraid that will not fit for the type of musical entertainment at the *Geisterstunde*. I do most of the singing. Operatic arias usually. Any accompaniment must therefore be from those with trained voices. You have no such training?"

Meier shook her head as her eyes began to tear. "I desperately need the work, Frau Kaplinsky. I must take care of my parents. They can no longer operate the family tailoring business.

Kaplinsky was silent for a moment. "Why is that?"

Meier broke into tears. "The SA destroyed the shop and broke father's hands."

"You are Jewish?"

"Yes. Is that a problem? I have not found work in three weeks."

"No, it is not a problem. Several of my employees are Jewish. That however is never to be discussed." Pausing for a moment, Kaplinsky continued. "I realize you have other aspirations. Right now, I can only offer you a position as a waitress. Are you interested?"

Deflated at the prospect of how little that must pay, Meier said, "How much does it pay?"

"Well that depends a lot on you. I will pay you 100 Reichsmarks a week as a salary. If you please the patrons, you should be able to double that with tips."

The amount surprised Meier. "Please them how? Does that mean I must sleep with them?"

Kaplinsky smiled. "To the contrary. I do not run a brothel. The patrons, including women, come to the *Geisterstunde* for entertainment and fine dining. Like you, my waitresses are all attractive, complementing the luxury interior decor. The rules are absolutely no soliciting.

"Was exchanging sex for money part of your past jobs?"

"Only if you wanted enough money to get by."

"Of course. These are difficult times. Attractive women like you must use their assets to survive. After all, is that not what marriage amounts to?"

Meier smiled. "Along with other burdens." She instantly liked Kaplinsky.

Kaplinsky said, "I have nothing against providing sex for money, only it must not detract from the reputation of the *Geisterstunde.* You will hear talk among some of my waitresses that they have found a way to enhance their income. Here is s card with a telephone number. If you are interested, discuss the particulars with Herr Fischer. Any liaisons you choose to arrange must be made exclusively through this escort service. Freelancing will be cause for dismissal."

The card read *Zeitarbeitsvermittler, Walter Fischer* and a telephone number. In English, simply *Temporary Employment Agency.*

"Is that understood, Fräulein Meier?"

"Yes."

"Very well, you may start tomorrow. The hours are from seven o'clock to three in the morning. Come early to select a gown from our wardrobe. I see you do a good job with your makeup. That will do nicely. I am hiring you because you are attractive and seem intelligent. Do not disappoint me."

* * * *

That was a year earlier. Genevieve Meier did not disappoint. Neither Valeska Kaplinsky nor patrons of the *Geisterstunde* or the *Zeitarbeitsvermittler*. She developed what she hoped was a sophisticated flirtatious style. That with her overt sex appeal earned her good tips. Selling her body doubled her waitress income.

It was through the escort service that she met Heinz Bauer. A tall handsome blond-haired man in his early thirties. Surprisingly considerate in his lovemaking. She welcomed regular repeat engagements over the following weeks.

Bauer claimed to be the son of a wealthy industrial family on his first liaison with Meier. They always met at the same modest apartment. He said his principle residence was outside Berlin, closer to the family's industrial operations. He used this central Berlin address when staying in Berlin on business.

This night he left the bed naked for the small kitchen. Their ritual was to make love, relax with a bottle of Champagne, then resume again.

While he opened the Champagne, Meier retrieved his shirt to cover her shoulders to ward off the chill of the room. Returning to the bed, she pulled the covers over her legs. She left the shirt open to display her breasts knowing it added to his arousal.

Handing Meier a glass of Champagne, Bauer said, "I need to tell you something important, Genevieve. Something you must never reveal."

She looked up at him with an expression of concern.

"My name is not Bauer. I am Mikhail Borisovich Gekht. I am Russian. Like you, Jewish."

The revelation left her speechless and shaken. A Jewish communist? Was this a trap by the Gestapo?"

"I am no Jew. Why do you say that?"

"Because I know all about you. I know about your parents. What the Nazis did to your father. I want to help you."

"Help me? How?"

"Arrange for your parents to leave Germany."

Angry at his deceit and not necessarily believing him, she said, "Why would you do that? So you can fuck me for free?"

He smiled. "It is not about money. I make love to you because you are beautiful and satisfy my sexual desires. My job is to gather intelligence on the Nazis. Many of them your clients. You also talk with the other women. Like you, most work at the *Geisterstunde*. Men tend to boast to women in sexual circumstances. I simply want you to pass along useful information to me. I know that two of your regular clients hold high-level positions. One in the foreign ministry, the other in the SS."

"Who do you work for?"

"Russian intelligence. Hitler makes war on Jews now but will someday make war on Russia."

"Where would my parents go?"

"Somewhere safe. Perhaps Denmark or the Netherlands. It will take some time to arrange. Time for you to gather useful information and show a good faith effort for our support in helping your parents."

Desperate to save her parents from the growing persecution of Jews by the Nazis, Genevieve Meier entered the employ of Soviet Red Army GRU intelligence.

Meier agreed to Gekht's proposal for the simple reason she already passed information gleaned from her clients to Kaplinsky. Kaplinsky told the women engaged in the prostitution service the information collected from their clients goes to the Gestapo. In return, the nightclub suffers no interference from the police. A necessary arrangement for doing business.

It also avoided speculation among the women that this was some sort of anti-Nazi conspiracy. An understandable extension of the ubiquitous German secret police apparatus gathering information by every conceivable method. Never to be discussed even among the other women. Keep your mouth shut and just listen. Not likely the women would admit to anyone about being an informer for the Gestapo.

The Gestapo knew of the escort service. A virtual brothel for the wealthy and influential. Many important Nazis known to be clients therefore, the criminal police understood they were not to interfere.

Meier feared confiding to Kaplinsky the identity of this Russian spy. Once discovering she was a Jew, the Gestapo would send her to a concentration camp. Possibly execute her and her parents as spies. Whether Bauer or Gekht or whatever his real name was telling her the truth, she had no choice but play along.

* * * *

As Major Kaczmarek's control agent for the Kaplinsky network, Bruno Goettner kept watch over the call girls while staying well out of sight. His only direct contact was with Kaplinsky to take gathered information and transmit to Warsaw. His cover as the sales representative for the liquor distributor for the *Geisterstunde* provided the means for frequent visits with Kaplinsky.

Part of his job was reviewing client bookings for the escort service. Not all yielded intelligence from the sexual liaisons but the fact these men of means sought out prostitutes was itself of potential value. These were the most attractive prostitutes in Berlin, commanding rates prohibitive to the average man. Sexual engagements for the night rather than charged by the sex act of the typical prostitute.

Goettner was particularly interested in the regular clients. His task was to identify everyone on the list. No telling where that might lead. He assumed Kaczmarek probably deployed other assets in Berlin. Among the booking records of those he did not recognize was the name Heinz Bauer.

Bauer made repeat bookings over a six-week period. Always with Genevieve Meier. The same prostitute favored by an SS officer named Pfeiffer. If Bauer was someone of note, possible to mine him for information since he may feel a special relationship with Meier.

The name Bauer might be associated with the wealthy family owning controlling interest in major German machine tool manufacturer. The booking gave the address for the rendezvous. Always the same. An apartment in a middleclass neighborhood. As required, the women filed a report after each engagement. The man's profession, a physical description, and if his behavior was acceptable to ensure each woman's safety by blacklisting any dangerous sexual deviants or violent clients.

If the name was false, that alone did not make Goettner suspicious. Nothing more than avoidance of scandal or blackmail. Yet why would a young man of means choose such a plain apartment rather than a hotel?

Over the next week, Goettner spent many hours each night for several days watching the apartment. No one fitting Bauer's description arrived at the address. The specific apartment always remained dark.

The following week, Bauer booked another night with Meier. Goettner staking out the apartment building. A man fitting Bauer's description drove up and parked in front. Thirty minutes later, Genevieve Meier arrived by taxi.

Unlike their prior engagements lasting most of the night, both Bauer and Meier left the apartment and left in Bauer's car after only two hours. Goettner followed in his car.

After dropping Meier at her parents' home in a Jewish neighborhood, Goettner continued following Bauer, extinguishing his headlights to avoid Bauer noticing the tail. Interestingly, Bauer did not return to the apartment. Instead, he parked at what appeared to be a warehouse in an industrial sector of Berlin. Goettner sat awake in his car watching until dawn without seeing Bauer leave. The entire sequence of events suspicious.

Working alone, it took Goettner weeks before discovering what Bauer was doing. Ultimately, it was headquarters in Warsaw that identified the warehouse. Owned by a construction firm according to public records. Purchased two years ago by someone known to Polish intelligence. A communist with an interesting background. An associate of Vladimir Lenin during Lenin's exile in Germany. A German by the name Schmidt.

Schmidt avoided association with known German communists in order to function clandestinely in Germany. Received intelligence training in Moscow, now believed to head Soviet GRU foreign intelligence operations in Germany.

Kaczmarek must consider Bauer a Russian agent. Genevieve Meier possibly compromised or knowingly cooperating.

Regardless, Kaczmarek could not risk the productive Kaplinsky network. His coded orders to Goettner read, *eliminate both Bauer and Meier making it appear a sexual encounter gone violent.* The details left to Goettner.

As a former Polish separatist, Goettner was no stranger to violence. For three years, he fought remnants of the defeated German army in Upper Silesia to free historical Polish lands from the German Weimar Republic. He had killed before, but never a woman. Not understanding her motivation, or even if she was knowingly complicit with Soviet intelligence, made killing her troubling.

* * * *

Goettner's plan was simple. At the next scheduled rendezvous between Bauer and Meier, Goettner would be waiting. In his pocket was a letter addressed to Meier. An angry letter of unrequited love tinged with angry condemnation. Rejecting him in favor of a life of debauchery as a prostitute. Burst into the apartment, shoot Bauer first then Meier. Leave the letter and the gun.

To escape, he counted on less than a minute to perform the deed and make an exit down the one flight of darkened stairs after disabling any lights. His car parked over a block away with other cars. Once back at the car, he could drive away quietly into the night far enough removed from the aftermath of the shooting.

The letter in his pocket was short, scrawled in a violent script consistent with the tone of an obsessive stalker.

Why was I not good enough? I told you I would pay anything to keep you for myself. Your repeated refusals to see me leave me only this choice.

The opportunity arrived within days with another booking by Bauer. The rendezvous set for eight o'clock.

Goettner sat in his car at a distance with the car running to keep the interior warm on the bitterly cold December night. A streetlight cast illumination on the entrance to the apartment building. Bauer arrived half an hour early.

Once Meier arrived shortly after by taxi, Goettner waited thirty minutes before relocating his car to the next perpendicular street. Bundled in a heavy wool overcoat and scarf, he walked briskly back to the apartment. In his pocket the letter and a loaded 9mm pistol.

Approaching the apartment building, he could see the lights were on in the corner apartment. Perhaps not yet in bed. However, for all he knew sex was not part of these meetings. More risky with both Bauer and Meier up and about but he was anxious to be done with this. Standing about in the cold might invite suspicion for anyone looking out a window.

Once inside the building entrance he disabled the single light on the landing to the second floor. The room at the end of the short hallway to his left placed it at the front corner of the building. With his ear to the door, he could hear voices. He removed the pistol and stepped back several paces.

With a running start, he crashed his left shoulder into the door. The impact great enough to smash the door frame around the handle and lock. Unfortunately, the safety chain kept the door from swinging fully open. It gave Bauer enough time to scramble to his gun sitting on the nightstand next to the bed.

Dressed in only her undergarments sitting on the edge of the bed removing her stockings, Meier screamed. Goettner's first bullet caught Bauer in the back causing him to stumble to one knee dropping his weapon. Meier jumped off the bed and Goettner shot her twice.

Having retrieved his weapon while Goettner shot Meier, the wounded Bauer fired repeatedly hitting Goettner. Although mortally wounded, Goettner got off another two shots killing Bauer.

* * * *

The following day, Otto Decker of the Gestapo reviewed that day's reports from the criminal police. The triple homicide of a prostitute and two men caught his attention. Of interest was the prostitute. Associated with a unique prostitution ring known as a *call girl* service with sexual liaisons arranged by telephone appointment rather than operating as a brothel. The prettiest women and very expensive, their clientele therefore predominately men of financial means. Decker was familiar with this particular prostitution service. The female victim Genevieve Meier, like most of the prostitutes, worked as a waitress at the nightclub the *Geisterstunde.*

Many high-ranking Nazi members of the government were clients of this exclusive prostitution service as well as patrons of the *Geisterstunde.* Including SS. Decker knew that even Reinhard Heydrich and Johann Pfeiffer frequented the nightclub and this prostitution service. It fell to Decker to delete any documented records of Heydrich's known associations with prostitutes.

The police knew the ownership of *Zeitarbeitsvermittler.* Walter Fischer, a lawyer, was also the accountant for the *Geisterstunde.* Obviously, Valeska Kaplinsky was a silent partner supplying the women. Because of the clientele, both enterprises enjoyed official protection.

The police report was thorough. Two weapons involved both 9mm semi-automatics. The woman shot twice in the chest. The male victim, identified as Heinz Bauer, shot twice in the abdomen and once in the head. The other male hit three times, survived long enough to crawl to the door before collapsing and dying from blood loss.

The scene of the murders a modest apartment leased for the past six months by the victim Bauer. The investigating detectives reported the apartment likely intended for sexual rendezvous since there were few personal articles in the drawers and closet. By evidence found in his coat, Bauer apparently lived at another address not far away. A search at that location also revealed surprising little in the way of personal articles other than clothing. No personal papers other than a bank account statement with a small balance and regular monthly deposits.

The police report at this point turned interesting. Bauer listed his parents in the civil records as part of the family with controlling interest in a large German machine tool manufacturing corporation. His position as operations manager at one of the Berlin plants. However, when police investigators showed up at the company offices, they discovered the real Heinz Bauer. Suitably surprised, he could offer no information as to the identity of the murder victim. The report concluded the identity of the victim remained unknown.

Perhaps nothing. Someone masquerading as someone more important. Yet how could he afford two apartments in good neighborhoods and regularly pay for high-priced whores?

The second male victim, Bruno Goettner, appeared more straightforward. Of German-Polish descent from Poznan, employed as a sales representative for a liquor distributor. The supplier of spirits to the *Geisterstunde* nightclub. The letter in his pocket explained his infatuation for the prostitute Meier. He may have even intended a murder-suicide when the other man unexpectedly produced a weapon.

The unidentified other man remained sufficiently intriguing to pass along his concerns to Sturmbannführer Johann Pfeiffer of the Sicherheitsdienst. Pfeiffer undoubtedly would be interested since he regularly used the call girl service. Perhaps he knew Genevieve Meier? The thought brought a smile to Decker.

CHAPTER 22

Berlin, German Reich | January 1936

Fleming sat in his office at the embassy when the receptionist downstairs telephoned. He had a visitor. A Polish diplomatic officer by the name of Henryk Zieliński. Fleming did not recognize the name.

Descending the stairs, he recognized the visitor as Major Feliks Kaczmarek, obviously wishing to remain incognito. "I am Lieutenant Colonel Fleming. May I help you?"

"Sorry to intrude unannounced, Colonel. Warsaw instructed me to personally deliver certain sensitive information."

"Very well, please accompany me to my office."

Once behind closed doors they shook hands, both sharing smiles. Kaczmarek said, "Sorry for the surprise. You will understand when I tell you. You have been busy on your own. The information you are sending to me must come from very important sources. Impressive for someone new to espionage."

"Had a good mentor. Now, what is so urgent, Feliks?"

"One of my agents is dead. He controlled my most productive network."

"What happened?"

"Discovered an infiltration by a Soviet intelligence agent. I ordered my man to eliminate the Russian. While successful, it cost him his life."

"Is the network secure?"

"I believe so. My man made it appear as a love triangle gone violent. That is what I am here to determine. Would like to ask for your help if you are willing?"

"How can I help, Feliks?"

"Take over control of this network?"

Stunned, Fleming stared at Kaczmarek for a moment. Already actively engaged in espionage through his own sources, Kaczmarek's suggestion was not all that absurd.

"Depends on the details, Feliks. You see the intelligence you receive from me comes through military contacts in the course of my official duties as the American military attaché. For much the same reason you provide me intelligence on Germany. They fear Hitler is again taking Germany to war."

Kaczmarek said, "These sources you found are seriously anti-Nazi by the tone of their information. My compliments.

"This network I want you to run has been productive. A good deal of the material I forward to you comes from them. Particularly the internal maneuverings of high-ranking Nazi officials and their indiscreet revelations. The stuff that sounds like gossip. Insiders passing on secrets about their colleagues. Essentially, it is gossip, usually malicious. The kind of material a man reveals to impress a woman of his importance."

"What is this network, Feliks? A brothel?" Fleming said jokingly.

"A brothel of sorts you might say. Very exclusive. Very expensive. By appointment only. Do you know of a nightclub called the *Geisterstunde* on Leipziger Strasse?"

"Of course. I go there often. A bit pricey but the singer is extraordinary."

"Yes, Valeska Kaplinsky is certainly that."

"Are you saying she is involved with running a brothel and harvesting gossip for Polish intelligence?"

"Little more to it than that. Kaplinsky owns the nightclub. She is Polish. A tough survivor. Our association goes back a couple of years to when the nightclub nearly failed during the onset of the Great Depression. Polish intelligence helped out financially."

"In exchange for what, Feliks? Running prostitutes?" Fleming raised his voice slightly realizing a sense of disillusionment about the beautiful and cultured Valeska Kaplinsky."

"When I approached her, she was already engaged in this prostitution service. She prefers the name female escorts or call girls since arrangements are by telephone appointment. Her accountant runs this temporary employment service as a separate business. Many of those attractive young waitresses you notice at the *Geisterstunde* serve as the prostitutes. Voluntarily. A source of extra money in these difficult times.

"I do not moralize. If it mitigates your judgment about Valeska Kaplinsky, several of the women are Jewish. While Kaplinsky pays well for waitressing, the women can more than double their income."

"Therefore, these prostitutes gather information while they are sexually servicing their influential clients. They then give that information to your agent who is now dead?"

"No. The women know nothing of my agent. They pass the information to Kaplinsky."

"The arrangement sounds insecure. What if one of the prostitutes reports this to the Gestapo? Pissed off at someone, or gets in trouble and wants to bargain her way out by giving up what even they must recognize is spying. Obviously, the Soviet agent found the arrangement productive."

"Kaplinsky raised the same question when I approached her. The answer was simple. Kaplinsky tells them the information goes to the Gestapo. A requirement to remain in business. Everyone fears the intrusiveness of the Gestapo intruding into every corner of German life. Therefore this arrangement appears a logical bargain considering their clients are influential and the Gestapo is interest in anything suggesting disloyalty to the Führer."

Fleming reflected for moment before saying, "So Kaplinsky edits the gathered information for importance and gives it to your agent. Who becomes me if I accept?"

Kaczmarek nodded.

"Let's talk further over lunch," Fleming said.

It was an easy sell for Kaczmarek. Fleming rationalized the idea after the shock wore off of Valeska Kaplinsky's involvement with not only prostitution but also high-risk espionage. Already engaged in active espionage provided by Hans Oster of the Abwehr, why not add this?

The Abwehr proved a logical conduit for an ill-defined group of senior military officers fearful of Hitler involving Germany in another war prematurely. His personal friendship with Wehrmacht Colonel Strobel confirmed a strong thread of opposition existed within the military. Accepted into Strobel's intimate circle of army officers with ranks from major to full colonel, the level of distaste for Hitler was astonishing.

Running the Kaplinsky network allowed for immediate access of the raw intelligence gathered by the prostitutes. His initial reaction of hearing of Kaplinsky's involvement replaced with a sense of curiosity. A close association with Valeska Kaplinsky also an intriguing prospect.

* * * *

Once Kaczmarek installed Bruno Goettner as the control for the Kaplinsky network, he never established a direct communications link with Kaplinsky. Too risky in a police state capable of monitoring all communications. Should something happen to Goettner, she should resume activities as normal until contacted by him personally.

Fleming booked a table for the following evening at the *Geisterstunde*. On arriving, the maître d' said, "Your usual table up front, Colonel Fleming?"

"Not this evening, Oscar. Something well toward the back. This is an official evening with a foreign diplomat. We have much to discuss and I do not want to appear rude to the orchestra."

Kaczmarek remarked, "Your usual table? Then you have met Frau Kaplinsky?"

"Casually. She greets me by name, and we exchange a few pleasantries. However, she makes a point of greeting every table after her first performance."

Fleming felt it was more than just friendliness toward a regular patron to her expensive establishment. A reciprocal chemistry seemed to exchange with their eye contact. Perhaps his imagination or just transfixed by her looks and voice.

With the dimmed lights, Kaplinsky likely did not recognize either Fleming or Kaczmarek sitting in the shadows until she turned from another table and started to approach their table. Startled for a moment, she regained her composure as both men stood. "Colonel Fleming, so good to see you."

After kissing her offered hand, Fleming said, "This is Henryk Zieliński a visiting diplomat from the Polish Foreign Ministry. May I present the extraordinarily talented Valeska Kaplinsky."

Kaczmarek kissed her hand and said in a hushed tone, "Is this a good time to talk for a few minutes? We seem out of earshot from the other tables."

"I suppose so," She said while looking at Fleming, her eyes flashing anger.

Kaczmarek said, "Goettner discovered one of Genevieve Meier's regular clients was a Soviet agent. Went by the name Bauer. Goettner intended to eliminate Bauer. Things went wrong."

Kaplinsky glared at Kaczmarek. "Wrong? He went there to kill this Bauer and Genevieve Meier. The newspapers say it was a love triangle. Goettner apparently wrote a note."

"What else was he supposed to do, Valeska? Bauer's interest was to use Meier as a source to gain information about her other clients. Why she agreed to spy for the Soviets is unknown.

"Right now, the Gestapo appears not to know Bauer was a Russian. If they do, it is better that Meier is dead. No reason for them to assume she was passing information to the Soviets. The Gestapo has done nothing indicating suspicion the operation as compromised. The homicides still look to be a love triangle gone violent. Entirely plausible that Goettner as an unmarried man of modest means became infatuated by the sexual allure of a woman like Meier. As a supplier to the *Geisterstunde,* explains how he came to notice Meier since she worked as a waitress here."

"I should shut down the operation. This is more than I bargained for," She said angrily.

Kaczmarek shook his head. "To do so would raise suspicion among the women. Why would the Gestapo suddenly cease having interest in the gossip they previously collected from their male clients? You cannot afford the liability of even one of them speculating their information went somewhere other than the feared Gestapo."

"So I have no choice?" Turning to Fleming, she said, "How long have you been involved with Major Kaczmarek?"

Kaczmarek answered instead. "I have used Colonel Fleming as a back channel to provide intelligence to the Americans. He knew nothing of your operation as a source of information until yesterday.

Kaplinsky caught the eye of a waitress. "Bring me a glass of Champagne and another round of drinks for these gentlemen, Frieda."

After the waitress left, Kaplinsky said, "Why do you do this, Colonel Fleming? Even as a foreign diplomat, spying must be dangerous. The Nazis murder people for far less."

Fleming answered, "I am a soldier. Volunteered for this. Hitler and the Nazis are a danger to the peace of Europe. My personal view, the Nazis are a criminal enterprise led by a deranged madman. Eventually they will become enemies of America. Hitler can never beat America, but he can ignite another great European war. America will not allow a Nazi Europe."

To Kaczmarek, she said, "What if something again goes wrong, Major? Am I also to be sacrificed like Genevieve Meier?"

This time Fleming answered, "No. I can promise you that, Frau Kaplinsky. If your situation ever appears threatened, I will do everything possible to extricate you from Germany. Agreed, Major?"

Kaczmarek nodded in agreement. "Colonel Fleming is in charge here in Berlin."

"Very well. Do you have a good memory, Colonel Fleming?"

"I believe so. Why?"

"Because I do not put anything in writing. Bruno taught me that as a security measure. The women bring anything they believe of interest to me verbally. Bear in mind, they understand this information goes to the Gestapo. If valuable, I pay them a bounty. Major Kaczmarek's money of course. I then verbally relayed information I determined of value to Bruno using the guidelines he instructed."

"That is satisfactory. How often?"

"Weekly unless I had something of particular interest or time sensitive."

"Since Bruno was a supplier of liquor to the nightclub, easy to telephone him on some business pretext. What do you suggest in my situation?"

Kaplinsky gave the question some thought for several moments then adopted a mischievous smile, "Since you are already known as a regular customer, why not encourage the rumor that we are having an affair? Therefore, calling you anytime is easily explained should the police monitor my telephone calls."

Fleming could not resist a smile of his own. "The perfect solution. Delighted to be rumored as the lover of the beautiful and talented Valeska Kaplinsky."

Kaczmarek liked the irony of recruiting the American Fleming to run the Kaplinsky network.

Fleming realized he was sailing close to the shoals. Running a spy network of prostitutes spying on Nazi officials while thinking they were gathering incriminating information for the secret police. If discovered, his diplomatic status unlikely to protect him. In a police state, enemies just disappeared.

He also realized he served a unique role as the sole foreign intelligence source for the United States. Oster and Kaczmarek used known foreign intelligence agents for British MI6 and the French Deuxième Bureau. Their concerns for thwarting Hitler's territorial ambitions rested with the uncertainty of British and French resolve. Although he discouraged both Oster and Kaczmarek about any expectation of the United States weighing in against Hitler, Fleming felt obligated to contribute his services as a backdoor channel to U.S. policy makers. Who was he to gauge what President Roosevelt might do?

Dulles at least confirmed interest in the intelligence he provided. While provoking disgust for the criminal aspect of the Nazi regime, unlikely enough to nudge the United States to declare military support for an allied action with the British and French against Germany.

Kaplinsky now returned to her usual charming demeanor. "Here is the first piece of confidential information for my new intelligence supervisor. Hitler intends to remilitarize the Rhineland, probably by March."

An astounding piece of information if correct. The French and British removed occupation troops from the Rhineland in 1930 under threat by the former German Republic to discontinue war reparations payments. The French turned their attention instead to completing the Maginot defensive fortifications to defend against future German aggression. However, reoccupation by German military forces remained a direct violation of the terms of the Treaty of Versailles and the Locarno Treaties of 1925 specifically defining the territorial boundaries of Europe. Hitler was clearly testing the extent of French resolve.

"The origin of the information?" Kaczmarek asked.

"A senior aide to Foreign Minister Neurath. A man named Gottfried von Schumacher. Like Neurath, from a wealthy aristocratic family. You know his name from prior reports. Late fifties in age. A regular with the escort service. Tips lavishly. Rendezvous always at the Hotel Adlon. Not concerned with being discrete. Champagne and caviar. Demands only brief sexual activity. Seems to prefer spending several hours with beautiful young women that listen intently to his every word rather than the sex. Boasts that he is the principle policy maker of the Foreign Ministry."

"Any further details on the planned reoccupation?" Fleming asked.

"Schumacher said that on a diplomatic mission to Paris, he spoke with a minor politician known to be close to French Premier Laval. This official said that French economic problems have reduced military expenditures. France would likely not oppose German reoccupation of the Rhineland. Schumacher boasted that he convinced Neurath to assure Hitler that a military move into the Rhineland would not be opposed by the few French troops remaining on the west bank of the Rhine."

"Any details regarding German military strength for the re-occupation?" Fleming asked.

"Remember, Colonel, this is just listening to the client talk, not an interrogation. However, Schumacher also rambled on by saying he recommended caution by deploying only a limited German force that could be quickly recalled should the French resist."

"A remarkable piece of intelligence work, Frau Kaplinsky," Fleming said.

"Thank you. Since our relationship has changed, you need to play your part. I am Valeska and you are Spencer. Please reserve a table for this coming Tuesday. A typically slow night. I can spend more time discussing how best to pursue our new arrangement."

Turning to Kaczmarek, she said without warmth, "I suspect I will not be seeing you again, Major Kaczmarek. Have a safe journey back to Warsaw."

* * * *

Otto Decker of the Gestapo personally delivered the report on the triple murder of the prostitute and two men to the office of Sturmbannführer Johann Pfeiffer of the SD. Both had offices in the same building on Prinz-Albrecht-Strasse.

Decker relished in the anticipation of Pfeiffer's reaction.

"This is a report from the criminal police of a triple murder. Something of interest I thought you should see."

Decker handed the report to Pfeiffer then waited a moment as Pfeiffer looked at the report to gauge his reaction. He was not disappointed. Pfeiffer's face stiffened with a sharp intake of breath with his coloring turning pale.

Lifting his head to stare at Decker, "What is so interesting? A prostitute murdered by some deranged client?"

It was more than that as he slammed the folder shut in disgust. The instant he saw the name Genevieve Meier then the photos of her bloody body brought back visions of their recent tryst. Her bare breasts rubbing the inside of his thighs as she performed oral sex on him with her hair cascading across his loins. Never again to be experienced.

"Not that, Sir. The mystery is the identity of one of the two men."

"What do you mean?"

Knowing full well Pfeiffer used the *Zeitarbeitsvermittler* call girl service, he nonetheless said, "This prostitute service is by appointment only. The dead prostitute appeared to be servicing a regular client according to the person booking appointments. According to his records, the client's name is Heinz Bauer. Repeatedly booking this same prostitute for months."

"So where is the mystery, Decker?"

"It is undoubtedly a fake identity. There is a real Heinz Bauer from a wealthy industrial family. Seems this imposter Bauer just used the name, probably to masquerade as an aristocrat."

"So what is your point?"

"We have spent considerable effort in trying to establish his actual identity which remains unknown. At this point in the investigation, we cannot rule out the possibility he might be a foreign intelligence agent, or even some subversive element."

"Based on what evidence?

"Bauer rented two apartments in good neighborhoods about the same time less than a year ago. The building tenants where the murders occurred said the apartment was seldom occupied. None could even describe Bauer. Sparsely furnished with no personal effects. Appears to be just a meeting place. Nothing personally revealing as to the true identity of Bauer found at the other apartment where he apparently resided. Both modest residences inconsistent with someone of wealth. Extensive effort went into hiding his identity. Maintaining two apartments and regularly paying for an expensive prostitute suggests the real possibility that Bauer might be a spy."

Pfeiffer said, "Who is the second man?"

"A sales representative for the liquor distributor to the nightclub *Geisterstunde*. You see, most of the prostitutes of this temporary labor agency front work as waitresses at the *Geisterstunde*. He likely knew of the prostitute having seen her at the nightclub. It appears he came to this rendezvous intending to kill the prostitute out of a sexual obsession. Things went wrong. Bauer had a weapon. All three died in the exchange of gunfire. The details are in the report, Sir."

"Very well. Continue investing to uncover Bauer's real identity. Is there anything else that suggests Bauer was engaged in subversive activity?"

"Not yet, Sir. The thought however occurred to me that recruiting high-class prostitutes servicing influential clients might represent access to confidential information. Over the course of several hours with a beautiful woman after enjoying sex, conversation might lead to unguarded talk."

CHAPTER 23

Berlin, German Reich | Spring 1936

After that evening with Kaczmarek at the *Geisterstunde,* Fleming returned several nights later to discuss with Kaplinsky specifics related to their new arrangement. Admittedly, the cover of acting as Kaplinsky's lover invoked sexual fantasy. Beyond her beauty, there existed an indefinable attraction when she was close to him.

Arriving early, the maître d' greeted him. "Good evening, Colonel Fleming. Frau Kaplinsky told me to bring you to her office when you arrived."

After knocking, Kaplinsky answered the door. "Thank you, Georg."

Kaplinsky looked different this close up with her performance makeup in the bright light of her office. Dressed in a robe, Fleming took in her figure with the belt pulled snug around her waist accentuating her full breasts.

"Good to see you, Spencer. Please come in. Champagne?"

"Thank you."

Kaplinsky motioned him to an easy chair while she poured two glasses from a bottle in an ice bucket. Returning with the drinks, she afforded a view of deep cleavage as she bent forward. As she sat down, she swung a bare leg across her other knee exposing her thigh. Obviously she knew what she was doing.

Flirting or just her way of rebelling against Kaczmarek's manipulation?

"Did Major Kaczmarek tell you why I spy for him?"

"He said he approached you with a financial proposition when your business was struggling. I suspect it is more than that. The *Geisterstunde* appears successful now. I doubt you need the added income any longer. You do realize how dangerous this has become?

"Yes. The Gestapo merging with the state police gives them broader powers."

"Far worse than that. They are now exempt from judicial oversight. They can imprison anyone for whatever reason. So why do you continue?"

"Not sure I even know the answer to that. Kaczmarek is a Polish patriot. I am not doing this out of Polish patriotism. I was born in Silesia but spent my adult life in Berlin. I am as much German as Polish. In the beginning, it was about the money. Like everyone, survival was difficult during the never-ending hard times. As a woman alone, I endured much to get where I am today. I care nothing about politics, but instinctively I hate Adolf Hitler and the National Socialists thugs.

"Hitler is no mere politician though. A murderous madman. His rants on the radio disgust me. Perhaps I do this as my way of resisting something so evil. Treatment of German Jews particularly troubles me. Do you know there are millions of Jews in Poland? Far more than in Germany. I grew up in a largely Jewish neighborhood in Wrocław. Kaczmarek fears a future invasion by Germany. I fear the fate of Polish Jews. Perhaps that is why I continue to do this."

Fleming shook his head. "Not my place to dissuade you, but you should think seriously about leaving Germany. With your voice and looks, you could become another Marlene Dietrich."

"Really, Spencer? I am almost forty. A little old for a movie career."

"All the more reason to make a move know, Valeska. Germany is no place for someone with your talent."

"Thought you were supposed to use me to gather intelligence rather than encourage me to get out of Germany."

"That is Kaczmarek's job. I saw how you reacted to hearing that Kaczmarek ordered Goettner to eliminate the Soviet spy and the Meier woman. This is a dangerous and dirty business, Valeska. I have limited immunity with my diplomatic status. You do not. Germany is a police state run by criminals. Only getting worse. Get out before it is too late."

She got up to refill their glasses. Tears clouded her eyes as she touched his cheek with her hand. "Been a long time since a man appeared concerned about my well-being."

The tender moment passed quickly as she retrieved the Champagne bottle, refilling their glasses.

"Something you should know, Spencer. Among my working girls, three are Jewish. Genevieve Meier was Jewish."

Fleming's face tightened. "My god, Valeska, you know that only adds to the risk."

"Yes, of course. These women sell their bodies to support their families. Was I supposed to turn them away?"

Fleming sighed, "Why do these women pass along confidential information from their sex clients?"

"Prostitution is illegal. They believe I give the information they gather from their clients to the Gestapo as a way of protection. A requirement to stay in business. They rationalize passing along gossip as nothing more than spreading the secrets of men they despise. Presumably, the Gestapo uses the information for leverage or blackmail. Just another Nazi trick. Kaczmarek suggested it prevented anyone from going to the Gestapo with them thinking it was already an undercover police operation."

They spent further time discussing specifics of handling the information, including exchanging telephone numbers. Kaplinsky said, "Your calls must always sound like two lovers. If an emergency, use the phrase *just received some distressing news about a close friend.* And speaking of elaborating on our romantic affair is next Tuesday evening convenient?"

Convenient for what he wondered? "Certainly. What did you have in mind?"

Smiling warmly, "A late dinner. On Tuesdays, I only do the one early performance. Afterwards, we can enjoy a dinner in my apartment upstairs. It will give the staff reason to gossip. Word will get around. The perfect cover for your frequent presence."

* * * *

With Abwehr and OKW headquarters within easy walking distance of the United States Embassy, Fleming's frequent meetings with Abwehr Major Richter at a nearby coffee shop easily explained as friendship rather than official business. Fleming occasionally visited the Richter residence as he did with Wehrmacht Colonel Strobel. Natural for a foreign military attaché to establish a circle of friends with other military officers.

"Colonel Oster told me to convey these thoughts to you, Spencer. There should remain no doubt that Hitler intends to expand German territory by military means if necessary. We believe he will move much sooner than previously expected. His first objective is Austria, already internally weakened. Hitler realized the mistake of the clumsy failed putsch in 1934 by the Austrian Nazis.

"Since that time, he is pursuing the same strategy that brought him to power. Weaken vulnerable institutions by subversion to fragment already opposing factions. Destroy the opposition by indirect means where possible. When necessary, resort to coercion and selective murder. Then use seemingly legal methods to seize power in the political chaos.

"Since the failed putsch by the Austrian Nazis, relations with Mussolini are much improved. Sources report a directed effort of the Foreign Ministry to draft an agreement of mutual understanding with Rome. A necessary prerequisite for Hitler's bloodless annexation of Austria into a greater Germany.

"Hitler has also squeezed Austria. Chancellor Schuschnigg is on the verge of concluding a treaty with Germany. The deal trades German assurance of Austrian sovereignty for relaxing restrictions on Austrian Nazis. Placing two known Nazi collaborators on his cabinet and several others in sensitive government posts. Even releasing several thousand Nazis from prisons."

"That is absurd. Schschnigg must know he cannot trust Hitler," Fleming said.

"Seems obvious. However, Schschnigg is playing with what Colonel Oster believes to be a weak hand. Mussolini put an end to Hitler's backing of Austrian Nazis to seize power and ultimately annex Austria. Having his own designs on Austria, Mussolini threatened Italian military intervention into southern Austria. Since that miscalculation, Hitler and Mussolini are now looking increasingly friendly. You can report to Washington that negotiations are expected to soon produce a German-Italian agreement."

"How did the Nazis turn around the situation since the murder of Dollfuss in the failed putsch?"

"Heydrich again. The devil's henchman. The SD has been busy. The border is a sieve. SD and Gestapo agents move back and forth fomenting political turmoil at every level. Austria is nearly bankrupt. With a limited army of questionable loyalty, Schschnigg must cope with armed opposition from internal paramilitary forces."

"So Oster believes Austria will topple?"

"Almost certainly."

"What is the likely British reaction?"

Richter's expression showed disgust. "The British have no backbone. They prefer to wait for Hitler to rearm to a point when it becomes too late. Where does the United States stand?"

"Tell Oster I just met with my connection here in Berlin. A personal friend who understands European affairs. He assures me your intelligence product reaches President Roosevelt directly. Several of his most trusted foreign policy advisers told my intermediary the material provokes much interest. However, you should tell Oster my personal view is that means very little in the way of influencing policy."

"Why?"

"If you cannot get the British and French to be more aggressive, how can you expect the United States to make a difference? Questionable if they might back a British-French stand, but taking an independent aggressive stance will never happen. Hitler will continue to play his enemies until it becomes too late to stop him as you said, Konrad.

"My friend put it best. If a viable resistance exists within the officer corps, their only hope is to remove Hitler. Ridding Germany of Hitler also means eliminating the Nazi Schutzstaffel. Everything therefore rests with the Wehrmacht."

"Not that easy. Even those general officers that despise Hitler feel bound by their oath of allegiance."

"Well fuck all, Konrad. Then Germany is doomed. Hitler is a psychopath. He will destroy Germany and a good part of Europe if he starts another war. Remove Hitler and you can negotiate with Britain and France. The United States will back even a conservative government. Germany can then renegotiate the oppressive terms of the 1919 treaty and move forward."

"I will convey your comments to Colonel Oster as the likely position of your government."

Richter descended into a gloom. Fleming knew he agreed with his comments. "Is there any sort of organized discussion among enough generals that it could lead to eliminating Hitler through a military coup?"

Richter took a deep breath. "Several I know might. Colonel Oster keeps his network highly secret for security reasons. Only he could answer that question. Is there a possibility the United States might secretly provide inducements should Hitler be removed?"

"I do not know. Tell Colonel Oster this. If he can provide more specifics on such a possible likelihood, I will see that it gets to President Roosevelt. Roosevelt is very much hands-on. A clever politician that likes schemes. Who knows? It presents an alternative that addresses the root problem. Perhaps with foreign support for a more agreeable Germany, the generals may find the backbone to act."

Richter nodded. "Very well. Now to something more immediate. I believe I am under surveillance. Notice the fellow at the table near the door. He walked behind me for a block at a distance. Then that other fellow to our left. They look out of place. Both reading newspapers just drinking coffee. This is lunchtime but they are not eating. I might be wrong, but keep your eyes open. You might be followed too."

"Why would they be following you, Konrad?"

"As you said, the Wehrmacht is the only German institution capable of stopping Hitler. I interact with many foreign diplomats and military attachés. Perhaps the SS is concerned with a Wehrmacht conspiracy supported by a foreign power. Not sure what else you are up to poking around as military attaché, Spencer, but stay alert. Being an American diplomat might not be protection."

* * * *

After a laborious day of encrypting messages, Fleming readied himself for dinner with Valeska Kaplinsky with anticipation. A very long time since he felt this way. Not since Dominique seventeen years ago. A lifetime.

Readied with a haircut, freshly cleaned dress uniform, and polished boots, he set off for the *Geisterstunde*.

Good evening, Colonel Fleming," Georg the maître d' said. "I will inform Frau Kaplinsky of your arrival." Motioning to one of the attractive waitresses he said, "Anna, please show Colonel Fleming to table five."

Fleming followed Anna admiring her shapely behind in a tight gown. He wondered if she was one of Kaplinsky's prostitutes.

The orchestra was playing soft American jazz. Only a few other patrons this slow night. Mostly men. None in uniform.

Kaplinsky approached his table in the soft light. As usual, she looked magnificent. This evening she wore her signature fitted gown with revealing leg accented by a long string of pearls. The cut of the gown shaped the fullness of her breasts with the pearls drawing the intended attention.

After he kissed her hand, she sat down at the small table for two. Smiling broadly and staring into his eyes she said, "I looked forward all day to seeing you. I spend too little time relaxing. Berlin under the Nazis seems to suck the oxygen out of life's pleasures."

"You look especially stunning tonight. I spent the day dealing with boring administrative duties while anticipating this evening."

She rested her hand on his hand. "Easy to play the part of lover to such a handsome man. You must tell me later the significance of those colorful ribbons on your chest. Tonight in your honor, I framed my performance around several American popular songs. Some in English, others that work well in German."

Glancing at the orchestra, she nodded. Turning to Fleming, she gave his hand a squeeze. "Show time. Meet me backstage when I finish."

Kaplinsky was waiting for him after the performance as she gave instructions to one of the orchestra musicians.

Grabbing his arm, "What did you think?"

"Marvelous as usual, Valeska." Calling her by her given name felt intimate.

She continued holding his arm as they climbed the stairs. She opened the door to reveal a fashionably decorated apartment. Please make yourself comfortable. You might open the Champagne chilling in the bucket over there."

"Coming close to him, "I am glad to see you this evening, Spencer." Giving him a quick kiss on the cheek, "Give me a few minutes to freshen up and change into something comfortable."

He cautioned himself to constrain his aroused fantasies. However, opening the Champagne reminded him to moderate his alcohol intake just in case.

None of that proved necessary.

It was not long before Kaplinsky returned. Dressed in a silk robe tied at the waist and still wearing her heels.

Fleming smiled then turned to pour her a glass of Champagne.

"Perhaps we can wait later for the Champagne, Spencer."

Turning back toward her, his surprised expression immediately changed to a grin of approval.

Having unfastened the robe and dropping it to the floor, Valeska Kaplinsky stood there completely naked except for her high heels and the pearl necklace falling between her breasts.

"I have seen you look at me, Spencer. I also want to make love to you. We can drink and dine later."

He crossed the space separating them. Embracing her, they kissed for the first time increasing their mutual arousal. His hands moved over her back then her butt, eventually traveling up to her breasts. His arousal increasing as she massaged his crotch.

Moving to the bedroom, she sat on the bed with one leg crossed as he hurriedly undressed. After he removed his shoes and trousers, she hooked a finger motioning him to come closer.

She pulled down his underwear. Caressing his full erection, "That is beautiful. A circumcised cock is so much more appealing." As he breathed heavily, she took him into her mouth eliciting a protracted groan of pleasure.

After a time, her took her head in his hands and said, "Save some of that. Now I want you."

She flicked off her heels and fell back on the bed. Instead of entering her, he stood there admiring the sight of her body as he gently probed between her legs with his hand. Dropping to his knees, he placed his lips on her pubic hair gently brushing over her clitoris. She groaned with delight.

He wanted to sustain her pleasure as long as possible knowing he could not last long once he penetrated her vagina.

Her groans grew louder as the muscles in her lower abdomen distended as she approached orgasm. Slowing his attentions with his lips, he quickly stood and entered her. Pulling him deeper by grabbing his butt with her hands, she worked her hips in rhythm with his measured thrusts as they both reached climax.

Raised on his arms, he caught his breath while still remaining coupled inside her.

She looked up at him, "I wanted to make love to you for some time. That is why I suggested the cover of you becoming my lover. No acting required."

"Did you realize I was also attracted to you?" He said. "Stupid question I guess. Every man is attracted to you."

"Yes I knew. It was in your eyes."

As he withdrew and rolled over on his back, she propped up on her left elbow letting her breast rest against his chest as she manipulated his cock with her hand. As her attentions eventually brought forth another erection, she said, "Pleasure me a little more?"

She threw her leg over to straddle him and inserted him inside her. Moving back and forth, she said in raspy whisper, "Relax and let me do it."

Both thoroughly spent, they stayed in bed caressing and kissing for some time. After dressing, they sat down to enjoy drinks before ordering dinner from downstairs.

Picking up his uniform tunic, she asked, "These ribbons. Awards? German officers do not wear these. Only the Iron Cross."

"Commendations and participation in campaigns."

"What is this light blue one with the small stars?"

"That is the Medal of Honor. America's highest award for valor."

"How did you earn this?"

"My first year as an officer in Mexico in 1916. Killed a lot of Mexican bandits."

"Are some of these others for valor?"

He pointed to his distinguish service cross, silver star, and French Croix de Guerre.

"You fought in the Great War?"

"Yes, but enough about my military career. Where did you train to sing opera?"

Telling him she lost her family to the Great War, she presented a version of her past omitting the affair she used to advance her circumstances and music career. Downplaying her pragmatic reasons for developing the exclusive prostitution service, she confessed to the emotionally unwise decision of agreeing to engage in espionage against the Nazis. She portrayed her success as nothing more than an opportunistic businesswoman surviving extraordinary times. A confident woman making no apologies.

After an excellent dinner, Fleming launched into his planned advice for Kaplinsky. After lovemaking, he felt more strongly about her leaving Germany. He did not want to lose Kaplinsky to a tragic death like Dominque Dumont. To hell with Kaczmarek.

For that matter, to hell with his involvement in useless espionage. He longed for a normal life.

"Valeska. I meant what I said before. You should leave Germany. The German economy is in serious distress for the simple reason Hitler is spending vast sums on military rearmament. Things will only get worse. He will lead Germany into another war if he annexes Austria and probably invades Czechoslovakia. Kaczmarek believes Hitler will also push east and attack Poland at some time. Hitler needs natural resources. If that happens, your business ceases to exist while trapping you in Germany. In the meantime, you are playing a dangerous game."

With the death of Goettner and Meier, she gave much thought to Fleming's suggestion about leaving Germany. Yet the thought held its own uncertainty. What would she do? What would happen to her employees? She felt an obligation. The *Geisterstunde* and even the call girl service was a lifeline for many. Excuses or just in denial?

She also knew nothing about Spencer Fleming other than their mutual attraction.

"Leave why you have the chance. I can get you to America. Do you have money?"

"Some."

"That could be problem. The government is restricting currency leaving Germany. Your bank will block any sizable withdrawal."

"Yes, I know. I keep most of my money carefully hidden in cash. Knew this time might come."

"Well there you have it. You go on holiday and never return."

"What about you?"

"I will take you to Paris then to America. Pursue your singing career. Been thinking about leaving the Army anyway. Germany under the Nazis makes my official duties irrelevant. I only agreed to stay on to try to make a difference. Time I did something different."

* * * *

Hitler dispelled any doubts about his military ambitions in July. Days after Nationalist Spanish rebels consisting of dissident right wing army officers began a rebellion against the leftist Republican government Hitler sent critical military support. Immediately forming a composite unit called the Condor Legion, the first act was to transport battle-hardened Spanish colonial troops from Morocco to southern Spain by German aircraft.

Consisting predominately of the Luftwaffe and armored elements of the German Army, the intervention afforded an opportunity to test new German military hardware and provide combat experience for officers. Spain proved the perfect testing ground for the German Junkers Ju 87 Stuka dive-bomber and the Junkers Ju-52 Trimotor transport-bomber. Aircraft that would soon terrorize the skies over Europe.

German military participation in Spain in support of the Nationalist Spanish Fascist Falange fostered further turmoil in Europe. Unprepared for provoking a broader confrontation with Britain or France by increasing German support to the Spanish Fascist rebels in the civil war, Hitler instead persuaded Mussolini to provide Italian ground troops. This limited German involvement while furthering Hitler's ambition to enhance Germany's military stature. Fostering ties with Fascist Italy, Austria, and possibly Spain if the rebels proved successful, provided Germany a loose European alliance.

CHAPTER 24

Berlin, German Reich | Autumn 1936

Within a few weeks of their last meeting, Fleming was again having coffee with Major Richter.

"No doubt about being followed," Richter said. "The Gestapo is careless in their surveillance. Perhaps they wish me to know as a way of intimidation. Also means they might have an interest in you. Nevertheless, assume you are under surveillance and keep vigilant.

"Colonel Oster is interested in the suggestion about possible U.S. support if the Wehrmacht removes Hitler. Understandably, he has many questions. He therefore wants to meet with you personally. Tensions between the Abwehr and Heydrich's SD have escalated. Such a meeting between you and the Colonel must remain secret. Any ideas?"

Fleming said, "Are you saying that Oster is part of some broader conspiracy among the General Staff?"

Richter shook his head, "No. I am not saying that. There is no conspiracy. Given his position within the Abwehr, Colonel Oster fosters relationships with a large number of senior army officers. As you can imagine, he knows many that share his concerns over Hitler leading Germany to a premature war we cannot win. He does not share every detail with me, but I can confirm there are many generals opposed to Hitler."

"Enough to engineer a coup?"

"That I cannot say. Since Oster wishes to further discuss the matter, you can perhaps infer the possibility exists."

"Is Admiral Canaris aware of Oster's ...*independent actions*?"

"No. Canaris is only devoted to preserving the military's independence and therefore the Abwehr. He generally supports Hitler. A clever old fox with years of experience running intelligence operations. For his own reasons, Colonel Oster prefers to stay clear of confiding in the Admiral."

After a few moments of thought, Fleming said, "If the Gestapo is following you then we must assume Oster is also under surveillance. What about something seemingly in the open? A reception at the U.S. Embassy for senior officers of the Wehrmacht. Canaris and Oster included. Perhaps another senior Abwehr officer and of course the senior army officers to allow Oster to remain in the background.

"I can perhaps convince Ambassador Dodd it is a good opportunity for him to discuss German rearmament directly with the military leadership. The entire exercise created for an opportunity for me to be alone with Oster. It need not be long. Oster should prepare his demands from the allies in exchange for the military removing Hitler."

"By removing Hitler, what specifically do you mean?"

Fleming paused realizing he was negotiating details of a coup d'état backed by the United States. "Assassinated. Killed immediately. If he survives, he becomes a rallying figure. To be successful, you must obviously dismantle the entire structure of the Schutzstaffel. Himmler, Heydrich, and all senior SS executed. The remedy goes beyond judicial process. The same brutal tactics they used to behead the SA in 1934."

"Hitler will likely protest to your ambassador inviting the Wehrmacht General Staff to the United States Embassy."

"Let him. Perhaps he will not risk making this an issue considering the start of the Olympic Games. I assume the Wehrmacht still enjoys a measure of independence?"

"I will convey your proposal to Oster and let you know soon," Richter said.

****

Although it had been months since the triple homicide involving an expensive prostitute and the mystery of the identity of one of the victims, Otto Decker remained interested. If for no other reason than Johann Pfeiffer of the SD frequently used this exclusive prostitution service. On his desk was a new report that rewarded his original suspicions.

Having infiltrated a Berlin communist cell, the Gestapo conducted a raid on a warehouse during some sort of gathering. As the group of a dozen tried to escape, one man attempted suicide by biting a cyanide capsule. In the scuffle, he dropped the capsule. Obviously, this marked the suspect as something more than a mere communist. Under torture, he eventually relented by admitting he was a Soviet agent. More than that, a senior field operative recently arrived from Moscow. He revealed the identities of several agents working for the GRU in Berlin. Among the names, Heinz Bauer. His real identity Mikhail Borisovich Gekht, a Russian Jew.

With this new evidence confirming his earlier suspicions, Decker seized the opportunity to use the discovery for personal advantage. If the Russians saw the intelligence value of using these prostitutes as a source of information on their influential clients, the Gestapo should do the same. He took the idea to Pfeiffer.

"What is it you hope to achieve, Decker?" Pfeiffer asked.

"We will know the personal habits of these men of importance. Useful information in many ways I should image. Since we shall know the venues of the sexual rendezvous, it offers the possibility of recording the indiscretions of the clients. Might uncover anyone engaging in subversive activities against the Reich. At the least useful leverage."

Knowing Pfeiffer used this prostitution service, Decker enjoyed imagining him trying to recall any indiscrete remarks he may have made.

"Good work, Decker. I like the idea of using whores to gather information useful for achieving our objectives. Proceed with setting this in place. However, order that all intelligence gathered comes directly to you. Considering the sensitivity of what you may uncover, you will then submit your reports only to me, not through the usual Gestapo chain of command. Understood?"

"Yes, Sir."

* * * *

Decker with two other Gestapo officers confronted Walter Fischer in his nondescript office. With Fischer's private office door closed, his terrified secretary tried to continue working despite a Gestapo agent going through the files next to her desk.

Seated at his desk, a terrified Walter Fischer said to Decker, "What is this about?"

"Let me warn you, Herr Fischer. You are in serious trouble. I expect your complete cooperation. If I do not get what I want, you will come with us for further questioning at headquarters. That is not something you want. Rumors do not exaggerate about what happens to those that are uncooperative."

Sweating profusely, Fischer dabbed his forehead with a handkerchief. Middle-aged, he suffered from hypertension. His heart rate increased to a dangerous level.

"Therefore listen carefully. We know all about *Zeitarbeitsvermittler.*" Decker took a business card from the holder on Fischer's desk. A temporary employment agency is a clever cover for an exclusive prostitution ring. How much do you charge?"

Fischer swallowed before saying, "600 Reichsmarks for an evening."

The figure surprised Decker. Almost his month's pay. Even Pfeiffer could only afford the extravagance because of his family's wealth.

"A significant fee. A select clientele I imagine. Tell me, how was Heinz Bauer able to afford the frequent services of Genevieve Meier? "

Fischer's face twitched. "I believe he was from a wealthy industrial family."

"Well, I am sure you read that in the newspapers. Yet he did not come from wealth. He was not even German. His money came from Moscow. You see he was a Russian spy. A Jew. The whore Meier was also Jewish. The Russian used her to extract information from influential clients during long evenings of sex and drinking. I assume many of her clients are in the government or military?"

Fischer took a deep breath trying to calm his fear. "Yes."

"How many whores do you employ?"

"Eighteen."

"We know at least three are also Jews. Not only employing young Jewish women in a criminal enterprise, but also facilitating fornication between Jews and Aryans. Are you aware of the penalties for violating the racial laws?"

Fischer nodded.

"Here is the deal, Herr Fischer. You now work for the Gestapo. You will provide a list of appointments daily, including the location for the rendezvous. You will provide me with a key to this office. Every evening someone will come in to pick up that night's schedule. Place it in a sealed envelope marked confidential.

"This arrangement is to remain known only to you. Your secretary is not to know."

"How will I explain your visit today?" Fischer asked.

"A follow up to the triple murder involving the Meier woman. I also presume that Valeska Kaplinsky is your silent partner. After all, she supplies the women. She is also not to know of our special arrangement. Tell her the reason for this visit was our discovery of the real identity of the other dead man. The son of someone important looking to avoid scandal. A follow up report therefore necessary. Nothing more. Understood?"

Fischer nodded.

* * * *

Major Richter sent word that Colonel Oster liked the idea of a reception at the embassy, even suggesting some dates.

Fleming approached Ambassador Dodd with the idea. Since arriving in Germany, Dodd's tenure proved increasingly difficult. The Nazis held him in little esteem. They saw him as a bill collector, constantly lobbying to ensure repayment of American reconstruction loans while not offering relief of reparation payments. His fellow diplomats regarded him as odd.

Dodd's frugality became notorious. His official U.S. Embassy social affairs offered only sparse food and drink. Understandable since the Department of State provided inadequate funds to support the expected social status of the embassy of the world's most powerful nation. For that reason, most important ambassadorships went to wealthy political contributors of the ruling party, supplementing the meager social budget with personal funds. Dodd came from academia without the typical financial resources of most ambassadors.

Fleming sold Dodd on the idea as largely to heighten his work as military attaché. To that end, he told Dodd the War Department authorized paying for the reception. He also told Dodd it was a good opportunity to expand his understanding of German rearmament. After all, it was those massive expenditures causing the current German economic crisis, thereby impacting servicing the debt on the American loans.

Dodd argued about how the German Foreign Ministry might view independent interaction with the Wehrmacht. Fleming responded, "Do you really care, Mr. Ambassador? They treat you with disrespect.

"This will demonstrate U.S. initiative. We send out the invitations before those Nazi knuckle-draggers in the Foreign Ministry have time to complain formally. The Wehrmacht still enjoys substantial independence from the Nazi ministries and the SS. Hitler's avowed territorial ambitions require the support of the Wehrmacht."

The reception was set for the end of October. Fleming tasked Richter to confer with Oster and create the guest list with their contact information. Fleming arranged for an impressive array of hors d'oeuvres, Champagne, and assorted liquors. For entertainment, Kaplinsky formed a quartet from her *Geisterstunde* musicians. Dulles would reimburse him once told the reason for the unusual expenditure.

The reception was a casual affair starting on a Friday afternoon. Surprisingly well attended. These senior General Staff officers engaged in spirited conversation with both Fleming and Dodd. Their questions focused on the views of the Roosevelt administration toward Germany. To Dodd's credit, he adroitly found enough common ground in agreeing with their complaints of the terms of the Treaty of Versailles to turn the conversation to rearmament and the effects on the German economy.

Ritter von Strobel accompanied his boss General Ludwig Beck. As a close friend, Strobel said in a hushed whisper to Fleming, "This is extraordinary, Spencer. I appreciate your audacity. This will drive Hitler to one of his rages."

Oster arrived at five o'clock with Admiral Canaris and another Abwehr army officer.

Oster introduced himself to Fleming then introduced his Abwehr colleagues. "Let me introduce Admiral Wilhelm Canaris chief of the Abwehr and Oberst Horst Ehrlinger head of our foreign branch, Amtsgruppe Ausland.

"Major Richter speaks highly of Colonel Fleming. They have developed a close friendship." Turning to Fleming, "Richter says you have a long history as a military intelligence officer. He also says you were decorated for valor several times."

"You saw combat in the Great War?" Canaris asked.

"Yes, Sir. Intelligence officer. I had a tendency of sticking my nose in the wrong places."

Canaris smiled. "That is what a good intelligence officer does, Colonel."

At that instant, Ambassador Dodd's gregarious daughter Martha approached. Attractive and charming, she typically served as embassy hostess instead of her more reclusive mother. The military officers warmed to her good looks and intelligent interchange in passable German.

Oster let Martha Dodd lead Canaris and Ehrlinger to the refreshment tables while motioning a waiter for drinks. Hanging back with Oster, Fleming steered Oster to a different table acting as a bar. After picking up glasses of Champagne, they moved off together to a secluded corner of the room where they could talk.

Oster began, "I held a number of discussions with like-minded officers. A sufficient number tacitly agreed to participate in a military coup to topple Hitler in exchange for assurances from the United States, Britain, and France. I have in my pocket a list of those conditions by which I believe a coalition of army officers could be assembled to proceed with such a move."

"Give me an idea of the Wehrmacht's demands, Colonel."

"Very well. Removal of reparations."

"What about repayment of reconstruction loans?"

"That should not be an issue. Next, allow German rearmament to proceed without restriction but recognizing it must not detract from rehabilitating the German economy. Removal of all tariffs on German exports and sanctions on imports to allow a return to normal economic growth. Most importantly for the United States to ensure German security."

"You do not trust the British and France I assume?"

"That is the consensus. Most of us blame them for the punitive terms of the Treaty of Versailles."

"What is this new German government offering in return?"

"Renounce any claims on Austria and Czechoslovakia. Respect the borders as defined in the 1919 treaty. Disband the SS and the Gestapo. End all persecution of Jews and other racial minorities."

Fleming nodded. "That should provide a basis for negotiation. Tell me this, Colonel, do you believe it possible to mount such an action against the Nazis?"

Oster looked straight into Fleming's eyes. "I believe that is possible if a pathway to a renewed Germany is assured by conditional foreign support. The British government may talk of threats of war should Hitler take military action against Austria or Czechoslovakia. Their resolve is questionable. They too are rearming but British public opinion is firmly against entering another war on the Continent."

Fleming said, "If the will to act in rebellion exists, does the military possess enough loyal troops to confront the armed SS? This may start to look like a civil war. That is why eliminating

Hitler immediately becomes essential. Kill Hitler and Nazism dies."

"I realize that, Colonel Fleming. Loyal troops will not be a problem. I can assure you, that if we move forward, Adolf Hitler will be the first to die for the good of Germany and the SS beheaded."

Fleming nodded. "I will send your proposal to Washington. A small group close to the President. I guarantee delivery of your offer to President Roosevelt personally. If the President wishes to consider your offer, how do you suggest we proceed?"

"I gave that some thought. Negotiations must involve representatives of the United States and Britain. I suggest London."

"What about the French?"

"France is in political turmoil. The Wehrmacht will not negotiate with the current leftist government of the Popular Front. France is too self-absorbed. That is why we have focused backdoor channels only to the British government. At least the British voice condemnation to Hitler's provocative remarks about Austria and Czechoslovakia. His vision of *Lebensraum* threatens all of eastern Europe. France will come around if Britain and the United States stand in support."

"Who should be approached in Britain?"

"We suggest Robert Vansittart. Permanent Undersecretary at the Foreign Office. A staunch opponent to appeasement to Hitler and outside the cabinet. He is less susceptible to political pressures. Certain of my associates have already engaged in confidential conversations with Mr. Vansittart.

"What previously was a speculative alternative if unable to dissuade Hitler from his disastrous course of action now appears the only course. Time is now critical. With the prospect of added reasons to pursue this remedy, we have assigned a code name. *Operation Krebs.*"

Fleming nodded. "Operation Cancer. Yes. Entirely appropriate. I will let Major Richter know how Washington views your proposal. Am I at liberty to discuss specifics with Richter?"

"Yes. He knows everything. Now to the document you requested outlining our expectations for a post-Hitler Germany. It is signed only by me. At this time, I agreed with my associates not to reveal their names for reasons of security. You can assure your President that those willing to participate in this coup are senior officers commanding formations loyal to them. The combined troop strength sufficient to execute the plan. Including eliminating the Schutzstaffel leadership of Himmler, Heydrich, and others."

"I wish you success, Colonel. This could save not only Germany but Europe."

Fleming then deftly steered Oster around the corner to a hallway where they covertly made the exchange of Oster's exceptional document.

Recent initiatives by Hitler indicative of preparations for war caused Fleming to push Oster and his conspirators. In August, Hitler drafted the Four Year Plan to restructure German economics toward self-sufficiency while sustaining the rate of rearmament funding.

Hitler called for achieving a superior army by 1940. In a personally drafted memo, Hitler said, "The extent of the military development of our resources cannot be too large, nor its pace too swift. The role of the economy was simply to support Germany's self-assertion and the extension of *Lebensraum*."

In October, Hitler and Mussolini signed a pact recognizing mutual interests between Germany and Italy. In November, Germany signed an anti-communist alliance with Japan, continuing to fortify a coalition antagonistic to the Soviet Union.

Fleming realized his covert efforts meant he was helping shape United States foreign policy.

* * * *

Unexpectedly, Kaplinsky called Fleming one morning at the embassy a week after their first night of intimacy. "I need to see you this evening, Spencer. I miss you."

"Of course. I will look forward to it." Having agreed to minimize their telephone calls for fear of Gestapo monitoring, the tone of her call was alarming. Something possibly gone wrong, hopefully not urgent. He imagined all sorts of dire scenarios for the rest of the day.

He arrived early and Georg escorted him to Kaplinsky's apartment.

Distraught, she embraced him. She had yet to apply her makeup or do her hair for the evening's performance.

"What's wrong?"

"My accountant Walter Fischer. His wife called me. He collapsed this morning. A doctor was with him when I arrived. The doctor diagnosed a mild heart attack. Walter suffers from acute attacks of angina from a serious heart condition. Sit down, Spencer. There is much more."

"How is he?" Fleming knew that Fischer ran the prostitution service.

"Not good according to the doctor. Without his wife hearing, he told me what brought on the heart attack. A visit by the Gestapo."

Fleming was stunned. Circumstances deteriorating so soon.

"An officer by the name of Hauptsturmführer Decker told him the man called Heinz Bauer killed with Bruno Goettner and Genevieve Meier was a Russian spy. Said Meier was obviously the Russian's source for gathering material from her clients. She was also Jewish as are at least three other of the other women. Decker threatened to charge Fischer with criminal acts of engaging in prostitution and violating German racial laws. He faced a long prison sentence in a concentration camp if he did not cooperate. If Decker pressed collaboration with a Soviet spy, possibly death by guillotine. "

"Cooperate how?"

"Provide daily reports of the identities of clients booking the girls and the locations of the rendezvous."

"For blackmailing leverage on influential clients. Did Fischer say anything about you?"

She nodded. "Decker told him they knew of my involvement with the prostitution service. Warned him not to reveal this arrangement with the Gestapo to me."

"Yet he did."

"Walter said, we can perhaps still continue."

"Continue what?"

"Gathering information. Pass to the Gestapo and continue passing to Kaczmarek."

"Are you both mad? This is hanging by a thread. Everything hinges on a guy with a bad heart risking dying in a concentration camp, or death by guillotine. Why does he do this? Is he also Polish?"

"No. Walter is just a good man. Despises Hitler for his brutality. The persecution of Jews. Says Hitler is destroying his beloved Fatherland. Feels sorry for the girls selling their bodies.

"Walter smiled at the irony. The girls always thought they were just spying for the Gestapo. Said he is willing to go on if I am. He sees no other way out. We cannot just shutdown given the involvement of the Gestapo."

Fleming shook his head in disapproval. "No. Valeska, that is crazy. If anything goes wrong, your life is over. What if some high-ranking Nazi way over this Decker's head decides to shut you down. You and Fischer end your lives in a concentration camp."

Kaplinsky sat down and buried her head in her hands. Fleming got up and knelt in front of her. "Listen to me. I told you before you should leave Germany. Now I am telling you that you must leave. What do you say?"

"What about Walter and the women?"

"I will think on it, but that is unfortunately impossible. Getting just you out of Germany safely requires careful planning. You are undoubtedly a person of interest to the Gestapo. Difficult enough to evade possible Gestapo surveillance."

She pulled him closer and kissed him. "For the first time in my life, I am scared, Spencer?"

"Don't panic. I will personally take you out of Germany. Get you to America."

"Will you come with me to America, Spencer?"

"Yes, Valeska." He realized he wanted this unusual woman he knew little about. Yet what he felt went beyond his intense attraction to Valeska Kaplinsky.

For some time he thought about leaving the Army. This now became the catalyst to make the move. These last years as military attaché only interesting because the rise of German Nazism led by a psychotic megalomaniac dropped him into a web of intrigue. Now turning dangerous. Germany was rapidly descending into another European catastrophe. Unless Oster and his cabal of anti-Nazi generals could behead the beast. Nothing more he could do. The danger now coming closer. Time for him to leave Germany.

What exactly he wanted remained uncertain. Something stimulating, yet not necessarily the pursuit of adventure. Return to the United States. Furthering his military career no longer attractive. His background should afford a range of opportunities. Just a matter of being creative. More than anything, he wanted Valeska Kaplinsky as part of his life.

CHAPTER 25

Berlin, German Reich | Winter 1936

Fleming understood communicating Oster's proposal required more than simply transcribing a lengthy report. It meant a telephone conversation to communicate his impressions and field questions from Dulles circle of recipients of his intelligence product. He sent Oster's proposal and his own report in advance by diplomatic pouch to Dulles law office. This political intelligence was not material for the War Department. Telephone communications from within Germany were not secure. The Gestapo undoubtedly monitored foreign embassy signals traffic including telegraph. Although encrypted, this material was too sensitive.

The problem solved itself after making his commitment to get Kaplinsky out of Germany. If he was to get her to the United States, London was the logical choice. After drafting his report and sending it off with Oster's proposal in the diplomatic pouch, it would take more than a week before making its way to Allen Dulles in New York. That allowed time to exfiltrate Valeska Kaplinsky. Once safely out of Nazi Germany, he could telephone Dulles from the security of the U.S. embassy in a friendly country.

Exfiltrating Valeska Kaplinsky out of Germany must happen without delay. No easy task given the new circumstances. A miscalculation and she would fall into the hands of the Gestapo. A fate worse than death. With the Soviet intelligence penetration of the prostitution service, Kaplinsky was now under scrutiny and under the control of the Gestapo.

If the Gestapo connected Fleming's romantic association with Kaplinsky, that would increase their interest in him. According to Major Richter, he may already be under surveillance. With the melding of the state police criminal police, the Nazi police state expanded exponentially under the centralized command of Heinrich Himmler. No shortage of police manpower. Fear of being watched was not paranoia. He must act quickly.

How to evade the vast resources of Gestapo presented the challenge for getting Kaplinsky out of Germany.

Over the following days, he got off his report and Oster's proposal to Allen Dulles. He then sent an encrypted message to Dulles. *Anticipate receipt of sensitive package. Suggest immediate review with your associates. Will telephone within a week to elaborate and answer questions from a secure location outside Germany. SF.*

Also in the diplomatic pouch was a letter to the chief of the War Department Intelligence Division explaining his absence from his post in Berlin as a security matter. The delayed receipt in Washington avoided further explanation until safely out of Germany.

My activities during the tenure of my posting as military attaché involved probing many sources opposing the Nazi regime for several years. With the combining of the all police forces under Heinrich Himmler chief of the Nazi Party paramilitary Schutzstaffel, Hitler has solidified his creation of a police state with unchecked powers. With the conclusion of the Olympic Games, oppression is escalating with no regard to foreign condemnation. Oppressive measures include indefinite imprisonment without judicial process in their Konzentrationslager system of concentration camps, police torture, and unrecorded disappearances of the victims. Not only for political opponents, Jews, and Roma, but even foreign nationals.

Use of confidential sources within the Wehrmacht now places me at imminent risk beyond protection afforded by diplomatic status. To avoid an international incident should police or elements of the Nazi Party detain or attack my person, I therefore preemptively removed myself from my post in Germany. Will await further orders forwarded through the U.S. Embassy in London.

Lieutenant Colonel Spencer Fleming
Military Attaché Berlin, Germany

Separately, he drafted a letter of resignation. A difficult decision having spent twenty-one years in the Army. Intended for submittal once he concluded his obligation to expand on Oster's proposal for a possible military coup d'état to remove Adolf Hitler.

Torn between the twin fear of remaining in Germany and escaping arrest by the Gestapo, Valeska Kaplinsky continued with remarkable courage. Her nightly performances over the next several evenings at the *Geisterstunde* continued.

A new patron suddenly appeared at the *Geisterstunde* that solidified her decision to flee Germany. A man attending alone each night. After Kaplinsky described the man to Fleming, he observed the man the following evening. No doubt Gestapo or SD. The agent clearly out of place. Cheap suit. Drinking beer. Here to observe the other patrons. Who was talking to whom? Did any of these patrons also solicit sexual services by appointment with Fischer? Which of the pretty waitressed moonlighted as prostitutes? In a police state, control over the population was all about collecting and indexing every scrap of information. Sow fear and make organized opposition difficult.

Back in his office with only a day's absence to recover from his heart attack, Walter Fischer began delivering his daily reports to the Gestapo.

When the day arrived to put the escape plan into action, Fleming arrived at Kaplinsky's apartment at the *Geisterstunde.*

"Are you ready, Valeska?"

She embraced him. "Yes, but I am scared."

"It will be fine. I will be with you. Once we cross over into the Netherlands you are safe."

Troubling her beyond the fear was realizing the likely fate of Walter Fischer. Not wishing to burden Spencer with something he could not change, she remained silent about her feelings of guilt for abandoning him.

"It is not only that. I am scared of what is ahead of me."

"I will be there with you," He said and kissed her. "Time to leave."

He drove to Berlin's Anhalter Bahnhof railway station. With gasoline scarce, there was little traffic. A car following closely. Probably Gestapo surveillance. He must assume they both were under surveillance.

At the train station, Kaplinsky walked him to his train. Dressed in military uniform, he carried a single suitcase and a briefcase. He carried only a second uniform, a civilian suit, and toiletry kit. In the briefcase, his .45 Browning service sidearm and shoulder holster from his Mexico days. Since he was not returning to Berlin, he included *Charousek's Games of Chess* and *Webster's Revised Unabridged Dictionary 1913 edition*, necessary for constructing his personal cipher.

She embraced and kissed him just before he stepped onto the train. She then left, driving his car back to the *Geisterstunde.* For anyone watching, separating removed suspicion that Kaplinsky was planning to leave Berlin with him. The arrangement allowed him to lose any Gestapo following him before doubling back for Kaplinsky.

* * * *

Fleming did not tell her his suspicion the Gestapo followed them to the station. They had no reason to make a move against her. At least not yet, he hoped. Telling her would unnerve her further. He already factored the presence of a Gestapo tail on either of them or both into his plan.

That same afternoon, Kaplinsky left her apartment with a single suitcase. Inside were mostly sensible clothes and only one gown. Given the cold weather, she wore her expensive fur coat. Inside her handbag, all her jewelry, a few family photos, and a modest sum of cash in Reichsmarks stashed for such an emergency. Most of her liquid assets deposited in a secret numbered Swiss bank account. Those funds further secured in the form of stable Swiss francs. A lesson learned early when she invested her meager resources in Swiss francs during the years of German hyperinflation. A comfortable savings for starting a new life in America.

Driving southeast from central Berlin, Kaplinsky headed to Potsdam only thirty minutes away. The precaution seemed unnecessary, but Fleming insisted. She arranged to spend two nights over Christmas with her friend Bella Fromm. Fleming explained it provided him the means to leave Berlin separately, therefore avoiding suspicion if seen boarding a train together. He made a point of emphasizing it was his position as American military attaché that meant Nazi intelligence probably monitored his movements.

The train trip allow time to lose any tail by returning to familiar Koblenz in the Rhineland then doubling back to link up with Kaplinsky in Potsdam. From there they would journey west together by train to cross the frontier into the Netherlands. If under surveillance by the Gestapo, she could not escape Germany without his help. Even with his help, unpredictable and dangerous.

Kaplinsky relaxed slightly while telling Fromm what she was doing. Without revealing the seriousness of her situation, she simply said the Gestapo was suddenly paying the *Geisterstunde* uncomfortable attention. Asking questions about patrons. Business in decline, only getting worse. She did not feel safe in the Nazi police state.

With her wide circle of connections, Fromm of course knew the open secret of the prostitution service populated with Kaplinsky's attractive waitresses. Perhaps that was the source of Gestapo attention. Never understood Kaplinsky's motivation for the unsavory sideline given the success of the nightclub.

Fromm also knew of the romantic connection between Kaplinsky and Fleming. She bore no jealous feelings telling Kaplinsky, "Spencer is a wonderfully exciting man. We enjoyed our occasional intimacies, but we were never in love."

Kaplinsky said, "Thank you, Bella. First time I ever experienced being in love. When I leave here, he is helping me leave Germany. I will miss you."

Bella hugged her. "I am happy for you, Valeska. Not only about your relationship with Spencer but about leaving Germany.

I can see where the political wind is blowing. Hitler is eventually taking Germany into another war according to Spencer. He offered to help me leave more than once. I am sure I am foolish not to go. Yet leaving feels like I am abandoning my family and the very center of my life."

"Bella, you must reconsider. I have my own reasons for leaving, but you are Jewish. Staying is increasingly dangerous for you. Shall I speak with Spencer?"

"That is kind of you to offer. I will think about it more seriously. Write to me from America. Convince me I should follow."

The morning following Christmas Day, Kaplinsky said her goodbyes to Bella Fromm and drove the short distance to the Potsdam Hauptbahnhof railway station. Fleming thought it easier to watch for anyone following Kaplinsky while boarding the train at the smaller Potsdam station instead of busier central Berlin. If followed, the critical next part of the plan depended on adapting to circumstances. A long train journey ahead of them before crossing the border.

Fleming returned to Potsdam on Christmas Day taking a nearby hotel room for the night. His diversionary trip west took him to Koblenz. He rented a car and knowing the area, drove about making it difficult for anyone following. Never spotting a tail, he still drove to Bonn to catch a return train to Potsdam to make sure.

Spending the night at a nearby hotel, early the next morning he walked to the Potsdam railway station dressed in civilian clothes. Underneath his suit jacket, he carried the .45 semi-automatic in his modified shoulder holster that saved his life in Koblenz. If circumstances turned bad, he would not allow the Gestapo to arrest Kaplinsky. At the station, he bought two tickets to Amsterdam. From Potsdam, the route made brief stops at Magdeburg and Brunschweig before arriving at Hanover where they must change trains for the final leg to cross the border into the Netherlands.

Assuming Kaplinsky might be under surveillance, she was to purchase a ticket to Braunschweig just minutes before departure. If a Gestapo agent following her had time to find out her destination, no reason it should arose suspicion. This was Christmas. Perhaps she was visiting another friend for the holiday. She was to board a railway carriage in the center of the train at the last possible moment just before the train began moving. Fleming stressed that as important. This allowed him to watch for anyone following her by forcing the watcher to reveal himself by rushing to board as the train pulled away.

Positioning himself near the last car for a full view of the train. Fleming spotted Kaplinsky holding back until the conductor announced the train's departure walking the length of the platform blowing his whistle and shouting *alle einsteigen*.

Kaplinsky timed it perfectly. A short man in a trench coat holding his hat ran to catch the railway carriage step as the train began to move. Watching from a position close to the last carriage of the train, Fleming then boarded.

Fleming made his way through the train, stopping at each car to peer through the door to locate Kaplinsky. He told her to take a seat near the front of any carriage making it convenient for anyone tailing her to take a seat behind her.

Once he found her, he spotted the short Gestapo agent sitting in the last row of the carriage. Close enough for Fleming standing on the connecting platform between the railway carriages to see his face in profile through the glass window of the carriage door.

As the train pulled out of the station and picked up speed, Fleming took a seat in the railway carriage behind Kaplinsky's. Once the conductor made his rounds, he returned to the platform between the carriages to observe Kaplinsky and her watcher.

To escape across the border meant eliminating the Gestapo agent somewhere in route. No way to anticipate how to accomplish that. He could easily kill the unsuspecting agent. However doing so without creating a scene or risking discovery of the body, presented a problem. Discovery of a dead Gestapo agent identified as following Kaplinsky would close the borders and make Kaplinsky a wanted fugitive. Several hours yet before reaching the border, but Fleming did not have that much time.

Fleming knew he must make his move before reaching Hanover where they must disembark to change trains. The Gestapo agent would suspect Kaplinsky as fleeing Germany if she boarded the westbound train to Amsterdam. He would summon police at the Hanover train station to detain her before she boarded.

Fleming's best opportunity was for the agent to go to the toilet or dining car located several cars forward according to the signs. If the man did not leave his seat before Hanover, Fleming would sit down next to the agent and stick his .45 in his side. An improvised desperate move seriously jeopardizing escape from Germany.

After leaving Magdeburg, Fleming could see other passengers removing their heavy coats. A small coal stove at the front heated the carriage. The agent removed his fedora but not his trench coat. Wiping his forehead with a handkerchief suggested the coach was overheated. Fifteen minutes later, the agent stood up and opened the door in front of Fleming watching from the platform.

The agent replaced his hat and looked at Fleming.

Fleming said, "Colder than the devil out here, but way too hot inside."

The agent merely looked at him without commenting. Turning back to view Kaplinsky through the glass, the agent reached into his pocket and extracted a pack of cigarettes.

Fleming said, "Might I borrow a cigarette?"

The agent said nothing but shook out a cigarette from the package.

Both men put the cigarettes to their lips. As the agent produced a lighter, Fleming leaned in as if to share the flame. After striking the lighter wheel repeatedly, the wind repeatedly blew out the flame.

Fleming made the gesture of cupping his hands then pretended to lose his balance with the lurching motion of the train. To steady himself he used one hand to press against the side of the agent discovering the hard bulge of a handgun in a shoulder holster, then stepped back. "Sorry."

The distraction confirmed Fleming's suspicion the man was Gestapo.

Turning slightly to disguise his next move, Fleming brought his arm around to deliver a powerful straight blow to the man's jaw with his gloved hand. As the agent slumped to his knees, Fleming caught him from falling from the platform with his left hand.

Fleming extracted the Lugar, the agent's Gestapo credentials, and wallet, sticking them in his overcoat pocket.

Looking into both railway carriages to ensure no one was about to walk out to the adjoining platform, Fleming bent down to the semi-conscious man. Placing the crook of his arm under the man's chin, he violently twisted his head sideways. The crack of the vertebrae heard even above the noise of the rails.

Stripping off the agent's overcoat, Fleming removed the shoulder holster, flinging it off the train. Checking again for any witnesses, he shoved the dead man off the train watching the body fall into some brush paralleling the track. The entire episode lasted less than a minute.

Nighttime would have been better to conceal the body, but at least it might be hours before another train passed. With no identification, it should be some time before the body was determined as that of a missing Gestapo agent.

Before joining Kaplinsky, he took several minutes to composed himself. He killed before but this was troubling. The feeling however passed quickly. He discarded the Lugar and the Gestapo agent's identification at intervals to scatter the articles a distance from the body.

Approaching her aisle seat from behind, he touched Kaplinsky on the shoulder causing her to stiffen and turn abruptly with a stark look of fear, immediately replaced by relief.

She slid over and he took the aisle seat. "My god, I have been worried sick. I did not know if you even boarded the train. Where have you been?"

"Taking care of some unpleasant business. Someone followed you. Spotted a man walking behind you on the boarding platform then running to catch up as the train pulled away. Then I watched him as he kept an eye on you from a seat in the back. He was Gestapo."

"Where were you?"

"Outside on the platform freezing."

She touched his cheek. "You are cold. Where is this man now?"

"He left the train the hard way. Dead."

Her eyes widened. In a muted whisper, "You killed him?"

He nodded.

"They will be looking for us now. Looking for me at least."

Shaking his head no, "Not for some time. By then we are safely out of Germany."

"But they will know something is wrong when their agent does not report in."

"Eventually, yes. However, they do not know where you are. You are also no longer Valeska Kaplinsky."

He handed her a well-worn American passport. Stamped with entry stamps to Britain, France, and Germany. A real passport of a deceased American citizen drowned with her husband in a boating accident during the summer in Germany. He pressured Raymond Geist the current American counsel and First Secretary of the U.S. Embassy in Berlin that it was necessary for a Jewish woman to escape arrest by the Gestapo. He was also in love with the woman. Fleming knew Geist helped many other German Jews get to America, and detested the Nazis. Geist agreed to the forgery by replacing the photo of the deceased woman with a photo of Kaplinsky provided by Fleming.

Geist admonished Fleming not to use the forged passport for entry into the United States. For that, he provided a legitimate U.S. visa in Kaplinsky's name.

"If they demand to see our documents at the border before leaving Germany, you are now Rachel Allsburg. My wife. Recently married. Let me do any talking at the border. Note your place and date of birth." Smiling to lighten the atmosphere, he said, "Note you are now several years younger."

"You mean I must go by this new name?"

"Only for deceiving German border guards. Once we are out of Germany you again become Valeska Kaplinsky. I have an American visa in your real name in my pocket."

At the border, the train stopped as plain clothes police moved through the carriages checking documents. Only a police state concerned itself with people leaving the country. Fleming offered his regular passport rather than the diplomatic passport to avoid unusual scrutiny. Kaplinsky's fake passport raised no questions. Fleming remarked to the guard examining their documents, "My wife and I are taking a holiday in Amsterdam."

As the train crossed into the Netherlands, Kaplinsky grasped Fleming's hand as tears of relief and the prospect of a new life unfolded.

CHAPTER 26

Berlin, German Reich | Spring 1937

Decker was furious after informed of the disappearance of Valeska Kaplinsky. He ordered the arrest of Walter Fischer and the three prostitutes known to be Jewish. Under abusive interrogation supervised personally, he became enraged after learning the truth behind the prostitution ring.

With everything now lost and suffering terrible physical abuse, Fischer revealed the prostitutes collected information from loose talk of their clients. He passed the information to Kaplinsky but says he did not know her purpose. He tried to stick with the deception given to the prostitutes that he believed the gossip picked up from their clients went to the Gestapo as a necessary means for remaining in operation.

"Frau Kaplinsky said the information went to the Gestapo. Necessary for being allowed to operate."

"Yet you knew that was not true when I confronted you after discovering that one of your whores was working with a Russian agent."

Several more blows from a practiced torturer caused Fischer to give in knowing Kaplinsky had disappeared and hopefully was now safe. "Frau Kaplinsky said she passed the information to Polish intelligence."

Also under interrogation, the Jewish prostitutes revealed the nature of the information they collected. Examples they recalled astounded Decker by the stupidity of several high-level Nazis named as clients.

Fischer never left the basement interrogation room alive. He knew too much. The Jewish prostitutes sent to a concentration camp.

No alternative but for Decker to report the disastrous facts to Sturmbannführer Pfeiffer of the Sicherheitsdienst. Unfortunately, it was Decker's idea to compel Fischer and his prostitutes to report the names of their clients to the Gestapo. Never a Soviet penetration, he then overlooked the arrangement as an ingenious Polish intelligence network.

Worse yet, Decker allowed the principal spy to escape. Kaplinsky vanished several days ago with her Gestapo tail still missing. Likely helped by Polish intelligence and undoubtedly now in Poland. A personal disaster for Otto Decker.

* * * *

"Sonofabitch, Decker! This gross incompetence will be a mark on your record. You mishandled this from the beginning."

Decker seethed at Pfeiffer's criticism. After all, he uncovered the Russian penetration. Furthermore, Pfeiffer was a regular client of these prostitutes. Perhaps he even fornicated with the Jewish whore Meier that worked with the Russian spy. Unwittingly giving the Poles confidential information.

"This Kaplinsky woman was having an affair with the American military attaché. The one that is friendly with two suspect Wehrmacht officers. Where does he fit in this?"

Decker was not going to admit to surveillance on Fleming that also went wrong with the assigned Gestapo agent losing Fleming in the Rhineland.

"That is unknown. Fleming left Berlin almost a week ago. Perhaps he left Germany. That was before Kaplinsky went missing. The Gestapo observed her sending him off on a train from Berlin. She may have left Berlin using Fleming's automobile which we found at the Potsdam railway station. We are checking all border-crossing records for both Fleming and Kaplinsky. Considering

Fleming's intimate relationship with Kaplinsky, he is possibly involved with her disappearance. No way to determine if Fleming knew Kaplinsky was feeding information to the Poles."

Decker did not admit to his failure going deeper. He avoiding mentioning the missing Gestapo agent assigned to follow Kaplinsky. Nor the knowledge that Kaplinsky spent Christmas with the well-known Jewish journalist Bella Fromm. Admitting to either might escalate Decker's failure to above Pfeiffer, making his situation worse. The best course of action was to take Pfeiffer's reprimand and let the matter blow over.

"We searched Kaplinsky's residence. Most of her clothing and personal effects remain. Her bank accounts show no unusual withdrawals. If she has left Germany, she abandoned everything."

"Clean up this mess quickly, Decker. I want all copies of the records you confiscated from Fischer on my desk. Destroy any reports mentioning names of clients of these prostitutes.

"What about the American Fleming?"

"If he reappears, place him under close surveillance. I do not trust him. His relationships with certain Wehrmacht officers are suspicious. Now this. If you find any evidence he is working against the Reich, he must be eliminated. Yet not before we learn everything about his subversive activities. Since he enjoys diplomatic immunity, he must disappear without a trace to avoid an international incident. However, you will act only on my orders. Keep me informed of any developments, Decker."

* * * *

It was evening when Fleming and Kaplinsky arrived in Amsterdam. Both relaxed after the intense stress of the day's journey. Neither knew Amsterdam other than from photographs. Both were anxious to see the canals in the daytime. Yet even nighttime showed the unique charm of the city as the taxi traversed the many bridges crossing the canals decorated for Christmas.

Fleming made arrangements before leaving Berlin, booking a suite at the elegant Hotel De L'Europe, situated at the confluence of two major canals. Raymond Geist recommended the hotel and it did not disappoint.

Kaplinsky was buoyant when the bellman showed them their room. As soon as the man left, she fell into Fleming's arms and began kissing him. She disengaging her embrace and checked out the room. When she returned from the bathroom, he smiled relishing her happiness. "You must be hungry."

Removing her fur coat she embraced him again and said, "Yes. Hungry for you. There is a huge bathtub. Large enough for both of us. I want a good soak then make love. Celebrate the beginning of our new life, Spencer."

* * * *

The next day was cold but clear with bright sunshine. The view over the wide canal was breathtaking. It was too early in the winter to freeze over as possibly the case with the smaller canals.

"I must telephone New York after breakfast because of the time difference. There are several matters I must clean up before we continue our journey. May take several days. I booked us here for a week. Thought it would be more relaxing than London."

She said, "After breakfast, can we walk around? I love Amsterdam already. I shall remember it as our first special place."

"Good idea. We could shop for some additional clothing."

After breakfast in the hotel restaurant, Fleming sent Kaplinsky upstairs telling her he would make his transatlantic call and be up when finished.

The desk put the call through to New York. He sat in a wooden paneled telephone cubicle in the lobby.

"Allen? This is Spencer Fleming."

The line carried a background crackle so Dulles raised his voice. "Spencer, where are you?"

"Amsterdam. Did you receive my package?"

"Yes. What's your opinion about the possibly of the German General Staff pulling this off?"

"The question remains the commitment of as yet unidentified senior Wehrmacht officers? Do they collectively have enough troop strength to overcome the Schutzstaffel? Can these dissident commanders rely on the loyalty of their troops? Are there enough troops to deal with the SS? I don't have enough information to answer that, Allen.

"Colonel Oster has not shared specifics about his conspiracy. I can tell you that Oster is both intelligent and motivated. Not some wild-eyed radical. He is clever and charming. Held in high regard among senior officers of the Wehrmacht. I have another high-placed reliable source that confirms Oster's standing among general officers known to harbor anti-Nazi or anti-Hitler sentiments to varying degrees. I told Oster that to secure assurances from the United States and Britain he needs to convince us of the capacity of the conspiracy to carry this off."

"The encrypted material you have transmitted for over two years, does it come from Oster?"

"A good deal of it does. The Abwehr is not only an effective foreign intelligence service, but has tentacles into every German governmental sector, including the SS given their counterintelligence function. As part of the military, they also represent Germany's foreign intelligence service. Far beyond the role of American military intelligence."

"How did you connect with Oster?"

"He found me. Same motivation as Polish intelligence. Without an American intelligence service, to use me as a backchannel to United States decision makers. Whether the Poles or dissident Wehrmacht officers and others in Oster's loose conspiracy, the fear is premature war. My sense is not so much about the prospect of war, but a war Germany cannot win. They realize that a repeat of the defeat of the war twenty years ago would likely destroy Germany.

"As the most powerful nation in the world, they see the United States as the only power sufficient to confront Adolf Hitler. I tell you, Allen, Hitler will engage in some military action within a few years that will force war in Europe. There is no doubt in my mind."

"So where do we go from here?"

"I promised Oster I could guarantee the President of the United States sees his letter. A bold step for Oster. Exposing himself to a firing squad if found out. Told him I would try to broker a meeting in London if the President wished to pursue the matter. Can you make that happen, Allen?"

"Of course. The President is already invested in the intelligence you forward. I will get on it right away. Will you be returning to Berlin soon?"

"No. In fact, I am not returning to Berlin. While here in Amsterdam, I will resign my commission effective immediately."

"What? My god, why? You have a brilliant career ahead of you."

"As what? A spy for a country that has no foreign intelligence service? Besides, it is more complicated than that. The Gestapo shutdown the intelligence network in Berlin run by the Poles that provided my early intelligence product. Before that happened, I took over direct control for that network. I am in Amsterdam after helping the former head of Polish Berlin network escape the Gestapo."

"So you escaped the Gestapo? Didn't your diplomatic status afford protection?"

"I do not know if I was even compromised. Certainly cannot rely on diplomatic status as protection. I have lived in this pesthole where those suspected of opposition to the Nazi regime disappear. This is a fucking police state. Hitler is preparing for war. Why should his secret police concern themselves with the subtleties of international law?

"However, that is irrelevant. I am done with the Army. What would be my next assignment? Some dreary command in a remote backwater? Ascend in rank to a star on my shoulder? To a boring administrative job? No thanks. Time to leave the army.

"There is also another reason. The head of the Polish network in Berlin I rescued is a woman. You met her in Berlin. The beautiful singer at the nightclub. Much of the Polish intelligence material came from an exclusive prostitution ring picking up gossip from clients within the government. The Gestapo closed in so I pulled her out. Under Germany racial laws, she also classifies as a Jew. She is here with me in Amsterdam. I promised to take her to America. I intend to do that, Allen."

Fleming did not know if Kaplinsky had any Jewish grandparents, but it added weight to his assertion to help Kaplinsky.

"Good grief, Spencer. I understand. Yet I do not think you realize the importance of your service to American interests. You are America's only spy in Germany. Impossible, to gauge the impact of your intelligence. I can assure you though it shapes a clearer understanding of the Nazi regime for this administration compared with relying largely on journalistic reporting. "

"Thanks, Allen, but that becomes irrelevant. I will stay on here in Amsterdam to do what I can to facilitate this meeting with representatives of what I call Oster's Conspiracy."

"Have you submitted your resignation yet?"

"No yet."

"Can you hold off for a couple of days? I want to confer with my associates."

"I guess so. I can make some official excuse for being in Amsterdam. I am staying at the Hotel de L'Europe."

With that out of the way, he set out with Kaplinsky to shop for clothes and see Amsterdam. Still anxious over the uncertainty of what lay ahead, Fleming's spirits soared by seeing a new side of Valeska Kaplinsky. Her intensity softened with the unburdening of fear. She easily smiled and laughed. She told Fleming for the first in her life she felt safe. "I love you Spencer."

****

Two days later, Dulles telephoned early in the morning. Two in the morning in Washington D.C., "I spoke to Sumner Welles immediately after you called. I've been busy since then. We all have."

"Who else?"

"Welles, several other career foreign service officers he trusts, and Bill Donovan. We even met yesterday for two hours with President Roosevelt. The President is personally taking the lead in this. If it blows up, he wants to contain any collateral damage by limiting the number of people involved."

"Does the President wish to pursue this initiative, Allen?"

"Yes. That is also the consensus of the rest of us. If the potential exists to replace Hitler and the Nazi regime with a German government willing to remain within its current geographic boundaries, we must explore that possibility. The President is sensitive about avoiding the United States seen as sanctioning an act of war by conspiring to overthrow a legally installed government by a military coup d'état."

"Christ, Allen, Hitler's rise to power had nothing to do with a democratic process. He circumvented every legal convention by intimidation and violence. Removing the opposition by force does not constitute legal means. Now there is no other way to eliminate the psychopathic bastard than by a bullet."

"We just finished a marathon meeting today and substantially agree with your assessment, Spencer. Besides establishing confidence in the success of this Oster Conspiracy, we need assurances that replacing the Nazis with a military dictatorship is a better deal for peace in Europe. That needs to be impressed upon Colonel Oster to provide a convincing argument."

"I imagine Oster realizes that. He is a German nationalist as are his fellow conspirators. Post-Hitler, their concern is the threat of the Soviet Union. No different from much of the rest of Europe. They are not however willing for Germany to go to war over Hitler's irrational territorial ambitions."

"We have agreed to meet this morning in the Oval Office. Can you arrange to be at the U.S. Consulate in Amsterdam to receive the call at five o'clock this afternoon Amsterdam time? President Roosevelt wishes to speak personally with you."

"Of course."

* * * *

Alone in a consulate office, Spencer Fleming took the call from the White House.

The voice of President Franklin Roosevelt was unmistakable, "Colonel Fleming, let me first compliment you on your extraordinary initiative in the service of your country. What you have accomplished in your posting to Berlin is no less courageous then your actions that earned your commendations for valor in combat."

"Thank you, Mr. President."

"Do you think these military conspirators can pull this off?" Roosevelt asked.

"Colonel Oster has not shared details with me. If sufficient Wehrmacht units can be coordinated, it should be possible. Oster has the benefit of effective intelligence penetrations into the Nazi SS. The SS represents the physical obstacle to removing Hitler. Those covert intelligence sources represent a good deal of the information I pass through Mr. Dulles."

"This is Sumner Welles, Colonel Fleming. Why does Oster not include the French in his proposed discussions?"

"He does not trust the French. The current government is in too much political turmoil and too left leaning. Oster feels if he can gain assurances for a post-Nazi Germany from the United States and Britain, the French will agree. Oster places the greatest reliance on America's power and influence.

"Oster fears the lack of resolve of the current British government will waver further as German rearmament accelerates. Britain is proceeding with rearmament recognizing the potential German threat but devoting less financial resources than Hitler. Oster fears an eventual arms gap. He has sympathetic sources inside the German Foreign Ministry that report a troubling inclination among certain prominent British politicians believing they can negotiate with Hitler."

Roosevelt chuckled. "That is exactly what Winston Churchill said. Winston and I are old friends. He firmly agrees that Hitler represents an imminent danger. Appeasement will only lead to disaster. Should we go forward with these talks with this German resistance group, he agreed to take part personally. He also offered to recruit Robert Vansittart, Permanent Undersecretary at the Foreign Office, an ardent hardliner against Nazi Germany to participate as Oster suggested."

Fleming continued. "Oster believes any attempt to dissuade Hitler from territorial ambitions by negotiation is naïve. I firmly share that opinion. I lived in this charged environment. Adolf Hitler is a mentally unstable demagogue. He is not rational. If not removed from power, he will start another war in Europe."

Roosevelt responded, "That seems to be the consensus of the gentlemen in this room, Colonel. I see little alternative but to take the matter to the next level. Please inform Colonel Oster the United States will join exploratory talks in London. Will you continue to serve as the intermediary with Colonel Oster?"

"As I informed Mr. Dulles, I left Germany to escort one of my intelligence sources to safety to escape the Gestapo. I am not sure if I am under scrutiny. After all, I have engaged in espionage against the host country. Spies are shot."

"Colonel Fleming, this is William Donovan. You are the recipient of the Medal of Honor as a young second lieutenant. You then distinguished yourself in France. You have risked your life repeatedly in the service of your country. I cannot pretend to know the dangers you might face by returning to Berlin. Based on your own intelligence, this mission however could be instrumental toward averting another catastrophic war. As one soldier to another, I can understand the concern when asked again to risk your life. All of us including the President believe it vital to American interests. This is a volunteer mission subject solely to your call."

Fleming knew Donovan by reputation. As an officer leading from the front, he earned the nickname Will Bill. Like Fleming, also a recipient of the Medal of Honor, Distinguished Service Cross, Silver Star, and Purple Heart. A little heavy-handed, but then the whole idea was Fleming's. Difficult to walk away now.

Roosevelt added, "This is not however to be a suicide mission. If you assess the risk as acceptable, are you willing to return to Berlin, Colonel Fleming?"

After pausing for several moments to consider what he was doing, "Yes, Mr. President."

"Excellent. I shall call General Simonds personally. You will receive new orders within days at the consulate. It will state you are hereby assigned to detached duties in a classified capacity, reporting directly to the office of the Commander in Chief while still retaining your post as military attaché to Germany. What that means, son, is that you are on your own to do as you see necessary to complete your mission."

"Yes, Mr. President. There is one request I wish to make. The intelligence source I brought out of Germany is also my fiancée. She cannot return to Germany. I promised to take her to America. The U.S. Consul in Berlin issued her a U.S. visa. However, should something happen to me that is not adequate insurance. She becomes a stateless refuge. I therefore respectfully request she be given United States citizenship and issued a U.S. passport. Without resources, I need the Amsterdam consulate to also provide for her hotel accommodations for the duration of my tenure in Germany."

Roosevelt said, "Given you are leaving her in Amsterdam to risk your life for your country that seems the least we can do. Any problem with that, Sumner?"

Welles replied. "No, Mr. President. I shall make the arrangements immediately with the Amsterdam consul general. What is the woman's name, Colonel?"

"Valeska Kaplinsky. Thank you. Mr. Welles."

Donovan said. "Mr. Dulles shall remain your point of contact. The President recruited Allen and me to represent American interests in negotiating with these Germans. You will shuttle between Berlin and London to participate in the talks when necessary. Do you have the means for secure encrypted telegraphic communications outside regular military and diplomatic channels?"

Dulles answered, "Yes. Colonel Fleming has intelligence training. He devised a clever cipher based on chess games to relay his information to me. My longtime secretary has become proficient in unscrambling the groups of numbers into intelligible text. Without the encryption key, it is unbreakable. I will share the basis of the cipher with you and Mr. Welles."

Fleming said, "If I may, Mr. President, I need to offer my opinion regarding Oster and his conspirators. They wish to rid Germany of Adolf Hitler but hope to continue many of his nationalistic aims. Rearmament with economic stability is paramount. These are military men. They do not fear war, only a premature conflict that Germany cannot win. They are nationalistic conservatives to varying degrees. Not parliamentarians. This will be a military coup d'état with a great level of uncertainty for how Germany will fit within the European community of nations. A post-Nazi government will not be a western European democracy given the failed Weimar Republic experience."

"Well stated, Colonel Fleming. We appreciate your insights," Roosevelt said. "Now if there is nothing else, I believe that concludes the matter, gentlemen. I wish to express my gratitude again for your continued service to our country, Colonel Fleming. Good luck and God speed."

* * * *

Fleming downplayed the substance of the telephone call after returning to Kaplinsky at the hotel. She was dressing for dinner in the elegant hotel's French restaurant. "A few more days before I can conclude arrangements for leaving the Army."

Something he needed to do before breaking the distressing news that he must temporarily venture back to Berlin before they could leave for America. While devastating her, he must at least make her feel secure should something happen to him. A U.S. passport was essential but he also needed to make sure she was financially secure and not left alone in a strange country. The only person outside of Germany he knew well was Allen Dulles and his wife Clover. Perhaps they could look after Valeska in New York and manage his affairs if events turned out badly.

* * * *

The following morning he broke the news to Valeska. The prior night they enjoyed dinner followed by lovemaking. He could not ruin her euphoric mood without thinking through how to mitigate her distress by their separation and concern over his return to Berlin. A sleepless night but nevertheless he determined to tell her in the morning.

Following breakfast in their room, he said, "I have something difficult to tell you?"

Her expression frightened him, realizing that it perhaps sounded like some revelation damaging to their relationship.

"It has nothing to do with my love for you, or some dark secret. It is about my immediate circumstances. My obligation as an American Army officer. Yesterday the President of the United States spoke to me on the telephone. You see I have been engaged in other spying beyond your network working for Kaczmarek. The United States has no foreign intelligence agency. I am the only direct source of secret information. The President wants me to temporarily return to Berlin."

Kaplinsky violently shook her head. "No. You cannot leave me. We were to go to America. Together."

He approached her trying to take her hand, which she pulled away. Tears flowed freely.

"Valeska. We will. I promise. I just have to complete a specific mission then I am done. It is important. I am the only person that can accomplish what is necessary. After that, I will leave the Army."

"What is this thing you must do?"

"I cannot reveal the specifics. It is so secret that only a few people know. It might prevent almost certain war in Europe. It is that important."

"What am I supposed to do while you play spy in Berlin?"

She now allowed him to embrace her. "We are going to discuss that today. I also have a couple of pleasant surprises in store for you today. So, get dressed. Do your hair and makeup for a photograph."

"A photograph?"

"A portrait actually. For me. Our first stop of an interesting day I assure you, my love. I cannot change what I must do, but I can try to make you happy."

Still holding each other, she kissed him as more tears flowed. "You do make me happy. You must not leave me."

Her kisses became more intense. He was partially dressed but she only wore a hotel robe. Naked underneath, he quickly opened the robe and began caressing her body.

Shedding the robe and pulling him to the bed, she undid the buttons of his shirt then removed his trousers. "At least your timing is right. I will do my hair and makeup after you show me how much you love me."

The photographer took several shots. Kaplinsky was unaware the principle reason for coming here was to get passport photos. The photographer promised the photos to be ready by early afternoon.

The next stop was Fleming's special surprise. A pawnshop he passed on his way to the consulate yesterday. He spent an hour there attracted by a violin in the window. Forced to leave her prized violin behind in Berlin, he thought this might brighten her spirits when he must tell her of his leaving.

The Jewish proprietor told him the story behind this violin. Fleeing Nazi persecution required an elderly Jewish couple to forfeit their wealth in order to leave Nazi Germany. They managed to smuggle out the violin and some jewelry.

"The poor fellow told me it was very valuable. I do not know musical instruments but I felt sorry them. He wanted far more than I could offer. It is two hundred years old by the inscription inside, but that does not make it valuable. The wife offered some nice jewelry so I gave him more money than I should have for the violin."

Fleming knew nothing about violins. The instrument was beautiful and appeared in perfect shape. He scrapped the bow over the strings and it made a pleasing sound, proving nothing to the untrained ear. Still, it might please Valeska. She would know if it was worth the equivalent of one thousand U.S. dollars when he brought her here tomorrow.

Slightly puzzled as the taxi stopped at a pawnshop, she stopped before entering to look at the violin in the window.

"Ah, Herr Fleming. Good to see you again. And this must be your beautiful fiancée," the proprietor said in German.

Kaplinsky turned to Fleming giving him a smile, "Fiancée? That is sweet."

"Herr Fleming said you play the violin. The instrument in the window caught his eye. Let me get it for you."

The little man proudly presented the instrument and bow to Kaplinsky. After examining its condition, she looked inside the left f-hole, the usual location for identifying the maker.

"Do you have a magnifying glass?" Kaplinsky asked.

As the proprietor went to retrieve the glass, she tucked the violin under her chin and began playing. The sound captivated both the proprietor and Fleming.

"That is magnificent, madam."

Several minutes later, Fleming said, "What do you think? Is it a good instrument?"

With an expression of concentration, she answered distractedly, "Yes. Very good." She was now intent on what the inside revealed.

Moving to catch the natural light coming through the shop window, she could see the maker's name and date inscription. She remarked to Fleming in a whisper, "My god. Unless a fake, this is a Del Gesù."

"Is that a big deal?"

"The common trade name of one of the great Italian violin makers from Cremona, Italy. Bartolomeo Guarneri. Perhaps second only to Antonio Stradivari."

Fleming smiled. To the proprietor, "You can see madam loves the instrument. We will take it. Now to the other item I found interesting yesterday."

Absorbed with running her hands over the violin, Kaplinsky looked up as Fleming pulled her toward a glass jewelry case. The proprietor reached in and withdrew a diamond ring.

Placing the ring on a velvet cloth, both men waited for Kaplinsky to turn her attention to the ring. After picking it up, she turned to Fleming with a questioning expression.

He took it from her and slid it on her finger. "For my fiancée."

"Oh my god!"

At lunch, she could barely contain her joy. Twisting the ring to catch the light. At her feet rested the violin case. "I love you, Spencer."

"I love you, Valeska. To make this a very special day, I have one more surprise this afternoon."

"Spencer, please. You are not wealthy. I do not know how much you spent at the pawnshop but I saw you hand over a large amount of money. Then the expense of our hotel."

"I know what I am doing. This final surprise did not cost money, yet it may be the best of all."

After stopping at the photographer's to pick up the passport photos and portrait prints, they took a taxi to the U.S. Consulate.

Entering the consulate, they approached a receptionist and signed the log after showing their identifications.

"We are here to see Mr. Mathews."

The clerk said, "Yes, Colonel. The Consul General is expecting you." She then placed a call. "Mr. Mathews will be right down."

Walking into Consul General Mathew's office, another consular official and a military officer stood up from their seats. In uniform, Fleming saluted his counterpart a full colonel. Everyone took a seat after introductions.

Consul General Mathews said, "A most unusual call yesterday from Under Secretary Welles. Said the request came straight from the President. Then Colonel Laughlin arrived this morning from our embassy in the Hague. Colonel Laughlin is our military attaché to the Netherlands. Mr. Barnes here will prepare the passport."

"Do you have the photo and the personal information for Frau Kaplinsky?" The junior consular officer asked.

"Here are the photos." Turning to Valeska, "Mr. Barnes needs your birth certificate."

Fleming knew Kaplinsky carried all her important documents in her purse. Extracting the birth certificate, she looked at Fleming with a questioning expression.

"Yes, Valeska. They are preparing your American passport. You are now an American citizen."

She grabbed Fleming's hand as tears came to her eyes.

"This should take no more than thirty minutes, Colonel," The man said and left the room.

"Colonel Laughlin has some confidential military business to discuss with Colonel Fleming. Can I offer you some coffee while you wait, Frau Kaplinsky?"

Once in another office, Laughlin handed Fleming an envelope. "I received new classified orders for you this morning by encrypted telegram and ordered to deliver them to you personally here in Amsterdam."

United States War Department
Office of the Deputy Chief of Staff
United States Army
April 8, 1937

Lieutenant Colonel Spencer Schneider Fleming is hereby promoted in rank to Colonel in the regular army effective this date. Colonel Fleming will return to his duties as military attaché to Germany but will operate under independent instructions from the War Department chain of command under detached assignment reporting directly to the Office of the President of the United States until such time as countermanded by future order.

Major General George S. Simonds
Deputy Chief of Staff
United States Army

"Thank you, Colonel.

Laughlin then surprised him with small box. "Congratulations on your promotion. With orders like that, perhaps a dangerous mission. Might be difficult to obtain the insignia of your new rank in Berlin. Here are a couple of sets of eagles. Maybe they will bring you good luck."

Fleming took the box and shook Laughlin's hand. "That is particularly thoughtful of you, Colonel. Can you also send this telegram for me? It is to Polish Military Intelligence, Warsaw headquarters. To Major Feliks Kaczmarek."

Laughlin took the handwritten notation of Fleming's chess-based cipher in the form of numerical groupings of six numbers. The standard army cipher used five-number groupings. "A special code?"

"Yes. As you might guess, my mission is classified *eyes only*. The message read: *Kaplinsky network compromised by Gestapo. Kaplinsky safely out of Germany. I return to Berlin embassy by end of week. SF.*

Before leaving the consulate, Fleming placed a telephone call to Major Konrad Richter. Disguised as a personal call, he affirmed *Operation Krebs* should move forward with an agreed upon coded reference. "Glad to report the doctors are optimistic about the surgical removal of the cancer."

CHAPTER 27

Berlin, German Reich | Spring 1937

Once outside the consulate, Kaplinsky turned and embraced Fleming. "That was your real reason for stopping at the photography shop."

He smiled. "I wanted to surprise you. Make you feel secure. You are now an American citizen. I also wanted a photograph to carry."

By secure, she understood he meant should something happen to him. "How long must you remain in Berlin?"

"Hard to say. Not something I can control. I hope not long. Could be a couple of months though. My mission might involve trips to London. If so, that means I can spend a day or two with you here in Amsterdam. Once I am done with this mission, we leave for America."

She sighed then kissed him. "Will you be in danger?"

"I do not believe so. It was you that was in danger not me. I maintain certain contacts within the Wehrmacht that the President feels are vital to interests of the United States. Only involved with my duties as military attaché no longer involved with spying for Kaczmarek. The Gestapo has no reason to connect me to your activities other than our romantic affair. Besides, I have diplomatic immunity."

"When must you leave?"

"In three days. I need to get you settled financially. I have some cash I will leave with you which should hold you for a while. Tomorrow we set up a bank account for you. Fortunately, you will not have to move from the hotel. The American government will pick up the bill. As an American citizen you can always seek help at the consulate."

The weather turned warmer and they used the time to walk about Amsterdam. Both fell in love with the city and deeper in love with each other.

Departing was understandably difficult but Valeska Kaplinsky was a strong person. She took life's setbacks and moved forward. She was stoic as Fleming boarded the train. Yet fearing for his safety was more wrenching than her flight from Germany. Having found the love of her life, losing him became unimaginable. They still knew little of either's past but it did not matter. Their connection at a deeper level transcended their pasts.

Fleming's final parting comment lifted her spirits slightly. "If my duties in Berlin extend longer than anticipated, I will return to Amsterdam periodically for a few days. I will call you as often as possible. We must be careful should the Gestapo be listening to telephone calls, even from the embassy. I will ask for your room number. Remember you are registered under the false American passport in the name of Rachel Allsburg. Therefore, I will call you Rachel. Be careful to avoid anything other than talk among newlyweds."

Fleming arrived in Berlin that evening. Arriving at his apartment, careful inspection revealed it had been searched. Nothing obvious, but small details out of place. As a career soldier, his habits of organization were precise. Underwear folded in a certain manner. Books carefully aligned. Bed meticulously made. Clothing evenly spaced on hangers in the closet. Since he avoided keeping anything incriminating at his residence, there was nothing for the Gestapo to find.

Confirmation of their interest in him heightened his concern. This enemy was determined, ruthless, and possessed unlimited resources. Possibly followed on his diversionary trip to the Rhineland before backtracking to rendezvous with Kaplinsky in Potsdam now seemed likely. He must assume their interest involved his association with Kaplinsky's activities and disappearance.

Possibly compounded by his associations with Richter and Strobel. Unlike suspected foreign intelligence operatives disguised as minor consular officers, as a military attaché, his activities were largely transparent. A good cover but engaging in espionage against the Nazi Reich, he must avoid underestimating the enemy.

He called Richter the following morning to announce his return and arrange to meet that afternoon. The United States Embassy was located at 39 Bendlerstrasse, only a block from the great complex of buildings housing the headquarters of the Army, the Oberkommando des Heeres, or OKH, and the Abwehr. The coffee shop was just north of the embassy.

"Is everything in order, Spencer?"

"An unusual question, Konrad?"

"Your relationship with Valeska Kaplinsky is no secret. Neither is her disappearance from the *Geisterstunde,* which is now closed. Just a coincidence with your absence?"

"You have good sources, Konrad."

"We are an intelligence organization. Considering our association, you are part of the family so to speak. We put surveillance on your apartment while you were gone. You had an unwanted visitor late one night."

Fleming nodded. "Not surprising. Nothing to worry about though. There is never anything incriminating at my residence. As for the Kaplinsky woman, she was the reason for my absence. I took her out of Germany. The Gestapo wanted her waitresses to spy on her influential clients."

"You mean her prostitutes. Our counterintelligence people from Abwehr III know about her prostitution ring run by her lawyer and accountant, Walter Fischer. Unfortunately, the Gestapo arrested Herr Fischer, his wife and the prostitutes. All probably now in a concentration camp."

"Okay. Actually, her situation was more precarious. The Gestapo discovered a Soviet GRU agent infiltrated the service using one of the women to spy on her important sex clients. I convinced her to leave Germany. Since we are not only friends but also conspiring against a common enemy, I was using the prostitutes to gather information from the loose talk of their clients. The irony being the women thought all along the loose talk of their clients was given to the Gestapo as the means to stay in business."

Fleming chose not to complicate matters by revealing Kaplinsky's network was a Polish intelligence operation.

Richter actually laughed. "You are a clever devil, Spencer. A real spy at heart. That will please Oster. Especially with what he wants me to tell you. He is bringing you into our circle of conspirators as you call us."

"Understood. My orders are to advise my government and facilitate this mission. You can tell Oster I spoke directly with President Roosevelt. He is personally in charge of any American initiative. Only a handful of foreign service officials know of this, so security is tight. The two negotiators he is sending to London are not even government officials. One is my personal friend. Experienced in foreign affairs. He is the one that induced me to pursue gathering of political intelligence on the Nazi regime. Information beyond the sphere of interest to the U.S. War Department. The other is a decorated officer of the war in France and a prominent New York lawyer."

"Colonel Oster is committed to moving forward. Removing Hitler appears the only way to save Germany. If he can broker a deal with the Americans and the British to back our demands for installing a new government, he believes he can convincingly press the generals to act. He trusts you. Besides the negotiations in London, he believes your involvement is critical to reaching an agreement since you know the situation in Germany intimately."

"When I met with Oster at the embassy reception he said I can speak freely with you, Konrad. Therefore, a couple of things. First of all, I can send messages directly to the American negotiators using a special cipher I use for all the intelligence you provide to me. Tell Oster I suggest your negotiators come prepared with detailed tactical plans for decapitating the Nazi regime. With one of the Americans a former army officer, I suggest one of your negotiators also be an army officer since this is a military operation. They must be convinced of the viability of your plan before committing themselves. When can you be ready to present your plans in London?"

"That is up to Colonel Oster. Lots of moving pieces involved. I will get back to you as soon as possible."

"Equally as important as the takeover plan is defining the composition of the new government."

Richter said, "What is your side expecting? Not likely to look like the government of the former republic."

"I told them that. They are realistic. If it were up to me, I would demand some concrete assurance of no German territorial expansion by force. After all, that is the reason for the risk of war if left to Hitler. How you convince the other side of that I do not know."

Richter nodded his understanding. "All of us are under scrutiny from Heydrich's SD. He has vast manpower resources in the Gestapo also under his command. As you might imagine, Oster must be careful to stay in the shadows and therefore it is difficult for him to interact with the senior officers necessary to pull this off. His solution therefore is to use a number of middle rank officers like me. We shuttle between the generals involved to obscure our intentions as part of regular duties.

"That has been underway for many months. Testing the views of those senior commanders that might resist orders by Hitler that risk war with Britain and France. This alternative for a preemptive coup represents something far more complex and urgent."

"Speaking of the risk of war, Konrad, I believe that among many of your generals it is not war they fear, but rather a premature war that Germany cannot win. Tell Oster that is a concern he needs to surmount in his negotiations. The other side needs something more than just replacing a maniac like Hitler with a more pragmatic German military government. A Germany better prepared in a few years' time to embark on the same military territorial conquests."

"I will convey your thoughts to Colonel Oster. Now to a practical matter. Since you are critical to providing information from Germany to your people in London, I will sometimes need to pass on material not easily conveyed verbally or transmitted by cipher.

Such as the material I passed through Frau Fromm. Material you can personally courier to London as necessary. One of our field agents suggested a method of espionage tradecraft that I adapted to our situation."

"Speaking of tradecraft, are we being watched now?" Fleming asked as he casually looked around.

"Yes. The man and woman seated behind you and to the right. They came in after you."

"How can you tell?"

"Having been under surveillance for some time provides practice. Subtle tells. They are more interested in their surroundings rather than each other. Have not spoken a word to each other. Seem disinterested in their coffees. As for my shadow, that older gentleman to the left reading a newspaper. I have seen him before outside my apartment building."

Fleming made a slight nod in acknowledgment. "So tell me how we exchange documents with the Gestapo always watching?"

"A variation on what is called a dead drop. A location where one person hides something for subsequent retrieval by another. Since we are both under surveillance, we must use intermediaries and various locations for the pickup.

"We continue meeting as we normally do to explain the nature of the material and the arrangement to make the exchange. For example, the newspaper kiosk outside your embassy is one such location. The older fellow that runs the stand of international newspapers works for Abwehr counterintelligence. He displays small flags of the nationalities of the publications. If the American flag is absent, it means the drop is compromised."

"I know the newspaper stand. I buy the New York Times there almost every day. So it already is my normal routine."

"Excellent. As a contingency, I am working on infiltrating someone into the cleaning staff at your embassy. Perhaps you can get this person hired by constructing some reason for your personal recommendation. That has the benefit of a secure handoff of confidential material. The cleaning woman just leaves the envelope on your office chair.

"One other security protocol. In any exchange of information whether written or even encrypted, never use actual names. Names of the enemy or any of our names. Everyone has a three-digit number. The numbers are random with no significance of importance. It is just security shorthand. I am 121. Oster is 112. You are 167. Hitler is 188. As I pass information, I will tell you verbally the identity of those people referenced."

"What next?" Fleming said.

"The SD has increased subversive operations in Austria. We have fragmented information on simultaneous activities in the Sudetenland region of Czechoslovakia. I am putting together a package accompanied by intelligence assessments. Perhaps you can bring this material to the first meeting of the talks in London.

"Bear in mind, the tactics are different for Czechoslovakia compared to Austria. The majority of Austria is already ethnically German. The Austrian Nazi Party remains a threatening force. The Austrian army is limited in strength by the Treaty of Versailles. Czechoslovakia is an artificial multi-ethnic state. SD subversive activity in the Sudetenland continues but internally destroying greater Czechoslovakia from within is not possible. Military invasion is the only way Hitler can annex Czechoslovakia. It will eventually be the fuse that ignites war.

* * * *

After eight years in German military counterintelligence, Oberleutnant Dieter Vogel felt underappreciated. Recently passed over for promotion to head the desk of Abwehr section IIIC-2, charged with countering foreign espionage, also meant passed over for promotion to the rank of captain. For a university graduate from a prosperous family, his military career seemed a disappointment. The thought of joining the family construction business an admission of failure. His dismal financial circumstances caused his fiancée to break off their engagement.

Depressed, Vogel easily fell under the influence of a cousin in the Sicherheitsdienst des Reichsführers-SS, the Nazi Security Service, or SD. The cousin held the rank of Hauptsturmführer, the equivalent to that of captain in the Wehrmacht. The cousin regaled him with the sheer excitement of being associated so close to the seat of real power in the Reich. Boasting that he reported to Sturmbannführer Pfeiffer who in turn reported directly to Brigadeführer Heydrich, head of the SD and the Gestapo. Heydrich was the operational head of the entire SS and Heinrich Himmler's number two. Instead of recruiting Vogel to the SD, the cousin suggested Vogel first make a name for himself by secretly providing confidential information from within the Abwehr.

Dieter Vogel represented Heydrich's first serious penetration into Abwehr headquarters.

Vogel's access to information was better than the two low-level clerks currently feeding information to the SD, but still limited in scope. As within any intelligence organization, compartmentalization was a fundamental security protocol. From his counterintelligence subsection, his duties involved monitoring espionage activities of Western powers. This included known officers of British MI6 and the French Deuxième Bureau, operating under the cover of consular officers, and military attachés. Therefore, Fleming fell into this group as the sole American of interest since the United States had no foreign intelligence service.

Like Heydrich's SD, the Abwehr kept current dossiers on the activities of these Westerners operating out of the embassies. Additionally Abwehr IIIC-2 kept tabs on German officials of the Foreign Ministry as possible sources of foreign espionage penetrations. Vogel therefore had no direct insights into Oster's conspiracy. For his part, Oster left no trail of his treasonous activities within the Abwehr. Not only to preserve security but simply because only a small number of Abwehr officers were involved. Even Abwehr chief Admiral Canaris was unaware of Oster's activities.

Yet Vogel was still able to stumble on reported activities of certain individuals singled out in counterintelligence files for casual attention either because of their positions or expressed views. These included Theodor Kordt, Chargé d'Affaires at the German Embassy in London and his brother Ernst, counselor at the Embassy. Carl Goerdeler, the former major of Leipzig who resigned after long running disagreements with Hitler over economic policy. Currently Director of overseas sales of Robert Bosch GmbH and traveling extensively outside Germany. Unknown to Vogel, these individuals represented some of Oster's negotiating team with the British and now possibly the Americans.

Fleming became part of a watch list of people Vogel passed along to his cousin in the SD. Nothing incriminating existed on any of them other than routine log entries of recent activities and movements. Pfeiffer did not expect anything of substance. Heydrich made it clear they just needed names from which to populate a believable fiction of a military resistance movement. Heydrich's exact words, "Creating effective propaganda requires building on a foundation of facts to create a plausible narrative."

However, Fleming provoked Pfeiffer's special interest. There remained the collapse of the prostitution ring as a source of intelligence on influential persons for the Gestapo. Decker's failed idea with Kaplinsky's disappearance and discovery instead of a Polish espionage operation. Was Fleming actually having an affair with Kaplinsky or was that a cover?

Vogel's information placed Fleming in Amsterdam at the time Kaplinsky disappeared. Dutch Abwehr sources identified Fleming as staying at a hotel with an American woman named Allsburg. Might that actually be Kaplinsky? Were Kaplinsky and Fleming working with Polish intelligence? Perhaps an American-Polish joint espionage operation with the Russian agent just a red herring?

It made little difference. Pfeiffer could craft an incriminating scenario involving not only British and French subversive efforts, but also perhaps the Americans. The premise directed toward a foreign conspiracy involving dissident Wehrmacht middle rank officers to topple the government. Far less an improbable fiction than the unrealistic script conceived to justify the Night of the Long Knives purge of the SA.

Although Vogel's information was not yet significant, Pfeiffer took credit for recruiting the sole source within Abwehr headquarters. No telling what Vogel could produce if properly coached.

After three months, the value of Vogel's information produced only meager results. Nothing obviously incriminating. Nothing that pointed to Oster much less Canaris. Enough however to begin forming a foundation for a fictitious script of a Wehrmacht resistance conspiracy to remove Adolf Hitler.

In reality, Oster's conspiracy within the ranks of the Abwehr extended to only a very few officers, including several general officers. The conspiracy originated with Oster and General Ludwig Beck the principal sponsor within the Wehrmacht General Staff. Vogel's information was nothing more than routine travel reports of Abwehr officers. Specifically those of Major Konrad Richter, Captain Friedrich Wilhelm Heinz, Captain Georg Hansen, and Major Helmut Groscurth.

Using Vogel's information, Pfeiffer's team pieced together a record of contacts. Nothing unusual could be discerned by these officers' activities. Their contacts did not necessarily discriminate toward those generals with SD dossiers noting questionable alliance to the Führer. However, interaction with those general officers known to hold military views at odds with those of Hitler did show a marked higher incidence of interaction. Whether indicative of anything did not matter to Pfeiffer. He had no reason to believe a conspiracy representing a threat to the current regime actually existed. Simply following Heydrich's order to develop a fictional conspiracy case against the Wehrmacht General Staff. Constructed on a foundation of circumstantial information and hearsay, it needed only the casting of conspirators to provide the appearance of credibility. It did not need to pass critical scrutiny, only feed the paranoia of the Führer.

Heydrich did not share with Pfeiffer the intended use of this contrived conspiracy. Only told that it must carry more credibility than the brazenly improbable narrative behind the purge of the SA years earlier. Therefore, based on SD dossiers of the Wehrmacht General Staff, he began populating the fictitious conspiracy with generals known for voicing opposing views to those of the Führer. Included were Generals Beck, Olbricht, Liebmann, Adam, Witzleben, and Weichs.

Heydrich did not know how close he was to identifying several key figures in the real Oster-Beck conspiracy.

Pfeiffer then connected these generals to lower ranking subordinates linking supporting entries in SD records where possible to fortify a circumstantial case for conspiracy. Among those names was Oberst Ritter von Strobel, chief of planning for General Ludwig Beck, Chief of Staff of the Army High Command. Strobel had many entries in his SD dossier for anti-Nazi and anti-Hitler remarks. Also recorded were the names of personal friends that included two other officers from General Witzleben's staff in Berlin. Again, there appeared the name of American Lieutenant Colonel Spencer Fleming. Perfect for tying in the foreign connection, Pfeiffer cast Fleming in a leading role in this fictitious conspiracy.

CHAPTER 28

Berlin, German Reich | Summer 1937

A month earlier, Heydrich summoned his senior SD subordinates and Gestapo operations chief Standartenführer Heinrich Müller to a meeting. "We have a new assignment. The Führer harbors concerns about the willingness of the Wehrmacht to carry out orders should military action become necessary with Austria or Czechoslovakia. Reichsführer Himmler therefore has directed us to determine if there exists organized opposition to the Führer among the General Staff.

"It is my belief that not only does opposition exist but there is likely the real threat of something more extreme. I am speaking of a possible military putsch to topple the Führer and replace the current government with military rule by the Wehrmacht."

Sturmbannführer Johann Pfeiffer and his colleagues stiffened with Heydrich's pronouncement.

Heydrich continued. "For some time, I have suspected active subversion exists within the Wehrmacht. Ever since Admiral Wilhelm Canaris took over the Abwehr. I know Canaris well. He is smart and clever. A schemer. I have my own reasons to believe Canaris is involved and perhaps even leading a dissident faction of Army generals."

Heydrich's leap from suspicion of the General Staff to outright claiming some secret resistance organization actually existed surprised even Pfeiffer. A high stakes game typical of Heydrich. Naming Canaris specifically suited Heydrich's own interests. The

Abwehr was part of the Wehrmacht and therefore a rival to the SD as the foreign intelligence service of Germany.

"All of you are directed to search your records to assist in identifying Wehrmacht officers opposed to the Führer. Sturmbannführer Pfeiffer will head the investigation. Standartenführer Müller, you will provide Pfeiffer with whatever manpower from the Gestapo is necessary to investigate officers suspected of active subversion.

"Understand we must be cautious to avoid directly antagonizing the Wehrmacht. A committed leadership in the Army is necessary for achieving German national objectives. Do not make waves. That is all, gentlemen. Please remain behind Pfeiffer."

Once alone, he said to Pfeiffer, "Your assignment is slightly different from what I explained to the others. The Wehrmacht can harbor whatever views they wish as long as they execute the Führer's orders efficiently when the time comes. However, a problem exists with opposition from the very top of the Wehrmacht leadership. The Führer expects a creative solution. You shall work with me to find that solution."

* * * *

Having reached the pinnacle of power, Adolf Hitler became increasing impatient with the Wehrmacht. He attributed their consistent objections and offering alternatives of archaic military strategy as belonging to an earlier era. Few appreciated his genius. Interaction with the General Staff often ended in one of Hitler's ranting diatribes with the generals shrinking into silence.

On November 5, 1937, Hitler called a meeting in response to complaints from commander of the Navy Admiral Raeder that the Navy was receiving insufficient allocations of steel and other vital materials. Attending the meeting were Foreign Minister Konstantin von Neurath, War Minister Field Marshal Werner von Blomberg, Army Commander General Werner von Fritsch, Grand Admiral Erich Raeder, and Luftwaffe Commander Hermann Göring.

Hitler was not there to resolve factional disputes between branches of the military. Instead, he used it as a forum to launch his larger vision for German imperialism. In answer to Germany's increasing economic crisis fueled by rearmament, Hitler categorically stated the only solution was to embark on a policy of aggression by seizing Austria and Czechoslovakia. The timing critical before British and French rearmament closed the gap in military capabilities with Germany.

Blomberg, Fritsch, and Neurath rigorously opposed the policy. Germany needed more time to rearm while stabilizing the economy. Brushing aside Raeder's needs, Hitler realized building a navy of capital ships to compete with the British was impractical. His territorial ambitions required resources for the army supported by a technologically superior air force.

The pushback only served to heighten Hitler's impatience with the entrenched military high command. All lacked the vision of seeing the genius of his plans. Given their positions, Hitler saw Blomberg and Fritsch as the principal obstacles to his ambitions for expanding the German Reich.

* * * *

Hitler was averse to giving specific orders, favoring instead to make broad statements revealing his thinking. To an ambitious acolyte like Heinrich Himmler, gaining favor with the Führer required interpreting his thoughts and acting accordingly. No one was better at this than Himmler. In terms of power within the Third Reich, Himmler was second only to Hitler.

To Himmler, it was clear that Hitler needed to find a way to bring the Wehrmacht firmly under his control before moving against Austria and Czechoslovakia. Everything Hitler envisioned required a motivated military to carry out his orders without hesitation. Himmler set out to accomplish just that. His plan called for removing the current OKW high command and reorganizing the General Staff in a manner to inhibit organized resistance.

Decapitating the SA was a different scenario. Once purged of the leadership, the SA immediately retreated into irrelevance. In contrast, the Wehrmacht was the linchpin to a remilitarized Germany. Himmler's plan was to find a way to remove the current Minister of Defense Blomberg and the commander-in-chief of the German Army Fritsch. Both respected officers. Diminishing the power of the Wehrmacht conversely increased the power of the Schutzstaffel.

As he did with the task of eliminating Ernst Röhm and the SA leadership, he turned again to Reinhard Heydrich.

Heydrich was essential because he took Himmler's vague orders and translated them into action. In Heydrich, Himmler had a ruthless conspirator with a proven ability for organization and consistently achieved results.

It fell to Heydrich to attack the problem with a nuanced plan. A plan that went beyond Hitler simply removing Blomberg and Fritsch. After two weeks, he presented his ideas to Himmler.

"Removing Blomberg and Fritsch is a delicate manner. Both enjoy wide respect. Therefore, the only approach is to discredit them in a way that reflects badly on military traditions. Personal scandal making their departure palatable to their fellow officers. The issue concerning Blomberg already exists. As for Fritsch, I have found a basis for scandal but it will require additional evidence to add credibility."

Himmler interrupted. "What is it you are suggesting for Blomberg?"

"His mistress, Reichsführer. Sources close to the field marshal suggest he plans to marry her soon. Gestapo sources within the criminal police discovered an extensive criminal record of twenty-four year old Erna Gruhn."

"What sort of crimes?"

"Prostitution. Not a moral lapse but a career. Several convictions. Records exist in seven different cities. Also sentenced by a Berlin court for distributing indecent personal photographs."

Himmler said in his deadpan manner devoid of emotion, "Therefore, we let Field Marshal Blomberg cut his own throat by marrying his whore. What about Fritsch?"

"Fritsch is more complicated. Over a year ago, a report came to my desk. An obscure allegation of homosexuality."

"Is there any merit to the allegation?" Himmler asked.

"Perhaps. Fritsch never married. The allegation rests solely on testimony of a known homosexual prostitute and blackmailer. To make the accusation credible will require manufacturing supporting evidence."

Himmler nodded. "Fritsch is known to despise the Führer. His removal is in the interest of the State."

"Another thought I had, Reichsführer. Removing Blomberg and Fritsch may not be enough to achieve obedience from the high command to act on the Führer's orders. Unless the Führer replaces them with someone of their liking, they will find ways to subvert his authority. Reshuffling the Wehrmacht General Staff will disrupt their sense of fraternity. It needs only a believable justification for the Führer to act. I therefore have another parallel plan of attack to bring the Wehrmacht into line. It will serve as a basis for reshuffling the Wehrmacht command structure to reassign officers of questionable loyalty."

"This is a delicate balancing act, Reinhard. The committed performance of the Wehrmacht is essential when the time comes to invade Austria and Czechoslovakia. Bringing them into line without reservation is essential. We can counter pockets of resistance but not outright revolt."

"I understand, Reichsführer. My plan will leave senior officers untouched directly, but sufficiently warned against taking any contrary action. I rely on their self-interest to preserve career and prestige. Most will fall into line and observe their oath to the Führer by devoting themselves to the military tradition of following orders. Historical traditions of duty and honor shall prevail above all else, Reichsführer."

"What is your plan, Reinhard?"

"Over the last two years we have intensified our surveillance efforts of activities of the Abwehr. Ever since Admiral Canaris took command. I know Canaris well from my early days in the Kregsmarine. Canaris is a master of intrigue. Perfectly suited to intelligence work. Our paths intersect frequently."

Himmler and Heydrich both chafed at the competition between the military intelligence branch of the Wehrmacht's Abwehr and the SS security Service the SD. Himmler coveted not only control of all German intelligence and counterintelligence operations, but also to deprive the military of an important element of power.

"We know that among the Wehrmacht General Staff, serious opposition exists to the Führer's objectives. How deeply this goes and if there actually exists any organized resistance, we do not know. Regardless, I believe an opportunity exists to erode the independence of the Wehrmacht further. Something to follow along with the removal of Blomberg and Fritsch. Something that will support a reshuffling of command assignments to disrupt any organized resistance when the Führer moves against Austria and Czechoslovakia.

"My plan is similar to the script justifying the purge of the SA."

Himmler scowled. "Are you suggesting a purge of the Wehrmacht?"

"Certainly not, Reichsführer. Such a move would be counterproductive. Even those generals that disagree with the Führer remain militarily useful. I am suggesting something more subtle. A fabricated plot for a putsch instigated by a conspiracy of middle-ranking officers. Colonels and majors. We move against a list of selected officers using a body of manufactured evidence built on a circumstantial basis using documentation records. We make no attempt to directly incriminate any general officers but leave the implication as they are reassigned to other duties."

"What role does the Abwehr play in your script?"

"They play the lead role. A number of Abwehr officers travel extensively visiting all military districts. Their travel records based on our surveillance therefore interpreted in such a way as to reinforce a conspiracy. We now have placed our own spy within Abwehr headquarters to build on this scenario."

"Who is the head of this fictitious conspiracy, Reinhard?"

Heydrich's thin lips parted slightly in an expression more a sneer than smile. "That is the best part. Admiral Canaris. Canaris is vulnerable since his position requires foreign interaction. A career working with foreign countries. Speaks six languages. Easy to create a fictitious treason with Britain, France, and possibly the United States. We thereby destroy the influence of the Abwehr at the same time.

"Admiral Raeder is known to dislike Canaris. He approved his appointment only as a comprise candidate to place a navy officer at the head of the Abwehr. He is unlikely to defend Canaris."

Himmler said, "That may be too much following the scandals to remove Blomberg and Fritsch."

Heydrich responded, "I suggest we move against this plotting of a putsch by lower ranking officers immediately following exposing the evidence that will blacken the honor of Blomberg and Fritsch. Those personal scandals will work like a disease within the Wehrmacht and create a major distraction. Separate events that will appear unconnected. I believe it will unbalance the General Staff thereby inhibiting Wehrmacht resistance to the Führer's orders. They will choose to abandon politics and follow the Führer to preserve their careers."

Himmler remained silent for several moments. "An intriguing scenario, Reinhard. Proceed with your planning. It must prove compelling enough for the Führer to authorize moving forward. How much time do you need?"

"No more than sixty days, Reichsführer."

* * * *

Pfeiffer got busy with creating a body of circumstantial evidence for those Abwehr officers key to the fictional conspiracy of a putsch to overthrow Hitler. His targets included Major Helmut Groscurth of Abwehr Department II, Hauptmann Georg Hansen of Abwehr Foreign Armies West, Hauptmann Friedrich Wilhelm Heinz of Abwehr Department III, and Major Konrad Richter, Abwehr Central Division.

Spreading outward into various commands of the Wehrmacht, Pfeiffer began adding names of officers frequently contacted by these Abwehr officers. To add weight of suspicion,

Pfeiffer's team would single out lower ranking officers subordinate to senior officers with records of anti-Hitler views. When moving against this fabricated cabal of these subordinate officers, Pfeiffer rationalized many of their superiors might decline to mount vigorous defenses for fear of the accusations tainting them.

Among those added names was Oberst Ritter von Strobel. As operations chief to Army Chief of Staff General Ludwig Beck, he long ago fell under SD scrutiny. The outspoken Beck clashed with Hitler's initiatives on many occasions. Strobel was little better at concealing his views than his boss. Spreading outward from Strobel, Pfeiffer added several other names known as frequent visitors to his home.

Within Strobel's circle was another officer on General Beck's staff, the intelligence officer on the staff of the commander of the Hanover military district, and the chief of staff to the commander of the Dresden military district. Pfeiffer had much from which to stitch together an imaginary military coup.

Pfeiffer had no way to know that he was close to identifying several of Oster's actual conspirators. Not the least of which was General Beck, the designated head of what essentially was the conspiracy creation of Oberstleutnant Hans Oster.

The Strobel connection also added another name. That of American military attaché Colonel Spencer Fleming. Recently promoted after returning from Germany. Easy to expand that into an American espionage penetration. Impossible to refute.

Given Fleming's personal friendship with both Strobel and Major Richter of the Abwehr, Pfeiffer could weave Fleming into his conspiracy narrative. Perhaps make Fleming out to be the principal connection of the conspiracy to foreign powers interested in removing the Führer?

For security, Heydrich kept those aware of the broader intent of developing this fake military coup conspiracy to a minimum. Other than his select team, the secretive Heydrich excluded other ranking SS officers from knowledge of the audacious scheme to run in parallel with removal of the two top Wehrmacht generals. Head of the Gestapo Müller designated Otto Decker to work with Pfeiffer and marshal whatever manpower resources proved necessary to support the operation in the field. Everyone but Heydrich and Pfeiffer compartmentalized to knowledge of project details based on their need to know.

CHAPTER 29

Berlin, German Reich | December 1937

Fleming resumed his military attaché cover duties after leaving Kaplinsky in Amsterdam. While assuming still under surveillance, nothing overtly happened to heighten his sense of being at risk. Obviously, his association with Kaplinsky raised questions. Impossible to guess how much more the Gestapo knew. The *Geisterstunde* closed down. The newspapers alluded to illegal black market activities without providing details. Fleming could not make enquiries without drawing attention. No reason to fear anything worse than expulsion from Germany if he limited his associations only to Richter and Strobel. Explained as both personal and professional relationships of long standing.

Expecting to conclude his espionage mission within a few months proved optimistic. It was the beginning of summer before Oster even declared he was ready to commence secret talks in London.

1937 proved a tumultuous year for Great Britain. In December of the previous year, the neurotic Edward VIII, the British king for only a year, abdicated the throne in favor of his younger brother who became George VI. The marriage to an American divorcee already an embarrassment, the now Duke of Windsor also expressed an affinity for Nazis Germany. This followed b seventy-year-old three-time prime minister Stanley Baldwin resigning. Neville Chamberlain became the new prime minister.

Recognizing the potential threat of Nazi Germany, Britain began rearmament in earnest. The Chiefs of Staff reported that by May, German Luftwaffe would have 800 bombers compared the RAF's 48. Baldwin badly underestimated Germany rearmament throughout his third term as prime minister. Britain realized it lagged far behind in the arms race. Given this and ample evidence of Hitler's belligerency, the new government of Neville Chamberlain continued Baldwin's conciliatory attitude toward Nazi Germany.

For Hitler's part, his militaristic ambitions became more transparent. After backing the Spanish Fascist Falange rebels by airlifting colonial troops to Andalusia to start the Spanish Civil War, the Luftwaffe Condor Legion took an active part in the fighting. In April, German bombers destroyed the town of Guernica in the Basque region on market day. The act of terror against 10,000 civilians proved a tactical training exercise for the reequipped Luftwaffe.

France recognized the growing threat of Germany by beginning expansion of the Maginot Line, the elaborate defensive fortifications spanning the entire border between France and Germany.

On the American front, the growing threat of Japanese territorial ambitions burst forth in a brazen Japanese attack on Northern China from Manchuria in July. The beginning of the Second Sino-Japanese War that would stretch on for years. Clear evidence of Japanese imperialism to acquire vital military resources. The aggression posed a direct threat to British colonies and American economic interests in the Pacific.

Japanese aggression in the East shifted immediate attention from Germany to Japan for both Britain and the United States. What seemingly should increase American, British, and French interest in indirectly supporting German military dissidents' removal of Adolf Hitler, instead distracted foreign policy attention away from Germany for months.

Adding to Fleming's frustration, in June Richter informed him that operational planning still required more time.

"God damn it, Konrad. What is taking so long?" Fleming asked while sharing coffee at their usual café.

"Communication. For security, Oster must largely interact with the key general officers through intermediaries like me. Everything verbal. The back and forth makes for a slow process to avoid being obvious. Are your people in Washington pressuring you?"

Fleming wondered if the delay might be due more to doubt among the conspirators. "Not really. My friend says the Japanese invasion of China is dominating foreign policy concerns in Washington. I am more worried that delays on your part may dampen Roosevelt's confidence about the Wehrmacht pulling off this coup."

"I assure you that is not the case. You can see by the intelligence we continue to pass to you that military planning related to invasion of Austria and Czechoslovakia continues in earnest. As does active SD subversion efforts. Tensions are only increasing the urgency to act."

Richter's material these past months included more documents. Provided to Fleming by a woman on the housekeeping staff of the U.S. Embassy. An envelope placed on his chair. Exceptionally sensitive material. Battle formations, maps, commanders, troop strength, mechanized assets, aircraft, and the list goes on. It appeared Oster was holding little back. Fleming had no way to verify the material but felt it was not disinformation. Yet deception was Oster's business. The numbers suggested a stronger Wehrmacht than Washington believed. Was Oster's overstating German military capacities? If so why?

With these delays, Fleming took a week's leave in May. His first return to Amsterdam since returning to Berlin in January. A special holiday with Valeska. He flew to Amsterdam where they flew together to Paris. Valeska's first plane ride and first time in Paris. A glorious sunny spring week. A suite at the Regina Hotel, next to the Louvre and only a fifteen-minute walk to the Paris Opera.

Fleming could not explain to Valeska why the President wanted him to remain in Berlin but vowed to be done by the end of the year regardless. For his remaining time, he promised to come to Amsterdam each month for a few days. His absences explained within the embassy as necessary to conduct secure telephone communications from outside Germany. Allen Dulles assured him the President still supported the removal of Hitler. Fleming assured Dulles the Oster Conspiracy remained committed with Hitler's increasingly brazen actions. Candidly, he told Dulles he believed Oster was possibly encountering an erosion of resolve from some of the conspirators.

* * * *

Fleming returned again to Amsterdam in December 1937 for what he hoped signaled the end of his mission. This time the secret joint talks in London were finally to begin. Fully a year since he rescued Valeska and embarked on this fateful assignment. A year of frustration and personal sacrifice. Making the trip to Amsterdam to see Valeska only occasionally. The circumstances largely of his own making for pushing to assassinate Adolf Hitler. If this meeting did not move things to conclusion imminently, he was done. Time was also running out before events overtook any attempt to remove Hitler before he started another war.

Winter was approaching. A dusting of snow covered the city. Even with the signature flowers gone from the bridges over the canals, Amsterdam held its charm. All the more delightful anticipating seeing Valeska after several weeks.

Since he returned to Berlin, the stress of taking part with Oster's grand plan was unrelenting yet frustrating with recurring delays. Should the venture not succeed, Fleming knew Europe would eventually fall into another war.

Oster's plan was nonetheless precarious. Fleming had no way of assessing the commitment of those generals integral to the plan. The first casualty of war was the battle plan. At every juncture, many things could go wrong and some will go wrong. Developing the organizational aspects of the complex undertaking made more difficult by operating in secrecy against an advanced police state.

Seeing Valeska waiting on the platform as his train pulled in, Fleming shelved his apprehension over concerns for the success of Oster's coup for the next two days before proceeding to London.

After smothering him with kisses, Kaplinsky grabbed his arm leading him through the train station to a taxi. "I have missed you, Spencer. You do not call often enough."

Holding her hand, "Cannot trust the telephones. Not even placing calls from the embassy. The Gestapo likely monitors my calls. I have to go to creative lengths to call you from locations where I am cannot be identified."

"Then you are in danger?"

Of course he was. He was participating in the violent overthrow of Hitler and the Nazis. Just continuing his duties as American military attaché made him of interest to the Nazi police state. Yet he had a mission to carry out. Downplaying the threat for Kaplinsky, "Your sudden disappearance probably raised suspicion with the Gestapo. If I place repeated calls to a Rachel Allsburg in Amsterdam, they will believe it is you. Safer not to reveal your whereabouts."

Following lovemaking, Kaplinsky said, "I have a surprise for you tonight."

"Really? I thought you just gave me your body as my coming home present."

"Dinner at a special place. French cuisine. It will remind you of the *Geisterstunde.*"

"Wonderful."

* * * *

After relaxing with drinks, she stood up from the table at the restaurant. "Now the surprise."

Approaching the lone piano player, she picked up a microphone. In passable French, she announced, "Tonight is for my fiancé just returned to Amsterdam."

She sang several songs in French to enthusiastic applause of the patrons. Later she told him, she sang here on the weekends.

The charm of Paris with their trip in May motivated her to learn French. Something else they could share.

A special evening. In two days, he was off to London. After the first round of talks, he would return to Amsterdam to spend Christmas with her before returning briefly to Berlin. If the talks stalled, or Oster did not make his move, he was done.

Living within the horrors of Hitler's Third Reich, Fleming emphatically believed the only solution was to kill Hitler. Execute him immediately affording no time for Nazi followers to recover. The idea of German national socialism eradicated like a disease. That meant a bloodbath to destroy the SS.

His contribution was to convince the former Allies to provide Oster with foreign assurances of support for removing Hitler. Assurances necessary to convince those generals still wavering to participate without hesitation. He understood the details of Oster's plan. The order of battle was far more than a list of forces. It was an intricately interlocked sequence of maneuverers. Timing critical. Anticipating the many variables made planning alternatives difficult. Success rested on key individuals adapting to the fluidity of developing events. Everything directed toward achievement of the objective.

* * * *

Fleming flew to London and headed straight for the United States Embassy to meet with Allen Dulles and William Donovan.

A warm reunion with Dulles followed with William Donovan's effusive greeting.

"Honored to be working alongside a fellow officer with such a distinguished career in the service to America. Allen filled me in on the details of your working outside official channels these last few years. What made you single-handedly become America's only real spy, Colonel?"

"Fell into it you might say. Much of it due to Allen's internationalist views during our years together in New York. He recruited me. Then when posted as military attaché to Warsaw I developed a relationship with the head of the German desk for

Polish military intelligence. Even in 1932, the Poles saw the implications of Adolf Hitler coming to power. Reading *Mein Kampf* leaves no doubt of his militaristic ambitions. Czechoslovakia likely followed by invasion of Poland at some future time."

Dulles said, "That was Spencer's first intelligence he passed to me although he did not reveal the source at the time."

"This was political intelligence. Of little interest to the War Department. Furthermore, they might question how I obtained this information in my official capacity."

Donovan said, "This idea of Hitler leading Germany to war is the driving reason for what we are calling the Oster Conspiracy?"

"Precisely. However, for different reasons than the Poles. The barbarity of the Nazi regime is repellent to many Germans, including many within the Army. To varying degrees, most disagree with the persecution of German Jews as immoral or simply a distraction. The overriding concern of the Wehrmacht conspirators is a premature war. Germany not sufficiently rearmed thereby likely to suffer another catastrophic defeat by a demented leader with no understanding of the military.

"My reports to the War Department point to German weakness in the military readiness. Hitler has placed his bets on a strong air force and a well-equipped, well-trained mechanized army. He has neither the money nor the patience to develop a navy with capital ships to counter British naval superiority.

"Hitler of course realizes the shortages of vital war materials to enable his ambitions. Petroleum, iron, rubber, aluminum, tungsten. To obtain these resources he must seize territory within a few years. The timing critical to prevent collapse of the economy under the weight of military expenditures. War therefore becomes inevitable."

Donovan said, "Well summarized, Colonel."

"Why does Oster need assurances from Britain, France, and the United States to move against the Nazi regime?" Dulles asked.

"I will let his negotiators make that case in the talks. However, I believe that his conspiracy has a coalition of senior officers with varying degrees of commitment. Remember, this goes against their military code of honor. Allied assurances of a better deal for a post-Hitler Germany will significantly bolster their resolve. Provides an overriding nationalistic context for abandoning their oath to the Führer to save the Fatherland."

Donovan said. "Over dinner this evening, you must regale us with further details of your espionage penetrations of Nazi Germany. A remarkable achievement."

Fleming said. "Is everything arranged for the talks to take place at the Connaught Hotel in Mayfair?"

"Yes. An excellent hotel. All three of us also have rooms there. Do you know who Oster is sending to negotiate?"

"No. Only until a few days ago did I even know the names of the key generals designated to take part in the actual coup. I know that only because I told him that he must present specific details to convince the Allies and he wanted my opinion. Oster understandably plays things close to his chest. Told him that besides me, one of the American negotiators is a former military commander so he needs to sell us on the viability of the operational aspects of the coup."

Donovan nodded. "Oster is placing great reliance in the United States to nudge the British from their position of appeasement of Hitler. That might be a tall order."

Dulles added, "Which brings me to another subject. We do not meet here at the embassy again. Joseph Kennedy is currently going through confirmation hearings for appointment as Ambassador to the UK. Kennedy holds sympathetic views toward the German Fascist regime. We are therefore *unofficial*. The President expects our mission to remain deep and dark."

* * * *

The following day the first session got underway. Everyone, including the Germans, surprised to see Winston Churchill actually attend. Although a member of parliament, he was no longer part of the current government cabinet. Nonetheless, he still loomed large in British politics.

The other British negotiator was Robert Vansittart, the Permanent Undersecretary at the Foreign Office. He despised Adolf

Hitler and stood firmly against the appeasement policy of the new prime minister Neville Chamberlain and Foreign Secretary Lord Halifax.

Leading negotiations for Oster's Conspiracy were Ernst Kordt, counselor in the London Embassy and his brother Theodor, chargé d'affaires at the embassy. For the past year, they actively collaborated with Oster to probe the British government's position regarding Hitler's rearmament efforts and abandonment of the restrictions of the Treaty of Versailles.

Backing up the Kordt brothers was Ewald von Kleist-Schmenzin a German lawyer, conservative politician, and a longstanding opponent of Nazism from even before 1933. Personally acquainted with Winston Churchill and Robert Vansittart.

Major Helmut Groscurth of the Abwehr, experienced in unconventional warfare using special forces, added to the delegation to explain the operational plan for carrying out the coup.

All the Germans spoke fluent English.

Following introductions, Winston Churchill launched right to the heart of the matter. In his gravelly unmistakable baritone voice, "Why is it, gentlemen, you need our participation?" Why not simply get rid of Hitler?"

Ernst Kordt replied, "As you might well imagine, there are many that hesitate in taking the extreme step of deposing Adolf Hitler. Some remain hopeful if the British government were to hold firm with the threat of war, it would deterred Hitler from military aggression in Eastern Europe. As you and Mr. Vansittart realize, that posture is unlikely with the Chamberlain government's decided inclination toward appeasing Hitler."

"I might add that even if the threat of war forestalled Hitler's ambitions, German invasion eastward is inevitable," Kleist-Schmenzin said. "At the rate of German rearmament, in a few more years the German military will become too strong for even the combined forces of the Britain and France to act without repeating something worse than 1914."

Churchill countered, "All the more reason to move forward with your planned coup. Are not assurances of Britain and our

American friends needed largely to convince those generals still undecided about the undertaking?"

Theodor Kordt responded, "There is some truth to that, Mr. Churchill. However, those in command of essential military resources for executing the operation are fully committed. Colonel Oster instructed Major Groscurth to present the operational plan as evidence of the viability of the operation. Those named commanders remain steadfast in their resolve. Foreign assurances to recognize a new German government with a peaceful path forward will immediately establish support for the transition government across the entire Wehrmacht.

"We will present our list for key positions in the provisional government to provide a sense of what a post-Nazi German will look like. For security reasons, several of these individuals are unaware of preparations to remove the Nazi regime by force."

Dulles said, "Who exactly leads this conspiracy? Colonel Oster?"

As the designated lead negotiator, Ernst Kordt answered, "Colonel Oster is the originator of the idea. The operational head and facilitator. The senior officer that has both the authority and the respect to command the enterprise is Generaloberst Ludwig Beck, Chief of Staff of the Army High Command. It was General Beck and his operations chief Oberst Ritter von Strobel that prepared the tactical elements of the military operations."

This was the first Fleming learned of the active involvement of his friend Ritter von Strobel. While surprised, it fit what he knew about the outspoken Strobel. A man of action willing to act on his convictions. It was also likely that Strobel knew of Fleming's involvement with Oster and therefore passed along information disguised as indiscreet comments passed to a sympathetic trusted friend.

Following a break for lunch, William Donovan said, "Colonel Fleming convinced President Roosevelt the military coup outlined in Colonel Oster's document is both essential to world peace and the best immediate alternative to remove the Nazis from power. Like Mr. Churchill and Mr. Vansittart, President Roosevelt is pursuing this outside normal diplomatic channels. Involvement in supporting a military coup d'état of another nation carries all manner of international ramifications if it becomes known.

"This is something better suited to a foreign intelligence collaboration. Given the stance of the present British government regarding Nazi Germany, hardly suitable for the British Intelligence Service to be the instrument of collaboration. Hence, Mr. Churchill and Mr. Vansittart represent a vehicle for backdoor diplomacy into the British Parliament. The same holds true for the United States. President Roosevelt chooses to avoid any direct involvement of the Department of State to preserve security. Therefore, I am here along with Mr. Dulles and Colonel Fleming working outside his role as military attaché to Germany. Colonel Fleming provides the conduit for direct communication with Colonel Oster. May I then suggest we get to the business of exactly how you intend to eliminate the Nazi regime?"

Major Groscurth took over. "Let me first provide an overview then progress to details and answer your questions. Colonel Fleming has seen the plan which incorporates certain suggestions he offered."

Fleming interjected, "Before Major Groscurth continues, I stressed to Colonel Oster that to secure immediate success of the takeover, they must kill Adolf Hitler. Arrest and trial invites counterattack by the Schutzstaffel. Hitler's immediate death is essential to success. A harsh reality but necessary. Colonel Oster agreed."

Groscurth said, "Colonel Fleming is correct. In fact, Hitler's death is the linchpin of the operation. The precursor to everything that follows. A select detachment of Abwehr officers backed by a full regiment of elite Brandenburger special forces will carry that out. The two officers leading the assault are willing to sacrifice their own lives if necessary to kill Adolf Hitler.

"The location is Hitler's residence in Munich. A luxury nine-room apartment occupying the entire third floor of a five-story building at Prinzregentenplatz 16. Hitler actually spends more time there then in Berlin. His Berlin residence is an apartment located within the Reich Chancellery. A vast building guarded by a battalion of Hitler's personal security Leibstandarte SS Adolf

Hitler. The Munich location is not as heavily defended and more consolidated.

"The Munich military district is under the command of General Wilhelm Adams. General Adams is nearing the end of his career and despises everything about Hitler. Fully committed to saving Germany. His best field commander will attack the Munich apartment building and secure the perimeter while the Abwehr detachment makes penetration and kills Hitler. Their orders are to take photographs then remove the body to a secure location."

Donovan interjected. "So this represents your opening action. I assume the majority of subsequent attacks will take place mostly in Berlin. Communication will be the key to coordination. How is that accomplished?"

"Once the Führer is eliminated, a number is telephoned at Army headquarters in Berlin. Confirmation of Hitler's death will trigger initiation of the following simultaneous actions to seize control. Participating military districts outside Berlin receive telephone calls to commence operations. Since most of the critical seizures are within the Berlin sector, each unit in the field is equipped with wireless radio capability to coordinate with central operation control."

"Who commands this central control?" Donovan asked.

"General Beck supported by Oberst Strobel and Oberstleutnant Oster."

Vansittart asked, "What about the others that must be removed, particularly the SS? Is this to be another massive purge like the SS perpetrated against the SA in 1934?"

Ernst Kordt replied, "In some respects. Hitler holds power through the SS that now represents the Nazi police state. The top SS leadership must be eliminated or civil war could result between the Wehrmacht and the SS with the SA adding to their ranks."

"Which other leaders are targeted for summary execution?" Vansittart said.

"Göring, Goebbels, Himmler, Heydrich, Müller the head of the Gestapo, and all SS over the rank of obersturmbannführer, in

English, lieutenant colonel. A total of less than sixty. Not the bloodbath of hundreds perpetrated by the SS against the SA during the *Night the Long Knives*. However, we expect combat casualties since the SS defends many of the targeted objectives."

Dulles asked, "What about the thousands of SS disarmed and detained?"

The lawyer Kleist-Schmenzin responded, "For SS officers of command rank, the only option is trial by military tribunal. For the vast numbers of lower rank, simply disarmed and returned to civilian life. The post-Nazi government will not engage in internment in concentration camps."

Groscurth continued, "We have strongly committed senior command general officers in seven of the most important military districts. In Berlin, General Erwin von Witzleben commands Army Corps III, along with General Fritz Fellgiebel, Chief of the Army's Signal Establishment, and of course Army Chief of Staff General Beck. Ample manpower with transport and tanks exists to assault all target locations.

"I brought copies of the operational plan and the order of battle indicating key commanders down to the regimental level and their specific assignments to further our discussions. However, my instructions are not to leave behind any copies for security reasons. Colonel Oster presents this as his way of communicating the scope and commitment of those willing to risk everything to save the Fatherland from disaster."

A political cynic, Churchill was characteristically blunt with little concern for diplomatic protocols. "Before we adjourn for the day, we are particularly interested in the government that will replace the Nazis. Oster's letter states the commitments Germany will make. How are we to assume that a government created by the military will be any better for peace in Europe than the Nazis? You will undoubtedly continue with rearmament. Why should we believe this is not a move to buy time while you get your economic house in order before continuing to embark on territorial adventurism?"

A practiced diplomate, Ernst Kordt took no offense. "Here is a list of those that will be asked to form a provisional government.

The names arrived at by consensus of all involved in this conspiracy. Many are unaware that resistance to Adolf Hitler has progressed to the level of organized plotting of his overthrow. For example, Colonel Oster's superior Admiral Canaris remains an outsider. As does Hjalmar Schacht who is well known in the international finance world.

"To your question, Mr. Churchill, the exact form of government has not been determined. That shall be for the provisional government to determine. Perhaps by plebiscite. We make no specific promises. However, we understand the assurances Colonel Oster outlined are a quid pro quo for Germany honoring its territorial commitments.

"Let me offer this comment. Germany seeks to rejoin the European community with equal stature, militarily and economically. We believe it better to fulfil German aspirations through non-military means rather than by threats as a pariah state. Hitler's aggressive rearmament is bankrupting the country. His only recourse is to annex land and resources within a few years. Britain and France are also rearming. Hitler must act soon or risk insurmountable forces within a few years.

"I believe Colonel Fleming forwarded copies of a secret meeting Hitler called of his military leaders, the so called Hossbach Memorandum. In clear terms, it states the economic imperative of acting soon against Austria and Czechoslovakia. Whatever government follows the Nazis must slow rearmament and reestablish an economy that advances the standard of living in Germany or risk civil unrest."

This first round of talks lasted two days. Little more to discuss. What was there to negotiate? The Americans and British representatives committed to providing a response by the week after Christmas.

The Germans would spend that time refining the plan and solidifying the resolve of those general officers essential for pulling this off. Fleming sensed the solidarity of some, or perhaps many of those identified in the operational plan, perhaps wavering. If this coup failed, all faced a firing squad. Beck and Oster wanted some document attesting to support from the British and Americans.

Fleming doubted they would get anything in writing. If he were Oster, he would bluff by reporting favorable results of the London talks. Tell the generals that because of the sensitivity of the matter and powerful political opposition, the British and Americans would not risk putting their commitments in writing. Overreach by affirming that Roosevelt and Churchill support assassinating Hitler and recognition of a non-aggressive new German government without stipulating its form.

Before departing London, Allen Dulles gave Fleming some disheartening news. In January, a new U.S. ambassador to Germany was to replace William Dodd. Unlike Dodd who despised the Nazis, the career diplomat Hugh Wilson praised Hitler for restoring the Germany economy, while portraying the American press as Jewish controlled and fomenting a climate of hate.

Fleming angrily said to Dulles, "Fuck Wilson. For that matter, what kind of game is Roosevelt playing? Are we here just pissing in the wind, Allen? First he appoints that asshole Joseph Kennedy to London now another neo-Fascist to Berlin."

"I don't know, Spencer. I would guess for unknown political reasons. Anti-Hitler sentiment is not exactly pervasive in America. Isolationism seems the only constant."

Fleming intended to enjoy Christmas with Valeska in Amsterdam before returning to the Berlin. The only comfort, the end was now in sight. Complete his commitment then get the hell out of Germany. Find a new career and make a life with Valeska.

CHAPTER 30

Berlin, German Reich | January 1938

Under Heinrich Himmler's orders, Heydrich sprung his trap to destroy War Minister Werner von Blomberg the commander-in-chief of the armed forces. Within days after Blomberg's marriage to the thirty-five years younger Erna Gruhn, Heydrich met with Hermann Göring. Presenting a thick folder, he informed the Reichsmarschall of a shattering discovery involving General Blomberg.

He explained to Göring that as a standard security precaution, he ordered the Gestapo to investigate Blomberg's marriage to such a younger woman of unknown background. At the least, she must not have any taint of Jewish ancestry.

"Unfortunately, Reichsmarschall, investigators found something equally as damaging. Erna Gruhn has an extensive criminal record as a prostitute. We discovered her mother was also a prostitute. Such a marriage violates the code of conduct for German military officers.

"This must be brought to the Führer's attention before a public scandal erupts. You know General Blomberg personally. Reichsführer Himmler thought it best to bring the matter to you."

The news shocked Göring. Yet immediately he saw possible personal advantage in a scandal causing the removal of Blomberg as head of the military. Göring coveted control of the entire German military.

"Yes, I must inform the Führer. He must order Blomberg to annul the marriage."

Heydrich said, "Annulment or divorce is clearly in order. However, should the information become public, General Blomberg's stature as head of the Wehrmacht remains compromised. The Führer must persuade Blomberg to resign or consider removing him from his position to maintain respect among the General Staff."

Presented with the facts, Hitler was furious. When confronted, Blomberg refused to end the marriage. After Göring threatened to make the criminal records of Erna Gruhn and mother public, Blomberg succumbed to the pressure and resigned.

While the downfall of Blomberg was self-inflicted based on undeniable evidence, the matter of removing the popular Generaloberst Werner von Fritsch, Supreme commander of the Army was tenuous. The sole basis for a scandal rested on the dubious allegations of a single unreliable source. Just weeks after successfully removing Blomberg, Heinrich Himmler however wanted to move against Fritsch.

Heydrich brought to Himmler's attention old allegations of a notorious homosexual prostitute and blackmailer's accusations against a military officer named Fritsch.

Heydrich could not however discover corroborating evidence to strengthen the allegation against Fritsch. Never married, Fritsch expressed little interest in women, devoting his life instead to military duties. Perhaps odd, but it added nothing of substance. Heydrich instead developed an idea to reinforce the allegation by introducing something much more inflammatory. He tried to convince Himmler to hold off taking the dubious allegation against Fritsch to Hitler. He told Himmler he had something more solid with which to reinforce the case for Fritsch's removal.

Heydrich needed only a little more time to finalize reshaping Pfeiffer's idea about manufacturing a coup conspiracy involving middle ranked military officers. Although entirely fabricated, it built on a foundation of circumstantial evidence adding a veneer of credibility. The strength of the plot rested on introducing foreign players conspiring against Germany. Difficult to refute beyond the evidence the SD produced. Not only damaging to the Abwehr, indirectly it entangled certain targeted senior officers. It would reinforce the removal of Fritsch based on something far more damaging than a deniable accusation of a single homosexual incident years earlier.

* * * *

Reinhard Heydrich was the Machiavellian dark prince of the Nazi regime. Among the obese Göring, the weak-chinned myopic Himmler, the clubfooted Goebbels, and the non-descript Hitler, Heydrich in contrast was well over six feet, blond, handsome, the ideal Nazi Aryan. The only hint to his dark character his piercing blue eyes that many commented as lacking any warmth. With good reason, Hitler commented on Heydrich as *the man with the iron heart*. The label an accurate reflection of someone supremely ruthless. Even among the psychologically malignant Nazi leadership, Reinhard Heydrich stood apart.

Heydrich knew many general officers opposed Hitler. He also felt that an organized resistance reaching the level of a putsch against Hitler was unlikely. These generals had too much invested in their long careers to venture into the uncertainty of direct revolt. However, the Abwehr represented not only German military intelligence, but also foreign intelligence and counterintelligence. The SD clearly represented a rival. If any active resistance against the Nazi Reich were to develop, it would at least involve the Abwehr. Populated with officers skilled in intrigue and secrecy, their ubiquitous involvement in every sector of the military would prove invaluable. Therefore, the Abwehr became the logical center of Heydrich's fictional conspiracy.

Kaplinsky's disappearance forced Pfeiffer to inform Heydrich of the failed Gestapo operation to use the prostitution ring for gathering information. Under brutal interrogation, the prostitutes confessed to providing information obtained from their sex clients believing it went to the Gestapo. Walter Fischer confessed that he believed Kaplinsky passed the information to Polish intelligence.

Heydrich thought to redeem the counterintelligence failure by using the *Geisterstunde* nightclub and Kaplinsky's prostitution service in his manufactured Wehrmacht conspiracy scenario. Ordering the arrest of all the employees of the *Geisterstunde* the Gestapo drafted coerced testimony casting Kaplinsky as a spy working for the American foreign agent Fleming posing as Kaplinsky's lover. Heydrich would simply ignore Fischer's admission this was a Polish intelligence operation and make it American. He ordered the Gestapo to dispose of all these victims by dispersal to various concentration camps.

Heydrich enlarged the complex plot of foreign espionage penetration as one of conspiring with elements within the Wehrmacht to overthrow the Third Reich. The American Fleming cast as the foreign connection with the United States working behind scenes. Fleming linked to the Abwehr by his friendship with Major Richter. His personal friendship with the outspoken Oberst Strobel provided connection to the equally outspoken critic of the Führer's authority, General Ludwig Beck. Fleming conveniently became the lover of Valeska Kaplinsky heading a network of useful prostitutes as spies. All this while operating with diplomatic immunity as the American military attaché. The perfect cover to interact with British and French foreign intelligence operating from respective Berlin embassies.

Within the United States Embassy, the SD discovered that Martha Dodd, the daughter of the former U.S. ambassador was intimately involved with the Soviet press attaché, a known Soviet spy. Another element to weave the Soviets into the fictional narrative of international conspiracy against Germany.

Heydrich's plot involved fabricating a case for collusion of the former allies opposing Germany in the Great War. Britain, France, Russia, and the United States. Fleming cast as the liaison to conspirators within the Wehrmacht, directed from within Abwehr. A body of circumstantial, hearsay, distorted, and falsified documentation intended to add weight to the baseless allegations. Sufficient to convince his audience of one, Adolf Hitler, already inclined to believe in opposition conspiracies within the military.

The objective to provide a firmer basis for not only the removal of General Fritsch as head of the Army but to disrupt any form of organized opposition of the Wehrmacht against the Führer.

The plan called for arresting Major Richter. Under torture and threats against his family, force Richter to confess to a broad conspiracy implicating selective Wehrmacht officers. The names of those officers drafted by the SD. Incriminate general officers known to oppose the Führer. General Fritsch and Admiral Canaris among those names.

To add weight to the manufactured conspiracy, a wholesale arrest of middle-rank officers representing the core of the active plotters, backed by more circumstantial and falsified documentation. This would allow the Führer to place the General Staff off balance. Discourage any attempt for a putsch while maintaining overall willingness to follow his orders as supreme commander.

As for the American Fleming, arrest and intense interrogation. Kill him after extracting what he can add to reinforce the military conspiracy narrative. His body to disappear leaving the impression he fled Germany.

Heydrich was however not able to persuade Himmler to forestall taking the allegations of Fritsch's homosexual activity and blackmail prematurely to the Führer. Heydrich's concern was everything rested solely on the testimony of an unreliable witness. An old allegation with no supporting evidence. Heydrich argued for springing his trap to expose a broader conspiracy first. The dubious case for Fritsch engaging in homosexual behavior then obscured by the weightier issue of widespread treason within the Wehrmacht.

With Blomberg removed with only a manageable backlash from the officer corps, Hitler pressured Himmler for the means to remove Fritsch. Anxious to provide Hitler an avenue for removing Fritsch, Himmler ignored Heydrich's caution and brought the allegations of the old homosexual incident and blackmail to Hitler. Ignoring Fritsch's popularity among the General Staff, Himmler believed it another breach of military code of conduct similar to Blomberg, with the anticipated same result.

Seeing the opportunity for consolidating his direct leadership of the Army, Hitler immediately confronted Fritsch. The aristocratic Fritsch strenuously denied the charges, but then foolishly resigned.

Unlike the removal of Blomberg for an uncontestable breach of military conduct, the furor of Fritsch's resignation quickly grew out of control. Hitler compounded matters by arbitrarily removing thirteen generals from their commands and reassigning or retiring forty-four others. He also used the opportunity to eliminate the Ministry of War, substituting it with the creation of the Oberkommando der Wehrmacht, the OKW. This weakened the traditional Army High Command, the OKH, now subordinate to the overarching OKW with Hitler in supreme command.

The move not only denied Göring overall command of the military, it preempted Heydrich's scheme to reorganize Army command following exposure of the fictional putsch conspiracy by the Wehrmacht.

Hitler's blunder set off tangible resistance among the Army General Staff. Fritsch chose to fight the charges. With widespread support, the Wehrmacht demanded a court of honor of senior officers to examine what they called the Fritsch Affair.

For those colleagues in the Army's high command, the Fritsch allegations were beyond absurd. Many made no attempt to disguise their disgust. Making matters worse, the Gestapo discovered the homosexual prostitute could not identify General Werner von Fritsch as the army officer he blackmailed since 1934. The incident instead involved a junior officer with a similar name. The discovered truth would exonerate Fritsch during the military hearing. Hitler likely to blame Heinrich Himmler for the political debacle.

A revolt by the Army High Command could jeopardize Hitler's immediate plans for annexation of Austria. Concern over loyalty of the Army forced Hitler to agree to the Army's demand for military judicial review. In a panic, Himmler turned to Heydrich suggesting he move immediately to implement operations against his contrived putsch conspiracy as a means to counter the Army's opposition to the Führer. Heydrich understood the timetable for

Austria and the personal rewards if he could salvage the situation and deflect fault from the Reichsführer-SS.

* * * *

To add substantive evidence to the foreign espionage conspiracy, Heydrich would provide actual operational plans for invading Austria and Czechoslovakia. Conveniently planted on one of the conspirators. The two operations connected by the first incursion into Austria. With German troops in Austria, this allowed complete encirclement of the Czechoslovakian Sudetenland perimeter region of western Czechoslovakia to overwhelm expected stiff Czech military resistance.

The plans would come from within Wehrmacht military intelligence, the Abwehr. The undisputable incriminating evidence planted in the quarters of Pfeiffer's own SD spy within the Abwehr. Adding weight to other planted materials incriminating senior Abwehr staff, including Admiral Canaris.

Heydrich advanced the timing of setting the operation in motion knowing of Hitler's timetable for Austria.

Following increased violence in Austria from the Austrian Nazi Party and Heydrich's SD provocateurs, Austrian Chancellor Schuschnigg met Hitler at Berchtesgaden on February 12 in an attempt to prevent a takeover of Austria. Schuschnigg caved into Hitler's demands further weakening his bargaining position. A week later Hitler made a speech to the Reichstag where he said, "The German Reich is no longer willing to tolerate the suppression of ten million Germans across its borders."

Heydrich knew that Austria either would fall to a bloodless political union or suffer invasion by German forces scheduled within weeks. With Wehrmacht high command relations already compromised from the fallout from the Blomberg-Fritsch Affairs, Hitler needed the Wehrmacht fully committed to the military venture. A larger move against the Wehrmacht as Heydrich originally planned was now out of the question. However, a scaled down version implicating the Abwehr at the center of a foreign espionage plot might still produce useful results.

****

Heydrich convened a meeting with his select team to launch the attack against the Abwehr and by extension the Wehrmacht. It was two weeks since Fritsch's resignation. Once the military tribunal convened, it would expose the charges against Fritsch as baseless, fueling widespread resentment among the Wehrmacht of all ranks. Heydrich must act immediately to not only salvage the disaster, but also regain dominance of the Schutzstaffel over the Wehrmacht in the eyes of the Führer.

Heydrich opened the meeting, "Reichführer Himmler has scaled back our plans to execute our initial plans to cast a wide net among those Army officers targeted for arrest. This affair involving General Fritsch has created a backlash from the Wehrmacht. We shall reverse that by acting with a narrower scope. I believe sufficient however to accomplish our objectives.

"Once we have established the foundation of a foreign intelligence penetration we will gradually expand by exposing additional conspirators as they are uncovered. A rolling wave of revelations directed at middle ranking Wehrmacht officers conspiring with foreign powers to topple the Führer and the Schutzstaffel.

"We will force the Army High Command into an impossible defensive position. New evidence and arrests will deflect concerns about Fritsch. In fact, we will implicate Fritsch indirectly and settle the matter. The Führer will seize the opportunity to regain firm control of the military. We shall benefit by irreparably damaging the Abwehr. The Führer will then turn to the SD on matters of intelligence, distrusting the Abwehr as agents of the Wehrmacht.

"Our initial move will be against Abwehr Major Richter and the American military attaché Colonel Fleming. They become the foundation and the first thread for unraveling this treasonous conspiracy within the Wehrmacht and foreign powers. What has your new source in the Abwehr produced, Pfeiffer?"

Oberleutnant Dieter Vogel of Abwehr counterintelligence produced prodigious amounts of information. Unfortunately, lacking in substance. Movements of certain people in the German Foreign Ministry such as the Kordt brothers, and routine reports of foreign nationals and diplomats amounted to nothing of value other than use as background material. His efforts nothing more than untargeted forays into confidential records. Nothing directly incriminating. Seemingly of little use in spinning a web of conspiracy. Vogel was a disappointment to Pfeiffer.

"Unfortunately, nothing of particular value. Nothing suspicious in itself, Obergruppenführer."

"Any material useful toward making a case against Canaris or other senior officers?"

"Not yet, Sir."

"It seems that Vogel has not measured up to expectations. Therefore, we shall put him to better use. Sacrificed to further the case against Richter and the American. I will secure highly sensitive military orders. Sufficiently convincing in scope to make the case that Vogel was a foreign spy. Working for Richter who in turn worked directly with the American foreign agent Fleming. Vogel shall give his life for the Fatherland. Simultaneously with moving against Richter and the American, Vogel will commit suicide to avoid arrest.

"Select a quiet place. Make it appear a mortal wound to the head inflicted by his personal service pistol. Have his body discovered by the criminal police from an anonymous tip. Because of his sensitive position, the Gestapo will search his quarters thus producing the secret military war plans. Plant additional evidence incriminating others within the Abwehr."

"What is the plan for Richter and the American Fleming?" Pfeiffer asked.

Heydrich said. "Prepare similar packages of incriminating original documents for each. Add other incriminating forged documents. Once laid over a mass of circumstantial evidence, this will produce irrefutable evidence of espionage and treason."

"What is to happen with Richter and Fleming? Their deaths will risk serious backlash." Müller said. Heydrich was a risk taker, and equally treacherous. If circumstances went badly, he would not hesitate to cut his losses and deflect blame."

With no expression of emotion, Heydrich replied, "Obviously, they must die. Differently from Vogel, but in such a manner as to serve the larger narrative. Two separate teams will move simultaneously against both. Therefore, communications are vital to coordinate the timing and placing of each target. Pfeiffer will command one team, Decker the other. The overriding stipulation is to do it quietly. No witnesses."

"What about Richter's family?" Pfeiffer asked.

"Obviously we cannot keep Richter's detention quiet if his wife and two children remain free. Isolate and detain them. Useful as bargaining leverage for forcing Richter to confess to treason and incriminate Canaris. When we are done with Richter, he will hang himself in his cell. His family will disappear into the camps."

"Colonel Fleming is an entirely different problem. Holding diplomatic status, we must avoid creating an international incident with the Americans while extracting maximum value from planted sensitive documents. His role is essential for creating a cohesive narrative of a larger conspiracy involving foreign provocateurs. Expulsion from Germany is not an option. Dispose of his body in such a manner as to prevent discovery. His disappearance to leave the unanswered speculation that he simply fled Germany."

Looking at Pfeiffer with his piercing dead blue eyes, Heydrich said with a hint of malice, "The details are for you to work out, Sturmbannführer."

CHAPTER 31

Berlin, German Reich | February 1938

Fleming received a message from Allen Dulles the first week in January. *Talks proceeding. Roosevelt, along with Churchill and Vansittart support removing Hitler by force. Still pressing for better understanding of the post-Hitler government. Regardless of the current conciliatory diplomatic tone of the British government, once Hitler is dead the path forward seems clear. Churchill declares even the vacillating Chamberlain government will agree to German demands to renegotiate the terms of the Treaty of Versailles once Hitler is removed. The French will protest to exercise their independence but have no choice but to agree.*

Weeks later, the Blomberg-Fritsch Affair settled further debate. A megalomaniacal Hitler seizing direct control of the military signaled German military aggression against Austria and Czechoslovakia all but certain. The likely outcome, war in Europe. Oster was not going to receive anything in writing to convince generals still sitting on the fence. It no longer mattered. To the Oster conspirators, the assassination of Adolf Hitler represented the only way to avoid plunging Germany into another disastrous defeat.

* * * *

Given the green light by Heydrich to proceed with the first phase of moving against the Abwehr, Pfeiffer set the time for the night of Thursday February 17, 1938. A cold moonless night with few people about. The plan called for first arresting Abwehr Major Richter inside his apartment. Less likely for Richter to violently resist in the presence of his wife and two young children.

A team led by Johann Pfeiffer would ransack the house as if looking for something. Pfeiffer would plant a bulky envelop in a location such as a closet. Questioning the wife about the discovered documents to gain her affidavit later as witnessing the seizure in the apartment after threatening her and the children with arrest.

A second team led by Otto Decker was to seize the American Fleming. Both Richter and Fleming then taken to Gestapo headquarters on Prinz-Albrecht Strasse. The Gestapo maintained holding cells for detainees and interrogation facilities equipped with various means of torture in two subterranean levels of the massive building. With no judicial oversight, once inside the building the prisoner lost all hope. Most brought to this medieval dungeon of horrors either left for concentration camps, often with severe injury, or simply disappeared without any record of arrest.

The night of the seizure, Pfeiffer and Decker each led two-man teams of Gestapo agents. In separate black Opel 4-door sedans, Pfeiffer followed Richter and Decker followed Fleming. On this night, both teams sat outside a restaurant. Fleming picked up Richter in his car at Abwehr headquarters earlier that evening and continued to the restaurant.

Pfeiffer approached Decker's car on foot. "When they leave, if Fleming deposits Richter back at his apartment, follow Fleming. Proceed to take him outside his apartment building. He will likely protest his diplomatic immunity loudly. Bludgeon him and place him in a cell at headquarters. There is to be no record of his detention.

"I will join you there after seizing Richter. Remind your team this is top secret. No discussion with anyone outside their immediate assault group."

Pfeiffer was in a foul mood after sitting for two hours in the cold. He was not a field officer. The Opel's heater inadequate to the task of warming the interior of the vehicle and the air heavy with stale cigarette smoke.

As Fleming and Richter exited the restaurant, Pfeiffer's vehicle took the lead position followed by Decker. Both expected to move according to the original plan once Fleming dropped Richter at his apartment.

As Fleming pulled to the curb in front of Richter's apartment building, Pfeiffer decided to change the plan. Why not simply seize both Richter and Fleming together given this opportunity? They had enough manpower with six against two. Avoid the added risk of something going wrong by making separate seizures.

Pfeiffer ordered his driver to pass Fleming's car then abruptly cut them off forcing their car to the curb. He expected Decker to immediately adapt to the change in plans and assist with his two other agents.

As Pfeiffer's car braked to halt at an angle in front of Fleming's car, Fleming slammed on his brakes. Realizing what was happening, Richter reacted without hesitation. Jumping out from the passenger side of Fleming's car, he withdrew his service pistol from its holster.

Pfeiffer and his driver exited their car. Richter stepped closer to the other Gestapo agent holding a Lugar while trying to exit the passenger side of the same vehicle. Knowing the risks of his activities with Oster, Richter long ago determined never to allow capture by the Gestapo. A clean death preferable to torture and threats to his family. With escape useless, kill as many of his attackers as possible.

Richter shot the man twice through the car door window from only a meter away then begin exchanging gunfire with Pfeiffer and the driver on the opposite side of the car. Multiple rounds struck both Richter and the driver in the exchange of gunfire.

Pfeiffer then came around the rear of the car firing at Fleming still behind the wheel of his car. By now, Decker and his two Gestapo agents exited the second Gestapo car stopped ten meters behind Fleming's car.

As one Gestapo agent approached to check on the downed Richter, Fleming engaged his car into reverse. With the passenger door of Fleming's car still open, the door clipped the Gestapo agent sending him to the ground. Decker and the other Gestapo agent begin firing at the rear of Fleming's car joined by Pfeiffer firing from the front.

Hunched low for cover, Fleming shifted into first gear and accelerated forward running down Pfeiffer. The front end of the car lifted up as it bumped over Pfeiffer's body. Assuming these to be Gestapo, Fleming realized there was no escape if arrested. He must take out the attackers and make a run for it or die in the process. A flashback to the WWI trench situation where he almost died.

Braking to a stop after running over Pfeiffer, Fleming reversed bouncing again over Pfeiffer, scattering Decker and the one Gestapo agent still firing. Fleming stretched low across the front seat to avoid repeated rounds smashing through the side and rear window.

After scattering the attackers, Fleming shifted into first gear accelerating toward the two Gestapo agents now on the sidewalk while Decker remained across the street. He intended to take out at least one more attacker using the car. The man previously knocked down by Fleming's door tried to rise to his feet from the sidewalk.

Fleming smashed into him hurling him backward, and then braked to a stop. Reversing, he accelerated as fast as possible steering into the side of the second Gestapo car. The collision pushed the car sideways into the street knocking the Gestapo agent now firing from behind the cover of the car to the pavement.

Of the entire Gestapo attacking force, only Decker remained standing. Realizing his exposure, he frantically reloaded a new magazine into his Lugar.

Exiting his stalled car, Fleming moved to the attack quickly. From his shoulder holster, he extracted his Browning .45 service pistol. Coming around the Gestapo car, he shot the downed Gestapo agent flung to the ground by the collision. Two shots, one to the head.

Reloaded, Decker fired several rounds wildly from his Lugar. Fleming steadied his hand and took a breath squeezing off one round hitting Decker in the chest. Decker dropped to the street.

Not yet out of the danger, he must check on Richter and the condition of the downed attackers before making his escape. Determine their identity.

The identification of the last man he shot read Hauptsturmführer Otto Decker, Geheime Staatspolizei. Gestapo. Decker is unconscious and bleeding out rapidly. By the location of the wound, he took the bullet in the heart.

The first man he ran over twice is lying in the street. A bloody mess but still alive. He is wearing an SS uniform. Sturmbannführer Johann Pfeiffer, Sicherheitsdienst des Reichsführers-SS by his identification. A SD major and a Gestapo captain named Pfeiffer and Decker. An attack against a Wehrmacht officer and an American diplomat meant this action sanctioned at the highest level. At least by Heydrich, possibly Himmler.

Fleming checked on Konrad Richter. No pulse. Struck several times in the upper chest.

Fleming must finish the grisly task of dispatching any of the attackers still alive. Leave no witnesses, although that was probably irrelevant. Might at least provide more time to escape the scene.

The Gestapo agent Fleming ran over on the lawn was conscious but disabled with probably a broken arm and leg. Locating the man's Lugar on the ground, he shot him in the head.

Fleming retrieved his briefcase from his disabled car and moved quickly to the car that first cut them off. Now his only means of escape.

The SD major still not dead. His eyes wide open in terror. With every breath, condensation rose as he expelled a gorge of fresh blood. Fleming asked who ordered this, but the man could not reply as he slowly drowned on his own blood. A bullet to the head ended his suffering.

Fleming purposely slowed his breathing rate to regain control by tamping down the adrenaline rush. In the midst of deadly combat situations, he found he possessed the capacity to slow down his perception of time. This quelled the instinctive survival response allowing his training and rational mind to direct his actions. That is how he survived Mexico, France, and the attempt on his life in the Rhineland.

Now what? Escape in a Gestapo vehicle to where? He could not rely on diplomatic immunity in a police state to save him. Asylum within the American Embassy out of the question. The Nazi regime seemed to hold little fear of international condemnation of all manner of state-sanctioned acts of murder. Taking his chances for escape by measures under his control preferable even if the odds were long. Capture meant protracted torture and an ugly death in the end. If it came to a gunfight, he would take out more of the enemy before a quick death.

The immediate concern was leaving the site of this carnage. Obviously, there were numerous residents in the surrounding apartments hearing the gunfire and probably watching the battle in the weak light of a couple of streetlamps. He drove blocks away and parked behind several other cars. He needed a few minutes to let the adrenaline subside while considering his next move.

Escape seemed impossible. Way too far to travel by automobile from Berlin to any frontier border. That also meant stealing another car since he must quickly abandon the Gestapo vehicle. The police alerted at all points leaving Germany. Trains and commercial aviation impossible. His only chance was finding help.

With the American Embassy out of the question, so too were any of the consular officers. He also had no right to risk their lives. With Konrad Richter dead, that left only Ritter von Strobel. Perhaps Strobel was also compromised if what Fleming just experienced was part of a larger SS operation. Perhaps Oster's entire conspiracy was compromised. He also could not endanger Ritter or Adele nor risk walking into another trap.

Then he realized there was someone else. Bella Fromm. Did he have the right to place her in this kind of danger? She knew everybody that was anybody in Berlin, particularly influential civilians and foreigners opposed to the Nazis. Perhaps she could connect him with someone willing to smuggle him out of

Germany. Given the opportunity, Bella had enough guts and motivation to ram a stick in the eye of the Führer.

Less than twenty miles to Potsdam, he could likely make it in the Gestapo car before a widespread alert went out. He would dump the car among other parked cars at the Potsdam rail station to obscure his trail. A long walk to Fromm's residence but at least not bringing the Gestapo to her doorstep.

His overcoat concealed his military uniform. With his service cap stuffed in his briefcase, he might pass as just another businessman. Except for walking hatless in winter in the middle of the night. Given what he just went through, a difficult walk on this cold night weaving his way in the shadows avoiding any illumination from street lamps.

At a telephone booth, He called Fromm. "Bella, this is Spencer. Sorry for calling so late. I have somewhat of an emergency. I need to stay out of sight for a couple of days. Could I impose on you?"

* * * *

Arriving at midnight, she answered her apartment door and embraced him giving him a kiss. "My lord, I thought you returned to America taking Valeska with you. I have not heard from either of you since she vanished. What happened? Is she safe?"

"Valeska is safely out of Germany. Waiting for me to join her. Sorry I did not stay in touch, Bella. For your protection.

"My emergency involves my association with Oster and Konrad Richter. Been working with them since January. That association now places me in extreme danger. Richter is dead. Killed tonight by the Gestapo. I narrowly escaped after killing several of them. They are now after me. If they catch me, it means a bullet to the head if lucky enough to die that quickly."

She took a deep breath. "Sit down. How about some whisky?"

"Thanks, Bella. It's been a very long night."

"You look like you had a rough time."

"About ready to keel over. Just need some sleep."

Fleming told Fromm the story about the attempted coercion of Valeska's activities with the call girl service by the Gestapo and his involvement in helping her flee Germany. Safely tucked away in Amsterdam waiting until he finished something in Berlin before taking her to America.

"She is fine, but I had to return to Berlin. Obviously involved in dangerous work. That is why I did not contact you. Feel guilty about now putting you at risk, but you are my only chance for getting out of Germany alive."

"Nonsense. We can discuss this in the morning after you get some rest."

Fleming slept on the sofa. He awoke to the morning sunlight as Bella brought him a cup of coffee from the kitchen. "Feeling better?"

"Much. Thanks, Bella."

"So you want me to help you get out of Germany?"

"Without risking your life, Bella. You know people that might help me. All I need is for you to connect me then I will be out of your life."

"I would never want you out of my life, Spencer. We had good times together. Happy that you and Valeska found each other. I will always consider you as someone special in my life."

"You should also consider leaving Germany, Bella. Join your daughter in America. If I get out of Germany alive, my offer still holds to get you to America."

Fromm smiled. "Right now, go take a hot bath and I will fix you something to eat."

In the bathtub, an idea for fleeing Germany came to him. The only sure way was by air. Since commercial air travel was not possible, why not hijack a small charter aircraft? He even knew of such an airfield.

The Broitzem Flugplatz German air transport school was a clandestine training center to disguise prohibited training of military pilots under the terms of the Treaty of Versailles. All that changed in 1935 when Hitler went public announcing German rearmament. The Luftwaffe took over converting the facility to military use. Watching the facility periodically as an important military installation, Fleming knew that civilian aviation operations relocated to the newly constructed Braunschweig-Waggum

Airport in 1935. Braunschweig was located only 125 miles west of Potsdam. A three-hour drive. A better alternative than risking a much longer automobile trip then attempting a border crossing.

Finishing a meal of bread, eggs, and sausage, Fleming said, "I feel like a new person, Bella. Thank you so much. I think I have an idea how I can get out of Germany. All I need is a car and a change of civilian clothes. I kept plenty of cash always in my briefcase in case of emergency."

"Where can you go in a car? All the borders west, south, and north are many hours away. As each hour passes, police across Germany are alerted to your name and description."

"Yes, I know, but I only need to drive to Braunschweig three hours west. There is a civilian airport there. Small private aircraft, probably something available to charter."

"Sounds like a desperate plan," Fromm said as she sat across the table sipping coffee.

"Not if I can find a pilot to get me to Cologne to see my terminally ill mother. Once in the air, I force him to divert and fly to Amsterdam. About the same distance so his calculated fuel load is enough to make it that far. My escape not likely discovered until too late. Once in the air, impossible for the Gestapo to locate the aircraft, much less do anything about it."

Fromm nodded, her face suggesting she was wrestling with what to do.

He said, "Something wrong, Bella? Tell you what, can you at least get me some clothes. I will just steal a car."

She laid a hand on his forearm, "No it is not about getting you help and transport. I know people willing to help. I was actually thinking about a better alternative. What if I took you?"

"No, Bella. That is far too dangerous. After what I did, the Gestapo will seek out everyone I ever knew in Germany. I debated about even coming here."

"Glad you did. I am offering to not only drive you to Braunschweig but also accompany you all the way to Amsterdam. I made up my mind last night after listening about what you and Valeska went through. I must leave Germany. Waited too long already. The Nazis shut down our wine business. They mean to destroy all German Jews. Nothing left to keep me here."

He grabbed her hand in his. "Are you serious? It means leaving right away. Tomorrow morning. Once the Gestapo car is discovered at the Potsdam train station, they will eventually connect you to me and come asking questions."

Fromm nodded. "I can be ready. Knowing this day would come, I gradually withdrew money from my bank account over the last year. You know Jews cannot leave without forfeiting almost everything. Will you take me?"

"Of course. But it's still a terrible risk accompanying me."

"I am willing to take that risk, Spencer. Can you still get me to America?"

"You bet. All three of us will go together."

"Are you sure Valeska will understand you taking an old flame along?"

Fleming laughed. "You helped Valeska flee Germany. She is also well aware of our prior relationship, Bella."

Fromm smiled and nodded.

"Now how about buying me some traveling clothes before the shops close. I will write down my sizes. A complete outfit. Suit, shirt, tie, shoes, overcoat, and fedora. Make me look like a prosperous businessman. We must leave early tomorrow while still dark. Get to Braunschweig by mid-morning. Here is some money."

* * * *

At four o'clock the next morning, they set out in Fromm's small Opel coupe. They looked the part of a prosperous couple. Fromm looked smart dressed in fashionable slacks and sweater with wool overcoat and hat. With Fromm's eye for style, Fleming looked the part of a prosperous businessman in a new suit, wool overcoat, and fedora.

With her two suitcases. Fromm made ready to leave her apartment, never to return. Watching as Fleming secured his shoulder holster and placed a spare magazine for his .45 in his pocket, brought a look to Fromm's face that he interpreted as possible second thoughts.

"Everything all right, Bella? Is it the gun?"

She smiled. "No. Just sadness. Leaving Germany, probably never to return. Will I like America, Spencer?"

"I am sure you will, Bella. You even speak English. Imagine never again fearing a knock on the door in the early morning hours by secret police. And you will be with your daughter."

Three hours later, they arrived in Braunschweig. Fleming drove slowly checking out the civilian airport. A bitter cold day yet more importantly a clear sky with only scattered high clouds. A good day for flying. Minimal airport activity given the early hour.

Fleming was not a pilot but as part of his job, he knew aircraft for their military value. Two Junkers Ju 52 tri-engine 17-seat commercial aircraft with the Lufthansa logo sat on the tarmac in front of a small terminal with a large sign reading Braunschweig-Waggum. Further on there was a collection of small aircraft. Fleming spotted the perfect choice for making their departure out of Germany.

He pulled into a parking spot in front of a building displaying a sign reading *Braunschweig Flugdienste*. A flying service. Possibly offering small aircraft for charter.

Fleming and Fromm entered the building. A man stood behind a hotel-like desk counter in what looked to be an operations center populated with several desks and radio equipment. Off to the side was a lounge area.

The man greeted them.

Fleming said, "Do you charter aircraft? My sister and I need to get to Cologne urgently. We just learned our ailing mother has taken a turn for the worse. Doctor says she may not have long."

"Oh my. So sorry to hear that. Yes, I have aircraft for hire."

"Excellent. What about the Bf108 I saw sitting out there. I am not a pilot but I saw one perform at an air show. It is very fast. Time is of the essence."

"Yes, it is available. Depends of course on getting the pilot here on such short notice."

"Please try," Fromm said, putting on a suitable display of emotional distress. "You can see this is very difficult for both of us. We are willing to pay double if we can leave quickly."

The Messerschmitt Bf108 was a four-seat German single-engine sport and touring aircraft. Built for aeronautical competition flying, it saw use for training future Luftwaffe pilots. Fleming knew it capable of 190 miles per hour. Something over two hours flying time to Amsterdam. Half the time compared to the other small aircraft on the runway.

After a brief telephone conversation, the man smiled. "Good news. The pilot will be here in twenty minutes. Let me get someone to fuel the 108 then we can do the paperwork."

Fleming turned to Fromm. "Easier than I thought. Let me do the talking. He will want to see our papers. I have a regular American passport so I will not raise questions by using my diplomatic passport."

Fromm smiled. "I see why I became your sister instead of your wife. Avoids explaining passports with different names. You are good at this cloak and dagger stuff. What were you and Richter up to I wonder? Are you a spy, Spencer?"

"Not anymore."

The man returned. "Everything should be ready when your pilot arrives. His name is Ulrich Loewen. Experienced pilot. Lots of hours in the 108."

Showing their passports, the man remarked to Fleming, "American? Your German is excellent."

"I was raised in Cologne then educated in America. Combining business with visiting family. We spent the holidays with mother, now this unexpected turn of events."

"I do hope your mother recovers. I am charging you only our standard rate."

"Thank you. That is most kind. Let me then give you something extra for your exceptional service."

Fleming handed the man 300 Reichsmarks.

"I shall give the same to Herr Loewen. Getting to Cologne so quickly is a blessing."

Before their pilot arrived, Fleming studied the map on the wall. Cologne was southeast of Braunschweig at a compass heading of roughly 120 degrees. Amsterdam due east at a heading of 90 degrees.

Fleming asked to sit in the front next to the pilot. "Never been in an aircraft cockpit."

Once off the ground, Fleming asked the pilot about all the instruments. After twenty minutes, he said. "There is a slight change in plans, Herr Loewen. We are not going to Cologne. Our new destination is Amsterdam."

Loewen looked at Fleming with a scowl, "That is not possible, Herr Fleming. Our flight plan cannot be changed."

"I am afraid you will have to make an exception. The good news is there is a handsome bonus in it for you. You just claim a man with a gun hijacked you."

"I refuse. Can you fly this aircraft without me?"

Fleming answered, "No. However, we intend to go to Amsterdam at all cost. You do not have a choice. None of us needs to die."

Fleming removed his Browning .45 from under his suit jacket and rested it in his lap.

"Do you understand now? I also know the compass heading to Amsterdam so do not try to deceive me."

Loewen nodded.

"Will you be able to navigate to Amsterdam?"

Loewen nodded again and reached between the seats withdrawing a chart. "Put away your gun and open this chart. I need to determine the waypoints to make course corrections to take us into Amsterdam's Schiphol Airport."

EPILOGUE

The murder of his key subordinate Major Konrad Richter did not deter Oberstleutnant Hans Oster. The disappearance of the American Army officer Fleming suggested he and Richter likely were responsible for killing six SS. Although never made public, Oster's sources within SS headquarters provided details of the incident. If intended as part of a wider attack on other conspirators, nothing further materialized.

Within a couple of weeks, the military tribunal found General Fritsch innocent of the allegations to his character. Furthermore, they condemned the evidence as a fabricated plot by the SS. The backlash directed at Heinrich Himmler. Hitler made it known the SS was to take no aggressive action toward the Wehrmacht that would distract from his next major move against Czechoslovakia.

Adolf Hitler was in a state of euphoria as the Fritsch debacle became irrelevant. A week before the military tribunal verdict on Fritsch, Austria capitulated in what became the Anschluss, or the annexation into the Greater Germany. The German Army marched across the border unopposed to cheering crowds of Austrian Nazi supporters. Even the Wehrmacht high command applauded Hitler's brilliant move of annexing Austria without a shot. Czechoslovakia however likely meant a military invasion.

The effect of the Austrian Anschluss dampened the resolve of several of the key Wehrmacht conspirators. Fleming's report of events forcing his escape from Germany cast doubt on the willingness for the Oster-Beck conspiracy to overthrow Hitler. The backchannel talks in London collapsed. No record remained that it ever took place.

Oster's conspiracy collapsed completely in September 1938, through the timidity of the British and French to stand against Hitler's aggression. In an ignoble act of cowardice and naivety, British Prime Minister Neville Chamberlain led negotiations that ceded the Sudetenland region of Czechoslovakia to Germany. All without having any such authority, and without the participation of the Czech government.

Oster's entire basis that an invasion of Czechoslovakia would result in a greater European war evaporated. Yet war would come one year later. Emboldened by his success in annexing Austria and subsequently all of Czechoslovakia without military action, Hitler ordered the invasion of Poland bringing about the start of WWII in 1939. The apprehensions of Oster, Beck, Strobel, and Kaczmarek over war materialized into a destructive conflict exceeding their worst fears.

Hans Oster never relented in his opposition even during the first four years of WWII. Most of those earlier conspirators continued subversive efforts against Adolf Hitler. On July 20, 1944, Hitler survived another in a series of failed assassination attempts. A bomb placed by Colonel Claus von Stauffenberg in a conference room at Hitler's field headquarters in East Prussia killed many, yet by a quirk of circumstances, Adolf Hitler survived with only minor injuries. Oster and Beck's *Operation Valkyrie* fell apart once information spread of Hitler's survival. A bloodbath of retribution of suspected conspirators and anyone even thought to oppose Hitler followed. Hans Oster and General Ludwig Beck were among the many conspirators executed.